# THE
# INFINITE
# FUTURE

WITHDRAWN

PENGUIN PRESS | NEW YORK | 2018

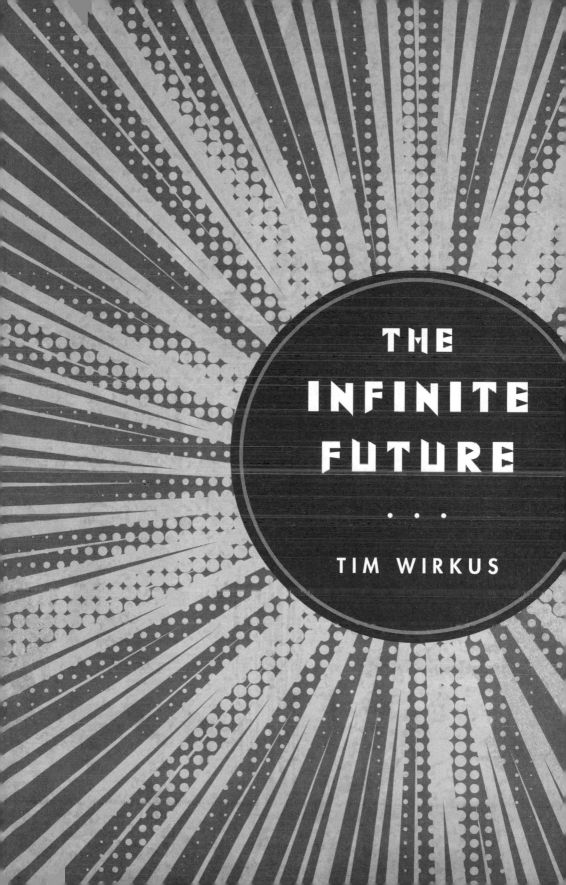

PENGUIN PRESS
An imprint of Penguin Random House LLC
375 Hudson Street
New York, New York 10014
penguin.com

LIBRARY OF CONGRESS CATALOGING-IN-PUBLICATION DATA

Names: Wirkus, Tim, 1983- author.
Title: The infinite future / Tim Wirkus.
Description: New York : Penguin Press, 2018.
Identifiers: LCCN 2017025119 (print) | LCCN 2017027797 (ebook) |
ISBN 9780735224339 (ebook) | ISBN 9780735224322 (hardcover)
Subjects: LCSH: Quests (Expeditions)—Fiction. | Authors—Fiction. | BISAC:
FICTION / Literary. | FICTION / Satire. | FICTION / Science Fiction /
General. | GSAFD: Science fiction. | Satire.
Classification: LCC PS3623.I754 (ebook) | LCC PS3623.I754 I54 2018 (print) |
DDC 813/.6—dc23
LC record available at https://lccn.loc.gov/2017025119

Printed in the United States of America
1   3   5   7   9   10   8   6   4   2

Designed by Gretchen Achilles

# THE
# INFINITE
# FUTURE

# FOREWORD

## by TIM WIRKUS

Really, this foreword should take place in the lamp-lit reading room of a classy Victorian gentlemen's club—or, better yet, in a grand old house on Christmas Eve where party guests swap strange tales next to a crackling fireplace. As I understand it, those are the two most appropriate locations for receiving a peculiar manuscript whose provenance is nearly as intriguing as its contents, and as it happens, the book you currently hold in your hands began its life as just such a manuscript. In a perfect world, the story of my first encounter with it would take place in a fittingly mysterious locale. Unfortunately, real life is rarely so obliging, and so this story, or at least my very small part in it, begins in the refrigerator section of a Texaco Food Mart a few blocks from Weller Book Works in Salt Lake City.

Having worked up an appetite giving a reading from my first novel at the bookstore earlier that evening, I was currently on the prowl for a local brand of chocolate milk my sister had told me I needed to try before I left town. My flight back to California left first thing the next morning, and so my window of opportunity on the milk was closing fast. A cursory glance at the Food Mart's glass-doored refrigerators did not bode well—slim pickings in the dairy department, which comprised one shelf of one refrigerator practically hidden behind a rotating rack of five-dollar DVDs. I was leaning in to get a better look when my phone buzzed—it was Danny Laszlo, an old classmate from BYU.

"Hi Danny," I said.

I peered into the refrigerator, and in a stroke of good fortune, among the three brands of chocolate milk that the Food Mart carried was exactly the one I was looking for.

"Hey," said Danny. "Do you have a minute?"

I'd seen Danny in the audience at the reading earlier that evening but hadn't had a chance to talk to him before the event had ended.

"Sure," I said.

"To talk in person, I mean," said Danny.

This caught me off guard. I had no idea what Danny Laszlo could want to talk about that couldn't be discussed over the phone, and quite frankly, by that point in the evening I just wanted some chocolate milk and a good night's sleep.

"In person?" I said, trying to think of the best way to turn him down. I squeezed past the DVD display and, opening the refrigerator door just wide enough to fit my arm through, reached to the back of the single-file line of chocolate milks to select the coldest container from the rear of the refrigerator. Excuse-wise, I was coming up empty.

I said, "Where are you?"

"I'm at the gas station," he said. "Just out front."

I let the refrigerator door swing shut.

"This gas station?" I said.

"Yeah," he said.

I turned around to look out the windowed front of the Food Mart. Sure enough, Danny Laszlo stood just outside, phone to his ear. He gave me a sheepish nod and raised his free hand in a short, businesslike wave.

"Did you follow me here?" I said.

"Well," he said. "I needed to talk to you."

I didn't know what to say. Chilled pint bottle in one hand, I stood there for a moment, staring dumbly. We were close enough to see each other but too far away to talk without using our phones, a situation that never fails to make me very uncomfortable.

"I'll be out in a second," I said and hung up as quickly as possible.

Danny Laszlo and I first met back in 2005, in an undergraduate creative writing workshop at BYU. I was a recently returned missionary at the time, still reacclimatizing to civilian life. I'd gotten back so recently, in fact, that I still sported the unmistakable tan lines that result from wearing a collared shirt and tie in the sun all day, every day.

I felt conspicuous and awkward, even, or especially, at BYU.

I was relieved then, on the first day of class, to spot somebody else sporting missionary tan lines of their own: a tall, solidly built guy who would have been a dead ringer for a young Orson Welles if not for his light-blond hair. I sat in the desk next to his and introduced myself. He said his name was Danny Laszlo. I asked him if he'd just gotten back from a mission. He said he had, and a bit more small talk revealed that we had both served in São Paulo, Brazil, although in different parts of the city.

It quickly became apparent, though, that Danny had little interest in swapping anecdotes of missionary life in Brazil. Instead, he asked me what music I'd been listening to since getting home. I told him the Strokes and the White Stripes. The Shins, a little bit.

"That's pre-mission stuff, though," he said. "What new stuff are you listening to?"

I told him I was still catching up.

"You need to be listening to the New Pornographers," he said. "*Twin Cinema*—just came out a couple weeks ago—best album of the year. You like power pop?"

And so we talked music until class started. Then, while the instructor, the other students, and I went over course objectives, policy, and scheduling, Danny worked his way through a crossword puzzle he kept screened behind his copy of the syllabus.

Based on initial impressions, I expected to become good friends with Danny Laszlo. Over the next three years, however, our acquaintanceship followed an asymptotic path in which our interactions grew increasingly genial without ever reaching a state of true friendship. Though chronically affable, Danny maintained a tight seal over the personal details of his life, which kept me and others at a perpetual distance.

During this time I worked as a peer tutor at BYU's student writing center, which employed a team of undergrads, mostly English majors, to dispense unwelcome and occasionally ill-conceived writing advice to our fellow students. When business was slow, the other tutors and I sat around the staff table trading gossip and dog-eared copies of our favorite books. Several of us became very good friends, forming a loose cadre that socialized both on campus and off during our time together at BYU.

I bring this up because the writing center crowd developed a minor fascination with Danny Laszlo. Most of us had classes with him and could testify to the skill with which he camouflaged himself behind a blind of false transparency. He might widely broadcast his interests and opinions—he loved James Joyce, thought Bob Dylan (and singer-songwriters generally) were criminally overrated, and he refused to associate with anyone who'd ever been a member of a high school or collegiate choir—but when it came to concrete details concerning his history or his off-campus lifestyle, he revealed nothing. All of us in the writing center crowd wanted to be his friend—or rather, wanted him to consider us a friend and thereby grant us access to the secret life he concealed so completely. To this end, we repeatedly invited him to our extracurricular parties, and he repeatedly and breezily turned us down.

The truth is, in our heart of hearts, none of us believed that Danny's private life would be that much more interesting than any of our own, but still, we wondered. I suppose the point of all this is, I knew Danny at BYU but not extremely well. Not surprisingly, we lost touch after graduation, and now ten years later, I was curious to know what he'd been up to in the meantime.

. . .

Outside the Food Mart, we shook hands and I asked Danny where he wanted to go to talk.

"Right here's fine," he said.

So we stood a few feet from the entrance to the Food Mart, in a little gap of cement between the pebble-surfaced garbage can and the locked display of propane tanks.

"Are you sure?" I said.

"Yeah," he said, rubbing his chin. His clothes had that unostentatious but perfectly tailored look that whispers *money* in polite undertones. Clothes like that are magic, endowing their wearer with an instant boost to their looks, charm, and credibility. Standing this close to him, though, I could see a ragged, haunted quality clinging to his features. If, when I'd first met him, he'd resembled the youthful Orson Welles of "The War of the Worlds" publicity stills, now he looked like Welles at the end of *The Lady from Shanghai*, hollow-eyed and shaken.

"So how are you?" I said, genuinely curious.

"Fine," he said.

Danny had clearly retained his reluctance to discuss any details of his private life. Only with considerable effort did I learn that he was an associate at a prominent Salt Lake law firm, one that even I had heard of. This was a group of attorneys who, by all accounts, shaped the very fabric of the city according to their—or rather, their clients'—whims.

"Wow," I said. "How do you like it there?"

"It's exhausting," he said.

"Long hours?" I said.

"Yeah," he said. "That's part of it."

A car drove slowly past us, pulling in next to the nearest pump.

"Listen," said Danny. "I don't mean to change the subject here—well, actually that's exactly what I mean to do, so let me get to it. You have connections in publishing, right?"

"Kind of," I said.

"You don't have to be modest," he said.

I was not being modest.

"Anyway, you're better connected than I am," he said. "And that's why I wanted to meet this evening. I have a manuscript for you."

"You wrote a novel?" I said. Danny's writing had always impressed and intimidated me, and if he'd written a novel, I'd be very interested to read it.

"No, I don't write fiction anymore. It's a terrible way to live," he said. "No offense."

This surprised me. Danny had always looked down on anyone not pursing the so-called artist's path. A dark SUV circled around the pump across from us, its headlights briefly shining directly into our eyes. As they did, Danny grimaced, turning his face from the glare and ducking his head, resembling, just for a moment, a cowering dog. This was a much different Danny than the one I'd known at BYU. Somehow all his prickly charisma had become obscured within an ashy cloud of melancholy. He blinked his tired eyes.

"The manuscript then," I said. "What is it?"

"Okay," he said. "So, about six years ago I had an experience that completely changed me. I mean, that's such an empty thing to say, to describe what happened, because people say that kind of thing all the time, but you need to understand that I'm talking about a real and significant change here—like a true shift in who I was."

"Wow," I said, impressed partly by his willingness to open up like this, but mostly by his ability to do so without disclosing a single specific detail.

"Yeah," he said. "And to describe it externally, you know, the actual external reality of what happened, it doesn't sound that dramatic. But inside, it affected me more than anything else I'd ever experienced. And that's where the manuscript comes in."

"So it's a memoir?" I said.

"Not really," said Danny. "There's more to it than that. Part of the manuscript is a translation I did of a story by this extremely obscure Brazilian science-fiction writer, but really it's all kind of wrapped up together—the translation and my own story, I mean. They're inseparable, in my opinion."

"Huh," I said.

The manuscript sounded intriguing. It also sounded completely unpublishable.

"Honestly—"

"No," he said. "Before you weigh in on this book, you have to read it." He pulled his phone from his jacket pocket. "What's your email?"

A spark of Danny's former vitality animated this desperate plea. I gave him my email address. In response, thumbs tapping the screen of his phone, Danny said, "I'm sending you a pdf."

"All right," I said. "I'll take a look."

My first read-through of the manuscript, while waiting for a much-delayed flight at the Salt Lake City International Airport the next day, prompted a mild panic attack. I had no idea what to make of what I'd just read, and immediately I began formulating an apologetic email to Danny in which I explained that the whole venture was a lost cause. Luckily, my flight boarded before I could send off the email, because in the meantime, the book's odd memorability had become duly apparent to me.

The great Argentine writer Jorge Luis Borges once argued that reading Edgar Allan Poe's stories is never as satisfying as *remembering* Poe's stories. I initially read that sentiment as a gentle insult, but the more I think about it, the more complimentary it seems. After all, any story that creates a more potent and delightful version of itself in the reader's memory has performed a not insignificant act of transmutation. On the page, Poe's fictions might trip over their own overly wordy feet, but in the imagination they move with a deft and sinister grace, lingering long after the reader closes the book. *The Infinite Future* has similarly haunted me. It's not a scary book, and isn't supposed to be, but its peculiar contents have insinuated themselves into my consciousness with the persistence of a wronged and fretful ghost.

I should add as a postscript that Danny Laszlo remains as elusive to me as ever. I had wondered if our reacquaintance might yield both a published book and a new friendship, but after that initial conversation at the Food Mart, Danny withdrew himself behind the same genial veil that concealed him throughout the three years I knew him at BYU.

*May 2017*
*Irvine, CA*

# TRANSLATOR'S NOTE TO THE READER

## by DANIEL LASZLO

first heard of Eduard Salgado-MacKenzie and his impossible novel on an otherwise lousy research trip to São Paulo. The city itself wasn't the problem. I was back after four years away—I'd lived there for two years as a Mormon missionary—and was as pleasantly confounded by São Paulo as ever. *Hallucinated City*, as Jack E. Tomlins dubbed it in his loose translation of Mário de Andrade's iconic poetry collection, *Paulicéia Desvairada*. I can see where Tomlins was coming from, but in spite of São Paulo's mind-boggling immensity and the dream logic of its juxtaposed neighborhoods, I've always found the city much too tangible to be a hallucination—the warm, gritty air against my skin; the bouncily sardonic Paulistano Portuguese in my ears; the oregano-seasoned fillings of warm salgadinhos on my tongue; the aggressively uneven sidewalks beneath my tired feet.

No, the city wasn't the problem.

Funded by a Young Religious Novelist Grant, I was in São Paulo to research my first book, an expansive roman à clef based on my time as a missionary and buttressed by exhaustive research conducted in the city where I'd worked. That's what I was aiming for, anyway, but four days into my trip I ran into serious trouble.

At the time of this trip to Brazil—summer 2009—I was living below a doughnut shop in Provo, Utah, in what some (my landlord) might call a studio apartment, and others (anyone but my landlord) might call a windowless basement storage room with a shoddy, RV-style bathroom in the corner and the constant stench of rancid cooking oil in the air. I'd graduated from college at the same time the economy had gone belly-up, so job prospects had been grim. I found part-time work at a nearby flower shop called Nothing But Flowers! and was barely getting by.

My original plan had been to wait out the economic storm in grad school, but after two rounds of applications to seventeen different MFA programs had resulted in nothing but rejections, it seemed clear that this wasn't going to happen. During my second round of applications, though, I'd also applied for a handful of fellowships and grants, and about a month after my last MFA rejection, I got a letter informing me I'd been awarded a Young Religious Novelist Grant. I would be given seven thousand dollars to research and compose a novel "that elucidated the joys of twenty-first-century religious experience."

You've probably never heard of a Young Religious Novelist Grant before. (Okay, you've definitely never heard of a Young Religious Novelist Grant before, because that's not what it's really called. This seems like as good a time as any to let you know that I've changed the names and distinguishing characteristics of several people and institutions who appear in this account. As I think will become clear, I have good reason for doing so.) I hadn't heard of the grant before I'd applied, but the prospect of seven thousand dollars thrilled me. I was less thrilled when the contract arrived. Even though I couldn't understand a lot of the legal jargon, I did get the sense that there might be some pretty thick strings attached to the money. I couldn't find much about the YRNG online— only that the grant's sponsoring organization was a group called the Coalition of Aggrieved Christians, whose name made me nervous. They had virtually no Internet presence, which worried me even more.

The letter did include a contact number, so I gave it a call. When I introduced myself to the man who answered, he sounded glad to hear from me. He said his name was Wayne Fortescue and his job was to answer any questions I had about the grant.

"Perfect," I said. "What can you tell me about the Coalition of Aggrieved Christians?"

"Our sponsoring organization!" he said. "You've done some research!"

"Yeah," I said. "I actually couldn't find much about them online."

"That's a very deliberate move," said Wayne Fortescue, like it was supposed to impress me.

"Why?" I said.

"They don't like to toot their own horn," said Fortescue. "They're very modest. In short, though, the CAC's mission is to defend and enhance the quality of religious experience in America for folks like you and me."

"All right," I said evenly, like his answer hadn't set off all sorts of alarm bells. "And what does that involve exactly?"

"Just like a writer," he said. "Full of questions."

I thought I detected a hint of warning in this response.

"If you're not comfortable talking about this—" I said.

"Are you kidding me?" said Fortescue. "I love nothing more than talking about the Coalition. Ask me whatever you want."

He said it cheerfully but with a sharp undertone that suggested I should be sorry for asking any questions at all. That alone would normally be enough for me to end the conversation right there.

Seven thousand dollars, though.

"What I'm looking for," I said, "is a basic overview of what the Coalition does."

Fortescue rattled off a boilerplate response that was high on praise for the Coalition's virtues and low on concrete information regarding what they actually did or believed.

I decided to explore a different avenue.

"I guess my biggest question," I said, "is whether the novel I write needs to conform in any way to the Coalition's ideologies. Whatever those might be."

"Oh no," said Fortescue, a little too quickly. "Of course not. That's not what this is at all. Not. At. All."

"So I can write about whatever I want," I said.

I needed an explicit yes.

"We're here to help you," said Fortescue.

"I *can* write about whatever I want, then," I said.

"The grant committee was very interested in the novel you proposed—Mormon missionaries in Brazil? That's the novel we would hope you'd write."

"And that is what I'm planning on writing—" I began.

"Good," interrupted Fortescue.

"But what I'd like to know is if there's any situation where you guys would—I don't know—ask for your money back or something."

I'd meant the question as a joke, but it came out with an involuntary tremor.

"That rarely happens," said Fortescue, his voice low and soothing.

"Rarely?" I said.

"There *was* a grant recipient a few years back," said Fortescue, not missing a beat, "who ran into some difficulties with her novel, and made some poor choices as a result. Unfortunately, we had to repossess her funding."

"What kinds of poor choices?" I said.

"I'd rather not say," said Fortescue. "Furthermore, papers were signed, and I'm obliged to maintain a level of confidentiality regarding the situation."

At some point we had slipped into the sinister realm of legalese.

"I'll be honest," I said. "That worries me."

"Shoot!" said Fortescue, all homespun joviality. "I've spooked you! Let me assure you that you have no need to worry, Dan. Can I call you Dan?"

"Sure."

"Dan, I'll level with you," he said, all man-to-man. "That young woman I mentioned, she was not CAC material. Just not a great fit, ultimately—our mistake as much as hers. But you, my friend, are a whole different story. A *whole* different story."

I thought of all the reasons why that response should concern me. Then I thought of how behind I was on my student loan payments. I thought of my doughnut grease–infused apartment. I thought of the frozen potpies and instant oatmeal that had made up my primary diet for the past several months.

I thought of everything I could do with seven thousand dollars.

I thanked Wayne Fortescue for his help. I got off the phone, and before I could change my mind, I signed the contract and dropped it in the mail.

Now, four days into my trip to São Paulo, the money was gone (student loan payments, travel expenses), the novel was dead in the water, and Wayne Fortescue, still unaware of those last two developments, was not going to be happy.

The moment I realized I would never finish my novel, I was sitting in an air-conditioned study room of the Biblioteca Anita Garibaldi, one of the University of São Paulo's forty-five libraries, reading a densely written monograph on the city's architecture during the coffee-boom years. I turned a page halfway through a chapter critiquing Ramos de Azevedo's Theatro Municipal, and realized I couldn't bring myself to read another word. It was so much to take in, and the more research I'd done over the past few days, the more research I realized I'd need to do to make the novel even halfway decent. That would have been fine, if I hadn't also finally admitted to myself that I had no interest in writing the novel I'd pitched to the CAC. Not that novel or anything like it. I closed the architecture book and set it back on top of the to-read pile that I'd ambitiously stacked there when I arrived at the library that morning.

Every failure deserves a soundtrack, and on that sorry day at the Biblioteca Anita Garibaldi, mine was "There She Goes," by the La's. I know you've heard this song before. The album version is a rom-com staple, a jangly, Steve Lillywhite–produced pop confection. But the band also recorded a live version for BBC radio that's not as warm or polished. The vocals are rougher, the guitars more jagged, the production more spare, and it totally skews the feel of the song. The album version has a sweet, wistful vibe to it, but the BBC version, even though it's not *that* different, sounds like the aural instantiation of pure anxiety, especially once the song hits the 1:40 mark and the backup vocals come in, pleading and echoey.

I spent the rest of the morning listening to that song on repeat through a pair of crummy earbuds, drenched in flop sweat. As disappointed as I was by this artistic impasse, I was more worried about the financial consequences of my failure. I thought of the contract I'd signed for the Coalition of Aggrieved Christians, and of all the vague yet sinewy strings attached to the money I'd already spent. To keep my nervous hands busy, I collaged all of the tiny sticky notes I'd brought with me into a colorful seascape on top of my desk—a vivid orange ship floating on electric-blue waters, and beneath it all, a colossal pink squid reaching its tentacles upward toward the unsuspecting ship. I was tearing a bit of notebook paper into a circle to make the squid's right eye when I felt someone watching me.

I looked up.

Sérgio, my liaison at the library, stood in the doorway of the study room, hands clasped behind his back. I pulled out my earbuds and set down the paper.

"Excuse me," he said. "I didn't mean to interrupt."

I couldn't tell if he was being sarcastic or extra considerate.

"No problem," I said.

I placed Sérgio somewhere in his fifties, broad and slightly paunchy, with long, graying hair that he kept back in a neat ponytail. His accompanying beard was carefully trimmed, and overall he cultivated a distinguished, countercultural air—a diplomat from the underground. That morning, he wore faded jeans, a Raul Seixas T-shirt, and a gray linen blazer.

"And your research," he said. "It's going well?"

Again, I couldn't tell if he was being sincere or not.

"This is a prewriting exercise that I do," I said, nodding at the sticky-note collage. "It helps me."

"I'm happy to hear it," said Sérgio.

He slipped his hands into his pockets and stepped into the study room. Lips pursed, he gave the paper squid on top of my desk a long hard look.

"Today I'm researching the architecture of São Paulo," I said. "Interesting stuff."

"The coffee-boom era," said Sérgio, noticing the cover of the book I'd set aside.

"Yes," I said, but had nothing to add.

I knew that Wayne Fortescue had been in contact with Sérgio to coordinate my time at the library, but I wasn't sure in what capacity Sérgio currently operated. Was he liaising solely between me and the library or between me and the library and Fortescue? Was he sending the CAC updates on what books and articles I consulted and how I used my time? I wasn't sure how careful I needed to be around him, so I opted for full discretion.

"Yes," I repeated. "The work is going very well."

Sérgio said, "I found a story you wrote."

This caught me off guard.

"Really?" I said.

"Yes," he said, a tension in his voice that I couldn't read. "About a woman's visit to an art museum."

"That's the one," I said.

A small but respectable journal had run the story when I was a junior at BYU. It was my only publication to date, a cosmic fluke apparently. I'd written reams of short stories since then and gotten back nothing but rejections. I had hoped a novel might turn the tide, but that obviously wasn't going to happen.

Sérgio pointed to my backpack slouched on the floor.

"Please pick that up and come with me," he said. "Leave the books for now."

I grabbed my bag and followed Sérgio out the door. I had no idea what he was up to, but it seemed serious. We walked past the restrooms, past some more glass study rooms, past a long bank of multicolored reference books. Sérgio opened a door marked "Authorized Personnel Only" and we descended a flight of stairs, passed through another door, and descended another, even narrower staircase. The deeper we went, the more nervous I got. Finally, the stairs opened onto a long hallway lined with dented metal doors. Sérgio reached into his pocket and pulled out a cluttered ring of keys. As we made our way down the hall, he fumbled through the keys until we came to a door, identical to the rest except for a plaque at eye level that read, "Sérgio Antunes, Sublibrarian." Sérgio unlocked the door, opened it, and gestured for me to enter. It was a tiny broom closet of an office, which contained in total three items: a metal folding chair, an attached desk-chair combo of the type used in public high schools, and a two-drawer filing cabinet. Even with so little furniture, there was barely enough room inside for the two of us.

"Please," said Sérgio, "have a seat."

I sat down on the folding chair. Sérgio left the door, which opened into the hallway, slightly ajar and sat down at the desk. I wiped my sweating palms on the sides of my pant legs.

"You're a missionary?" he said.

"I used to be," I said, "a few years ago. Now I'm trying to write a novel about it."

"Cashing in on your experience," he said.

"Well," I said.

I shifted in my chair. Sérgio folded his hands on the desk in front of him.

"So who do you read?" he said. "I mean, who are your favorites?"

I told him James Joyce, Flannery O'Connor, Sherwood Anderson. I wondered where he was going with this.

"Any science fiction?" he said.

"Not really," I said. "A little Bradbury, I guess."

"But you do know Salgado-MacKenzie, correct?" he said.

"Who?" I said.

"Salgado-MacKenzie," he said. "Eduard Salgado-MacKenzie."

"No," I said, "I've never heard of him."

Sérgio slapped his palm against the surface of his desk with such force that the sound echoed off the bare walls of the room and into the hallway.

"You must have," he said.

I shook my head. This was getting intense.

"Are you sure?" he said.

"I'm pretty sure," I said.

"I was positive you had read him," he said, a note of accusation in his voice.

"I'm sorry," I said.

Sérgio leaned his elbows on the desk and ran his hands through his hair with a sigh.

"Your art museum story," he said, his voice softer now, deflated. "What was it called—'The Gallery Within'?"

"Yeah."

Sérgio nodded.

"That story reminded me of one of Salgado-MacKenzie's—'Without Anger or Fondness,' it's called. The premise is, there's a museum on Mars that displays great works of art that were salvaged from Earth before Earth was essentially destroyed by nuclear war. One day, a woman named Dolores da Gama visits the museum; Dolores was born on Earth, but her family fled to Mars just before everything went haywire.

"Dolores is at the museum, then, looking at the art on display, and at first she's enjoying herself, but then she starts to feel like something's off. She's not sure why, but something about these paintings makes her very uncomfortable. Finally, she gets to *Le Déjeuner sur l'Herbe*—you know, Manet's picnic painting—and figures out what's wrong. Instead of lounging in a verdant French grove, the picnickers have reclined in the middle of a severe, red rock Martian landscape. Everything else is just as it should be—the man in the round black hat, the inexplicably nude woman, the fruit spilling artfully from the basket—but they are unmistakably picnicking on Mars. More confounding still, the style of the landscape is completely appropriate. If Manet had ever painted the surface of Mars, this is exactly what it would've looked like, which somehow upsets Dolores even more.

"Now she goes back through the rooms she's already visited, and sure enough, each painting is subtly but unmistakably set on Mars: Raphael's *The Alba Madonna*, Hopper's *Cape Cod Evening*, El Greco's *Laocoön*, Botticelli's *Primavera*, Gainsborough's *The Painter's Daughters Chasing a Butterfly*, and on and on—all of them featuring red rock landscapes painted in the unmistakable styles of the original artists.

"With each altered painting she sees, Dolores grows angrier and angrier. Who would perpetrate such an elaborate and senseless prank? In a room with Delacroix's *Girl Seated in a Cemetery*—altered like all the rest—she grabs the security guard by the arm and asks what happened to all the original paintings. The security guard has no idea what she's talking about, so Dolores demands to speak with the museum's curator. The guard obliges, leading her to the main offices, where the curator listens politely to the woman's concerns and then patiently explains that the paintings have not been altered since being brought from Earth. Dolores argues with the curator, tries to prove somehow that these are not the original paintings, but she can't. She has no photographs or prints of the original paintings, so it's ultimately her word against the curator's. Eventually, Dolores gives up.

"In the next scene, she's standing again in front of *Le Déjeuner sur l'Herbe*, and at first she's still angry, but the longer she looks at the painting, the more the Martian version resonates with her. She can still remember the non-Mars version, but this new red rock setting seems so *right* somehow. It just fits, and Dolores finds it harder and harder to imagine the painting looking any other way. On her way out of the museum, she stops by the gift shop and buys a framed print of the painting—the Mars version—and goes home feeling oddly vindicated.

"So there you go. Obviously, there are some key differences from your story, but there were enough similarities, even some turns of phrase, that I thought your story had to be an homage to Salgado-MacKenzie."

There actually was a strong similarity there; my story's about a woman who insists that a painting by her late husband has been altered by the museum that displays it, although she can't pinpoint how exactly. But I'd never heard of Eduard Salgado-MacKenzie or read his Martian art museum story.

"No," I said. "I'm sorry. I don't know that story."

Another sigh from Sérgio. I felt bad disappointing him.

I said, "So this—what's his name again?"

"Eduard Salgado-MacKenzie."

"Right," I said. "This Salgado-MacKenzie. Is he a Brazilian writer?"

"That's a good question," he said, brightening a little. "Open up the top drawer of that filing cabinet, would you?"

I had to scoot my chair nearly out the door, and when I opened the drawer I found a hypochondriac's arsenal: blister packs of tablets for diarrhea, allergies, motion sickness; bottles of brightly colored syrups for coughs, sore throats, insomnia, the flu; bottles of pills for migraines, dizziness, fatigue.

"The antacid tablets," said Sérgio. "The yellow lid."

I found the bottle and handed it to him. With an expert flip of his thumb, he opened the snap-top lid and shook five of the chalky tablets into his palm. He tossed them back and proffered the open bottle in my direction.

"No thanks," I said. "I'm fine."

Nodding, he shut the lid and tossed the bottle back into the drawer with a clatter.

"You can shut that now," he said when he had finished chewing. A fine white powder dusted his lips. I shut the drawer.

"Eduard Salgado-MacKenzie," Sérgio said and then paused, wincing. "I'm sorry." He put a hand to his chest. "Disappointment gives me heartburn."

He took a breath.

. . .

So (began Sérgio). Eduard Salgado-MacKenzie. As you probably guessed, he's my favorite writer. His stories—most of them anyway—feature Captain Irena Sertôrian, commander of a spaceship that gets separated from its fleet at the end of a long, drawn-out intragalactic war. Her ship doesn't have the power to make it back home on its own, so she and her crew go from planet to planet in an obscure and dangerous system at the edge of the civilized galaxy—kind of a frontier situation. And that's pretty much it. Each story is a different adventure on a different planet.

As far as science fiction premises go, it's pretty conventional. People, at least the ones who've heard of him, dismiss Salgado-MacKenzie for that reason. They say his work is derivative and flat, but they're missing the point. They're not seeing what he *does* with that premise. I'm not sure how to explain to you . . .

Sérgio paused.

I was fifteen years old (he continued) when I first came across him in this magazine, *Contos Fantásticos*. I'd never heard of Salgado-MacKenzie before, but back then, when I read a magazine I read it cover to cover. So this story by Salgado-MacKenzie, it's called 'If You Seek a Pleasant Peninsula,' and it's about a planet where all of the living people live on one side, the light side, but then once they die, they go to the dark side of the planet, where they populate whole cities. They're not ghosts—they have substance—but they're dead. In fact, they have an entire dead society that mirrors the living one on the light side of the planet. Businesses, dance clubs, churches. And how the story starts is, Captain Irena Sertôrian and her crew land on the dead side of the planet, and it baffles all of the residents, because Irena Sertôrian and her crew are all alive and no living creature has ever been to the dark side of the planet.

Well, everyone starts asking questions—both the planets' residents and Sertôrian's crew—and this leads to a big tribunal that culminates with a really eerie examination by a dead-person doctor who uses a kind of stethoscope, but with a long needle instead of a drum, to listen to the soul, basically, of each member of the crew. I loved the story, and of course I had to get my hands on everything else this Salgado-MacKenzie had written, but that's where I ran into trouble. I riffled through the back issues of my magazines but came up empty. I subscribed to all the big ones, and some smaller ones too: *FC, Argonauto, O Planeta, Contos Astronômicos, Contos Intergalácticos, Contos do Astronauta*—the works. Anthologies too: stuff in translation by Asimov, Le Guin, Clarke, as well as Brazilian writers—Fausto Cunha, Jerônimo Monteiro, André Carneiro, Dinah Silveira de Queiroz, and some others. My father owned a newspaper—the *Paulistano*—so we were pretty comfortable and I had access to whatever reading material I wanted.

Even so, I couldn't find anything else by Salgado-MacKenzie in my collection. So what I did was I interrogated the owner of every bookshop in a twenty-block radius. I was a persistent little teenager, but nobody had heard of the guy. I kept looking, though, unwilling to give up that easily.

Sérgio's enthusiasm had an almost physical quality by this point—a tendril of intensity reaching across the room to hold me in its grasp.

Finally (continued Sérgio) in a three-year-old copy of a fifth-rate magazine called *Contos 'Science Fiction'* that I bought from a grimy used magazine stand at the train station, I found another one of his stories. In this one, Captain Irena Sertôrian lands on yet another undiscovered planet, in this case one that seems completely deserted. They poke around a little and are just about to leave, but then crew members start disappearing—just vanishing—and I'd tell you the rest but I wouldn't want to spoil it.

It's great. I enjoyed this second story as much as I had the first, maybe even more.

Unfortunately, finding his stories didn't get any easier from there. Over the course of five years, I only managed to track down another three. I loved them, though, as much as the first two I'd read, perhaps even more so because of the effort I'd expended in obtaining them.

Meanwhile, I'd also become interested in journalism and politics, and around the time I turned twenty-one, I got a job as a reporter for *O Trabalhador*, a minor leftist paper whose purpose in life was to criticize my father's right-leaning *Paulistano*. I liked to pretend that nobody on the staff knew my true identity—I worked under a pen name—and that I had been hired based solely on the merits of the handful of mediocre pieces of mine that had appeared in small newspapers around the city. I'd later find out that the editor knew exactly who I was and had hoped I might be a useful source of inside information about the *Paulistano*. Regrettably, for both me and the editor, I had never paid much attention to my father's mealtime shop talk, and once he heard I was working for the *Trabalhador*, he kept quiet about work whenever I was around.

Anyway, one day I was hanging around the offices of the *Trabalhador*, bending a colleague's ear about the greatness of Salgado-MacKenzie, when my colleague—fed up—stopped me and said that if I loved Salgado-MacKenzie so much, I should find him and tell him how I feel about his work, just to get it out of my system.

Why this idea had never occurred to me, I'm not sure. I'd forgotten, I suppose, that we occupied the same plane of existence, Salgado-MacKenzie having developed such totemic significance for me. But in all likelihood we actually lived in the same country, possibly even the same city. Who knows if I had already passed him in the street or stood next to him on a bus or sat behind him in a movie? The prospect left me dumbstruck.

Over the next few weeks, I managed to speak with every editor who had ever worked with Salgado-MacKenzie's fiction. Two of them had no idea who I was talking about; they had to look him up to verify that they had, in fact, published his work. Of the three editors who *did* remember his fiction, none had met him in person. His work had made an impression, though, and each of them offered up a different portrait—or, I suppose, theory—of the man, pieced together from whatever factual fragments they had managed to glean.

All three agreed that he had been born, or at least raised, in the United States, and that his mother was Brazilian, his father North American or possibly Scottish. The family relocated to Brazil when Salgado-MacKenzie was in his mid- to late teens, and so Portuguese was not his first language. Soon after moving, and here's where the details get even fuzzier, both parents died—a car crash, or a political hit, or a double suicide. Whatever the cause, young Eduard was left alone and spent his teenage years being passed around by distant relatives of his mother's. Or maybe he spent that time barely surviving on the streets. No one could say for sure.

Beyond those few tidbits, the editors I talked to agreed on very little. One editor claimed that Salgado-MacKenzie had written the stories decades and decades ago, in English, and had in the meantime died or moved back to the States. A friend or relative had discovered the manuscripts and was currently translating them into Portuguese, submitting them to various magazines as they were finished. This would explain the choppy Anglo sentence structure of the prose, as well as the stories' apparent unawareness of any scientific developments postdating the early fifties.

The second editor believed that Salgado-MacKenzie was actually a woman. This theory was based primarily, from what I could tell, on the fact that so many of his stories featured a female protagonist. This editor argued that the actual author felt a need to hide her identity and so adopted a male pseudonym. I asked why she would need to hide her identity, and the editor said she might be a government official, or maybe she was a serious artist dabbling in genre fiction. She might even have been the North American poet and noted lusophile Elizabeth Bishop, disguising herself with the stories' clumsy prose. It was not so far-fetched, really. Many respectable writers made secret forays into the sordid world of genre fiction. I told the editor I was not so sure.

The third editor I talked to believed that Eduard Salgado-MacKenzie was just a man named Eduard Salgado-MacKenzie, currently alive and writing odd stories in a language that was not his own. He was in all likelihood a very dull person and if I ever found him I would only be disappointed. This editor also gave me Salgado-MacKenzie's mailing address—a post office box—along with an assurance that I could try writing, but I'd never hear back from him.

I tried writing anyway, posting a brief but heartfelt letter in which I explained what his stories meant to me and asked if he would be open to speaking with me—perhaps I could profile him in the newspaper, or, if he shunned publicity, we could meet instead for a friendly cup of coffee.

I waited for weeks and then months, but as the editor had predicted, I received no response.

I was tempted at that time to take advantage of some government contacts I had established through my job. I knew they could get their hands on the personal information of the owner of that post office box, but in the end I decided to respect Salgado-MacKenzie's silence. Although his work remained a lodestar for me, I would leave the man in peace.

We'll jump forward about fifteen years, then: I was at a science-fiction convention here in the city. No, I should be more specific. I was three or four degrees removed from this convention. What I mean is, I had attended the convention during the day, and that evening I had gone to a party at a friend's house, a fellow SF enthusiast. The evening had worn on, and from that party I had broken off with a few people to go to a different party nearby. I had broken off from that party, and the one after that, and that's how, a little after midnight, I found myself in a cramped hotel room with a dozen or so fellow conventioneers that I had never met before in my life.

A few of us stood in the bathroom debating the merits of various first contact novels, but as the conversation grew heated and petty, I excused myself and made my way to the main room, stepping carefully over the lounging bodies of my fellow partygoers. The room reeked of cigarettes and sweat, but in a nice, intimate way. A relaxed, easy gathering, all in all: men and women sitting cross-legged on the two full beds, or sprawling out on the red-and-blue-patterned carpet, drinking and talking. In fact, everyone was sitting or reclining except for one slouchy middle-aged man who stood alone in the far corner of the room staring at an empty patch of carpet in front of him. He wore slacks, a threadbare blazer, and an unfashionably thick tie, the top button of his shirt still done up. He had a head like an upside-down egg and a sad, apologetic face.

I crossed the room toward the man, if for no other reason than to occupy the empty space of carpet in front of him; there was nowhere else to sit or stand.

"Sérgio Antunes," I said, holding out my hand. He shook it without looking me in the eyes.

"Eduard Salgado-MacKenzie," he said.

With the hum of a dozen conversations happening around me, I wasn't sure I had heard him right. I leaned in closer.

"Excuse me?" I said.

The man's already apologetic face assumed an even more remorseful expression as he opened his mouth to reply.

"I'm sorry, I know it's a mouthful," he said in a thick Anglo accent, his eyes still fixed on the carpet. "My name's Eduard Salgado-MacKenzie."

I couldn't believe it. I felt a rush of adrenaline, and the atmosphere in the room took on a vivid, dreamlike quality.

"Salgado-MacKenzie the writer? The Irena Sertôrian stories?"

"That's right," he said, looking up with surprise.

"This is wonderful," I said. "Mr. Salgado-MacKenzie. Sir. I'm a great admirer of your work."

He looked me in the eye, and for a moment—less than a moment—there was an expression of guarded pleasure, an expression that stretched his lips and cheeks into positions they seemed deeply unaccustomed to. He opened his mouth to reply, but then his eyes took in my face and something changed. His pale lips curled, his eyebrows clenched.

"You!" he exploded, and hit me in the chest, an awkward mix of a punch and a shove. I stepped back to keep my balance and knocked over the drink of the woman sitting on the floor behind me. She stood up, a ripple moved through the room, and then everyone's eyes were on me and the man in the corner.

"How dare you?" said the man, his finger pointed at my chest. "How dare you belittle me like that?"

The crowd in the room went completely silent.

"You must have misunderstood me," I said. "I'm truly a great admirer of your work. I can't even begin to convey what it's meant to—"

"No," he said, fury in his eyes. "I haven't forgotten how you treated me, and I refuse to allow it again."

"I'm sorry," I said, "but I think this is all a misunderstanding. You and I have never met before."

He winced at this.

"You'll pretend you don't know me?" he said.

Hoping to clear this up as quickly as possible, I said, "Truly, I don't recall—"

"Or have you forgotten?" he said, the fury now tinged with something much sadder. "Have you really forgotten?"

I lifted a placating hand. I said, "I can assure you, we've never met before tonight."

"Unbelievable," he said.

We were all a little tipsy by this point in the evening, but there was something frighteningly sober about this man, a clarity in his thin voice and his pale eyes. He had the attention of the entire room.

He said, "You lived for several years in a building on the corner of Imperiador and Machado. Apartment number 207. Am I wrong?"

He was not. That was my first apartment. I lived there when I was first starting out as a freelancer, up through my time with the *Trabalhador*. My hope that this was a complete misunderstanding shriveled inside me. I still didn't recognize this man, but he knew where I'd lived.

"That was my apartment," I said.

"I know," he said. "We were neighbors. I lived in 209."

He waited for me to process this, but still I didn't recognize him.

"I'm sorry," I said.

He said, "So you still claim we've never met?"

"All I'm saying," I said, "is that your face doesn't ring a bell."

"It figures," he said, throwing up his hands. He took a breath, composing himself, and turned to face the roomful of people, who watched us intently. When he began to speak again, it was to them, as if he couldn't bear to address me directly.

"This man," he said, his voice soft now, his audience straining to hear. "This man and I were neighbors for three years. We lived right next to each other, and although we were not friends by any means, we were friendly. I don't believe we were ever formally introduced, but we had a nodding acquaintanceship and exchanged pleasantries whenever we passed each other on the stairs or ran into each other at the mailboxes. During one of these exchanges, we discovered that both of us wrote professionally; he was a journalist and I earned my living translating repair manuals for industrial equipment.

"Once we found that common ground, we'd always talk books when we saw each other—not great, in-depth conversations, but updates on what each of us was reading. I was on a Flaubert kick in those days, and if I recall, Sérgio here was reading a lot of Hermann Hesse. There was the slightest edge of competition to our book updates, or if not competition then a desire to impress, at least on my part, which is why I might mention the latest Vargas Llosa novel I'd read, but not the latest Le Guin. Aside from books, we might complain about the building superintendent—a belligerent Southerner rumored to be the son of a Nazi in hiding—or commiserate over the building's unreliable plumbing. Standard neighbor small talk."

Salgado-MacKenzie paused and wiped at his pale lips. Personally, I could remember the bad plumbing, the superintendent with alleged Nazi ties, the building itself, but this guy's face was still completely unfamiliar to me, and so was our supposed book talk.

"As I said," Salgado-MacKenzie continued, "he and I were not friends—I recognize that—but when we greeted each other I thought I could detect a genuine warmth in his smile, a collegiality in his voice.

"We also shared a schedule in common—or rather, a lack of schedule. Unlike others on our floor, the two of us kept irregular hours. I translated from home, and so I worked when I felt like working and slept when I felt like sleeping. I often went for late-night walks and would return to see my neighbor here just getting in, or sometimes leaving.

"I still remember one chilly June midnight in particular. I'd just finished a translation and had no interest in sleeping. I decided, for starters, to check my mail. As I passed apartment 207, I saw light peeking through the crack at the bottom of the door and heard cupboards being opened and shut. Feeling that night owl's sense of camaraderie, I saluted the closed door and continued on to the stairs.

"When I got to my mailbox, my mood only improved; I found a letter inside informing me that I had won a short story contest put on by a magazine in Portugal. It was not a great prize but it was a good prize, and what's more, it was a contest I had forgotten I'd entered. I tucked the notice into my shirt pocket and ran quietly up the stairs. I walked down the hallway, past the door to my neighbor's still-lit apartment. I paused. I walked back several steps and, on a whim, knocked lightly on my neighbor's door.

"He answered almost immediately, pulling the door open wide, still dressed for work. Behind him, I could see an elaborate game of solitaire laid out on the battered kitchen table. Jaunty music played quietly in the background—Chico Buarque, maybe, or Caetano Veloso. My neighbor asked me what he could do for me. I told him I had good news, news worth celebrating, and would he like to join me for a drink, or maybe a bite to eat?

"He didn't respond right away. He waited for what must have been only a few seconds, but it felt to me like minutes, hours even, as I watched him consider my friendly proposal. I hadn't realized before I spoke how vulnerable I would feel extending this invitation. I'd suffered some personal losses recently and was—in ways that I understand now, but didn't at the time—aching for a human connection."

Salgado-MacKenzie paused at this point, lost in his own recollections. When he resumed his story, he spoke directly to me.

"You didn't even answer," he said. "Not a word. You just looked at me like I was nothing, and you shut that dark wooden door in my face. We never spoke again after that, until this evening."

His story over, Salgado-MacKenzie considered me through heavy-lidded eyes, and then shrugged back into the same cringing posture I had found him in, his gaze fixed on the carpet.

Naturally, I was horrified. I consider myself a basically kind person, and to treat someone that way would go against everything I believe in. My first impulse was to apologize, but the problem was, I had absolutely no memory of the incident, or of ever meeting Salgado-MacKenzie. His face remained stubbornly unfamiliar.

Part of me still hoped this was a terrible mistake, but I knew that voicing that possibility would only insult the man further. I had no idea what to say, and so I stood there, dumbstruck.

After a moment, Eduard Salgado-MacKenzie gave a snort of disgust, shoved past me, and left the party.


Sérgio shook his head. The tiny office had grown hot and stale over the course of his story. He leaned over and pushed the door, already slightly ajar, all the way open, and a soft rush of slightly cooler air drifted in. Sérgio brushed at something on the back of his hand and looked back up at me.

"It's a terrible feeling, being reviled by a lifelong idol," he said. "It's even worse to consider that I might have deserved it." He gave his beard a melancholy scratch. "More vexing still, though, is the question of why I don't remember the encounter or even the man's face. How could I forget someone that I'm supposed to have spoken with frequently?" He shook his head. "One possibility is that I was so wrapped up in myself at the time that the man next door never truly registered on my conscious-ness. Sad as that may be, it's very possible. I was young and fascinated by my own potential, and that can blind you to so much.

"I also, as a journalist, talked to a lot of people over the course of any given day, and that can blur conversations together, even make them dis-appear. So I can see how I might not have remembered him. But still, I can't imagine what would impel me to slam the door in the face of some-one who'd just made such a simple, friendly gesture."

Sérgio was looking increasingly despondent. I decided to throw in my two cents.

"Maybe he made the whole thing up," I said. "There's at least one inconsistency in his story."

"The mail?" said Sérgio.

"Right," I said. "If Salgado-MacKenzie had all his editorial mail sent to a post office box, then why was he getting an award notification at home?"

"Exactly," said Sérgio. "I've thought a lot about that. But it doesn't mean he was lying. It could be a minor misremembered detail, or maybe he sometimes submitted stories via his home address. Really, it's a small enough inconsistency that, if I'm being honest with myself, I have to admit doesn't invalidate his story."

He sighed heavily and stared into an empty corner of the office.

"I'm sorry," I said.

Sérgio nodded, eyes still distant.

He said, "I've tried to track him down since then, but with no luck. Salgado-MacKenzie put out a few more short stories during the early nineties, and then nothing. Radio silence."

Throughout Sérgio's story, I'd temporarily forgotten my own trou-bles, but as he wrapped up his account, thoughts of my failed novel came flooding back. I felt claustrophobic and queasy, suddenly desperate to get out of the tiny office.

"I should probably go," I said.

Sérgio scooted his desk/chair combo back, the legs screeching against the floor.

"Why don't you open that bottom drawer," he said, pointing to the filing cabinet. I swiveled around, knocking my shoulder against the front edge of Sérgio's desk, and opened the drawer. Instead of pharmaceuticals, I found hanging files, binders, and notebooks.

"That manila folder in front," said Sérgio. "Hand it to me, would you?"

I did, and while he leafed through its contents, I stood up and moved closer to the door, which only entailed taking a half step to my right. If I moved any farther, I'd be out in the hallway.

"Here it is," said Sérgio.

He pulled a stapled packet from the folder and held it out to me.

"It's a story by Salgado-MacKenzie," he said. "Take it. Read it."

didn't read the story. Instead I went back to my hotel and slept for eleven hours. Some people, when they're in trouble, can't sleep. Their problems rattle around their skulls like rocks in a polishing tumbler, and the noise keeps them up for hours. For me, it's the opposite. When I'm in a tight spot, it's like my brain overloads and there's nothing to do but shut down. Sometimes I don't even dream; I just lose consciousness for as long as my body can manage to stay asleep. It's great, until I wake up the next morning and my troubles return, reinvigorated by their own night's rest.

Sure enough, that's exactly what happened when I came to at 6:00 a.m. in my hotel room, still fully dressed in the clothes I'd been wearing the day before. I had managed to get my shoes off, so that was something. I sat up in bed, my clothes warm and wrinkled. The worst part was I had jeans on, and the only thing worse than sleeping in jeans is wearing them swimming.

I felt terrible.

This whole trip, Fortescue had been keeping me on a very short leash. Each morning I was required to email him an update on the research I'd done the day before, as well as the research I planned to complete that day.

My emails were vague yet positive, but I'd grown certain that Fortescue could smell the failure through my carefully worded missives and, like a bored tiger, was merely toying with me until he could administer the swift killing blow to my tender neck. I had no idea what I'd tell him in today's email, but I had to send it soon or I would miss his arbitrarily imposed deadline and incur whatever dire consequences lay in store.

I got out of bed, showered, and walked the half mile to the Biblioteca Anita Garibaldi as quickly as I could. Sitting down at the sleek, mid-century-modern worktable in the library's computer lab, I set to work on my email. I updated Fortescue on the previous day's research and then floated a hypothetical past him. Say I couldn't write this novel—what happens then?

I sent off the email, looked at a couple of news sites, and read an article from *SPIN* (or maybe it was *Rolling Stone*) arguing that power pop's true golden age ran from 1990 to 1997, and that the era's—and the genre's—greatest album, Matthew Sweet's *Girlfriend*, stands as a monumental testament to that fact. I was on board with the nineties-as-golden-age part of the argument, and I do like *Girlfriend*, but I certainly wouldn't rank it as the greatest power pop album of all time, or even of the nineties. (My top five nineties power pop albums? 1. *Kon Tiki* by Cotton Mather, 2. Fountains of Wayne's eponymous debut album, 3. *Frosting on the Beater* by The Posies, 4. *Girlfriend* by Matthew Sweet, 5. *Regretfully Yours* by Superdrag.)

I closed the article and was about to log off when I saw a new message in my inbox from Fortescue. His speed alarmed me, and with good reason.

His email started out positive, all rah-rah, halftime, go fight-win speak. He knew I could do it, blah, blah, blah. In the second paragraph, though, he answered my question. Failure to fulfill the terms of our contract would force the Coalition of Aggrieved Christians to repossess the funds they'd awarded me, pursuing legal action if necessary. Interest would be charged.

I read through the email a second time, and then a third. On the one hand, it was a relief to know exactly where I stood. On the other hand—and more important—I owed a shady religious organization seven thousand dollars, plus interest. I don't know if that sounds like a lot of money to you, but at the time, it was enough to demolish me. I was in bad trouble.

I know you must think I was overlooking the most obvious solution to my problem. Why not just write the novel? The truth is, I'd already been trying to for months by that point, since before I'd applied for the grant even. I'd always believed that writer's block was a luxury available only to established writers and smarmy, well-funded MFA students. Who else could afford to spend their time *not* writing, *not* moving forward on their next project?

And I guess my problem wasn't writer's block exactly. I was writing plenty—two thousand words a day, sometimes—but all of it was terrible. I would draft the novel's first chapter, spend weeks revising it, and then realize I hated it down to its bones and no amount of revision could save it. A few times I tried moving forward anyway, writing a second and a third chapter, but every time I did I despised each successive chapter even more than the one before it. I don't mean this to sound arrogant, but the problem wasn't a lack of talent on my part. Over the previous few years I'd developed a hard-won technical proficiency, but unfortunately even the most elegant sentence in the world couldn't mask the lack of heart in those failed drafts. You could almost hear rats' feet scurrying through the dry cellar that lay beneath every word I wrote.

I had hoped that my visit to São Paulo would imbue me with some grand sense of purpose. Instead, it had forced me to admit that this project as I'd imagined it—a grandiose *Portrait of the Artist as a Young Missionary*—was never going to happen. I don't want to get too much deeper into the details of why the novel didn't work out; that's not what this story is about. The short answer, though, is that I'd put too much pressure on the project. I was still stinging from all the grad school rejections. My financial situation was grim. I lacked conviction, artistic and otherwise. And so this novel needed to rescue me. It needed to radiate indisputable genius and it needed to sell a million copies. Instead, not surprisingly, it collapsed in on itself.

I read through Wayne Fortescue's email again, hoping that this time I'd notice a smiley face or a "J/K!!!" at the end of his paragraph of threats. No such luck. My fear was starting to go septic, and by the time I logged off the computer, I reeked with fury at stupid Wayne Fortescue and his stupid Coalition of stupid Aggrieved Christians, but most of all, at stupid me for signing the stupid contract to write a stupid novel that I now hated the thought of.

I needed to clear my head. I slung my backpack over my shoulder and headed for the nearest exit.

I was almost to the door when Sérgio stepped out from behind a bookcase, head buried in a newspaper. I had to skip to the side to keep from bumping into him.

"Daniel," he said. "So sorry."

Today's T-shirt, partially obscured beneath his buttoned blazer, featured Iron Maiden, a band more beloved in Brazil than maybe anyplace else in the world.

"It's fine," I said.

"A dangerous habit," he said, lifting up the newspaper. "Walking while reading."

"Really," I said, "don't worry about it."

I took a step toward the door.

"I am glad I caught you, though," he said, tucking the newspaper under his arm. "What did you think of the story?"

The truth was, I'd completely forgotten about it.

"Right," I said. "The Salgado-MacKenzie."

"The very one," he said.

I hadn't read it but a lie seemed like the quickest way out the door.

"Yeah," I said. "It was pretty good."

"Pretty good?" said Sérgio.

"Yeah," I said. "Not bad." Sérgio arched an eyebrow at this. I went on. "And also, I just want to thank you for all your help with the research and everything. I may not be coming back to the library before I fly home, because I'm going to be doing some on-the-ground type stuff for the next few days. You know, getting reacquainted with the city and whatnot. So, thanks."

Sérgio tapped his folded newspaper against his chin while he considered this, sphinxlike.

"It was my pleasure," he said finally. "Good luck to you."

Before I could get entangled further, I told Sérgio that I had to run and then stepped out the door into the eucalyptus-and-exhaust-scented air of the city. I walked, head down, earbuds plugged in, to the nearest metrô station, swiped my ten-day pass, and boarded the first train that pulled up to the platform.

I must have looked as angry as I felt, because the other passengers kept their distance, eyeing me warily, a toxic blond ogre stinking of huffy failure. As I watched the city pass by through the window—towering skyscrapers, bustling church-side praças, clusters of plywood shanties—I remembered the story that Sérgio had given me. I felt bad about lying to him—he'd been nothing but generous to me, and the story obviously meant a lot to him. I should just read it.

I found the pages, all crumpled, at the bottom of my backpack. I sat down in an open seat, smoothed out the creased paper, and started to read.

**III**

The story begins with Captain Irena Sertôrian and her crew, dangerously low on provisions, making an emergency supply stop on an unknown planet. They touch down in an abandoned rocket port near a small, picturesque village. The way Salgado-MacKenzie describes it, the village sounds like a painting by Norman Rockwell: broad, tree-lined streets; white picket fences; front-porch rocking chairs—the works. And next to the village is a beautiful blue lake.

As Sertôrian and her crew cautiously approach the village, they're met by a small welcoming party, all smiles. A man in a three-piece suit introduces himself as the mayor, and a kindly old woman presents them with a strawberry rhubarb pie still warm from the oven. Sertôrian thanks them for their hospitality and explains their predicament. She asks the mayor if the town could spare some fuel and basic provisions. The mayor thinks about this for a second and then says his town would be happy to help, but it will take them a day or so to get the necessary supplies together. In the meantime, Sertôrian and her crew will be the honored guests of the town. Sertôrian thanks him profusely.

The mayor bows and wishes them well, and then the kindly old woman, the one who gave them the pie, leads them to the boardinghouse she runs and tells them to make themselves at home. That evening, they all enjoy a hearty, home-cooked dinner together, the best food they've eaten in ages. While they're polishing off the last of the roast bisonium, the mayor stops by and invites them all to go for a swim with him in the lake the next morning. The lake, he says, is the village's pride and joy. Sertôrian says they'd be honored to swim in the lake, and the mayor wishes them a good evening.

That night, the crew sleeps extremely well, and the next morning, after a hearty breakfast, they meet the mayor down at the edge of the lake. He's there with two smiling villagers—tall, broad-shouldered men—and they're dressed in this iridescent dive gear that's kind of incongruous with the aesthetic of the story so far. They have extra gear for Sertôrian and her crew, and while they all suit up, the mayor tells them about the lake.

He says the lake is deeper than any other on their planet, and that to understand the people of this village, one must plumb the depths of the lake's dark waters. He says that to do so is an honor rarely extended to foreigners, but that, as they will soon understand, Sertôrian and her crew have earned it.

After that, there's a pretty tedious passage describing a short hike to a special cliff that they're all going to jump from. Not much happens, but the story goes on and on about the smooth pristine surface of the lake and the fathomless depths below. Eventually, though, they make it to the cliff and everybody jumps into the water.

That's where things really start to pick up. Down they all go, dive suits shimmering, and the deeper they sink, the uneasier Sertôrian and her crew become. They were on their guard already, this being an unfamiliar situation on an unknown planet, but now they really start to worry. They'd been anticipating something more recreational, but the mayor swims toward the bottom of the lake with this steely determination. This definitely isn't play, or unstructured exploration. They're headed someplace specific.

The other weird thing is that they're being pulled to the bottom of the lake somehow. Since they're actively swimming downward, nobody notices it at first, but then Sertôrian stops kicking for a second, and she doesn't slow down at all. She signals her crewmates and they see her, legs not moving, descending as quickly as the rest of them. This makes them all pretty nervous. One of them tries swimming upward, but it's no use; they all keep hurtling down toward the bottom of the lake.

And that's the other thing. They keep expecting the lake bottom to appear at any second because they've been descending for a really long time, but below them there's just more blue, darker and darker blue, and after a while, it's the same above them as well. No sunlight, just dark water. At this point they realize that the tech on this planet is much more advanced than it seemed at first. The dive suits are flimsy looking, but are helping their bodies withstand a crazy amount of pressure.

Well, they keep falling, and Salgado-MacKenzie keeps ratcheting up the suspense, doing a really nice job of it too, and then finally the shipmates see something. At first it's just a blurry outline below them, but the farther down they go, they see that it's an enormous building, all wavy metal and smooth contours, a really organic looking structure, but shiny too. As they get closer, it becomes clear that this structure is colossal, bigger even than the village they've just come from. As far as they can tell, the building has no windows or doors. It's all smooth, undulating metal.

Apparently there are doors, though, because one opens up directly below the divers. It's more of a hatch, really, but the important thing is, the opening is pulling everyone toward it. It slowly sucks them all into the building and then the hatch closes behind them. For a second everything's dark, but then a light goes on and the water drains out of the room very, very quickly, because that's where they are, in a little room like they have in submarines—an airlock?—and in just a few seconds all of the water's gone.

The mayor removes his diving mask, all smiles, and is about to make some speech, but before he can, Sertôrian pulls off her own mask and just lays into the mayor. He should have warned them about what was going to happen, and he had no right to drag them to the bottom of this lake without their permission, and what was he thinking?

The mayor looks pretty contrite about this, as do his two assistants. The mayor says he's mortified, just mortified. He thought it would be a nice surprise for everybody, but he can see now how maybe it wasn't the best idea, maybe not the type of surprise that everyone would enjoy. He says he hopes Sertôrian and her crew will accept his most sincere apologies.

This doesn't make Sertôrian any less wary, but she can see that the best tactical move is to pretend to accept the apology. So she does, but she still insists that they return to the village immediately. The mayor says it would be a shame not to take a tour of the Aquatorium—that's what this building's called—before they go. Sertôrian declines the invitation. The mayor presses. It goes back and forth like that until the mayor sneers at Sertôrian and her crew, tells them there's no point pretending anymore, and presses a button on this special wrist console he has on his suit.

Immediately, the dive suits of Sertôrian and her crew go completely rigid. Basically they're trapped. That's when the mayor introduces one of his assistants as the town judge. The judge gives a solemn little bow, and then pulls this sheet of parchment from a pocket of his dive suit. He reads some official jargon about Sertôrian and her crew committing grave crimes against the village of Lakeshore, and that now, for their own good and for the good of society, they're sentenced to life imprisonment in the Aquatorium.

Then things get a little convoluted in the story, or maybe it just stretched my Portuguese skills too far. As I understood it, though, the mayor and his assistants—the judge and the other guy—are able to leave somehow, but Sertôrian and her crew are stuck, and then their dive gear dissolves, or is taken away, and then they're inside the main hall of the Aquatorium with thousands of other people.

From here we learn that the Aquatorium is essentially a gigantic underwater debtors' prison. The people of the village have very strong feelings about self-sufficiency, or whatever you want to call it, so anyone who can't pay off their debts is cast out of town and sent to live at the bottom of the lake. That's why Sertôrian and her crew are there, because basically they just showed up on the planet and asked for a handout. Actually, it's a little more complicated than that. Salgado-MacKenzie spends eight pages explaining the philosophical underpinnings of the law, as well as its nuanced applications. In a nutshell, though, the Aquatorium is a debtors' prison.

The story picks right back up as it follows Sertôrian and her crew through their first few weeks in the Aquatorium. Navigating prison life requires every skill they've developed during the war and their subsequent years of imperiled wandering. The Aquatorium is surprisingly brutal for a debtors' prison, thanks in large part to the guards. They treat their charges with unrelenting cruelty, devising malevolent schemes to exploit existing rivalries between the inmates—rivalries that, thanks in part to these machinations, often erupt in violence. Within this turbulent environment, the shipmates are constantly having to prove themselves in bloody one-on-one fights that happen whenever the guards deliberately turn a blind eye. However, all of the shipmates, and Sertôrian especially, successfully strike a balance between being tough but not malicious, and eventually they win the respect of their fellow prisoners.

Their closest ally is a woman named Vera, who has attempted twenty-three separate escapes from the Aquatorium. She's kept in solitary confinement most of the time because of this, but Sertôrian's chief technician rigs up a way for Vera to communicate with them, and together they plan a daring prison break that will free everyone inside the Aquatorium.

Their escape plan relies on a crucial piece of intelligence: On her most recent attempt, Vera could have gotten away but instead chose to break into the warden's office because of a rumor she'd heard from the Aquatorium's most senior inmate just before he'd died. He'd told Vera that plans existed to safely evacuate the warden and all of the guards in case of emergency. He wasn't sure how, exactly, but if Vera could find out, she could use the plans to escape with a large number of her fellow inmates.

Sure enough, when Vera broke into the warden's office and cracked his safe, she found protocols and technical directions for turning the Aquatorium's recreation hall into a massive, temporary submarine that would safely carry its occupants to the surface. Elated, Vera committed the plans to memory, returned them to the safe, and then, to cover her tracks, deliberately got caught by a guard on the opposite end of the Aquatorium.

With this submarine evacuation capability in mind, then, Vera and Captain Sertôrian plan the prison break. One part of their escape team will draw the guards away from the recreation hall. Another will disable the locking mechanism that keeps all the individual cells closed. Another will guide all their fellow inmates to the recreation hall. And another will make the necessary technical preparations for the recreation hall to become an escape submarine.

The prison break itself goes better than any of them could have expected. In the cafeteria, Vera starts a small fire that temporarily distracts the guards, and from there everything runs like clockwork. The prisoners are freed from their cells. The guards are drawn out of the recreation hall, which is then filled with all the prisoners. Sertôrian's chief technician throws a lever. The wing seals itself off from the rest of the prison. An engine whirs to life and the vessel rises.

Inside the submarine, there's cheering, hugging, and tears. Everyone thrills at the prospect of seeing daylight again, of being able to move about freely. For a few minutes, the recreation hall is one big happy party.

When they reach the surface, though, the real trouble begins. Turns out, the warden and the guards were able to send word to the mayor about the prison break via a secret emergency radio, so when Vera, Sertôrian and her crew, and all the other prisoners finally make it to shore, the mayor and most of the village are waiting with heavy artillery.

It gets pretty ugly. They just start mowing down the prisoners, no questions asked. Bodies pile up, blood in the water, the works. The prisoners do have some makeshift weapons of their own, though, and there are so many of them that even though the casualties are severe, they manage to overwhelm the forces of the mayor eventually. They take control of the heavy artillery and, in turn, the village.

Things get more complicated from there as the former occupants of the Aquatorium disagree about how to proceed. Some of the people want to execute every last villager on the spot. Others, led by Vera, argue for a more temperate approach, at least for the time being—a resettlement elsewhere on the planet, maybe, or even a peaceful reintegration. By this point, Sertôrian and her crew have extricated themselves from the core of the action and are just waiting for the first opportunity to make a break for their ship. They've seen this kind of thing before, but that doesn't make it any easier to watch.

As the debate among the former prisoners heats up, the shipmates slip away. There's this moment just as they're leaving when Sertôrian catches Vera's eye, wanting to silently thank her for helping them escape the Aquatorium, and Vera looks back at her from the midst of this debate that's only getting uglier, and just looks completely overwhelmed, kind of defeated. Sertôrian turns away, and then she and her crew are off. They're boarding their spaceship when they hear renewed gunfire back in the village. Then they take off and that's it.

W hat I'm about to show you," said Sérgio, "has remained hidden from the eyes of the world for many, many years. Only a select and worthy few have ever laid eyes on this document, and you, Daniel Laszlo, having passed your initiatory trial, will now join that select fellowship."

I was back in Sérgio's office, my plans for the day having taken another unexpected turn. I'd been so engrossed in the Salgado-MacKenzie story that, without noticing, I'd ridden the train all the way to the end of the line and then back to the same station I'd started from just a few blocks from the library.

After apologizing to Sérgio for lying to him that morning, I'd told him what had just happened with the story—that it had drawn me in so completely that I'd lost track of my physical existence in the world.

"Very good," Sérgio had said. "Very good. I think you're ready now to hear the portions of my story that I withheld from you yesterday."

We'd then walked down to his office, where he'd removed a yellowing, business-sized envelope from a secret pocket on the inner wall of the filing cabinet.

Sérgio now held that envelope upright at the front edge of his desk.

"I wish I could tell you, Daniel," he said, "that the reason nobody else has seen this document is because a sinister cabal—the Illuminati, maybe, or the Rosicrucians—has worked for decades to suppress it, and that I only obtained it myself by deciphering a series of obscure clues I found concealed within the world's most treasured works of art, clues that led me to a labyrinthine archive below a centuries-old cathedral, where I snatched this document from its malevolent keepers at great risk to my own life.

"But the truth is, I found this document in a box of garbage, and nobody else knows about it because nobody else cares."

He set the letter flat on his desk and raised his hands in a gesture of rhetorical surrender.

"Nevertheless," he went on, standing the envelope back up on its edge. "I would ask you, are the forces of indifference any less sinister than those of hooded cultists bound together by arcane oaths to uphold ancient and bloody agendas? I would say no, mainly because I don't believe these secret cabals really exist. Indifference, though, is all too real. Indifference snuffs out idealism and enables tyrants. Indifference consigns millions of fascinating men and women to the dustbin of history. Indifference swallows people like you and me into its gaping maw, never to release us. *That's* what we're fighting against here, Daniel."

He waved the envelope at me.

The story of how I got my hands on this document (said Sérgio) picks up where yesterday's story left off. My unexpected meeting with Eduard Salgado-MacKenzie really rattled me, prompting some intense soul searching, as you can probably imagine. It also kicked off a four-year rough patch in my life. First, I lost my job because my editor was under government pressure to kill a story I was working on, and I wouldn't give in. This wasn't the *Trabalhador*—I'd moved on from there. I'd rather not say which paper it was because the editor's still around, and I don't really blame him for what he did, because those were complicated times. The upshot, though, was that I lost my job and became very disillusioned with journalism.

I told you that I'd moved on from the *Trabalhador*? I'd been fired there too, actually. I shouldn't obscure that fact. Office politics of a very different variety in that case. Anyway, I was sick of all that and ready for a career change, and maybe I could have found work at another paper, or maybe not, but I decided I wasn't interested.

I also got divorced around this same time, after being married for just fifteen months. Her name was Dina, and she was a theater critic for one of the big newspapers. A really terrific woman. I don't know. I don't really want to go through all the details again, or my theories of what went wrong. Things did go wrong, though. We both made mistakes and treated each other poorly, just shabbily, and were both devastated when it got to the point when we realized that neither of us could stand the sight of the other anymore. We wanted it to work, you see. And we thought it would, but it didn't.

During all this time, I was also trying—and failing—to track down Eduard Salgado-MacKenzie. The morning after that party, I called everyone I knew who'd been there. None of them knew Salgado-MacKenzie. I called the organizers of the convention, hoping he'd been a registered attendee, but no such luck. I wanted so badly to speak to him again, to apologize or try to work out what had actually happened between us. I wrote a long letter to the old post office box address I had, but he never wrote back. I wasn't even sure if the box still belonged to him.

Well, eventually I found a new job, albeit a temporary one. An old friend from the *Trabalhador* put me in touch with an extravagantly wealthy steel baron who was looking for someone with good research skills and a familiarity with pulp magazines. Agreeing that I certainly fit the bill, the steel baron and I arranged a meeting, and over caipirinhas at his glass-and-metal beach house, the man explained to me that he collected vintage literary erotica. To his knowledge, he had one of the finest collections in the world. A recent uptick in business, though, had left him short on time to pursue this hobby, and the thought of all the books and magazines that he wasn't collecting, that were simply moldering in storage rooms and used bookstores, was driving him a little crazy. Erotica, he explained, was such a fleeting genre. By and large, libraries, museums, and other archives expended scandalously little effort to preserve such publications, and if he and other like-minded individuals didn't collect the books and magazines themselves, they would be lost to humanity forever, doomed to rot in landfills or burn in garbage fires.

He said he understood his hobby might seem strange to me. I told him it didn't—not at all. I explained my lifelong interest in the work of Salgado-MacKenzie and the similar frustrations I'd encountered as I'd searched for his work in the highly disposable medium of the pulps. Thrilled that I understood, the steel baron hired me on the spot as his official acquisitions agent. He gave me a handwritten list of titles he hoped to obtain, and I set to work.

I enjoyed the job, although it ended up being very short-lived. My employer quickly realized that 80 percent of the joy he'd taken in his hobby had come from the thrill of the hunt, and to farm that part of the process out was to deprive himself of great pleasure.

Still, while the job lasted I was very good at it. I knew all the best places to look for old, disreputable magazines and cheap anthologies. Most pulp presses trafficked in multiple unsavory genres—science fiction, true crime, horror, erotica—so many of the contacts I'd developed in the publishing world during my decades-long quest for the works of Eduard Salgado-MacKenzie were able to point me toward the obscure titles that my employer wished to acquire.

I was also fascinated by the stories themselves. While many of them utilized hackneyed premises involving nurses, schoolteachers, and libidinous dukes, some of the more obscure stories featured scenarios as novel and elaborate as anything I'd ever encountered. I read stories featuring telekinetic nipples and lie-detecting scrotums. I read stories of nude astral projection, of invisible orgies held in empty deserts, of shape-shifting lovers alternately confounding and fulfilling their partners' desires with their ever-mutating forms. I read about yodeling vaginas and penises turned to gold. I read an erotic homage to Borges entitled, "The Erogenous Library of Babel," in which an infinite ziggurat contains a living catalog of every sex act that could ever be imagined. Each piece in the catalog embodies a steamy (or in a few cases, very, very cold) coupling (or tripling, or quadrupling, and so on) of wildly ecstatic participants. These carnal tableaux are curated by a rigorously trained order of scholars, whose understanding of human lust, over time, reaches divine, transcendent heights.

These stories explored territories of the human imagination I never knew to be so vast, so intriguing, or so delightful.

As I said, the job didn't last long, but the experience proved invaluable to me for two key reasons. The first was that it led me to my current vocation as a librarian, a career I've found far more satisfying and suited to my talents than journalism.

The second is this envelope, which I stumbled upon completely by accident. A few weeks after I accepted the gig with the steel baron, I got a call from a publishing friend who wanted to let me know that the owner of Venus House, a small press that had specialized in pulp anthologies—erotica, mainly, as well as some science fiction—had just died. Apparently, the man had kept in the second bedroom of his apartment a copy of every book he'd ever published, and this weekend his nephew would be auctioning it all off to whoever was interested. I thanked my friend for the tip, and immediately informed the steel baron.

My employer said he was very interested, and instructed me to buy as much of the collection as I could. Given my employer's deep, deep pockets, I was able to buy all of the deceased publisher's collected erotica, allowing with some reluctance the few boxes of science fiction he'd accumulated to be divided among the other attendees at the auction.

It turned out that buying these books was the easy part of the job. When the boxes arrived at his library, the steel baron instructed me to catalog each new volume, to read every book from every box, and to write a one-sentence summary of every story in every erotic anthology that Venus House had published. My employer was paying me well, though, so in spite of the staggering tedium that lay ahead of me, I acquiesced.

Even with some judicious skimming, it was exhausting work. I mentioned before that some of the erotica I encountered through this job truly impressed me. This was not the case with the fiction purveyed by

Venus House. The publisher's hallmark seemed to be uninspired clichés offered up at prices so low that they made the stories' banality sufficiently acceptable to its consumers. Up to this point, the job had felt like a lucrative busman's holiday, but now I was truly working for my wages.

I was about halfway through a box of *Naughty Nurse* anthologies—one of the publisher's most popular series—and feeling increasingly certain that if I read one more lazy description of heavy breasts beneath crisp white uniforms, my brain would get up out of my skull and walk away.

Then, I picked up *Naughty Nurses #27: Bedpan Babes*, and stuck to the back cover, I found this.

Sérgio raised his eyebrows, tapping the envelope on his desk with both forefingers.

In the moment (he said) I was so focused on the task at hand that I detached the envelope—obviously affixed accidentally—and was about to toss it aside without a second look. I set the letter down, and that's when I saw the return address on the back: "Eduard Salgado-MacKenzie," followed by a familiar post office box in São Paulo.

I couldn't believe it. For a second I wondered if I'd fallen asleep, the nurse stories' soporific powers having finally overwhelmed me. But no— I was antsily conscious, with three cups of coffee coursing briskly through my veins. The letter was addressed to Venus House and remained unopened. Trying not to get my hopes up—after all, the envelope was too small to contain a story—I carefully slit open the seal and, briefly savoring the moment, removed the unread letter.

Sérgio smiled at this memory, and then held out the envelope to me.

"Go ahead," he said. "Look inside."

**V**

9 May 1976

Dear Mr. Lobos,

I am an avid reader of the science fiction published by your press. *Through a Looking-Glass Darkly: An Anthology of Alternate Realities* contains one of my all-time favorite stories: Felipe Valentinês's "A Harsh Cry at Midnight." I also greatly admire a novel you recently published—*Alas the Stars* by Emília Montenegro—whose scope and ambition challenged and inspired me. For these reasons, I believe Venus House would be an optimal publisher for a long-gestating project of mine.

Strictly speaking, THE INFINITE FUTURE is not a novel. It is, instead, a prose-poem epic that discerns in the imagined empires of the future the germ of humanity's eventual henosis— its sublime and terrible union with the infinite future. It is, in other words, a prophetic text on a par with the Holy Bible or the I Ching.

To be clear, the union that THE INFINITE FUTURE prognosticates—humankind's sublime henosis—will not be achieved through the contemplation of warm homilies and gentle proverbs. No. Such a union can only be brought about through a bracing immersion in certain truths so occult and so challenging that the workaday world cannot now perceive them.

And from what source do these supernal truths flow? Thick and sweet as honey, they flow from the life and teachings of one Irena Sertôrian, a twenty-third-century space captain, who in the twilight years of her storied life was received four times—in vision or in actuality, she could not say—into the presence of the divine and elusive beings who shape and govern our vast and unfathomable universe. Sertôrian's accounts of these divine encounters are—or rather, will be, as I speak of things that are yet to come—unparalleled in their majesty and insight.

THE INFINTE FUTURE, however, does not contain Sertôrian's accounts of these visions, nor does it present a straightforward biography of the illustrious Sertôrian. To engage such grandeur so directly would be, to the mind of the average reader, equivalent to staring directly at the sun. For just as that blazing star that holds our simple Earth in its orbit burns the eyes of those who gaze directly upon it, the unthinkable visions of Irena Sertôrian sear the souls of any who have not been properly prepared to receive their glories.

It is as an initiatory text, therefore, that THE INFINITE FUTURE functions, preparing the hearts and minds of a blindfolded generation to be filled with a stark and challenging light. More a single-volume library than a unified narrative, THE INFINITE FUTURE presents devotional poems, clouded prophecies, scriptural exegeses, scholarly histories, mystic visions, and slippery allegories composed by various and sundry disciples of Sertôrian in the centuries (and millennia!) after her death.

To briefly delineate *just a few* of these narratives:

1. **The Vizio of Han-Tin Haantin**
   The oral history of a humble crentonium miner who received indescribable visions of Sertôrian's inner being while trapped in a collapsed mine shaft for three days with no food and very little water.

2. **The Agony and the Ecstasy of Sister Úrsula**
   An account written by a galactically revered nun-historian
   whose attempts to reconcile her scholarly methodologies
   with her latent mystic impulses is made all the more urgent
   by the approach from without of hostile armed forces, and
   the pressure from within of a long-kept secret that has
   tormented her for decades.

3. **Nebula Songs**
   A collection of psalms praising the wisdom of Irena
   Sertôrian and comparing her glorious ministry to the
   cloudy splendor of a distant nebula.

4. **The Apotheosis of CGJ-Gamma**
   An allegory, composed by an early follower of Sertôrian,
   in which an ambulatory robot claims to have achieved
   self-awareness through a felicitous irregularity in its
   programming. When asked to prove this by an
   interplanetary panel of scientists, the robot refuses.
   Instead, it hijacks a long-distance transport vessel and sets
   out to explore segments of the universe that have never
   been visited by humans. Its pilgrimage is described in such
   a way as to simulate for the reader the experience of being
   a self-aware machine.

And those are only four of the legion of prophecies, visions,
and wisdom-books that together form THE INFINITE
FUTURE, a volume whose significance will one day reverberate
throughout all of space-time. Where the sages of eons past
sought theosophical truths in homely seer stones and Aztec
mirrors of pure obsidian, those seeking such mystical insights
today must turn their gaze to THE INFINITE FUTURE, a

work as uncompromising as stone, and as effulgent as cut gems in the noonday sun.

Be warned before you embark, however, that books cannot be unread and—as much as you might wish to after absorbing the sublime and horrible truths contained within these narratives— there will be no returning to that prelapsarian state of innocence that constituted your existence before experiencing THE INFINITE FUTURE.

If this project interests you, it would be my pleasure to send the full manuscript. I thank you for your consideration.

Sincerely,
Eduard Salgado-MacKenzie

# VI

still remember that moment fondly.

Right now I'm studying for the bar exam. Not *right now* right now, obviously. Right now I'm writing this introduction. It's eleven o'clock at night, and I'm alone in the galley kitchen of my apartment. I'm writing right now because after bombarding myself for thirteen hours with sample MBE questions, I'm too keyed up to go straight to bed, and the writing helps me ease back into thinking like a human again.

Studying for the bar exam feels so different from what I was doing—or trying to do—on that research trip to São Paulo. Generally speaking, I don't look back on that period of my life with any degree of nostalgia. Financially, my situation was grim and about to get grimmer. Artistically, I was floundering, slowly coming to the painful realization that I didn't have what it takes to write a novel. Personally, I was lonely; I was so cloistered during my post-undergrad years in Provo that my existing friendships had dissolved in the acid bath of my solitude. Romantically, things were just as bad. I'd broken up with my girlfriend of two years the night after we both graduated from BYU, my ostensible reason being a desire to date other people before we committed to anything more serious, when in reality I hadn't wanted her there as a witness to the death of my once bright potential. I'd regretted the decision almost immediately, but by the time I called her three months later, she'd already started seeing someone else. And finally, spiritually, I was stagnant: I'd lost my missionary zeal long before and had failed to replace it with anything more compelling. Failure encroached from all sides.

I thought a lot during this time of some advice I'd once gleaned from a wilderness survival manual. Apparently, if you ever fall from a great height into a large body of water, it's very important that you clench your anus. The manual didn't explain why. My best guess is that if you're falling from high enough, the water might tear through your guts if it finds a way in, but I'm no doctor and that's just a guess. In any event, it's one of the most depressing pieces of advice I've ever come across.

To be clear, I'm not saying it's a bad idea to clench your anus if you ever find yourself in that situation, or even that it's not important. What I *am* saying is that if you're ever jumping or falling from a very high place *against your will*, then things are really not going great for you. And while some people might find it symbolically inspiring to maintain control over whatever elements you can, no matter how dire the circumstances—stiff upper lip, tight sphincter, etc.—for me that clenched anus is rife with nothing but pathos. Sure, it might help you a little, but really it's just a reminder of how terrible your situation is.

That, in a nutshell, is how I remember the Provo doughnut shop years—a free fall during which all of my grand plans amounted to so much anus clenching.

There were moments, though, that, however briefly, offered something more. The first time I read Eduard Salgado-MacKenzie's novel proposal was one of those moments. The sheer bravado of the document was contagious, infecting me, at least for a few minutes, with a robust confidence. What this novel promised was no less than a gateway to enlightenment, a path to the innermost secrets of the universe. Also contained in this promise was a hint of danger that I couldn't quite pin down, but on the whole, the proposal, rather than repel me, endowed me with a small glimmer of hope, both for my own future and humanity's.

I had to read this book.

"You can imagine the thrill I got," said Sérgio, "when I first read that letter."

"Yeah," I said.

The strange energy of the document had my hands jittering with excitement.

You see, this letter confirmed something I'd been unwilling to acknowledge, even to myself (said Sérgio). The fact of the matter is, though I'd never been a religious man, Captain Irena Sertôrian had, over the years, come to inhabit a place of reverence in my soul. Beneath her generic similarity to so many other fictional space captains, she pulsed with something unique, something intriguing. In empty and difficult times throughout my young life, I often found my mind turning to Sertôrian, not so much to wonder what she would do in my shoes but simply to contemplate her being, to dwell in her imagined presence.

Doing so filled me with a bristly kind of peace, for lack of a better way to describe the feeling, a grounding in something potent yet ethereal. As I've already mentioned, this connection I felt to Irena Sertôrian— a nonexistent person—deeply discomfited me, and I refused to admit to myself the great significance she'd gained in the inner recesses of my being. Though I was perfectly comfortable professing my enthusiasm for Salgado-MacKenzie's stories as compelling fictions, even I could recognize that this connection to Sertôrian was a bridge too far. And so I kept my strange faith buried, nourishing it only occasionally with quiet reveries on Sertôrian's occult divinity and otherwise refusing to fully acknowledge the depths of my devotion to this fictional being.

Then I read that book proposal, and everything came to the surface. If I'd developed delusional attitudes surrounding Irena Sertôrian, at least I knew now that they were shared delusions. Salgado-MacKenzie himself recognized—or should I say instilled?—the selfsame mystical qualities in the intrepid space captain that I'd discerned over my years of reading. It was indisputable, and so of course, I had to find *The Infinite Future*. I needed to absorb its teachings and discover where this discipleship might lead me.

My life had a purpose again. I got on the phone immediately and called everyone I knew who'd been involved in publishing during the seventies. I figured if Salgado-MacKenzie had queried Venus House, he had probably contacted other presses as well.

Well, I'm sure you won't be surprised to hear that the search went very poorly. Most of the people I spoke to just laughed when I asked them about Salgado-MacKenzie's book proposal. Did I realize how many queries passed through their hands on any given day, they'd say. And I was asking them to remember one specific query from the 1970s written by some nobody? I'd tell them yes, I was, and to please call me if they remembered anything.

The futility of my quest was not lost on me, but still, it was the happiest I'd been in years. Even contemplating the concept of the novel filled me with a faint, otherworldly light. I could only imagine what the text itself would do.

One Saturday, I stopped by the office of Vanda Soares—a friend of a friend from school—who I'd learned recently had worked very, very briefly as an assistant editor with LusoGalactica, a small science-fiction press, now defunct. Now she wrote telenovelas and did very well for herself.

I showed her the letter, and she said, "Yeah, I remember that book."

I was taken aback, certain that she was confusing *The Infinite Future* with some other more prominent novel. But she insisted that this was a query she remembered.

I said, "Did you see a manuscript as well?"

"Yeah," she said. "Cardoso, the editor, came out of his office one day holding a query letter that had ended up on his desk by mistake. I thought he was going to be angry it ended up there, but he'd read it and told me to contact the author and request the novel. It would either be brilliant or a train wreck, and Cardoso was dying to find out which.

"So I wrote to the author—Eduard Salgado-MacKenzie—and requested the full manuscript. It showed up within a week, and I kid you not, the manuscript was a foot high. When Cardoso saw it sitting on my desk, he laughed and told me to read the first ten pages. If they seemed brilliant—like earth-shatteringly good—then I should read some more. Otherwise we'd send it back."

"So?" I said.

"We sent it back," she said. "I wish I could say I remember anything else about it, but I don't. I probably would've forgotten the incident altogether, except I only worked there three months, so that experience stands out."

I asked Vanda some follow-up questions, but that was really all she remembered. I thanked her profusely for her time.

I realize it may not sound like much, but Vanda's sighting of the manuscript was all I needed to keep me going—it meant that *The Infinite Future* really existed, that I wasn't chasing a phantom—and I've been on the novel's trail off and on ever since. My devotion to Sertôrian has only grown in the meantime, as has my yearning to read the sacred tome that her elusive creator has composed for her. Now.

Sérgio reached under his chair for a brown paper package I hadn't noticed when I'd come in.

"This, Daniel, is where your apprenticeship begins in earnest," he said.

He handed me the package.

"Go ahead and open it."

I unwrapped the paper packaging and found a fat, purple binder inside, filled to capacity with photocopied pages. I breathed in the smell of fresh toner and new possibilities.

"Is this it?" I said.

"You mean the novel?" said Sérgio. "No. Absolutely not."

I must not have hid my disappointment very well, because Sérgio amped up his pitch from there in a valiant attempt to maintain the energy level in the stuffy little room.

He said, "What you have there is a comprehensive collection of every story Eduard Salgado-MacKenzie ever published. And here's what you're going to do with it. A twofold mission, if you will. First, translate the stories into English. You need to familiarize yourself intimately with the stories' contents, and I can think of no better way to do so than translation. Second, you're going to search the texts for clues pertaining to Salgado-MacKenzie's biography and potential current whereabouts."

As interested as I was in *The Infinite Future*, this was starting to get a little overwhelming. The spell cast by Salgado-MacKenzie's query letter was already wearing off, allowing my own failed novel and Wayne Fortescue's belligerent threats to pull my heart earthward. On top of that, Sérgio was going too big with his pitch, addressing me as if my time and attentions were his to command. Behind the forcefulness, though, I could sense cold desperation.

"So I take it you haven't found the novel yet," I said, hedging his commission, still unsure to what extent I wanted to entangle myself in this quixotic scheme.

"*The Infinite Future* continues to elude me, yes," said Sérgio. "But just as Galahad pursued the Grail and Novalis yearned for the Blue Flower, I continue to seek the quintessence of Captain Irena Sertôrian."

"And this is supposed to help you find it?" I said. "Searching through his stories, I mean?"

I hadn't meant to sound quite so incredulous, but Sérgio caught my tone and his body tensed.

"I recognize that the chances of finding *The Infinite Future* by this method are slim," said Sérgio. "But unfortunately, the more promising avenues of investigation have led nowhere, and this is what's left. So. I want very much to find Eduard Salgado-MacKenzie and his long-lost novel, and if that involves grasping at straws, then I will grasp at those straws as tirelessly as the situation requires."

"I can understand that," I said, hoping to smooth things over.

"I don't think you can," said Sérgio, the mood in the room turning sour. "Not yet anyway."

Chagrined, he looked at the overstuffed binder I held in my lap.

"I can see now how this all might be something of an imposition," he said.

"No," I said. "It's not. It's just a lot to take in."

Which was true.

"Yes," said Sérgio, looking suddenly exhausted. "Yes, it is."

## VII

Six weeks after I got back from São Paulo, the Wayne Fortescue situation came to a sulfurous boil. I'd spent three weeks dodging his emails before deciding that the best way out of this mess was to just give the CAC a novel. It didn't need to be good, it just needed to exist. My plan was to write very, very quickly, just type, actually, without prewriting or revision or thinking too much at all. I'm a pretty fast typist, so I managed to produce an eighty-thousand-word manuscript in about nineteen days.

Rest assured, the quality was terrible—just abysmal, stream-of-consciousness babble that would make even Kerouac blush. Here's a (mercifully) brief sample, littered with half-remembered quotations from *Portrait of the Artist as a Young Man*:

*Elder Byrne, several paces behind Elder da Silva, breathed heavily as they trudged up the hill, and with each breath he drew the hot, dusty air of the favela into his lungs, air that, in spite of its heat, failed to thaw the cold indifference that clutched Elder Byrne's chest, an indifference that inured him to the sights that surrounded him, sights that might otherwise have kindled a warmth in him— the stray dog with only three legs and mangy fur, the woman hanging her faded laundry, the gang of children chasing a downed kite, the crumpled lottery ticket, and other things like that, like a pipe he saw lying at the side of the road, the kind of pipe that is smoked, not the kind through which water or gas might run, and all of these things converged to inspire a non-reaction, or at least a non-warming reaction in Elder Byrne's chest.*

Four days after I emailed him a copy of the novel, I got a phone call from Fortescue.

"I just finished reading that manuscript you sent me," he said.

I waited for him to go on, but he didn't. This didn't bode well.

"And?" I said, bracing myself.

Through the speaker of my phone I could hear him breathing, each exhale almost a growl.

"Can I ask you something, Dan?" said Fortescue.

He spoke softly, but sounded like he wanted to crawl out of my phone and smash my face against a wall.

"Of course," I said.

Again, he waited to respond, letting the silence creep ominously forward for a few beats before asking me, "How stupid do you think I am?"

Another long pause told me he was not asking rhetorically.

"Zero," I said. "Zero stupid."

He said, "That's very interesting, Dan, because after reading that three-hundred-page pile of garbage, I can only assume that you think I'm some kind of imbecile."

"It's a rough draft," I said.

"Rough draft, nothing," said Fortescue, ablaze now with righteous indignation. "What kind of scam are you trying to pull here? Huh? You think because we're a religious organization we're not going to notice when you try to swindle us? Just a naïve bunch of Bible beaters? Is that what you think? Is it? You think you can take our money, piss it away, and we'll be fine with that?"

"No," I said, standing my ground. "I don't think that, but the thing is with grants, they usually—"

"Don't try to change the subject, Dan," said Fortescue. "What's at issue here is that your so-called novel fails to fulfill the terms of our agreement, and yet you appear completely unwilling to return the money we loaned you."

"See, that's the thing," I said. "I've been doing some research, actually, and the fundamental definition of a grant is that it's an award of non-repayable funds, so it's not clear to me—"

"I'm going to stop you right there," said Fortescue, "before you waste any more of my time. *Fundamental definition of a grant?* You know what you should have done instead of dicking around with online dictionaries? You should have reread the contract you signed, where you'll see it very explicitly stated that if the novel you produce does not meet our standards, then the funds we awarded you convert to a loan, repayable on demand, with interest, and penalties for late payment."

"Then why call it a grant?" I said, working up some righteous indignation of my own. "That doesn't make any sense."

"If it doesn't make sense, then why did you sign the contract?" said Fortescue.

He had me there, no getting around it. Obviously, I should have read the contract more carefully. I had nothing more to say for myself.

"Get the money together or the Coalition will be forced to take action," said Fortescue, and hung up the phone.

The next morning, Fortescue sent me a statement calculating how much interest had accrued on the seven thousand dollars—more than I would have expected—and reminding me that if payments were not forthcoming, the consequences would be dire.

By this point it was as clear to me as I'm sure it is to you that the Young Religious Novelist Grant was some kind of bizarre scam. Unfortunately, though, it seemed to be a legally binding one. After reading through the contract, I discovered that every condition Fortescue had mentioned was there in black and white, with my signature at the bottom ratifying the entire document. If there was a way out, I couldn't see it, and since I couldn't even begin to afford a lawyer, that was that—I could either pay the money or face the wrath of the CAC. And really, even there I didn't have much choice. I was broke, and so paying them back was not an option. I told Fortescue as much in an email, and then braced myself for the consequences.

For several weeks, I heard nothing from Fortescue or the CAC, which scared me even more than Fortescue's bluster had. Wherever I went—on my way home from church, or biking to work, or even checking my mail—I kept half expecting to be ambushed by muscular thugs who would break my fingers and burn my skin with cigarettes. At night, I only half slept, willing myself to stay alert to any noises that might signal an intruder's entrance into my dark and vulnerable apartment. At the flower shop, I regarded customers with a wary eye, vigilant for any sign that might betray them as CAC goons sent to surveil my place of business. But for two weeks I didn't see or hear anything suspicious, and I began to half wonder if Fortescue had decided to leave me alone.

Then one day I came home a few minutes early from work and found a woman I'd never seen before rummaging through my underwear drawer.

"Hey!" I said, reaching for my phone.

"Hey Danny," she said, apparently unconcerned by my presence. "Is that what people call you—Danny?"

Like I said, I'd never seen this woman before in my life. She was about my age, maybe a few years older, and couldn't have been much more than five feet tall. She wore a gray suit and a green blouse with one of these ruffles down the front, but what really caught my eye were the black leather gloves on her hands, not bulky burglar's gloves, ideal for lifting heavy appliances, but slim, elegant assassin's gloves, intimately tailored to the fingers so as not to interfere with precision knife work or the squeezing of a pistol's trigger.

"I'm calling the police," I said, more frightened now than surprised. Although she hadn't yet produced a gun, I couldn't help but imagine one tucked away beneath that smart gray blazer.

"You don't want to do that," she said, lifting the mattress of my bed and sweeping her arm under it. "You'll only embarrass yourself."

With the emotionlessness of a seasoned professional, she dropped my mattress and then crouched down to examine the stacks of CDs next to my bed. She wrote something in a steno pad she held in her left hand, and stood up. I took a step back as she passed me, the possibility of violence still hanging in the air.

"What are you doing," I said, unable to resist asking, despite my discomfort.

At my desk, she opened my laptop and turned it on.

"It's fine," she said, looking directly at me for the first time, taking me in with dispassionate shark eyes. "I'm with the CAC."

This was not fine.

"You work for Fortescue?" I said.

"I work *with* Wayne Fortescue," she said.

She waited for my laptop to finish booting up, then she wrote something down and closed the laptop.

"Listen," I said, "I'm really going to call the police if you're not out of here in, like, five seconds."

She said, "If you were going to call the police, you would have done it already."

"Oh yeah?" I said.

"Yeah," she said. "And for your sake it's a good thing you haven't. I'm not breaking any laws here—you agreed to all of this in your contract."

"Agreed to what?" I said as she lifted a fistful of pens from the mug on my desk and then looked inside the empty mug with those dead eyes of hers. She replaced the pens, and then one by one, she picked up the books from my desk and, holding them spine-up, flipped their pages to see if anything would fall out. Only my bookmarks did. She wrote that down.

"I'm cataloging your assets," she said. "Your meager assets, I should add. The contract stipulates that if you're not forthcoming with the scheduled loan repayments, the Coalition is entitled to a thorough catalog, prepared by a party of their choosing, of everything you own. Furthermore, the Coalition is not required to provide you with advance notice of this cataloging, and in signing the contract, you grant the party of the Coalition's choosing express permission to enter your residence, whether or not you are present at said residence at the time of the cataloging. So. Here I am."

The contract again. Of course.

She opened a kitchen cupboard.

"Is this a rice cooker?" she said.

"Yeah," I said, sitting down at the edge of my unmade twin bed.

"Does it work?" she said.

"It did the last time I used it," I said.

She wrote that down in her notebook. She gave my fridge the once-over and then opened the freezer door.

"Come on," I said. "The freezer? Do you really need to know how many chicken potpies I own?"

She poked around with her pen and made another note in her steno pad.

"You'd be surprised what people keep in their freezers," she said. "I once found twelve thousand dollars' worth of heirloom jewelry under a bag of mixed vegetables."

There was nothing so glamorous in my freezer, though, and she shut the door.

"So what are you?" I said. "Some kind of burglar-for-hire?"

"I'm a lawyer," she said, pulling the refrigerator away from the wall and then running a gloved hand up and down its back. "In-house counsel for the Coalition."

"Then I take it you're responsible for the contract I signed," I said.

"I wish," she said, bracing herself with a wide stance and pushing the fridge back against the wall. "It's an excellent contract. Elegant, muscular, and airtight. I *have* tweaked a few passages here and there at my employer's request, but not enough to claim authorship. Sadly. It really is a beautiful document."

She wiped the dust from her gloves on my kitchen dishtowel.

"It's funny you say that," I said, "because the attorney I've hired tells me the contract is so flimsy it'll fall apart the second we step into a courtroom."

She looked at me with a patronizing smile and said, "We both know that you're not meeting with any lawyers, and even if you were, no lawyer that you could afford is going to find any wiggle room in that document you signed. Trust me."

She walked across the room and opened the flimsy accordion door that separated my cracked toilet and dripping RV shower from the rest of the apartment. She lifted up the lid of the toilet tank and looked inside.

"Then why the gloves?" I said.

"Huh?" she said, replacing the lid of the toilet tank. She picked up my shampoo bottle from the damp floor and gave it a vigorous shake.

"The gloves," I said. "If this is so aboveboard, then why are you wearing gloves?"

"It's cold out," she said.

"Not really," I said. "Plus, we're inside."

"Okay," she said. "So, yeah. I'm wearing gloves. I would be stupid not to. I don't mean to hurt your feelings, but here it is: I'm coming into your apartment totally blind, right? I have no idea beforehand what kind of person you are, other than you're someone who can't fulfill his financial obligations. And I know I'll be going through your stuff, but what I don't know is whether or not this is a clean person I'm going to be dealing with. Are there going to be—I don't know—used needles hidden in piles of trash or something? I mean, that's an extreme example, but even just garden-variety deadbeat filth is not something I want to be getting all over my hands."

"Hold on," I said.

"Let me finish," she said. "I don't want that on my hands, and I don't think that's an unreasonable aversion. That said, in your case you have a reasonably clean living space. You are obviously a lonely person, and your apartment *does* make me sad, but nobody could accuse you of being a slob."

She pulled my desk chair to the center of the room, climbed up on it, and ran her hand over the top of the light fixture.

"Are you just about done here?" I said.

She looked around.

"Let's see," she said. "Kitchen area. Sleeping area. Bathroom. Desk. Check, check, check, and check. Tiny one-room apartment—makes my job a lot easier."

"Are we done then?"

She got down from the chair and pulled it back to the desk.

"What's the deal with that binder, by the way?" she said, pointing to the collection of Salgado-MacKenzie stories that Sérgio had given me.

"It's nothing," I said.

"You realize that only makes me more interested," she said.

"It's a translation project," I said. "They're photocopies of stories by a Brazilian science-fiction writer. Nobody's heard of him."

"What's his name?" she said.

"Eduard Salgado-MacKenzie," I said.

"Never heard of him," she said.

"Like I said."

She considered this for a moment.

"A translation project?" she said.

"Yeah."

"Good," she said. "I'm happy to hear you're pursuing something so lucrative."

"It's not about money," I said.

"Clearly."

She stood there a moment, hands on her hips, looking around my apartment.

"I did notice," she said, "that you have some orange juice in your fridge. Do you want to offer me a drink?"

And so, totally discombobulated by this request, I did. I didn't own a couch—there wasn't really space for one anyway—so the two of us sat at the edge of my bed, each with a mismatched cup of chilled orange juice.

"Is it Danny or Daniel?" she said. "Or Dan. You never answered my question."

"Danny's fine," I said, having given myself over to the warped logic of this unexpected, unwelcome interaction.

"Danny, then," she said. "Christine Voorhes."

"Nice to meet you," I said.

"Very polite," she said. "Can I give you a piece of advice?"

"I don't see why not," I said.

"And this is totally off the record," she said.

"Sure," I said.

"Give Fortescue the money," she said. "Just do what you have to do. Get the money together and give it to him. He's going to get it from you one way or another, and the longer the process drags on, the more humiliations lie in wait for you."

"A nice piece of unbiased advice from Fortescue's own lawyer," I said.

"I told you," she said, "I don't work for Fortescue. I work for the CAC—he and I both do. And anyway, are you aware that the penalties accrue weekly? Weekly, Danny. If you don't have the money—and I know you don't—then borrow from your family. It's embarrassing and awkward, I know, but trust me, it's the cleanest way out of this."

"No one in my family has that kind of money just lying around," I said.

"That's my advice," she said with a shrug. "Take it or leave it."

"I appreciate that," I said.

"I also have to say," she said, "you seem a lot smarter than the other grant recipients I deal with. I don't know if you actually are a smart person, but you've got one of those competent faces. That'll get you a lot further in the world than you might think." She turned the juice glass in her hands. "What I'm saying is you can do better than this." She waved her hand in a little circle that dismissed everything inside my apartment. "Ditch the writing. Ditch the translation. Put that competent face to better use."

"Like breaking into people's houses," I said as snidely as possible, hoping that a thick layer of sarcasm might conceal the delight I felt at being praised by someone I barely knew. I wasn't even sure if it was a true compliment, what she'd just said, but even her acknowledgment of the *appearance* of potential in my person exhilarated me. She also wasn't wrong about how I'd been spending my time. What good, after all, was fiction writing? What good was translating? What kind of freedom had either of those pursuits ever given me?

I caught myself, though, before this line of thinking carried me too far from whatever sense of principle I still possessed. Here I was lapping up praise from someone who made her living preying on the desperation of others.

"It's a stepping-stone," said Voorhes in response to my jab. "The CAC is very well connected."

"I'd never heard of them before I got the grant," I said, still fighting back envy for the life she led.

"Exactly," said Voorhes, and drained the rest of the orange juice from her glass.

Ten minutes after she left, my hands started shaking and I couldn't sit still. I'd been so caught up in the strangeness of the situation while Voorhes was in my apartment that the magnitude of the intrusion hadn't fully registered. While she'd been cataloging my things, her nonchalance had had a more or less placating effect on me—if she wasn't bothered by the situation, why should I be? Now that she was gone, though, that same lack of effect felt much more dangerous. Was she some kind of sociopath? Should I fear for my physical safety? Was it still okay to sleep here? Voorhes knew how to get through the door without my permission; once inside, what other nefarious deeds was she willing to commit with those gloved hands of hers?

I moved my desk in front of the door, and thus barricaded in, my next impulse was to hide the purple binder full of Eduard Salgado-MacKenzie's stories. Its monetary value was virtually nonexistent, but at the moment it was my most valuable possession. I realized that hiding the binder was an exercise in futility—if for some reason the CAC wanted to find it, they would—but I had to take some action. I owned two cook-books at the time: *The Joy of Cooking*, and *Skillet Dinners for One*, a thirty-year-old volume that I had picked up for fifty cents at a thrift store a few months earlier. *Skillet Dinners for One* was published in three-ring binder format, which would serve my purposes perfectly. I pulled open its rings, removed the recipes, and replaced them with the photocopied pages from the purple binder. I then returned the modified *Skillet Dinners* to its spot on the counter next to *The Joy of Cooking*, where it had at least a small chance of avoiding detection.

Although I had abandoned, once and for all, writing fiction of my own, I'd gotten a lot of satisfaction over the past several weeks from translating Salgado-MacKenzie's stories. More than anything else, trans-lating reminded me of doing a crossword puzzle. I spent plenty of time frustrated, straining to find the best word or phrase in English to approximate something from the Portuguese, but when I did, when I landed on a fitting gloss, it was like deciphering one of Will Shortz's foxiest crossword clues—an epiphanic *of course* followed by a rush of satisfaction.

The best part of the process, though, was spending so much time with the stories themselves. I hadn't pegged Salgado-MacKenzie as a writer whose work rewarded such close attention, but the more carefully I read his stories, the more I enjoyed and admired them.

I was especially taken with his ongoing portrayal of Captain Irena Sertôrian, especially the way in which each new story added another wrinkle to her ever-shifting persona, a mutable characterization that should have felt sloppy, but instead compelled me, drawing me deeper and deeper into the fictional universe that Sertôrian occupied. I still re-member some of those stories very well, even all these years later.

For example, there's this one where Sertôrian encounters the Church of the Blessed Excreta, a persecuted religious group that has taken refuge on Qyunah, a fringe Minoan desert planet. Basically, these people wor-ship human feces, which is why they're so reviled, and at first, Sertôrian finds them pretty off-putting as well, because frankly, given their beliefs, who wouldn't? The more time she spends with the members of this church, though, the more she respects them, and is even drawn to their tenets.

One thing in their favor is that the members of the church are actually very clean, because in outward practice, they don't treat their feces any differently than non-church members might. Sanitation-wise, they have toilets and sewers and everything else, because part of their religion is that feces must be respected. It's not totally accurate to say that excrement is their god, but they do view feces as a potent and far-reaching force in the universe. In support of this belief, the church points out that feces must be carefully managed; otherwise it can lay waste to entire civilizations as a carrier of illness and disease. And on a more personal level, feces play a salvational role as the vehicle by which excesses and impurities are removed from the body.

In light of these two irrefutable truths, then, the Church of the Blessed Excreta follows a complex liturgy that allows them, as a community of believers, to publicly acknowledge and celebrate their subservience to human waste. Each evening, they meet in small groups to sing hymns in praise of healthy digestion, and once every twelve days, they meet in larger groups to conduct a ceremony known simply as the Journey, in which a church member is selected by lottery to walk blindfolded through an elaborate hedge maze meant to symbolize the upper and lower intestines, while the rest of the congregation looks on from raised bleachers.

Outwardly, Sertôrian keeps her distance from these proceedings, but when her crew finishes its repairs of their ship, the *Circe*, it's with some reluctance that she leaves behind the planet of the Church of the Blessed Excreta. As she's walking away, one of the church members pulls her aside and presents her with a medallion of the ceremonial hedge maze. Tears in her eyes, Sertôrian slips the medallion into a pocket over her heart and says that she'll always remember it, always keep it close.

And it's her reaction that sticks with me, her affinity with the cult's tenets, which the story never really explains. The point is that it paints Sertôrian as being open to the mystical, a characterization that then gets contrasted in another story I remember well, one where Sertôrian is portrayed at her most analytical.

Basically, in this other story, Sertôrian and her crew fall into the clutches of a malevolent and hyperintelligent prospector, and in order to escape Muhnaan, the old mining planet where he's holding them captive, Sertôrian has to solve a series of complex riddles.

What's tricky, though, is that these riddles sound more like rambling anecdotes than tightly constructed puzzles, so Sertôrian has no idea which details to pay attention to and which ones to ignore. The prospector is just sitting there in his rocking chair telling a seemingly interminable story about three sisters who traveled by mule through one of the planet's deepest canyons, when he pauses his account, looks at Sertôrian, and says, *Now tell me, which sister was tallest, which sister was ill, and which sister spoke only in lies?*

Sertôrian is flabbergasted by this question, and tells the prospector that there's no way to determine the answers to those questions based on the meandering story he's just told her. He insists, though, that all the information was there, and she just needs to put together the right pieces.

Eventually, she does. It's a Sherlockian performance on the part of both Sertôrian and Salgado-MacKenzie, requiring the intrepid space captain to recall that a certain brand of tobacco carried by the sisters was produced exclusively by the Tropian Empire for a brief period in the years leading up to the Great Aurigan War. Once she summons that bit of trivia, though, the rest of the pieces click into place and Sertôrian is able to correctly identify which sister was tallest, which sister was ill, and which sister spoke only in lies.

The prospector is stunned by her success, and presents her with two more riddles, each one more rambling than the last. Each time, though, Sertôrian is able to solve the puzzle, which infuriates the prospector. He'd been certain he could outsmart Sertôrian, and his rage at Sertôrian's triumph leads to an amazing set piece—the story's climax—in which Sertôrian and the prospector track each other through a labyrinthine, crystal-walled mining tunnel that is slowly filling with water.

Anyway, translating these stories excited me, scratching my creative itch in a way that fiction writing no longer could. I read dozens of Portuguese-language Wikipedia articles on space travel, astronomy, and science fiction so I could get a feel for the register of the language Salgado-MacKenzie used, whether it was more colloquial, more technical, or a maddening blend of the two. I spent money I didn't have on a multivolume Portuguese dictionary that traced the history of each word it defined. And I could lose myself for hours constructing elaborate charts that tracked how, in each instance, I'd translated a word or phrase commonly used by Salgado-MacKenzie. *Ela sentiu saudades de Marte*, for example, became *She longed for Mars* in one story and *She felt a warm nostalgia for Mars* in another. This wasn't sloppiness, though. Each variant made sense to me in the context of the story that contained it, a phenomenon that further illuminated for me the enchanting elusiveness of language.

In addition to finding joy in the technical aspects of translating, I'd begun to discern in Irena Sertôrian something of the mystical power that Sérgio had described to me back in São Paulo. It was nothing dramatic, not like I was experiencing visions or deep, transcendent emotions. But when I thought of Irena Sertôrian as I translated the stories (something about how she fit within and reacted to the odd machinations of Salgado-MacKenzie's plots) I did feel a kind of low-grade joy—again, with a hint of danger—pulsing through my body. Of course, I told myself that the only reason I was experiencing anything unusual was because I was expecting to experience something unusual, primed as I'd been by Sérgio's wild account of his own relationship with these texts. Regardless of its source, though, this strange joy drove my translation work, pushing me through story after story in pursuit of whatever secret spark animated Irena Sertôrian.

It's a testament, then, to the CAC's sinister powers that they ruined translation for me too. Christine Voorhes's visit to my apartment shook me up enough that when I sat down that night to translate, I couldn't do it. The story was a good one too—Sertôrian gets captured by a vengeful theater troop that forces her to watch a tedious staged reenactment of her alleged war crimes—but I couldn't move, couldn't open the multivolume dictionary to check a definition, couldn't uncap my ballpoint pen, couldn't turn the gears in my brain that processed the Portuguese source text. All I could do was think about Voorhes's visit and what the CAC's next move might be.

If they were trying to mess with my mind, they were doing a great job. After the break-in, a fear enveloped me, dank as the air inside a forgotten terrarium. I would get home from work, push my desk in front of my apartment door, and then spend an hour or two trying to translate a new Salgado-MacKenzie story before giving up and going to bed, where I'd sleep for twelve hours in a welcome stupor. The enthusiasm I'd generated over the previous weeks was rotting away to nothing.

Three days into this unpleasantness, I got an email that broke the spell. It was not from Wayne Fortescue. It was from Sérgio Antunes, and its subject line said, "I've found him."

**VIII**

Daniel,

I hope this message finds you well and that you'll forgive me for dispensing with further pleasantries. I have pressing matters to discuss with you.

About a month ago, I was reviewing a list I'd made of every fictional place name mentioned in Salgado-MacKenzie's work. I'd analyzed this list before, searching for anagrams, cryptograms, any hidden message that might serve as a clue to the author's identity. In the past, these analyses have yielded nothing, but this time I stumbled upon something intriguing.

On a whim, I decided to read each place name aloud, but to do so using American English pronunciations. As I did, I rewrote the names to reflect these pronunciations, using more conventional, simplified English spellings so that, for instance, Ahyonaa (the horrifying city of wax where Sertôrian and her crew battle a horde of murderous sculptors) became Iona, and Gnampuh (a swampy military outpost) became Nampa, and so on, with all of the names from the list. I then cross-searched those transliterated names against lists of cities in the states of Iowa, Indiana, Illinois, and Idaho. (You might remember that one of the editors I spoke to reported a rumor that Eduard Salgado-MacKenzie hailed from the United States, specifically from a state beginning with the letter I.)

To my great excitement, I found several close matches between my re-transcribed list of fictional cities and a list of actual cities in the state of Idaho. No other state—I searched all fifty—yielded even a fraction of the matches that Idaho did. The Gem State, it seems, figured prominently in Salgado-MacKenzie's imagination.

But why? I was careful at this point not to jump to any conclusions. His reliance on Idaho city names as sources for science fictional locales *could* mean that he was born in Idaho, or lived there. But it could also be a private joke, or a purely random selection, or, I'm willing to admit, a complete misreading on my part. In and of itself, this connection was compelling but inconclusive.

Around the same time, though, I was pursuing another, unrelated line of inquiry—searching for a story by the Strugatsky brothers that I'd heard great things about but never read. I don't read Russian, and this particular story has never been translated into Portuguese or Spanish. I also couldn't find it in any of the English-language collections of their short fiction, so I started asking around to see if anyone else had stumbled across a translation of it anywhere. A friend told me he thought he remembered reading it in a Cold War–era anthology of Soviet science fiction published in the States called *Faint Constellations*. All he could recall about the book was the Strugatsky story, and the anthology's flag-waving introduction, which derided the very stories the book contained as indisputable specimens of Soviet inferiority.

This anthology wasn't easy to find, but I eventually tracked down a copy at a library in Porto Alegre and placed an interlibrary loan request. When the book arrived, I was very pleased to find the Strugatsky story I'd been looking for. Even more exciting, though, was the inclusion at the end of the anthology of three short stories written by Latin American writers. In an introduction to this final section, the anthologist explained that all Latin American countries, whether they'd admit it or not, harbored Soviet sympathies and an ardent desire for the kind of one-world socialist government that threatened the very foundations of democracy. Arising as they did, then, from such febrile aspirations, the three Latin American stories included in the anthology could never measure up to the work produced by their saner North American counterparts. The reader would be well advised to note their patent inferiority and learn from their authors' mistakes, both ideological and aesthetic.

As fascinated as I was by these sentiments, I was more excited by the stories themselves, or rather, by one story in particular penned by—you may have already guessed—our own Eduard Salgado-MacKenzie. It was one I'd read before ("All Quiet, All Dark"), so the treasure here was not the story itself but rather its presence in the anthology. Here was a bevy of new leads—a publisher, an editor, a translator—all of whom may have had contact with Salgado-MacKenzie himself!

The first two leads proved fruitless. I could find no record of *Faint Constellations'* publisher—Eagle's Landing Press—anywhere I searched. More frustrating still, the book's editor and introduction writer (probably the same person) had chosen to remain anonymous, thus cutting off another promising avenue of pursuit. Fortunately, the anthology did credit its translators with a small-print byline at the end of each story, and so it was that at the end of "All Quiet, All Dark" I found the name V. H. Kimball.

Fully expecting to be stymied yet again, I was delighted to learn that V. H. Kimball not only exists in the public record but also remains an active and prolific translator. I emailed her through the publisher of her most recent translation (*The End of Days*, a novel by Josefa Navarro, a contemporary Spanish writer), and asked if she was the same V. H. Kimball who had translated Eduard Salgado-MacKenzie's "All Quiet, All Dark" for *Faint Constellations: A Collection of Soviet Science Fiction*.

Three days later I received a response. I am, said her brief email. What can I do for you?

I explained my interest in Eduard Salgado-MacKenzie and asked what she could tell me about the anthology's publisher, or about its editor, or better still, about the reclusive author himself—had she had any contact with the man? Her reply began as follows:

> Eduard Salgado-MacKenzie was either a raving crank or one of the greatest minds of his generation, and the fact that I never got to find out which haunts me to this day.

Daniel, I could barely contain my excitement. I reread that first line twice, just to make sure my eyes were not deceiving me, before I continued reading:

It was a messy little incident, fraught with betrayal, shame, and typewritten manifestos, but before I get too far ahead of myself, let me answer your questions in the order you posed them.

First—the anthology's publisher. Eagle's Landing Press was the publishing arm of the Grandsons of American Liberty, a far-right-wing advocacy group that had something of a heyday during the Cold War. Their notable achievements include protesting the Civil Rights Act of 1964 (and the Civil Rights Movement generally), calling for the dissolution of the ideologically suspect American State Department, and generally making mainstream conservatives very uncomfortable.

Through Eagle's Landing Press, they published a handful of books meant to further their ideological mission—nonfiction works, mostly, if *nonfiction* is the right word for those dogmatic, poorly researched screeds. They published a few works of overt fiction as well, *Faint Constellations* being one of them.

The anthology's editor was Roger Ash, an ardent GAL member and the uncle of Karen Ash, a college roommate of mine. This was the early 1980s, and the Grandsons of American Liberty were experiencing a steep decline in popularity. *Faint Constellations* represented one of several desperate attempts to reach new audiences—in this case, readers of science fiction with underexplored far-right-wing sympathies.

When Karen contacted me about translating *Faint Constellations*, though, I had no idea the project was connected to the GAL (an organization I was all too aware of, thanks to a handful of enthusiastically affiliated relatives on my father's side). I don't think

Karen knew either, actually—she told me her uncle was putting together a science-fiction anthology for a little publishing company he knew of and was looking for someone to translate a story from Portuguese.

It would be my first professional translating job, so of course I said yes, even though my Portuguese was fairly shaky at the time. I was majoring in Spanish (double-majoring, actually—Spanish and history), just finishing up my undergrad, but I'd taken a couple of Portuguese classes and I figured I could pull the job off. I told Karen I'd do it, and within a week or so her uncle sent me a copy of the story, mimeographed from the magazine it had originally appeared in. (You'd probably like to know how Roger Ash encountered this story in the first place, and come to think of it so would I. As far as I know, he'd never been to Brazil.) Included with the story was contact information for its author, along with a handwritten admonition from Ash not to contact the man unless absolutely necessary.

I got started right away. I'd taken a class or two on translation, so I'd done this kind of work before, although not professionally. I was familiar enough with the process, though, to notice that this was a strange story. I'm not talking about the content, although that was strange too, something to do with a murderous, futuristic house painter and a wandering rocket captain. I'm talking about the prose style itself, which rejected the long sentences so common, as you know, in Spanish and Portuguese for a more terse English approach. Much of the story, in fact, read as if it had already been translated, but from English to Portuguese.

Not wanting to produce an unnecessary back-translation, I called Ash and asked if he was sure the story's original language was Portuguese. He said that of course it was, at least as far as he knew, and anyway I shouldn't worry about it. He seemed very uninterested by the question, but this was my professional reputation at stake—if my first published translation was of a story originally written in English, I would be very embarrassed.

Despite Ash's admonition, then, I decided to contact the author directly at his Idaho address, an address that had only added to my suspicions about the story's source language. In my letter, I told Mr. Salgado-MacKenzie that Roger Ash had hired me to translate "All Quiet, All Dark," an opportunity that I very much appreciated. I said that I admired the story's inventiveness. I then noted the qualities I'd pointed out to Roger Ash on the phone and asked if, by chance, an English-language version of the story already existed.

Mr. Salgado-MacKenzie got back to me very quickly, within a week, if I remember right. His envelope was much fatter than I expected, containing a long, long letter—over ten double-sided, typewritten pages. His response began very formally, thanking me for my attention to detail and confirming that yes, Portuguese was the story's original language, and no, no version existed in English, not yet at least, but he trusted that in my capable hands a fine translation would soon come forth.

So far, so good.

Then the letter took an abrupt philosophical turn. "I have a theory," Salgado-MacKenzie wrote, "that when two human beings enter into a deliberate relationship with one another—be it professional, personal, or otherwise—they become connected by a long, invisible filament that can never be severed."

He went on to explain that these filaments exist in a purely ideational realm whose intangibility did not diminish their significance in the least. To clarify: Just as the flow of electricity through a light bulb's filament heats the metal, rendering it incandescent, the flow of energy through a relational filament produces an illumination of its own.

Relational Filamental Illumination is what he called his theory, and a prime example of the phenomenon, he said, was the long, combative friendship between "your countrymen Thomas Jefferson and John Adams," as he called them. Copious energy flowed back and forth within their filament over the course of several decades as they wrestled a new nation into existence. The light produced from this filament, therefore, was stunning. Now I needed to remember, Salgado-MacKenzie wrote, that filaments illuminate what is close to but not directly connected with the two parties, so that the light produced by Jefferson's and Adams's filament did not illuminate the foundational principles of American democracy, as some might assume—Jefferson and Adams brought these ideas to light more directly—but instead illuminated something much, much bigger.

It is a well-known fact, he reminded me, that both men died not only on the same day, but on the Fourth of July, a date of recurring significance both to them and the country they'd invented, and it is by the light of this overly neat coincidence that a colossal hidden truth is (partially) revealed. The truth, he wrote, is this: that the forces of the universe have a woefully unsophisticated sense of narrative. How else to account for the triteness of the Jefferson / Adams / Independence Day death overlap? Such coincidence is the stuff of sentimental melodramas and shoddy adventure tales, of soap operas and ghost stories. The pat laziness of it practically turned one's stomach.

He also wished to clarify—though to do so with proper thoroughness would require an entirely separate letter—what he meant when he referred to "the forces of the universe." He did not mean God, at least not in the Judeo-Christian sense of the term. Instead, the Jefferson/Adams filament illuminated a governing intelligence (although that still wasn't quite the right term for it—both *governing* and *intelligence* missed the mark somehow) far more powerful than any Judeo-Christian deity, and far more diffuse, if that made any sense.

There was a lot more to the theory, pages more, but I've regrettably forgotten what they said. I do remember, though, that the letter ended with a very genuine, heartfelt thank-you for sticking with him for so many pages. He said he'd been thinking through this concept a lot lately, and it'd been helpful to get it all down on paper, and more helpful still to know that somebody else might read it.

Up until that point I'd been ready to dismiss Salgado-MacKenzie's ideas out of hand, but I found that sign-off so endearing that I sat down on my apartment's faded blue couch and reread the whole letter, all ten typewritten pages of it.

A second read left me unsettled. Was this man off his rocker, or some kind of genius?

Just then, my roommate Karen got home from her shift at the sandwich shop down the street. She sat down at the other end of the couch, put her feet up on the coffee table, and asked me how my day had been.

"Take a look at this, would you?" I said, handing her the letter.

"What is it?" she said, flipping through the pages.

"Just read it," I said.

So she did, the furrows in her brow growing deeper with each paragraph. When she finished the last page, she handed the letter back to me, shaking her head.

"Pretty creepy," she said. "I mean, the guy's obviously nuts, right?"

A few minutes earlier, I'd wondered the same thing myself, but something in Karen's tone triggered my inner contrarian, and I found myself disagreeing with her before I could quite say why.

"I actually think there might be something to it," I told her.

Too tired to disagree, Karen said maybe I was right and then went to take a shower.

I wasn't as sure about the letter's merits as I'd pretended to be, so I decided a further test was in order. Back in my room, then, I sat down and wrote a ten-page letter of my own, pointing out a dozen or so weaknesses I'd spotted in Salgado-MacKenzie's argument and asking for clarification on a dozen more points that had been unclear to me. The next morning I sent the letter off, and then I waited.

Here was the reasoning behind my strategy: The thing about crackpots is that they don't respond well to rigorous questioning of their pet ideas, and so Salgado-MacKenzie's response to my admittedly demanding letter would be a valuable indicator of his general mental soundness and rigor. And so I eagerly awaited his letter.

A few weeks later, I received his reply—fifteen typewritten pages filled with prose even more gracious and articulate than those of the previous letter. He thanked me for my questions and said he was thrilled to have someone engaging so enthusiastically with these ideas he'd been working through for so long in such stifling isolation. He then responded point by point to my questions, and while his answers were not quite as focused as I would have liked, they at least gestured toward compelling justifications for his claims.

The letter also included several meticulous hand-drawn diagrams, which for me almost sealed the deal. I wasn't convinced that his theory was completely sound, but all in all his reply had won me over, so I wrote back again, asking him to clarify a few more points for me. He again responded generously to my questions and we wrote back and forth like that over the course of several months and a half-dozen letters covering various angles of his Filamental Theory of human relationships.

(I wish I could remember more about what the letters said. I just spent ten minutes sitting here at the keyboard trying to dredge something up from my memory, but it's no good.)

Then, minor tragedy struck.

I'd long since finished my translation of Salgado-MacKenzie's story, and had almost forgotten its role as the impetus for our ongoing correspondence. It was with no small surprise and dismay, then, that I received a published copy of Ash's anthology in the mail one day. The first shock was the publishing house, Eagle's Landing Press, which I recognized from the bookshelves of my politically vituperative Grandsons of American Liberty–loving relations. Even more upsetting, though, was Ash's belligerently xenophobic introduction to the stories.

To have me translate Salgado-MacKenzie's story without telling me it would only serve as an incidental prop for the Grandsons of American Liberty's jingoistic claptrap—such underhandedness beggared belief. I was mortified and I was furious. I wrote one letter to Roger Ash requesting that my name be removed from all future editions of the anthology. I wrote another letter to Eduard Salgado-MacKenzie explaining the situation and apologizing for my unknowing part in it—I respected his story and if I had known what Ash was up to, I would not have participated.

I never heard back from either Ash or Salgado-MacKenzie.

I meant for this response to be short and to the point, but it's ballooned into something unwieldy. To (finally) get to your question, then—yes, I was in contact with Eduard Salgado-MacKenzie. At one point I had his address—somewhere in Idaho, but where exactly I couldn't tell you. Unfortunately I've since lost the letters he sent me. They disappeared along with my high school yearbooks and a set of much-loved china during an unpleasant period of transition in my life that I'd rather not get into here.

Eagle's Landing Press no longer exists, and neither do the Grandsons of American Liberty. At least I don't think they do. Roger Ash might still be around, though. I'm friends with his niece Karen online, so I could ask her. I'll let you know what I find out.

Until then,

Dr. V. Harriet Kimball

I thanked Dr. Kimball profusely for the information and after five days of eager anticipation, I received this follow-up:

Sérgio,

Glad to hear this has been helpful.

I have more.

I got in touch with Karen, and apparently Roger Ash passed away just a few months ago. I offered my condolences and Karen said he'd been sick for quite a while so his death had not been unexpected. I said again that I was sorry to hear he was gone. Karen thanked me and asked why I was looking for her Uncle Roger. I explained briefly about your search for Eduard Salgado-MacKenzie, and his connection to Ash through *Faint Constellations*. I said I realized that this was a long shot, but had Ash saved any letters from the Eagle's Landing Press days, and if so, had anyone hung on to them after he died?

Karen said we might be in luck. She said that Uncle Roger had become the unofficial historian of the GAL and had accumulated, over the years, boxes and boxes of photographs, pamphlets, meeting minutes, letters, and books from the society's more active days. He'd meant to write a history of the GAL, but hadn't gotten around to it before his health had declined. Karen said that as far as she knew, though, all of those boxes were still sitting in a storage unit in Orange County, California, not far from where Uncle Roger had lived. If I was interested, she said, she could get in touch with one of her cousins and they could give me the key to the unit—I'd be welcome to take a look.

I'm not sure if I've mentioned this or not, but I live in Danesville, Utah (a ten-hour drive from Orange County), so it's not the kind of thing where I could just pop over to the storage unit and take a look. Not normally anyway. As luck would have it, though, I'll be presenting a paper at a conference in Claremont, CA (not far from Orange County), during the second week of October. Karen assures me that there are no imminent plans to clear out the storage unit and that her cousin would be happy to let me look through Ash's papers while I'm in town for the conference.

I have to say that in the five days since I wrote that last email, I've been thinking about Eduard Salgado-MacKenzie a lot. I still feel strange about what happened between us—it was so intimate in its own way, and then it ended so abruptly. I still feel a need to clear the air.

What I'm trying to say is, I've realized that I've also become very interested in finding Eduard Salgado-MacKenzie. I don't know what your schedule is like, but if you'd like to meet me in California at the end of that second week in October, I was thinking we could go through Roger Ash's memorabilia together—two heads are better than one—and then follow the trail from there.

If I'm stepping on your toes here, let me know. I realize this is a project you've been very committed to for a very long time, and I know how that can be. If you're amenable to my collaboration, though, I look forward to working together on this.

Sincerely,

Harriet

It would only be a slight exaggeration, Daniel, to say my bags were packed before I even finished reading the email. What luck, to find another Salgado-MacKenzie enthusiast! What a treasure trove of new information! What an opportunity!

For years now, I've maintained an emergency travel fund for this very purpose, and I'm pleased to report that the trip is a go. Your government has even deigned to grant me a travel visa—no easy thing, but I have connections. I fly into LAX this coming Monday and fly home out of Salt Lake the Sunday after that. It's a narrow window—less than seven days in which to find Eduard Salgado-MacKenzie—but it will have to do.

The reason I'm telling you this, Daniel, is not just to share the exciting news but to invite you to join the expedition. I trust you've been diligent in your translation work and would serve the investigation well.

Time is of the essence, my friend, so make your decision quickly and get back to me as soon as possible.

Regards,
Sérgio Antunes
Sublibrarian
Biblioteca Anita Garibaldi

# IX

After reading Sérgio's email, it took me all of twenty minutes to pack a bag and reserve a bus ticket to California with my already overburdened credit card. The collection notices from Wayne Fortescue had grown even more alarming, and everywhere I went in Provo, I caught imagined glimpses of Christine Voorhes crouching behind bushes, lurking in stairwells. For three nights running, I'd woken up in a panic at 2:00 a.m., convinced I'd felt her gloved hands at my throat, holding it tenderly for a moment before tightening her grip and squeezing the life out of me. Each time I'd woken up gasping, my apartment empty, heart racing.

In California, I'd still be broke—I'd be even more broke, actually—but at least Fortescue and Voorhes wouldn't know where to find me. And so two days later, a fugitive from my creditors, I found myself standing at the locked door of Roger Ash's storage unit. At my side, Sérgio—looking tired and thrilled—rocked from foot to foot with nervous excitement. In front of us, Dr. V. Harriet Kimball—a short, scrappy woman with the look of a distance runner, somewhere in the neighborhood of fifty years old—consulted a note card on which she'd written down the combination for the storage unit's lock. After a moment, she turned around, gave Sérgio and me a here-goes-nothing shrug, and lifted the door's heavy lock.

It would not be totally correct to say I'd gotten off on the wrong foot with Harriet, but I will say that our introduction a few minutes earlier had not gone especially well.

"I'm sure you're familiar with Dr. Kimball's scholarly work," Sérgio had said to me.

In the split-second before responding, I'd noticed Dr. Kimball's narrow face tensing up slightly, as if she were bracing herself—whether for disappointment or something else, I couldn't tell.

"I'm sorry," I'd said. "I'm afraid I haven't," and her face had relaxed instantly.

"No need to apologize," she'd said. "And please—call me Harriet. As far as my scholarly work goes—I study Mormon history and do some cultural criticism as well. That's why I'm in town—a conference at Claremont on millenarianism in the twentieth-century Church. I presented a paper on the ways in which mid-century Mormon preparedness rhetoric positions food storage as a metaphorical bridge between temporal and spiritual salvation."

"That sounds very interesting," I'd said, unsure how I felt about this new acquaintance.

Now, standing at the door of Roger Ash's storage unit, Harriet dialed a combination of numbers into the hefty lock and then pulled down. The shackle came free of the latch, and Sérgio gave an enthusiastic "Ha!"

Handing the lock to Sérgio, Harriet grasped the dusty rope affixed to the base of the door and lifted it open, the metal segments rolling together with a sloppy clatter.

"Well," said Harriet, "it looks like we have our work cut out for us."

Morning sunlight streamed into the storage unit, illuminating hundreds, maybe even thousands, of yellowing bankers boxes stacked from floor to ceiling all the way from the back wall. And while thoughts of our task's likely futility muscled their way into my mind, Sérgio looked appreciatively at all the boxes and said that he had a good feeling about this, that the path to Salgado-MacKenzie often intersected with eccentric archives such as this one.

I did my best to embrace Sérgio's optimism. After all, there were three of us, and we had all day. Maybe we *would* find Salgado-MacKenzie's contact information inside one of these boxes. Stranger things had certainly happened.

"No time to waste," said Sérgio, removing his linen blazer and draping it over an abandoned hand truck. The short sleeves of his Ziggy Stardust–era Bowie T-shirt revealed meaty arms that immediately set to work removing the top box from the nearest stack.

And so, with meticulous haste, we began sorting through the boxes, searching for any record Roger Ash may have kept of his correspondence with Eduard Salgado-MacKenzie. Box after box yielded nothing we could use, although it quickly became clear that the contents of Roger Ash's storage unit could stock a whole library devoted to Cold War paranoia. We discovered hundreds of fliers, pamphlets, broadsides, and paperbacks that explicated with splashy rhetoric the key tenets of the Grandsons of American Liberty. It was fascinating stuff, and in spite of the urgency of our search, I couldn't help but peruse every fourth or fifth item that passed through my hands.

In one box, I found a pamphlet titled "Danger Drips from Your Kitchen Faucet," which alerted its readers to the perils of water fluoridation, warning that such mass drugging was only the first small step in a process that would eventually lead to the distribution of mind-control chemicals through the drinking water, chemicals that would set the stage for a global takeover by the collectivist New World Order.

In another box, I found a slim paperback called *The Inadvertent Arsonist?*, which accused former president Dwight D. Eisenhower of aiding and abetting the advance of Communism during his tenure as commander in chief by instituting policy after policy containing hidden and malicious socialist agendas. The cancerous damage these policies inflicted on American freedoms and the integrity of the Constitution was undeniable. The only thing up for debate, claimed the book, was whether Eisenhower committed these treasons knowingly, or if he was merely a patsy under the sway of Soviet controllers posing as American patriots.

On a more celebratory note, a framed poster-sized poem I found sandwiched between two stacks of boxes told a story of all the flags of the world attending an international flag convention. They're all mingling and talking to each other, but then the American flag arrives and all the other flags go silent. The American flag, which is a little worn and dusty, clears its throat and gives a speech about being just a simple flag for a simple country, and he may not be as sophisticated as all these other flags, but what he does know is that he loves freedom and is trying to do the best he can for his country. The poem ends with all the other flags of the world, duly humbled, bowing down before the American flag.

I saw the poem a second time on the back cover of a book making the case for the illegality of America's involvement with the United Nations, an organization second only to the Soviet Union in depravity and antipathy to the principles of democracy.

Another box contained a pamphlet from the early sixties—"The Problem with Civil Rights"—warning that figures such as Rosa Parks and Martin Luther King, Jr. were Soviet agents trained by their communist overlords to unfairly besmirch American democracy with slanderous claims of injustice and oppression. If these complaints were heeded, the pamphlet warned, the very fabric of our Constitution would be imperiled, and the way would be paved for the arrival of a dangerous New World Order.

"You know, a lot of Mormons really went in for this kind of stuff," said Harriet. She hefted a cardboard box down from the top of a chest-high stack, the ensuing cloud of dust further graying her faded jeans and worn flannel work shirt. She'd been tirelessly attacking boxes since morning, barely breaking a sweat and never breaking her rhythm—open, sift, close, repeat. She'd also been talking nonstop, delivering an incessant series of micro-lectures on selected topics from the world of Mormon studies.

"In fact," she went on, "a lot of Mormons produced material like this for similar organizations. It was a pretty wide-ranging phenomenon. I mean, I'm sure you're aware of Ezra Taft Benson's involvement with the John Birch Society when he was an apostle"—I was not aware, had never even heard of the John Birch Society, in fact—"but what a lot of people don't realize is that he was never actually a member. He aggressively supported them, but President McKay asked him not to join, so he didn't. It was a similar situation with a handful of other Mormon ultraconservatives—they were very interested in the Birch Society, but never actually joined. So instead, some of them founded little organizations of their own that promoted many of the Birchers's key claims, and then fused them with Mormon pseudo-doctrines. There were maybe a half a dozen of these little societies during the height of the Cold War. I don't think the Grandsons of American Liberty had Mormon roots, but it's a similar deal.

"Anyway, the effect was, you had these organizations bringing some very, very far-right-wing ideologies into the mainstream of Mormonism, fusing them, like I said, with supposed doctrines and passing them off as revealed truths.

"The craziest part is, we're still seeing the ramifications of that today in the Church. It's been—what?—twenty years since the fall of the Berlin Wall, and so much Mormon political thought still has one foot in Cold War paranoia. It's fascinating, isn't it?"

"Yes," I said, although really it wasn't, at least not to me.

As tiresome as I was beginning to find these mini-lectures, though, I did get a stronger and stronger sense the more time I spent with Harriet Kimball that I probably should have heard of her before then (a suspicion that would be confirmed later, as you'll see). I hadn't heard of her, though, and here's an oversimplified but useful dichotomy to explain not only why I hadn't but also why our interests diverged so sharply.

There are two kinds of Mormons in the world: Mormons who care about Mormonism qua Mormonism (to use the most pretentious preposition I'm aware of) and Mormons who don't. What I mean is, the first type of Mormon not only practices the religion but also spends a lot of time and energy thinking about Mormonism itself and participating in extracurricular Mormon-related activities. They might attend Church-history-themed pageants around the country, or listen to treacly Mormon pop music produced for summer youth camps. They might take

Book of Mormon tours of Central America. They might blog about Mormon history or sing in regional Mormon choirs. They might take summer road trips retracing (in reverse) the westward migration of the Mormon pioneers. They might also, if they're of a certain ideological stripe, attend Sunstone conferences, or read the complete works of Hugh Nibley or lobby for female ordination to the priesthood, greater transparency from Church leaders, or changes to Church policies regarding, say, gay marriage. Whatever the focus, though, Mormonism permeates every nook of these people's lives.

So that's the first type. The second type, the more laissez-faire Mormons, may be very devout, but they also compartmentalize their Mormonism to a much greater degree than the first type. It's like they have their professional life, their personal life, their social life, their religious life, etc., but the religious part doesn't bleed into all the others. I don't mean there's a hypocrisy there, or a lack of devotion—that's not it at all. Instead, it's more like there's a holistic concern with being a good person, but the Mormon-specific elements of that concern stay primarily in the Mormon compartment.

It's hard to explain in the abstract, so I'll use my parents as a concrete example. They attend church every week, they go to the temple pretty often, the whole thing. They're fully practicing Mormons. But they're also extremely unlikely to spend much of their leisure time doing Church-related stuff. Instead, especially these days, my dad will either be watching the History Channel (he's becoming an armchair expert on the Kennedy assassination) or trying to get my mom on board with some DIY scheme he's just read about on the Internet—for instance, saying that they should raise chickens out on the balcony of their condo, because wouldn't it be great to have fresh eggs whenever they wanted?

And my mom, when she's not talking my dad out of running down to the farm-supply store right away to buy some baby chicks (or whatever the scheme is on any given week), is probably playing or watching tennis with her friend Barb, or if that's not an option, rockhounding (as she loves to call it) out in the red hills of St. George just after sunrise, a new-found passion of her empty-nester days. Point being, Mormonism is not the overwhelming focus of their lives. It's one facet among many.

And like my parents, I just wasn't plugged into the kinds of conversations and debates that occupied people like Harriet Kimball. In terms of our shared religion, then, we actually didn't have that much to talk about.

In all honesty, though, my ambivalence toward Harriet grew less from her long-windedness on arcane points of Mormon history and culture, and more from an irrational fear that her presence had somehow rendered me superfluous in the quest to find Eduard Salgado-MacKenzie and his *Infinite Future*. I brought so little to the table to begin with—mostly I think Sérgio enlisted me because I was willing to listen to him talk—and now here was someone with significant experience as a translator, with legitimate academic chops, and with a general enthusiasm to rival even Sérgio's. I was redundant, although what the larger implications of that supposed redundancy might have been, I really couldn't have said. There was so little actually at stake, and yet I regarded Harriet with wariness, probing her persona for weaknesses like we were two neck-and-neck presidential candidates, and not just collaborating members of an amateur research team.

And as the day wore on, my gimlet eye did detect a weakness in Harriet. Though she spoke freely about her scholarship, she kept her private life—and especially her past—under heavy wraps.

For example, at one point late in the morning, I was sorting through a box of leaflets that warned of the perils of automobile safety regulations. At my side, Harriet sorted through a box of her own while delivering a disquisition on Joseph Smith's fascination with city planning and utopian sociality. At a conceptual break in this lecture, I jumped in, hoping to divert the stream of conversation away from the topic of Mormon studies.

"Did Sérgio say you live in Danesville?" I said to Harriet.

Setting aside her current box, which she had finished searching,

Harriet opened a new one and explained that actually she lived in a cabin at the mouth of Danish Fork Canyon, where she did her translation work ("My bread and butter," she added), primarily from Spanish but also from Portuguese, Italian, and sometimes French. Apparently the texts she translated ran the gamut from technical manuals to comic books to novels to poetry.

"You have to be flexible if you want steady work," she said.

"That makes sense," I said, opening a new box of my own. "I bet you come across some interesting stuff."

"I do," she said. "Last month I was working on the memoirs of one of the first female bullfighters in Spain—a remarkable story, really."

"And remind me," said Sérgio, wiping the sweat from his face with an already damp handkerchief and treading unwittingly into forbidden conversational territory, "what led you to pursue translating as a profession?"

Harriet had been pulling a new box down from an eye-high stack, but now she froze, arms extended, the box hovering at her chest.

"Did you hurt yourself?" I said, noting the extreme look of discomfort on her face.

"No," she said, unfreezing. "I'm fine. It's fine. You want to know why I translate?"

"Not if that would make you uncomfortable," said Sérgio, looking panicked.

"I said it's fine," said Harriet. "I got into translating when . . ." She shook her head. It was strange to see her so flummoxed. "I used to be a history professor, but then I got fired. I'd studied Spanish as an undergrad, so . . ."

She shrugged and set the box down on the floor, turning away from the two of us.

"My apologies," said Sérgio. "I didn't mean to pry."

"It's fine," said Harriet, over-cheerfully, but she didn't say anything more on the subject.

The more we talked that day, the more clear it became that Dr.

Kimball was a woman of many secrets. If our conversation ever veered toward details of her past, she would steer it sharply away, like a ship's captain avoiding a series of jagged rocks just below the water's surface.

There was another topic, though, that all three of us were avoiding— the possibility that we might not find anything Salgado MacKenzie-related in all these boxes of papers. We'd been working nonstop since morning, not even breaking for lunch, and that whole time the usually voluble Sérgio had been a picture of stolid absorption, moving with a barely contained agitation, his energies so concentrated on the search that he'd uttered only a sparse handful of sentences over the course of many hours. Sérgio's frenzy became less and less contained as box after box yielded up nothing pertaining to our search. His T-shirt grew more sweat stained. His long, normally neat hair became increasingly disheveled. And his eyes grew wilder until he became a picture of quiet desperation.

Harriet, too, seemed more affected by our failure as the day went on, her speeches growing less impassioned by the minute, so that by late afternoon she was speaking in a bleary monotone, her lecture on pre-Correlation-era Sunday school manuals sounding more than anything like a perfunctory filibuster against impending disappointment.

I myself was feeling lousier with each passing hour. Just being in Roger Ash's storage unit meant spending money I didn't have, and if our search through the dusty memorabilia of the Grandsons of American Liberty led nowhere, I wasn't sure I could handle it.

Morale seemed to be at a breaking point on all sides, but then nine hours into our excavation I justified my presence on the three-person team when, at the bottom of a box of anti-OSHA pamphlets, I found Roger Ash's old Rolodex, its circle of cards yellow with age.

"Look," I said, holding up the Rolodex like a stone idol.

When they saw what was in my hand, Sérgio and Harriet literally dropped what they were doing, their cardboard boxes hitting the ground with papery thuds as they bounded over the cluttered ground to reach my side. With Sérgio at my left elbow and Harriet at my right, I flipped the dusty cards to the S section. Four cards in, and there it was, typewritten in faded black letters:

```
EDUARD SALGADO-MACKENZIE
127 MAIN STREET
FREMONT CREEK, ID
```

"Wonderful," said Sérgio. "Wonderful, wonderful!"

little before 3:00 a.m. we made it to St. George, Utah. I'd been driving Harriet's near-pristine 1989 Toyota Celica since Bakersfield, and both Harriet and Sérgio had been asleep since Vegas. The streets of St. George were dark enough that I got turned around a couple of times before finally finding my parents' housing community. I'd only been to their condo twice before, so I might have had trouble finding it even if it hadn't been the middle of the night. They'd moved there three years earlier after my dad had retired and they'd sold their house in Salt Lake. The condo was a newish one-bedroom property, which was great for my parents but had precluded my moving back in with them during my post-college swan dive. Not that I would have been thrilled at the prospect, or that I'd expected them to put me up. All I'm saying is, the timing had been unfortunate.

As the car turned and slowed down, Harriet and Sérgio both stirred awake. I pulled into an open visitor spot, and we stepped out of the car into the chilly desert air. We got our bags from the trunk—we'd all packed light—and crossed the parking lot, shivering under our thin daywear. I'd called ahead, explaining the situation as concisely as possible, and my mom had said it all sounded very interesting and they'd be happy to have us.

I found my parents' spare key under a potted cactus and opened the door. They'd left a lamp on in the living room, and just inside the door was a neat pile of blankets and pillows. A note in my dad's handwriting on top of the bedding welcomed us and told us to make ourselves at home.

Moving as quietly as possible, we took turns in the bathroom and then rock-paper-scissored for the wide soft couch. Sérgio won, so Harriet and I took the two plush recliners, which leaned back far enough that they might as well have been beds.

I thought I would fall asleep immediately. We'd had an early start that day, and the drive had tired me out, but as soon as I lay down, my drowsiness disappeared.

It turned out I was eager to keep moving.

Rationally, I knew that even if we found Salgado-MacKenzie, Wayne Fortescue and the CAC would still be waiting for me at the end of the journey and I would be in no more of a position to pay them back than I'd been in before I'd left. Still, the search for *The Infinite Future* felt bigger than all that. During the seven-hour drive from Roger Ash's storage unit, I'd begun to cultivate a hope that Salgado-MacKenzie's long-lost novel might connect me to something bigger than myself and my lost ambitions, that it might lift me from my spiritual malaise into a transcendent state of being. Basically, I needed my life to mean something more than credit card debt and frozen dinners.

As I lay there on the recliner mulling this over, I was reminded of a Salgado-MacKenzie piece I'd translated about a month earlier. At the beginning of the story, there's been yet another engine malfunction that forces the crew of the *Circe* to land the ship on yet another unknown planet. They touch down at the edge of an enormous tent city, at the center of which sits a boxy factory whose smokestacks puff white, cheery clouds into the clear blue atmosphere. It all looks innocuous enough, but then again, who knows? To be on the safe side, then, Sertôrian sends out only a small party to make initial contact.

Hours pass. Hours and hours and hours. Captain Sertôrian, who has stayed behind with the *Circe*, starts to worry. Radio contact with the three envoys has been lost, and if their mission had gone according to plan, they would have returned already. Something has happened to them, so Sertôrian gathers up some guns and tools, and with two of her crew, she sets out to find her lost shipmates.

It doesn't take long. About a twenty-minute walk from the ship, Sertôrian finds her advance party lolling about on a sunny hillside behind the boxy factory at the center of the tent city. They're just lounging on the grass, propped up on their elbows, smiling and laughing. A handful of locals are there too, also lounging on the grass, all of them dressed in these loose-fitting tracksuits, all of them—just like Sertôrian's advance party—smiling and laughing.

When her crew members see Sertôrian, they give a happy shout, saying she has to join them, they're having a wonderful time. *I wouldn't want to intrude*, says Sertôrian, extremely wary of the whole scene.

*Don't be silly*, says one of the locals, getting to her feet. She's a tall woman who introduces herself as Theta and assures Sertôrian that they'd all be very happy to have more guests.

*Please*, says Theta. *Join us.*

The truth is, everyone does seem very happy, and not in a creepy, over-eager way, just in a warm, friendly, we're-glad-you're-here kind of way.

Then Sertôrian notices the sandwiches—everyone is eating, or has just finished eating what look to be mass-produced, diagonally cut sandwiches.

*What's going on with the sandwiches?* Sertôrian asks, and Theta, looking thrilled that Sertôrian has asked, offers the following explanation· The factory at the center of the tent city runs all day every day, and what it produces is a special sandwich that, when you eat it, makes you very, very happy. And everyone on the hillside has either just eaten or is currently eating one of these sandwiches, so they all feel amazing.

Theta insists on giving Sertôrian a tour of the factory, where she learns that the sandwiches' euphoric effect is produced by their filling, which looks and tastes quite a bit like egg salad but is actually a carefully engineered fungus mixed with a stabilizing paste and seasoned with salt and pepper. As far as Sertôrian can tell, there's nothing sinister about the production of the filling. It's not like it's made of recycled people, or anything sketchy like that, but still, Sertôrian refuses Theta's offer of a sandwich.

It's a funny thing—Sertôrian looks at her three shipmates, who have eaten these sandwiches, and they seem fine. Not narcotized, not brainwashed, just really, really happy. Very aware, very cogent, and very glad to be alive. The same seems true of the planet's residents, whose lifestyle, they tell her, consists of everyone working daily six-hour shifts in the factory and in the nearby farms and then just eating sandwiches during their time off and being very, very happy with their lives.

The story gets pretty talky at that point, with Theta giving a long speech extolling the virtues of the planet's lifestyle, and Sertôrian responding with extensive concerns (*The meaning of life can't be sandwiches*, she says at one point). The story culminates, though, with Sertôrian basically kidnapping her three sandwich-eating shipmates (they beg her to let them stay on this planet forever) and dragging them back to the ship. The *Circe*'s been repaired in the meantime, so they take off, never to return.

The general narrative is by no means original, but unlike, say, the lotus-eaters episode in the *Odyssey*, this story doesn't portray the sandwiches as being sinister. There's a pretty strong suggestion, in fact, that Sertôrian and her crew are making a big mistake when they leave the planet behind. In the closing lines of the story, one of the sandwich-eating crew members pleads with Sertôrian to send him back to the sandwich planet. Sertôrian refuses, reminding her shipmate that their objective as a crew is to return home together. Home, that's what he *truly* wants; he's just forgotten while in the grips of the sandwich.

At the mention of home, though, the crew member laughs—what does Sertôrian think she'll find there? Does she expect to find peace? To be loved? To be happy? Because if that's what she wants, she's just left it behind forever. *We found something meaningful*, says her shipmate. *We found paradise*. Sertôrian, unable to muster a response, stares ruefully at the empty sandwich wrapper in her shipmate's hand and then walks away.

Lying there in my parents' living room, I wondered if *The Infinite*

*Future* could do for me what those sandwiches had done for Sertôrian's crew—somehow transubstantiate my sorrows, failures, and frustrations into a light, playful gladness that would carry me through life more cheerily than my current sensibilities seemed capable of. In the past, I might have turned to Mormonism for this uplift, but at the time my life-long religion felt played out to me. It wasn't that I'd had a dramatic crisis of faith; it was more like the torrent of spirituality I'd experienced as a missionary had slowed to a gentle stream, then a trickle, then a drip. I still read the Book of Mormon every day, prayed, went to church on Sundays, but none of it worked for me the way it used to. Most of the time, in those days, I just felt hollow.

Reading Salgado-MacKenzie's fiction was the closest I'd felt to transcendence in years, and now that his masterwork was within our grasp (or could be with a little more detective work) I was tempted to wake my traveling companions and suggest we drive through the night. I wanted to get my hands on *The Infinite Future* as soon as possible. I knew, though, that we'd need our wits about us as we continued on our search, and so sleep would be essential.

As quietly as possible, then, I got up from my chair and found my MP3 player in my backpack. I didn't feel like lying down, so I sat on the floor behind the chair, my back against the wall, and listened to some Big Star, my favorite middle-of-the-night band. Their songs are catchy and propulsive, but tempered with just enough melancholy to stick not just in your head but in your soul. Actually, that's true of most power pop, maybe the most hangdog of musical genres. It's so aggressively sing-alongable, so eager to please, yet it's so often met with commercial indifference. Somehow it falls short of what it's trying hardest to do—to be popular music—and that failure is endlessly endearing to me. Earphones nestled in my ears, then, I listened to Big Star get looser and weirder over the course of their first three albums, until Alex Chilton's eerie vocals on "Holocaust" finally lulled me to sleep.

## XI

That night I had a dream.

I was in my parents' condo, asleep in the recliner, and I heard Wayne Fortescue's deep, drawling voice counting down from a thousand, saying it would help me sleep if I just paid attention to the numbers, the way they descended with such neat regularity.

In a panic, I opened my eyes, but instead of Fortescue, I saw Christine Voorhes sitting on the couch across from me. Or rather, I saw a kind of Voorhes/Fortescue hybrid. The entity was speaking in Fortescue's voice but looked exactly like Voorhes, wearing the same suit she'd worn on the day she'd broken into my apartment—the same green shirt, the same black leather gloves—except this time the gloves extended up past her elbows, hugging her biceps in a manner I found disconcerting, though I couldn't say why.

The other thing that worried me was the long wood-handled kitchen knife that lay across her lap. She wasn't doing anything with it, but I could see the knife had just been sharpened, little slivers of metal still clinging to the edge.

"You need to fall asleep," said Voorhes/Fortescue again, gripping the sharpened knife in one gloved hand. "You need to fall asleep so we can collect what's ours."

"No," I said, trying to sit up, but of course I couldn't. I'd been invisibly bound to the recliner, its soft cushions holding me fast.

Then, in one of those dream jumps that feel seamless in the moment,

Voorhes/Fortescue was standing above me, only now my clothes were gone. I was completely naked, still stuck to the chair, and starting to cry. Voorhes/Fortescue smiled at my tears, and without breaking eye contact, languidly traced the tip of her knife across the bare skin of my torso. I was definitely crying by that point, because I didn't want Voorhes/ Fortescue to see me naked, and I didn't want to die.

Teeth bared, Voorhes/Fortescue leered down at me.

Looking up into her gleaming, hungry eyes, I figured out what was going on in a sudden, intuitive burst.

"My heart," I said as the sharp tip of the knife paused in the middle of my chest. "You're going to cut out my heart, aren't you?"

Throwing back her head, Voorhes/Fortescue gave a full, throaty laugh and then leaned in close to me. Resting one gloved hand hard against my hipbone, and holding the knife to my throat with the other hand, she said, in Fortescue's laconic voice, "Why would anyone want your heart? There's nothing inside of it."

Things were looking pretty dire, but then suddenly I could move again, so I twisted my body out from under Voorhes/Fortescue's grasp, and then, with a jolt, I really was thrashing around, awake on the floor of my parents' condo, all balled up on a tangle of sweaty blankets behind the recliner.

I checked my watch. Quarter to seven. I crawled out from behind the recliner. Sérgio sat on the couch, his long hair still damp from a shower. He wore a neatly pressed pair of blue jeans, a Legião Urbana T-shirt, and a warm-looking camel-hair blazer. Arms folded, he was bouncing his leg up and down like a jittery grade-schooler.

"Morning," I said, sitting up.

He looked down at me with mild concern.

"Harriet's in the shower," he said, "so if you want to grab some breakfast while you're waiting, that might be a good idea. I'd like to get moving as soon as possible."

The night before, I'd been as eager as Sérgio to hit the road, but now I felt like a different person, and not in a good way. That dream had flipped a switch in my brain, and now our search for Salgado-MacKenzie felt like the boneheaded exercise in futility it probably was. Even if we found *The Infinite Future*, it wouldn't solve my problems with Fortescue and the CAC.

"I'm not really hungry," I said.

Sweaty blanket wrapped around me like a cloak, I stood up and switched on my parents' outdated desktop. It was an ancient computer, but it did—amazingly—have Internet capabilities, and so, moving the worn mouse across the souvenir mouse pad my parents had picked up on a recent trip to Wendover, I made the mistake of checking my email.

I had a new message from Fortescue, and it was an extra nasty one. He reminded me that, with penalties and interest, I now owed the CAC over ten thousand dollars, and he explained that if I didn't make a payment in two weeks' time, they would be forced to press charges. He closed the email by saying how disappointed he was in me, that I had seemed like such an honorable young man on the telephone, when in fact I was as lazy and entitled as the rest of my generation. This was the first time Fortescue had set a concrete deadline, and I feared that this signaled a true escalation in the CAC's aggressions.

"Everything okay?" said Sérgio.

"Fine," I said.

I was just logging out of my account when my parents walked into the room.

"Danny," they said. "How nice to see you."

They were a picture of lower-middle-class retirement, my dad wearing an ill-fitting golf shirt and unflattering shorts, my mom wearing a tennis dress she'd owned since I was a child. They were both tan, thinner than the last time I'd seen them, and somehow rangier looking. I gave them each a hug and then introduced them to Sérgio, who offered up the requisite pleasantries and was just beginning to take my parents' leave when Harriet stepped out of the bathroom drying her gray-blond hair with a striped beach towel.

My parents wished her a good morning.

"Good morning," said Harriet, laying her damp towel over the back of a kitchen chair.

"Now, I'm sorry," said my mom, "but you'll have to remind me of your name."

Harriet buttoned her wrinkled cardigan before extending her hand.

"Harriet Kimball," she said, shaking my mom's hand.

In return, rather than introduce herself, my mom said, "Harriet Kimball—isn't that the name of that angry college professor from a few years back?"

This was not the response I'd expected from my mom.

"It is," Harriet said, adjusting the sleeves of her cardigan.

"I bet you get mistaken for her pretty often," my mom said.

"Actually," said Harriet. "I am her."

She delivered this information coolly, and I don't think it quite registered at first.

"Excuse me?" my mom said.

"I am that angry college professor from a few years back," Harriet said.

I was as surprised that my mom had heard of Dr. Kimball as I was horrified by the turn the conversation was taking. The physical configuration of the people in the room had come to resemble a movie-musical knife fight, with me, Sérgio, and my dad circled around Harriet and my mom, who faced each other with unease. I wondered if I should intervene.

"But it's a common name," my dad said, stepping into the fray. "It would be silly to assume you were *that* Harriet Kimball."

"It *is* a common name," Harriet said, "but I *am* that Harriet Kimball."

"Anyway," I said, trying to defuse the situation. "We should probably let Harriet finish getting ready. We'd like to get going as soon as possible."

Rather than take the out I was offering, though, my parents insisted we all sit down to breakfast together before we left.

"We have plenty of Pop-Tarts," said my mom, almost defensively, "and I think some bananas."

And so the five of us crowded around the small round table in my parents' kitchen, eating Pop-Tarts and bananas in thick silence while Sérgio checked his watch every forty-five seconds.

Amid the crinkling of toaster pastry wrappers, I felt an anxious dread seep into my muscles. I'd forgotten for a moment about Fortescue's email and the strange nightmare that had preceded it, but now, sitting at the little table, I couldn't help but contemplate what Voorhes/Fortescue had said to me in the dream: *Why would anyone want your heart? There's nothing inside it.*

Was that true? *Was* there anything inside my heart? I thought of that line from Eliot, the one about hungry rats scurrying over broken glass in an empty cellar, and in spite of the kitchen's heat, I shuddered.

"So, Danny," said my dad. "How's the grocery store?"

"Grocery store?" I said.

"Yeah," said my dad. "Your job at the grocery store."

"Actually, I work at a flower shop," I said.

"Really?" said my dad. "I could have sworn it was a grocery store."

I shook my head and opened another pack of Pop-Tarts.

Something you should know about my parents, or I guess more so about me in relation to my parents, is that I'm the youngest of six kids, and more important, there's a nine-year gap between me and my nearest sibling. The first five kids are very regularly spaced—two to three years between each of them—and then there's that near decade that separates me from my older sister. As you can probably figure, my arrival came as a big surprise to everyone. My parents had thought they were done having kids and were already yearning for their empty-nester days. I befuddled them from their first awareness of my existence, and that befuddlement extended through my childhood, adolescence, and young adulthood, right up through the present moment in their condo. To an outsider (and to me), it might seem that my parents were just as uncomfortable talking to me as they were to Sérgio or Harriet.

"Well, anyway," said my dad. "How's your novel coming?"

"Don't you have a grant for it?" said my mom.

I glanced at my traveling companions. The frequency of Sérgio's watch-checking had just about doubled over the past few minutes, and Harriet was being uncharacteristically silent.

"The whole thing's a little complicated at the moment," I said, feeling a pang of dread at the thought of the Young Religious Novelist Grant.

"Complicated how?" said my dad.

I considered lying or forcefully changing the subject, but the sleep deprivation had rendered me pliant and confessional and I told them everything, from my failure in São Paulo to the latest threatening emails from Wayne Fortescue.

"No," said my dad. "That can't be right. Does that sound right to you?" He directed this last question to Sérgio and Harriet.

"It does sound fishy," said Harriet, folding her empty banana peel and setting it gingerly on the table.

Sérgio nodded in agreement.

I wanted this conversation—this whole breakfast—to be over, but my parents' line of questioning had gained enough momentum that there would be no stopping it. I started into a third package of Pop-Tarts.

"Have you told them this is outrageous?" my dad said to me.

"Basically," I said.

"It does sound very irregular," said Sérgio, who seemed as eager as I was to wrap this conversation up and get moving.

"Irregular nothing," said my dad. "It sounds criminal."

"You know who he should talk to?" said my mom, laying a hand on my dad's arm.

"Craig D. Ahlgren," said my dad.

At the mention of this name, Harriet looked up sharply from her strawberry Pop-Tart. Though it only lasted for an instant, an intense and unmistakable look of displeasure crossed her face.

"Exactly," said my mom. "That is exactly who I was thinking of."

"Do you remember Craig D. Ahlgren?" my dad said to me, then went on before I could answer. "He was our stake president during the last two years we lived in the Miller's Corner house. Great guy, and a brilliant attorney. *Great* guy. You remember Craig D. Ahlgren, right, Danny?"

"Yeah, I remember President Ahlgren," I said, watching Harriet from the corner of my eye. She, in turn, watched my parents warily, waiting, it seemed, to see where this discussion of Craig D. Ahlgren was headed.

My dad said, "I'm going to call him right now."

He stood up, unclipped his phone from his belt, and walked back to the bedroom, shutting the door behind him.

My mom said, "Danny, why didn't you say anything about this earlier?"

I didn't have a good answer for that.

Sérgio, head bowed, surreptitiously consulted a road map below the table. Harriet nibbled warily at her Pop-Tart.

A few minutes later, my dad returned with a triumphant grin on his face.

"Danny, you're in luck," he said as he sat back down. "Craig will be in Ireland for a month on a family history trip, but he's not leaving until tomorrow. He said he'd be happy to meet with you this afternoon and see what he can do to help. You all are planning on stopping in Salt Lake, right?"

Harriet had, in fact, made arrangements to meet with an old friend of hers who was on faculty at the University of Utah. This friend—Dr. Petra Robbins—was a major science-fiction enthusiast, and was especially interested in writers who lived, or had lived, in the Intermountain West. Harriet hoped to pick her brain about any science-fiction writers in the general vicinity of Fremont Creek who might have known Salgado-MacKenzie, or better still, who might have *been* Salgado-MacKenzie, working under a pseudonym. We all knew that a nearly thirty-year-old address might only get us so far, and we'd need all the help we could get.

"Yeah, we'll be in Salt Lake," I said. I turned to Harriet and Sérgio. "Maybe you guys can drop me off at Craig Ahlgren's house while you meet with Dr. Robbins."

Sérgio folded his map and returned it to his blazer pocket. Harriet nodded, her mouth a thin line. Something at breakfast had knocked her off balance, upsetting her more, even, than my parents' earlier faux pas had. It seemed pretty directly connected to Ahlgren, but I couldn't imagine how. What could this guy have done, I wondered, that the mere mention of his name could inspire such a sharp and visceral reaction in the illustrious Harriet Kimball? I was too tired to speculate, but I had an inkling that with Craig D. Ahlgren lay the secret of Harriet's dark and troubled past.

For that reason, if no other, I looked forward to our meeting.

# XII

woke up in a visitor parking lot at the University of Utah. Exhausted by my too-brief night of uneasy sleep, I'd conked out immediately in the back seat of the Celica and slept for the whole five-hour drive to Salt Lake.

"Awake now?" said Sérgio from the front seat.

He had a notebook open in his lap and was urgently jotting something down.

"What are you writing?" I said.

"Questions for Dr. Robbins," he said. "I want to be certain that we explore every possible angle with her."

His eyes shone, his enthusiasm having clearly bounced back since breakfast.

"Great," I said. "Where are we meeting her?"

Harriet turned around from the driver's seat.

"Sérgio and I are meeting Petra at her office," she said, "while you meet with Craig Ahlgren."

She handed me the car keys.

During my nap, I'd somehow forgotten about my meeting with President Ahlgren.

"You want me to take your car?" I said.

"I think that would be for the best," said Harriet, opening her door. "I'll text you when we're ready for you to pick us up."

"Wish us luck," said Sérgio.

Before I could say anything else, they were out of the car. Our abrupt separation left me uneasy. Alone now, I followed the handwritten directions my dad had given me to Hansen's Grove, a secluded neighborhood south of Salt Lake where multi-acre estates lie hidden away from the road behind layers of trees and iron fences. I turned down Sego Lane, the neighborhood's main artery, following it as it grew more twisting and narrow, the streets that branched off it becoming more poorly marked the farther I went. It was the middle of the day, but it could have been dusk for all the autumn-colored foliage overhead blocking the sun.

I drove at a crawl so I could read the obscured street signs, and even so, I nearly missed my next turn, which put me on a gravel path not much wider than my car. I wondered if I was in the wrong place until I came to a serious-looking iron gate with a keypad in a post that I could reach from my window. Craig Ahlgren had given my dad an entry code, so I punched it in and the gate swung open.

I headed down the gravel lane for another five or six minutes before the trees opened up, and suddenly I was on a neatly maintained cobblestone driveway approaching a grand chateau, complete with shuttered windows, stone façade, and a gray, sloping roof. I stopped on the little driveway loop and got out of the car.

To be honest, I was ambivalent about this meeting. On the one hand, I was pretty reluctant to entrust my fate to Craig D. Ahlgren; I had no desire to embroil myself with another powerful figure who could mold my life with his capricious and immovable whims. Because really, I knew very little about Ahlgren and what kind of person he might be. I'd heard him speak in a dozen or so church meetings back when I was in middle school, and that was pretty much it.

On the other hand, there was that morning's email from Wayne Fortescue—the two-week deadline, the ten thousand dollars. Even if throwing myself at the mercy of President Ahlgren constituted a frying-pan-to-fire situation, I'd at least welcome the change.

I rang the doorbell and steeled myself.

Craig D. Ahlgren answered the door in a pair of gray sweatpants and a blue oxford shirt whose untucked front and tails billowed at his thighs like a minidress.

"Daniel," he said, a smile wrinkling the corners of his eyes. "So good to see you. Come on in."

I stepped over the threshold.

"Thanks for doing this," I said.

"Of course," said President Ahlgren. "Right this way."

I followed him into a foyer of dark wood floors and clean white walls.

"Are you a sweatpants guy?" said President Ahlgren as he led me past a curving staircase.

"I'm definitely not opposed," I said.

"I love sweatpants," he said. "I've worn a suit to work every day for the past—boy, how long?—longer than you've been alive anyway. But sweatpants? Can't wait to get into my sweatpants at the end of the day."

"They do look very comfortable," I said.

We walked through a vast and tastefully furnished living room, weaving between linen armchairs, past a great stone fireplace, and into a narrow hallway.

"Right here," said President Ahlgren, stopping at a glass-paneled door at the end of the hall. "Go on in."

We stepped into his office, a little nook furnished with a broad, classy rug and a wooden desk so simple, sturdy, and elegant that you knew it cost a fortune. A tall, narrow window looked out on a rustic garden, and beyond that a tennis court and swimming pool nestled among a veritable forest of autumnal trees.

The only items not in keeping with the room's stately décor were two of those big rubber exercise balls that people use for Pilates or whatever. To be fair, though, they *were* both a tasteful, muted shade of gray. Craig rolled one of them up to the edge of the desk, opened a sleek laptop, and sat down on the ball.

"Make yourself at home," he said, rolling the second ball in my direction. I sat down on the bouncy surface, vaguely nervous that it would pop beneath my weight.

"I really appreciate this, President Ahlgren," I said as he removed a pair of reading glasses from his shirt pocket and perched them on his nose.

"It's my pleasure," he said. "And at home it's just Craig."

We sat there for a moment, both of us bouncing slightly on our inflatable seats as Craig pulled up a document on his computer.

"All right then," he said, peering through his glasses at the monitor. "I've written a letter to the people who awarded you this so-called grant. What it says, essentially, is that you've hired a lawyer and you're calling their bluff—because it *is* a bluff, I'm nearly certain of that. You probably even have grounds to go after *them*, if you're interested. In any event, this letter should get them off your back. I just need their address and the name of the person you've been in contact with."

He handed me the keyboard and I pulled up an email containing Wayne Fortescue's name and business address. After copying over the information, Craig printed off the letter on some official stationery, signed it, and put it in an envelope.

"I'll make sure it goes out in tomorrow's mail," he said.

I sat there bouncing on my exercise ball, waiting for Craig to add some unpleasant caveat, but none came.

"So that's it?" I said.

"That's it," he said.

And sure enough, a week later I would receive a brief, penitent email from Wayne Fortescue apologizing on behalf of the CAC for any unpleasantness that had passed between us. Of course I owed them nothing—there had been a misunderstanding, and our business together was now concluded. True to his word, Fortescue would never darken my inbox with his presence again.

Craig folded his glasses and tucked them back into his shirt pocket.

"Thank you so much," I said, laughing with relief.

"I'm happy to help," said Craig.

With a wave of his lawyerly pen, Craig D. Ahlgren had exorcised a legion of worries from my troubled heart. I felt like a person again, instead of a walking bundle of bad decisions.

"Really," I said. "Thanks."

"Please," said Craig. "It was no trouble at all. Have you had lunch yet?"

"No," I said.

With a spry bounce, Craig stood from his gray exercise ball. Bracing myself against the edge of the desk, I rose from my own.

"Neither have I," said Craig. "I'm going to rustle something up in the kitchen. Do you have time to eat?"

I checked my phone. Harriet hadn't texted yet.

"Absolutely," I said.

We walked around the corner to the kitchen, an open, airy space with a bank of windows on one side and a stone wall on the other that contained, within matching niches, the stove and the refrigerator.

"All right," said Craig, opening the fridge. "I'm leaving town tomorrow, so we need to take care of as many of these leftovers as we can."

He handed me a plate, which I loaded with roast beef, a spinach salad, and something with quinoa. Then we both settled in at the heavy wood table in the adjacent dining room.

"This is delicious," I said. "Thank you."

"I'd tell you to thank Bev," said Craig, "but she's out running a few errands before we leave town tomorrow. She's the cook around here."

He opened a bottle of mineral water and poured us each a glass.

"So," said Craig, screwing the lid back on the green glass bottle, "your dad tells me you're on some kind of road trip with Harriet Kimball?"

"That's right," I said and then explained a little about our search for Eduard Salgado-MacKenzie—who the man was and why we hoped to find him. I told Craig about the unpublished novel and the series of clues pointing us toward Idaho.

As I described our search, it became clear that Craig had no interest in Salgado-MacKenzie—not surprising, since no one ever did—but he did keep circling back to Dr. Kimball: *How had she become involved in all of this?* and *What exactly had she been up to in Southern California?* Stuff like that. And my answers to these questions seemed, somehow, not to satisfy him at all. He was obviously fishing for something specific, but I had no idea what.

Finally I asked, "Do you know Dr. Kimball?"

He chewed thoughtfully on a piece of beef.

"I used to," he said carefully.

He took a drink of mineral water as if that were a sufficient answer.

"But not anymore?" I said, prodding him on.

He shook his head, looking uncomfortable in this shift in roles from questioner to questioned.

"How did—"

"Wait," said Craig, waving his hand at me like he was erasing a chalkboard. "I need to tell you . . ." He paused, considering. "What I mean to say is, I want you to be careful."

This caught me completely off guard.

"Careful of what?" I said.

Craig pushed his plate back. Now we were getting somewhere.

He said, "I think I can understand, Daniel, the appeal that Harriet Kimball's work might hold for a bright young man like you. Her whole smarter-than-thou approach to Mormonism can make you feel like you're in on a secret that the rest of us are too naïve to pick up on. So I see the attraction there. I really do."

Did Craig think I was some dewy-eyed acolyte of Harriet Kimball's? If so, he was barking up the wrong tree. I had zero interest in Harriet's scholarship.

"Actually," I said, trying to set him straight.

"No," said Craig. "You need to hear me out."

"But—"

"No," he said. "Please?"

He said it like he was really asking. I nodded and he went on.

"I know I might seem like the bad guy to you—I don't know what Harriet's already said—but, for your own good, you need to listen to me." He leaned forward, elbows on his thighs, hands reaching imploringly toward me. "You're at a pivotal moment in your life right now; I can see it in your eyes. You're just drifting along, still figuring out what kind of person you're going to be, where your allegiances lie, and to a certain extent that's fine, just a natural stage in life. Sooner or later, though, you're going to have to decide whose side you're on: the Lord's or the world's. And there are certain people who will try to make those two sides seem much more muddled than they actually are.

"I can tell you, though, Daniel, that the contrast is actually quite stark. This might sound dramatic, but the truth is, you can either hold to the iron rod and follow the Lord, or stand in the great and spacious building and mock what's good and holy in this life. Those are your options.

"And do you want to know how to be sure you're always on the side of the Lord? The answer, Daniel," he said before I could respond, "is absolute obedience to God's chosen servants. It's that simple. Whatever happens, whatever we might think to the contrary, we follow the leaders of the Church. No matter what.

"Now, certain people might make arguments to the contrary, arguments that may be well intended, but I can assure you that these arguments will ultimately lure you away from the safety of the strait-and-narrow path. And the people who make those arguments . . ." He sat up straight and looked away for a moment. "Let me explain it this way instead," he said, looking me in the eye again. "Let me tell you about the most important decision I ever made."

"Okay," I said.

"And please," he said, "listen carefully to what I have to say."

"Of course," I said, putting on my best listening face.

"This experience is sacred to me, Daniel," said Craig, lowering his voice. "It's a decision that has served as a template for every subsequent decision, big and small, that I've had to make in my life. A watershed moment. Do you understand?"

"Yes," I said, nodding attentively.

"Good," he said.

He took a sip of mineral water and cleared his throat.

. . .

I had just turned seventeen (he began) and the one thing I wanted most in the world was to go to college. I know that for a lot of kids these days, college is no big deal, it's a given, but for me? Neither of my parents had ever even set foot on a university campus. We lived in Valley Park, out on the west side of—well, you're from Salt Lake, right? So you know where Valley Park is. And you probably know it's not the nicest neighborhood, very working class. That was the case back when I lived there too. Dad worked out at Kennecott, and there were nine of us kids, so we kept Mom pretty busy and the money spread pretty thin. We had to work hard—all of us did. Both of my parents had that work ethic, though, that salt-of-the-earth, pioneer-stock grit, which I didn't appreciate then like I do now.

Thing is, I was a very ambitious kid. I looked at how hard my parents worked, and I looked around at where we lived—you know, how little all that hard work got them (that's how I saw it, anyway)—and I knew I wanted a more comfortable life for myself, and I knew that college was the best way to do that. That's how I would better myself. That's how I'd get ahead in life. Problem was, I knew my parents wouldn't have any money to send me; some months they could barely put food on the table. I knew that if I wanted to get a university degree, it was all on me. So I started a college fund.

That was when I was fourteen years old. I told you, I was a very serious kid. Anyway, I did odd jobs around the neighborhood, worked harder in school than I had before, got involved in the honor society, played on the school basketball team—that was a little later, of course—and just did everything I could to give myself a good start.

Now, my parents raised us in the Church, but religion wasn't something I gave a lot of thought to as a boy. The state of my soul, what happens after we die, the nature of God—none of that held much interest for me. I was so focused on college and my future, you understand, that Mormonism was mostly an afterthought.

All of that changed, though, my junior year of high school.

I had just turned seventeen and was more determined than ever to go to a good college, and I'll tell you, I was burning the candle at both ends. I don't think I slept more than five hours a night that school year, I had so many obligations—my classes, the basketball team, student government, my job at the gas station, and then a social life on top of all that. I was young, though, and resilient. Somehow I pulled it off.

Well, one weekend, for a special stake conference, we were told that Elder Merle G. Roberts of the Quorum of the Twelve Apostles would be speaking to us. Obviously, he was before your time, Daniel, but Elder Roberts was such a beloved figure in the Church—a very warm, charismatic man; a former schoolteacher. He had striking, thick white hair, even when he got quite old, and he was an excellent public speaker. He had one of those warm rich voices—an old-fashioned way of speaking that you don't really hear anymore—and everyone loved the stories he told about growing up in Southern Utah. And his teachings on the gospel—when he expounded on the doctrines of the Church, he did it so clearly and lovingly that even a child could follow along. Our stake was very excited, then, that he would be visiting us.

And it was an interesting thing. When he met with our stake president in preparation for the conference, Elder Roberts told him that he'd received a strong impression the night before that in conjunction with this conference, he should speak one-on-one with all the high-school-aged young men of the stake.

Our stake president said that of course he'd be happy to make the arrangements, which was how, a few days later, I came to be sitting in the office of Elder Merle G. Roberts. I'm not going to lie; I wasn't thrilled to be there. I had so much going on at the time that I'd had to cancel some pressing engagement—a shift at work, maybe, or a study group, I can't remember for sure—in order to show up at this meeting. Like I said, Daniel, I was just college, college, college at this point in my life.

Elder Roberts was very gracious, though. He thanked me for making time to see him, and then in that rich warm voice of his, he asked me about my family, he asked me about school, he asked me about the basketball team. He was one of those people, Daniel, who, when I told him about my life, truly listened to what I was saying, listened with his whole being, if that makes sense. I had just told him about my desire to attend college when Elder Roberts nodded thoughtfully. He paused for a moment, and then he asked me if I planned to serve a mission.

The honest answer was no, but I told him that I would like to, the only problem was that I didn't know if I or my family could afford it. Back then, missions weren't quite as strongly encouraged as they are today, so my position was not necessarily unusual. At any rate, Elder Roberts nodded at my answer and then asked me if I had a job. I told him I did. He asked me what I did with the money I earned. I told him I saved most of it. Like I'd said, I had hopes of attending college after I finished high school.

Elder Roberts told me this was to be commended, and then he paused. He paused for so long, actually, that I wondered if I should leave. At one point his head was down and his eyes were closed, and I thought maybe he'd fallen asleep. Just when I was about to say something, though, he opened his eyes.

He said, "Craig, I feel prompted to make you a promise. I recognize that it won't be easy for you to gather sufficient funds to serve a mission, but it will be possible if you're willing to make a sacrifice. You've been saving money for an education, and as I said, that is commendable. I would challenge you, though, to consecrate that money instead to pay for a mission. While serving the Lord, you'll be educated by the Spirit and you'll bless the lives of countless souls. I promise you that, Craig. I also promise you that if you make this sacrifice, the Lord will ensure that you receive the college education you desire. So, Craig"—he paused, smiling kindly—"will you consecrate two years of your life to serving the Lord as a full-time missionary?"

This caught me completely off guard. As I said, I'd had no plans to serve a mission, and yet as I listened to Elder Roberts's invitation, I felt a warmth spreading through my chest, a strong impression that what he said was true.

Craig's eyes shone and I felt a once familiar warmth in my own chest, a resonant sympathy with Craig's sincere conviction.

"Still," he went on, "I wanted *so badly* to attend college, and if I did serve a mission, where would I find the money for school? Wouldn't I end up just like my father, working long hard hours at a wage that could barely support a family?

"Then again, I couldn't deny what I was feeling. I told Elder Roberts I'd need a little time to think it over, and he said that sounded like a good idea. He thanked me for my time and wished me the best in all my pursuits."

Craig wiped at his eyes with the heel of his hand, and I held as still as possible, not wanting to disrupt this heavy moment.

"I have to say, Daniel, that it wasn't an easy decision to make," he continued. "Every morning and every night for a month after that meeting, I prayed to know if what Elder Roberts said was true. And I don't want to go into too much detail—certain things are too personal and precious to be widely shared—but I can tell you that I did receive an answer, and that answer was that I needed to serve a mission.

"I followed Elder Roberts's counsel, and just as he'd promised, I had a tremendous experience as a missionary serving the people of New Zealand. Not only that, but I also received the education I'd so strongly desired. After my mission, I attended BYU on a scholarship, and from there I went to law school at Michigan. During those years I was blessed immensely. I had to work hard, and I certainly didn't have much money, but I always had sufficient for my needs.

"And you know, Daniel—you've served a mission, you've been a member of the Church your whole life, and I'm sure you could tell me similar stories of how you've been blessed by following the counsel of latter-day prophets. It's a thrilling time we live in, to have the Lord's Church restored on the Earth and prophets who receive regular, divine inspiration to guide us back to the Father.

"What breaks my heart, then, is when you get these members of the Church who look at our leaders, and all they can do is criticize and find fault. You know who I mean—oftentimes it's these academics or these feminists who think they know better than the men God called to lead His church. And it really is tragic, because not only are these brothers and sisters cutting themselves off from divine revelation—from the truth—but they're also trying to cut others off as well. And the fact of the matter is, Daniel, that people like that need a wakeup call. For their own good, and for the good of others. They need God's blessings just as much as I do and you do, and to receive those blessings they need to receive the counsel of the prophets.

"I'm a cause-and-effect guy, Daniel, and I can tell you that every blessing I've ever received has been predicated on my obedience to God's counsel. I've led a full, happy life because I've followed the leaders of the Church. When other people fail to live up to that potential, then, when they stubbornly refuse to receive that happiness, the most merciful thing you can do is try to snap them out of it, get them to see the stumbling stones they've placed in their own path. So do you see why I'm concerned, Daniel, that you're spending all this time with someone like Harriet Kimball?"

Warmth leaching from my chest, I said, "But I'm not really—"

"No," said Craig. "You don't need to make excuses."

"But—"

"Daniel," he said firmly, lifting his hand. "It seems to me that you've reached a crossroads in life, and all I'm asking you to do is to consider the state of your heart. Will you do that for me?"

In spite of all the bombast, I couldn't help but feel drawn to what Craig was saying. Here, finally, was someone who had his life together, a man who knew what he knew, and who wasn't going to be swayed from it. Here was someone solid, and while I may not have agreed with every single thing he'd just said, I couldn't argue with the general air of security that surrounded him.

"Yes," I said. "I will."

"Good," said Craig, wiping his mouth with his napkin. He looked at his watch. "Wow, I've really been talking your ear off! Can I steal you for a few more minutes, by chance?"

I looked at my phone. Still no text from Harriet.

"Yeah," I said. "I don't want to keep you, though, if you need to be getting ready for your trip."

"No, no—I'm fine," said Craig. "But there's something else I wanted to talk to you about before you go."

"Okay," I said, unsure what else there was to discuss.

Craig clasped his hands together and laid them on his sweatpant-clad leg.

"This morning on the phone, your dad was telling me a little about your situation," he said, emphasizing that last word as if to underscore that *situation* was the nicest term he could use to describe the mess my life had become. "And I hope I'm not overstepping here, but it sounds to me like you could use a better job."

"A better job would be nice," I said carefully.

I wondered again where he was going with this.

"Here's what I propose," said Craig. "I'm going to Ireland for a month, but I can set the wheels in motion to hire you as a filing clerk at my firm. I know you're probably qualified for better, but it's a place to start, and it'll give you a taste of how a law office works, because what you need to do, in my opinion, is go to law school—put that English degree to practical use. I think you'd be very successful—very happy—as a lawyer."

"Wow," I said, leaning back in my chair.

You might be tempted to read this moment as a test of my integrity, a will-the-struggling-artist-sell-out-his-ideals kind of thing, but here's the truth of it: I hated writing fiction—*despised* it—and although I'd enjoyed the few translations I'd done of Salgado-MacKenzie's short stories, that kind of work held no appeal for me, not as an actual career. Because by that point in my life, I wasn't looking for artistic fulfillment, or whatever it is you want to call that wispy mirage I'd been chasing with my failed novel. I say "wispy mirage," but I know exactly what I'd been pursuing; I'm just too embarrassed to say it, even after all these years. What I wanted was to forge in the smithy of my heart the unformed conscience of my people, or however that line from *Portrait of the Artist* goes. I wanted to write the Great Mormon Novel. But that really wasn't working out for me, so what I wanted now—what I wanted more than anything—was power.

I realize that sounds like something a James Bond villain might say, so let me clarify. I didn't want a *disproportionate* amount of power—no metal-toothed henchman or volcano lair for me. No, all I wanted was the kind of power Craig D. Ahlgren had wielded earlier when he'd composed that terse, bluff-calling letter to Wayne Fortescue. The words he wrote could actually *do* something in the world, unlike the pages and pages of fiction I'd produced. They had served as nothing more than deadweight in my pathetic downward trajectory.

I was tired of being at the mercy of crackpots and hucksters, of living in a storage room below a doughnut shop and eating microwave chicken potpies for dinner every night. During my undergrad years, I'd been so dismissive of my law-school-aspiring classmates, feeling smugly superior about my own more noble vocation. Now I could see that the pre-law kids had been right all along. There was nothing noble in penury and failure.

It was in that moment, as I considered Craig's job offer, that I understood the true danger of *The Infinite Future*. A book like that could destroy me, not through esoteric theologies or musty curses, but through its inveterate elusiveness. I could spend the rest of my life searching and hoping for a book like that to fill my life with meaning, but ultimately what would it bring me? It would bring me a life like Sérgio's or Harriet's, a life spent in the cramped, subterranean office of a university library, for instance, or in an isolated cabin in Danesville, Utah—the type of grim confinement where all prisoners of a certain type of idealism eventually end up serving their self-righteous sentences. That kind of confinement had felt inevitable to me, but now, talking with Craig D. Ahlgren in his lovely dining room, I realized I didn't have to end up like Sérgio or like Harriet. If I wanted to, I could still make something of my life. And I did want to.

"That sounds great," I said. "I'd really appreciate that."

"You'll come work for me then?" said Craig.

"Yes," I said. "Yes, I will."

"So it's agreed," he said, obviously pleased to have helped out.

"Yes," I said and Craig shook my hand, his grip warm and sure.

## XIII

Three days later, on the penultimate weekend of October 2009, Harriet and I sat waiting on a bench in front of the Spud Diner in Fremont Creek, Idaho. Inside the diner, Sérgio—deep in the grips of a formidable disappointment—sulked his way through a cheeseburger combo meal. The search had not been going well.

We'd arrived Tuesday evening to discover that the address from Roger Ash's Rolodex was now occupied by a shabby little video rental place: framed posters of ten-year-old movies taped to the dusty front windows, display shelves containing more dead flies than DVD cases, a half-deflated Mylar balloon tethered limply to the cash register. The proprietor had never heard of Eduard Salgado-MacKenzie. He had only been living in Fremont Creek for a few years, in fact, having more or less inherited the video rental place from an old friend who'd unexpectedly died. He suggested we ask around town, though—who could say what we might find?

Over the next three days, then, we'd visited city hall, the chamber of commerce, the Fremont Creek city archives, the police station, and the one-room office of the local paper, the *Fremont Creek Crier*. We'd talked to every shop owner, restaurateur, hunting guide, bartender, ex-mayor, local character, and octogenarian we could find, and not a single one of them knew or remembered any Brazilians or science-fiction writers who'd lived among them. Given the size of the town (1,237 residents, their WELCOME TO FREMONT CREEK sign proudly proclaimed), it seemed pretty likely that if no one recalled the name Salgado-MacKenzie, he hadn't lived there long, if at all.

We *had* learned that the video rental place was once a barbershop and that the more transient residents of the town used to have their mail delivered there. And so we'd spoken to every former employee of the barbershop still living. Like most citizens of Fremont Creek, these former barbershop employees—men and women in their twilight years—answered our questions with a perfunctory friendliness that belied a yawning indifference to us and our quest. Before arriving in town, I'd wondered if we might be met with suspicion or even hostility here, but the reality was, nobody even cared enough to treat us as the nosy and bothersome outsiders we were.

At any rate, none of the former barbershop employees could remember receiving letters for an Eduard Salgado-MacKenzie.

By Friday afternoon, then, we were running low on new places to look and people to talk to, and it was becoming harder and harder to deny that in a day and a half Sérgio would fly home empty-handed. The situation, in other words, was grim.

It should be noted, though, that there are much worse places to watch a dream die than Fremont Creek, Idaho. That, at least, was what Sérgio had kept saying during our first couple of days in town, although by day three he sounded less and less convinced each time he repeated the sentiment, until finally he stopped saying it altogether.

He wasn't wrong, though. In a lesser location, this petering out of a lifelong quest would feel all the more pathetic for the uninspired surroundings. Here, though, the failure had a Wagnerian heft to it. Just north of town was a wide, Rhinemaiden-friendly bend in the Snake River, and to the east were the craggy peaks of the Teton Range, where Valkyries might gather to do whatever it is that Valkyries do at the tops of impressive mountains. What I'm saying is, majesty oozed from the surrounding countryside—orange-leafed groves of quaking aspens, vast plots of rich farm soil, striking gray basalt cliffs—positively soaking our sorry enterprise with a vicarious grandeur.

Still, though, failure is failure, which is why Sérgio was currently sitting alone in the Spud Diner eating his feelings with a side of curly fries while Harriet and I waited out front, having sensed that our Brazilian friend could use a few minutes to himself.

"Do you think he's going to be okay?" I asked Harriet.

It was a cold October afternoon, and Harriet was wrapped in several wool sweaters, a stocking cap pulled tightly over her head.

"It's certainly a big disappointment," she said.

I'd just interrupted another one of her lectures, this one on the semi-matriarchal social orders that had existed within polygamous families in pioneer-era Utah.

"I hope we find *something*," I said.

"Yes," she said, a bit absently.

She was staring at something to the east, and I followed her gaze to the rugged silhouette of the distant Tetons. I wondered what was on her mind.

"Can I tell you something in confidence?" she said, turning to look at me.

"Of course," I said, eager to hear whatever secret from her personal life she was about to reveal.

Over the past few days, we hadn't really discussed Craig D. Ahlgren—neither of us had mentioned him at all, actually—and my partial, inferred knowledge of what had happened between them cast an awkward pall over our interactions. I worried that she assumed that I had learned more from Ahlgren than I actually had, and that I was keeping mum about it out of disapproval, embarrassment, or shock. And in fact, I *had* begun to evaluate her through the foggy lens I'd been given by Ahlgren. She'd been mixed up in something unsavory, but what? And how careful did I need to be around her?

I wanted to clear the air, but whatever had happened between her and Craig was also none of my business, and since she hadn't broached the subject with me, I figured she didn't want to talk about it. So we talked around the whole thing, whatever *the whole thing* was, which kept us at a perpetual distance from each other. The end result was that even after spending several days together, I felt like I didn't know Harriet any better than I had when we'd first met.

Now, though, it seemed that she was ready to break her silence on her haunted past.

"It's about Salgado-MacKenzie," she said.

Or not.

"Okay," I said.

Harriet leaned her head toward mine and lowered her voice. She said that before Sérgio had initiated contact with her, she'd only read one Salgado-MacKenzie story, "All Quiet, All Dark," the one she'd translated for Roger Ash's jingoistic anthology. On Sérgio's arrival to California, though, he'd presented her with a binder identical, I assumed, to the one he'd given me, jam-packed with the complete known works of Salgado-MacKenzie. Harriet had been working her way through the stories each night before bed, and although she enjoyed them more often than not, they'd failed to captivate her in the same way the elusive author's letters had so many years earlier.

"They're interesting enough, in their own way," Harriet said about the stories. "For instance, there's a modesty to them, even amid the grandiosity, that I appreciate. At the end of the day, though, I can't discern in them the quality that Sérgio finds so compelling. He's told me again and again, 'It's Sertôrian, it's all Sertôrian—that's what you have to focus on,' but she ultimately seems like a pretty by-the-numbers, stock science-fiction character to me. Really, it's a shame. So much of my scholarship focuses on bringing to light the lives and contributions of undersung Mormon women, and I would love nothing more than to read a canon of stories that features a potent new religion with a complex woman at its center, but like I said, for me Sertôrian just doesn't jump off the page like that." She glanced at Sérgio inside the diner and then back at me. "And I actually don't know why I'm being so furtive about this—I usually feel quite comfortable expressing my opinions—but the current situation feels delicate enough that I'm opting to err on the side of discretion. What

I'm curious about, I suppose," she said, finally getting to the point, "is whether you've felt any mystical connection to Sertôrian, or if I'm the odd one out here."

Just a few days earlier, I'd certainly thought I had. In my mind's eye, Sertôrian had glimmered like a lodestar at the distant edge of my sorry horizons. Since my meeting with Craig D. Ahlgren, though, Salgado-MacKenzie's inexhaustible protagonist had lost her guiding luster, and it was hard for me to think of those previous feelings as anything other than willful delusions, summoned to fill a host of gaping voids in my life. And now that those voids were filled, now that the CAC was out of my hair and I had a much better job waiting for me when I got back to Utah, now that I had the LSAT to study for and law schools to research, now that I had a bright future again for the first time in years, I didn't need Salgado-MacKenzie or Irena Sertôrian or *The Infinite Future* to save me anymore.

"I don't know," I said to Harriet. "Not really, I guess."

She looked at me intently for a moment.

"Nothing?" she said.

"Nothing," I said.

"Hmm," said Harriet.

I opened my mouth to elaborate on what I'd just said, but then I opted for silence, pulling my coat more tightly around me.

Gazing again at the distant mountains, Harriet said, "And I do have to acknowledge—we both do, really, you and I—that we could be missing something. His letters, after all, had a zip to them—a real *zip*, you know? They were much funnier than the stories, for one thing, and more audacious. And those qualities, I just don't see them in the stories. Or if so, only a glimmer." She shook her head. "That book proposal, on the other hand—*The Infinite Future*?—there's audacity for you. *There's* something I'd really like to read."

"If it even exists," I said.

As if summoned by this blasphemy, Sérgio stepped through the door of the diner and glared darkly at me.

"The waitress," he said, "told me we might try Stockton Funeral Home. The owner knows everyone in town, apparently."

And with that, he swung the loose end of his plaid scarf over his shoulder and started walking up Main Street, apparently uninterested in whether or not Harriet and I would follow.

Though Sérgio's stride was purposeful, I could see as I caught up with him that his face had been overtaken by an expression that was equal parts mourning and confusion. Feeling guilty that I didn't need *The Infinite Future* to fix my life anymore, while the book continued to matter so deeply to Sérgio, I thought I might try my hand at cheering him up.

"Maybe," I said helpfully as I walked alongside him, "this is one of those situations where the real treasure is in the searching for it, you know? Joy in the journey kind of thing."

We were making good time up the sidewalk as I said this, autumn leaves blowing around our feet. As soon as the words left my mouth, though, Sérgio stopped walking and grabbed me by the shoulder. He turned me so we faced each other.

"Let me make one thing clear to you, Daniel," he said. A few strands of hair had come loose from his ponytail and blew wildly around his face. "Although I might have implied otherwise in the recent past, if we don't find what we're looking for here, I will be very, very disappointed."

"Sure," I said, pulling free from his grip. "I get it."

"Do you?" said Sérgio, wrapping his scarf more tightly around his neck. He turned away.

"Come on," said Harriet, a few paces ahead of us. "We're wasting time."

It was hard for me to reconcile this surly, taciturn figure who moped his way up and down Main Street with the bold enthusiast I'd met just a few months earlier. Where, in the past, he might have fought back when the multifarious tentacles of disenchantment threatened to drag him underwater, now he seemed content to be embraced by their iron grip and conveyed without struggle to the beast's ravenous, clacking maw.

And unfortunately, our visit with Patricia Stockton did nothing to improve Sérgio's outlook. In the funeral home's muted, tastefully forgettable front lobby, Patricia—a woman whose demeanor was as far from funereal as could be imagined—told us she didn't know any Brazilians or any space-fiction writers who lived in Fremont Creek, but had we talked to Jack Phillips yet? We said we hadn't, and Patricia said that if anyone knew our writer friend, it would be Jack Phillips; he'd taught English for thirty years over at the high school and may have done a little writing himself. It seemed like an unpromising lead, but we thanked her warmly for her time and saw ourselves out.

"Should we give this Jack Phillips a call?" said Harriet as the three of us stood on the sidewalk outside the funeral home.

"I don't see why not," I said, although I had a pretty good hunch it would be a waste of our time.

Sérgio looked up and down the street. We'd been inside every shop, restaurant, and municipal building by now, which, given the size of the town, actually wasn't that impressive a feat.

"You two go," said Sérgio. "I'll head back to the motel."

We were staying at the Teton Motor Lodge, Fremont Creek's only motel. Located at the end of Main Street, just before the road became State Highway 49, the establishment consisted of twelve cozy log cabins that had been superficially renovated—a new coat of varnish on the logs, fresh paint slapped on the interior walls—by the current proprietor, an enterprising native son named Kenny who exhorted us, each time we saw him, to try out the new hot tub he'd just installed behind the main office building. If we hadn't brought our own bathing suits, he told us, we could rent them at the front desk. We'd noticed the hot tub, a secondhand affair that had seen better days, sheltered within a white vinyl gazebo, but so far, to Kenny's obvious disappointment, none of us had taken a dip.

"Come on," Harriet said as Sérgio started walking motel-ward.

"We could wait to talk to Jack Phillips," I said, "if you're needing a break."

A cold wind blew, cutting through my wool coat and sending an abandoned Styrofoam cup skittering down the sidewalk.

"I've finished for the day," said Sérgio. "Go ahead without me."

We watched him trudge up the street, head down, feet dragging.

Sans Sérgio, then, Harriet and I headed out in her old Toyota to meet Jack Phillips.

We drove toward the Tetons, their rugged outline still visible against the dim, early evening sky. On either side of us, empty potato fields stretched to the horizon. Inside the car, the heater blasted, not quietly. Neither of us spoke. Not knowing, though, when I'd have another chance to speak privately with Harriet, I decided that this was as good a time as any to clear the air.

"So how do you know Craig Ahlgren?" I said.

If the question bothered Harriet, she didn't let on.

Eyes fixed on the long straight road ahead of us, she said, "He was my bishop when I lived in Salt Lake."

I adjusted the shoulder strap of my seat belt.

"Did you know him well?" I said.

"Well enough," she said. "Why? What did he tell you?"

There was just enough of an edge to her question that I lost my nerve. If there were things she wanted to leave buried, they could stay buried.

"Nothing," I said. "Just that he hopes you're doing well."

"Hmm," she said, and that was the end of our conversation.

Jack Phillips turned out to be an even flimsier lead than Patricia Stockton had made him out to be. A short, broad-shouldered old man with a bushy white beard, he lived by himself in a small house on a lonely couple of acres he'd bought from a dissolute farmer decades earlier.

As we sipped hot cocoa around his Formica-topped kitchen table, Mr. Phillips recited for us a heroic catalog of grievances he had with Fremont Creek High School students, past and present. And every time Harriet or I tried to bring up Salgado-MacKenzie, Mr. Phillips would set off on a new rant about the sorry state of educational affairs in Fremont Creek—school-board politics, funding issues, etc. I think Harriet and I were both sympathetic to Mr. Phillips's plight, at least broadly, but it became clear pretty quickly that he had no information that directly pertained to our search. Each time we tried to politely extricate ourselves, though, a new rant kicked into gear. It took us well over an hour to convince him that, as much as we were enjoying his company, we really needed to go.

When we finally walked out of Jack Phillips's house, leaving him brooding in the kitchen, it was dark outside and fifteen degrees cooler than when we'd arrived. Amid flurries of snow—October storms were not uncommon in Fremont Creek—we drove back to the motel.

## XIV

I n a disconcerting development, we found Sérgio sitting in the Teton Motor Lodge's aboveground hot tub, his slouching torso wreathed in fluorescent-lit steam. As we drew closer, I could see through the illuminated water that he wore a pair of turquoise swim trunks with the words PROPERTY OF TETON MOTOR LODGE stenciled across the front.

"Hey," I said. "Everything okay?"

He drew a hand over his dripping beard.

"I'm drinking a milkshake in a hot tub," he said, lifting a paper milkshake cup for us to see. "Kenny's idea. He said it might be fun, the cold in the hot."

"The cold in the hot in the cold," said Harriet, gesturing at the snow falling around us.

"As you say," said Sérgio, closing his eyes and leaning back against the wall of the tub.

"I bet Kenny's thrilled," said Harriet.

"On cloud nine," said Sérgio.

Harriet seemed to be taking things in stride, but I was still trying to get a handle on the situation.

"So, Kenny suggested you drink a milkshake in the hot tub?" I said.

"No, he *insisted* I drink a milkshake," said Sérgio. "He went and bought it for me himself."

Sérgio appeared to feel nothing—not amusement, not pleasure, not embarrassment, or chagrin—about his current state, which worried me even more than his sulking had.

"That's a very specific request, with the milkshake," I said and then lowered my voice. "Do you think Kenny has, like, a webcam set up or something?"

"A webcam?" said Harriet. "Really?"

"Yeah," I said. "I mean, this has to be a thing, right? People who get off on watching people drink milkshakes in hot tubs?"

Harriet rolled her eyes. Sérgio shrugged.

"If he's filming then he's filming," he said.

The hot tub's heater hummed to life. Sérgio leaned back, eyes closed. Harriet zipped her coat up all the way to her chin and huddled down into it. I checked my watch.

"Listen," I said, hoping to snap Sérgio out of this funk. "It's Friday night. We should stop by the bar and the Spud again—catch the weekend crowd, talk to someone new."

"You can do what you want," said Sérgio, eyes still closed.

Snow had started to build up on my hair and shoulders. I stepped closer to the steam.

"Is the motel office still open?" said Harriet, blowing into her gloved hands.

"I believe so," said Sérgio.

"Then I think I'll join you in the hot tub," she said.

I looked at her through the steam. The evening had just taken another unexpected turn. Sérgio only nodded, though, as if everything was unfolding exactly as he'd imagined it might.

I took a step back from the tub, and Harriet turned to me.

"Daniel?" she said. "What about you?"

There was no question that the hot tub grossed me out. I'm no germophobe, but I'd once spent a queasy afternoon following links from a local newspaper article to CDC reports of fecal contamination in public swimming pools and hot tubs. Still, I had no interest in hunting for

Salgado-MacKenzie by myself, and what else was there to do in Fremont Creek on a Friday night?

"Okay," I said.

So we each borrowed a swimsuit from the box Kenny kept under the office counter, and fifteen minutes later all three of us—Sérgio, Harriet, and I—were sitting in the hot tub, the bubble and whir of the jets precluding any conversation. The awkward intimacy of being so nearly naked at such close quarters with two people I barely knew set me on edge. My two companions, however, seemed completely at ease, Sérgio allowing his generous, hair-covered belly to bob first above and then below the surface of the water as he reclined his body, and Harriet stretching her arms behind her, their nearly translucent skin loose along the underside.

I turned and watched the snow falling on the empty parking lot, the outside temperature having dropped low enough for the flakes to stick— little white dots on the black asphalt, then small clumps, then soon enough, a blank sheet of white. Occasionally a car or truck drove past on Main Street. Mostly, though, the night was still. The hot tub jets finished their cycle and shut off.

Sérgio lifted his body from the water to sit on the edge of the tub.

"So warm," he said. "And all this snow."

"It's the best time to hot-tub," said Harriet.

Sérgio looked up at the white vinyl roof of the gazebo.

"The steam," he said, pointing up. "It's collecting. Condensating? Condensing?"

"Condensing," said Harriet.

"It's going to start dripping soon," I said.

"A design oversight," said Harriet, hunching her bony shoulders in anticipation.

We all looked up and then, almost in unison, back down at the steamy surface of the water.

"I feel so foolish," said Sérgio.

For a second I thought he was talking about the hot tub and the gazebo, but then he went on.

"I understood going into this that we might not find the book," he said. "I understood that. I did." He took a long drag on the straw of his milkshake, loudly slurping up the melted dregs. "But still." He shook his head. "It's the cruelty of hope." He paused. "My life, or if not my life, then life more generally—I'd like it to mean something, although I have no idea what." Sérgio scratched his beard. "You see, I've tried philosophy, but philosophy feels far too cautious, too bound by human logic. And then there's religion—God, angels, sin—but none of that has ever appealed to me. Fiction masquerading as cosmology is what it feels like to me, and all too self-important, too self-serious."

Sérgio licked his lips and then gingerly dropped the milkshake cup over the side of the hot tub. "Salgado-MacKenzie's work, on the other hand—and Irena Sertôrian especially—feels like the absolute reverse of religion. Cosmology masquerading as fiction. Or at least I see the *potential* for that kind of transcendent meaning, something shimmering at the edges of all the Sertôrian short stories. Something brought to full light, maybe, in *The Infinite Future*. And I know—I've always known—how much meaning I impose on Sertôrian through sheer force of wanting meaning to exist there, but I've also hoped, in a secret part of my mind, that there really was something there, something *The Infinite Future* could elucidate for me." Sérgio eased himself down further into the water. "I'm embarrassed by how disappointed I am."

Harriet took this in, head bowed, nodding slightly.

I made what I hoped was a sympathetic face. I wanted to help.

"I know what you mean," I said. "I remember a couple of years ago—"

But Sérgio held up a hand to stop me. "I appreciate the gesture, Daniel," he said. "I really do. But there's a certain kind of existential disappointment you can only experience after you've passed the midpoint of your life, and right now I'm not sure if I can listen with much sympathy to your story of youthful travails. I hope you'll understand."

"Sure," I said, although I was getting pretty tired of Sérgio's moping.

In spite of the snow falling above us, the water was getting uncomfortably warm. I sat up straighter, exposing more of my torso to the freezing autumn air. The snow hadn't stopped falling since we'd left Jack Phillips's house, and it was beginning to overwhelm the black asphalt of the parking lot with soft whiteness. It was a strange feeling, being so warm on such a chilly night.

Sérgio had closed his eyes again and lay slouched there with his arms folded, the end of his ponytail dipped halfway into the water. Harriet, presumably as warm as I was, scooted over to the raised part of the underwater bench, adjusting the shoulder straps of her borrowed swimsuit as she did so, the fabric leaving behind a faint impression on her ghostly skin.

Clearing her throat, she said, "Earlier this evening, Daniel was asking me how I knew Craig Ahlgren—that attorney he met with in Salt Lake." She pushed a clump of loose hair back behind her ear. "I told Daniel that Craig was my bishop once, which is true."

She paused. Sérgio had opened his eyes and was listening intently. So was I.

Harriet said, "What I didn't say, because I don't readily admit this to anybody, is that Craig D. Ahlgren is my archnemesis."

She said it matter-of-factly, with only a pinch of malice, and even less irony.

"That's my big secret. Seventeen years ago, he excommunicated me from the Mormon Church. That part's common knowledge, at least in certain circles, but what I won't admit publicly is how much I hate him for doing it. When people ask me—at Mormon studies conferences, for instance—if I hate my former bishop for what he did, I tell them no, that what I feel toward him is compassion, that in some ways he's also a victim of authoritarianism run amok, and that I bear him no ill will." She shook her head. "None of that is true, but if I say what I really think, that I detest the man, I'm too easily construed as the unhinged malcontent that some church members need me to be.

"And just to clarify, I don't *hate* hate Craig Ahlgren. That's such a heavy thing, and I don't . . ." She looked away from me and Sérgio and gazed out at the falling snow for a moment before turning back to look at us. "Well, actually I do. I do hate him, but only a little."

She shrugged, not in apology but in defiance.

You have to understand (she continued), everything was going so well for me back then. This would have been early 1991—I'd recently been appointed chair of the Mormon studies program at Deseret State University, my biography of Eliza R. Snow, *A Variegated Life: Eliza R. Snow and the Birth of Mormonism*, had just come out and was getting some nice reviews from the right kinds of journals. I'd recently bought a house, a charming thirties-era bungalow, and to the extent that this is possible for me, I felt very content with my life.

If I had to pinpoint where the trouble started, I'd say it was when Ruth Taylor, the stake Relief Society president, invited me to speak about the Snow biography at a local Church fireside. I accepted the invitation. I was happy to do it, but then a week before the fireside was scheduled to happen, I got a call from Ruth letting me know that the fireside had been canceled. I assumed there must have been a scheduling conflict or something, so I didn't think too much of it until Ruth said, "Harriet, I'm sorry. It wasn't my decision." I asked her what she meant, and she said she'd canceled the fireside by the express instruction of the stake president. He'd told her my research was not an approved subject of discussion for a Church audience, and I was not to speak publicly about it in any official stake gathering.

I thanked Ruth for letting me know, and assured her I didn't hold it against her. I *was* tentatively furious, just not with Ruth. I got President Braddock on the phone and asked him why he'd canceled my fireside. He said he'd just received a letter from Church headquarters informing all stake presidents that I was not to be invited to give lectures or firesides relating to my book, *A Variegated Life*, in any Church-sanctioned settings, nor was I to be invited to speak on more general topics of

Church history. President Braddock explained that the letter cited my book's "unconventional portrayal of the Prophet Joseph Smith" as grounds for the speaking ban, such a portrayal being inappropriate for dissemination among the general Church membership.

It was true that a significant portion of my book dealt with the uncomfortable details of Eliza R. Snow's marriage to Joseph Smith. It was a secret marriage, at least to some people, including Joseph's first wife, Emma Hale Smith, although she did find out eventually. But that wasn't the most significant part of Snow's life, or my biography of her. The main focus of my book was on the influence she'd had on early Church cultures and structures through her poetry, her essays on Mormon scripture and doctrine, and her administration of the Relief Society and various other women's organizations. But in the long run, the section of my book dealing with her marriage to Joseph Smith ended up getting the most attention and raising the most hackles among top Mormon brass.

I asked President Braddock if he would send me a copy of the letter in question, and he said no, he couldn't. It was addressed to stake presidents only, and I was not a stake president, was I? Before I could answer that ridiculous question, or raise a few points of my own, President Braddock told me that if I had a problem with the decision, I should follow the prescribed channels of authority and take this up with my bishop. I told him I certainly would, and then, before I could get another word in, President Braddock hung up on me.

The next day was Sunday, and my bishop, Craig Ahlgren, beat me to the punch. After sacrament meeting, he stopped me in the hall and asked if I had a few minutes to chat. I said I did, that I'd been hoping to speak with him, and so we headed over to his office, a room identical in design and furnishing to hundreds of other Mormon bishops' offices of a certain mid-century vintage—prickly carpeting on the walls, red upholstered chairs, a dark wooden desk. A large framed print of the Salt Lake temple was hanging on the wall behind the bishop's desk.

I took a seat in one of the three padded chairs facing the framed picture of the temple, and Craig sat down in the soft red office chair behind the desk.

"Sister Kimball," he said, folding his hands and resting them on the desk in that universal posture of bishoply concern. "Thank you for taking the time to meet with me."

"I'm happy to," I said.

Craig responded with a beatific smile, and then compressed his face into an expression of thoughtful concern. He said he'd heard about the speaking ban and wanted to check in with me to see how I felt about it.

"Not good," I said.

A sympathetic smile from Craig.

"I'm sure you must have put a lot of work into that book," he said.

"I did," I said and then explained my frustration at being muzzled for writing about historically verifiable facts.

Craig said, "You should remember, Sister Kimball, that history's always up for interpretation."

"Certainly," I said as Craig leaned back, arms folded, looking inordinately pleased to have dispensed this historiographic nugget.

I explained, though, that I'd used the utmost rigor in evaluating my sources, that I stood behind the account of Snow's life that my book presented, that other historians had responded very positively to the book, and although I could see how some details of Snow's life might dismay some members of the Church, I wrote the book from the position that I continued to occupy, that of a believing Latter-day Saint. It was baffling to me, then, that Church leaders would want to suppress the biography I'd written.

"We're a religion that's supposed to love truth," I said.

"You're right," said Craig, "that truth is important. But just because something's true doesn't mean it needs to be discussed with everybody. Some truths are just not uplifting, and I have to say that your portrayal of Joseph Smith has the potential to shake some people's testimonies."

I tried my best to maintain my composure.

I said, "It's essential that we know our history."

"I'll agree with you on that," said Craig, although obviously he didn't, at least not past a certain point. He regarded me with those kind blue eyes of his. "Sister Kimball," he said. "I can see where you're coming from. I understand why you're upset. But I've always found in my life that even if I can't see the wisdom in certain counsel right away, I'm always better off following the Brethren."

"I appreciate that perspective," I said, "but I'd like to know what I need to do to get this speaking ban overturned. President Braddock told me to follow the prescribed channels of authority if I wanted to be heard, so that's what I'm doing. I'm following the rules. I'm talking to you."

"But I don't think you're listening to me," said Craig, a little less beatific now. "It's not for us to counsel the Brethren. Their job is to receive revelation from God, and our job is to follow it. What you need to do, then, is examine the state of your heart and figure out what *you* need to do to change. You're in a dangerous position, and I'd advise proceeding with caution."

I recognize a threat when I hear one, and I said as much to Craig.

"Let's not descend into paranoia," said Craig. "I'm trying to help you here, Sister Kimball."

I said that if he really wanted to help me, he would tell me who to talk to to get the speaking ban overturned.

He said, "I don't think you're hearing me, Harriet."

We'd obviously reached an impasse, so I thanked Craig for his time and left his office.

Unfortunately, that first meeting turned out to be more courteous and productive than any that followed. Over the next couple of years, I ended up meeting with Bishop Ahlgren dozens of times as I continued down a path that he deemed dangerously heterodox. Our first meeting had been civil enough, but each time he called me into his office after that, our exchanges grew more adversarial. According to Craig, my offenses were legion. Attending a handful of Mormon women's rights rallies. Writing a series of frank, factual articles for *Sunstone* that explained to an intended audience of high school seminary students sticky points from Mormon history, such as Joseph Smith's polygamy, the Mountain Meadows massacre, and the restriction of priesthood based on race, to name just a few. Joining the Mormon Defense Association, a non-Church-sanctioned group formed to identify and resist abuses of power within Mormonism.

Although the material circumstances prompting each meeting may have varied, our ensuing disagreements consistently pivoted on a question that continues to vex Mormonism: To what degree should public dissent be allowed within the Church?

As he'd stated in our first meeting, Craig felt that any public departure from the policies and teachings espoused by the Church's leaders constituted an open rebellion before God that damaged both the offending individual and the good name of the Church. On the other hand, I believed—and still believe—that free and open discourse is vital to the health of any community, and that Mormonism will never truly thrive as long as its leaders insist on suppressing dissenting opinions.

Early on, our debates were fairly academic, emotions and tempers kept well in check, but over time we gnawed at each other's patience until all that remained was acrimony and bile. I'm pretty sure that sooner or later we would have reached a crisis point on our own, but the process was sped along when, in the fall of 1993, six prominent Mormon intellectuals were formally disciplined by their local leaders—one of them disfellowshipped and the other five excommunicated. Over the previous months, each of the three women and three men had produced scholarship—ranging from feminist critiques of church hierarchy to heterodox interpretations of the Book of Isaiah, to detailed examinations of sticky moments in Mormon history—that had infuriated many Church leaders. A few of the six had also agitated publicly for Church reform.

Just to give you an idea, Sérgio, of how serious a punishment this was: Other offenses that merit excommunication include murder, rape, and child abuse, and the ecclesiastical consequences are accordingly dire. Your baptism is nullified, for starters, and if you've received ordinances in the temple, those are nullified as well. For couples, that includes your eternal marriage, which means that unlike other Mormons who marry in the temple, you will no longer be with your spouse after you die.

There are more immediate consequences as well. You're still allowed to attend church meetings—you're encouraged to, in fact—but you can't pray publicly, give talks, or take the sacrament, among other things. It's very serious, but it's not necessarily permanent, as apologists for the practice are quick to point out. And if, after at least one year, you've shown sufficient remorse for your offense, and met the conditions posited by your local leaders, the disciplinary council may consider your case and allow you to be rebaptized. That's a lot of *ifs*, though, and in cases involving ideological conflicts, rebaptism becomes even more elusive.

And so, the September Six, as the *Salt Lake Tribune* dubbed them, became the focal point of heated debates within Mormonism. Some felt that the disciplinary actions represented a miscarriage of church justice, a disturbing abuse of power that encouraged unthinking, unquestioning loyalty in rank-and-file church members. Others felt bad for the Six, but ultimately believed that their leaders had not been wrong to excommunicate them—it was the prerogative of the First Presidency and the Quorum of the Twelve to dictate inspired doctrines and policies for the Church, and lay members, no matter how well educated they might be, had no right to assume that role for themselves. Other members had even less patience for the disciplined scholars—they got what was coming to them and probably deserved worse.

There were also plenty of Mormons who really didn't care that much about it one way or the other.

I made my own position very clear and very public in an op-ed piece for the *Los Angeles Times*—the excommunications represented an abuse of power on the part of the bishops and stake presidents who actually carried out the councils, as well as irresponsible leadership on the part of senior Church officials, whose condemnatory rhetoric regarding Mormon historians and cultural critics fostered the environment of antagonism and oppression that had made the excommunications possible.

About two weeks after the editorial ran, Craig summoned me to his office for another meeting. He told me that this time I'd crossed an indisputable line—to so harshly and publicly criticize the Lord's anointed servants was a clear sign of personal apostasy. I was hurting myself, potentially leading others astray, and damaging the good name of the Church.

I told him I was doing no such thing. If the Church's good name was suffering damage, it was due to the reckless and reactionary authoritarianism exercised by the bishops, stake presidents, and general authorities responsible for the excommunications of the September Six.

Craig asked me if I truly believed that. I told him I did and that a healthy church depends on a free and open dialogue between its members and its leaders. Craig took this in, giving me one of those long, sincere, bishopy looks before saying, "Sister Kimball, it's clear to me that you *believe* you're doing the right thing here. What's just as clear to me, though, is that you are *not* doing the right thing. You're in a state of personal apostasy, and for your own sake and the sake of others, you need to begin the process of repentance. Because I believe you think your heart is in the right place, I'm not going to convene a disciplinary council at this point. Instead, the first step we're going to take together is an informal probation. As long as this probation's in effect, you won't partake of the sacrament. I'm going to release you as ward music coordinator, and you'll surrender your temple recommend to me."

I stopped him right there. In case you're wondering, Sergio, informal probation is a real thing. I think it's viewed as a more merciful action than a disciplinary council because it doesn't show up on your permanent membership record. It didn't feel more merciful to me, though. It felt like Craig was throwing aside what little due process exists in the Church for someone accused of major transgression.

I said, "If you want my temple recommend, you're going to have to convene a disciplinary council."

He said, "I don't think you want to do that, Sister Kimball."

I said, "I don't think *you* want to do that, Bishop Ahlgren."

I can admit now that this was a tactical error on my part, but I was so sure—and I'm embarrassed to admit this—I was so sure that God wouldn't let me be excommunicated. I'd thought and prayed so hard about the scholarship and activism I was participating in, and again and again I'd felt it in my heart and in my mind that I was doing what God wanted me to do with my time and my talents. I figured that in the formal setting of a disciplinary council, Craig would feel that too. He'd pray about my situation, and God would tell him that I was not an apostate.

Needless to say, that's not what happened.

The council was an ugly experience. I don't want to rehash all the nitty-gritty details of what was said—I still have panicky dreams about the meeting—but the end result was that Bishop Ahlgren and his two counselors decided I was, in fact, in a state of personal apostasy. (The phrase "flagrant apostasy" was thrown around quite a bit, actually.) My editorial in the *LA Times* was only the culmination of a years-long pattern of disrespect, disobedience, and open rebellion against God and his chosen servants. So that was that. I was no longer a member of the Church, and all saving ordinances that I'd received were no longer in effect, they said.

Harriet paused, the snow falling around us with renewed vigor. I could feel my wet hair freezing together. I lowered myself deeper into the warm water.

I'll tell you (Harriet went on), one of the worst parts about being excommunicated is all the rhetoric of love and caring that gets wrapped around it in an attempt to obscure the inescapable brutality of the act. During the meeting itself, Craig kept saying, "I like to think of this as a council of love. We're here to *help* you, Sister Kimball."

I'm usually not a violent person, but every time he said that I wanted to hit him with something. I was sitting there alone in a room with four men—the bishop, his two counselors, and the ward clerk off in the corner silently taking notes—who wanted to forcibly remove me from an institution I cared deeply about, who wanted to tell me what the state of my heart was and where I stood before God.

There's so much aggression there, so how do you respond when the person doing the excommunicating tries to pretend like he's just done you a great kindness? It's infuriating, but if you let that fury show, it becomes all too easy for Church leaders to portray you as hysterical, as another delusional feminist who's taken leave of her reason and her spiritual sensitivity. On the other hand, if you say *nothing*, they've succeeded in silencing you. You can't do anything, then, but respond reciprocally, professing love, compassion, and understanding for those who've wrongly excommunicated you.

Harriet gave a resigned shrug and leaned back against the edge of the hot tub.

The fallout from my excommunication was not pretty (she said). All of the confidence I'd felt going into the disciplinary council was replaced almost immediately by an edgy self-doubt, which was only aggravated when, right after my excommunication, I lost my job as chair of the Mormon studies program at DSU. Once word of my excommunication got out, the dean of the college pulled me aside and asked me not to come back after the Christmas break. If they needed to, they could find a way to fire me, but it would be much easier for everyone if I left of my own accord. DSU is a state school, so my excommunication should have had no bearing on my job, but Mormon studies programs get their funding primarily from wealthy Mormons, and since wealthy Mormons tend to be conservative on all fronts, my continued presence on the faculty would jeopardize the program's continued funding. My dean didn't state that in *quite* so many words—he couched the issue in terms of how my scholarship would be received now that I was outside the Church, etc., etc.—but funding was the real issue. Everyone was very sorry, he said.

So was I. This meant that no other Mormon studies program would touch me—I was damaged goods—and at the time, interest from mainstream history departments in Mormon-specific areas was scanty at best. Based on the scholarship I'd produced, I was unemployable.

And so I was in free fall—jobless, churchless, and soon to be houseless.

As per Maslow's hierarchy of needs, that third problem—my imminent houselessness—struck me as the most pressing. Decades earlier, my parents had built a cabin at the mouth of Danish Fork Canyon, where we'd vacationed often when I was a girl. Summers, in fact, we'd spend weeks at a time there, and plenty of weekends during the fall and winter. We'd used it less and less as we'd all grown up, though, and since Mom and Dad had died, my siblings and I only made it down there a few times a year. It was sitting empty, then, when I lost my job, and so, capitalizing on the resources still available to me, I sold my house in Salt Lake and, loading as many of my belongings as I could fit into my four-year-old Celica, I decamped to the family cabin, where I could live rent free until I figured out my next move.

Those first weeks at the cabin nearly destroyed me. Our cabin is a small one, relatively speaking, well under a thousand square feet—certainly not one of these palatial second homes that people build in the woods these days and then bestow with a rustic moniker that tries to downplay the cabin's opulence. No, our cabin is a simple one-story, two-bedroom affair with a small kitchen, a single bathroom, a cozy living room, and a wide back porch. There's an adjacent meadow that, in the summertime, is perfect for pitching a tent or dragging down an Adirondack chair from the porch and just sitting, listening to the rustle of the trees, and watching for birds, squirrels, and the occasional deer. My point is, in the summers, the meadow makes the cabin feel much bigger than it is, or at least less confining, as it more than doubles the amount of usable, habitable space available.

When I first arrived, though, it was the dead of winter, and the combination of freezing outdoor temperatures and aggressive internal despair kept me under effective house arrest. I moved my suitcases and boxes from the car to the cabin's second bedroom, brought in the groceries I'd picked up from town, started a fire in the living room's iron woodstove, and then I pretty much fell apart. Slumping down on the sun-faded living room couch, I started mentally replaying every decision I'd made that had brought me to this sorry state.

In a distant part of my mind, I knew that I should be doing something other than sitting around and thinking, but every other possible course of action, even something as simple as making myself a sandwich, seemed too frightening, too fraught with peril to attempt. So instead I remained in the cabin's compact living room, huddled on the threadbare couch, where I stared through the glass door of the corner woodstove, trying to ignore the jangling panic that ran just below the surface of my thoughts as the flames inside the stove steadily consumed the wood that I fed them.

I was convinced that I'd made a terrible mistake, scotching my chances for personal salvation forever. I couldn't be a hundred percent certain that Craig had been wrong to excommunicate me, because I'm not sure we can ever be a hundred percent certain about anything, so I tormented myself with the possibility that I'd been eternally cut off from the presence of God.

I'd intended to use my time at the cabin to compose an article I'd been researching for several months—a piece on women and the priesthood in the Nauvoo-era Church—but writing was out of the question. Not only could I not focus on any one thing for more than two minutes at a time, but my computer had also broken somehow during the trek from Salt Lake. When I switched it on I was greeted with an unintelligible garble of symbols followed by a flashing black-and-white screen. It was beyond my meager abilities to fix the problem, even under the best of circumstances. Given that making a sandwich was currently beyond me, taking my computer to be repaired or shopping for a new one was entirely out of the question.

During this time, to their great credit, many friends and associates called and offered to take me to lunch or on a vacation or to just come sit with me, any one of which would have been a great help, but I felt so internally out of control, so contaminated somehow, that I turned them all down, telling them I needed some time alone to process everything. Obviously, that was the last thing I needed—I was on such dangerous ground, and looking back now, if I'd gotten any worse, I'm not sure what could have happened.

Things didn't get worse, though.

One night, I woke up in a panic, as I often did, but instead of pacing the living room to calm myself, I decided to go out to the deck. Wrapped in all my blankets, I stepped out into the bracing midwinter night. The sky was clear, the air so cold I could feel my nostrils freezing together. I walked a few circuits around the deck to keep warm. The movement helped. I felt warmer and happier—or more precisely, less terrible.

Even today, there's a pretty good view of the stars from that deck, but back then Danesville was so small and isolated and dark at night that you could see absolutely everything from the deck, or that's what it felt like. Staring up at the bright jumble of stars above me, I tried to pick out a constellation or two. There was the Big Dipper, obviously, but aside from that one, I just knew names—Virgo, Sagittarius, the horoscope constellations, basically. I did seem to remember something about following the handle—or was it the cup?—of the Big Dipper to find the North Star, and so I spent a good ten minutes trying to find it, and even narrowed the search down to a few extra-bright candidates, but I couldn't be sure about any of them.

What did occur to me, though, was that I'd just spent ten minutes focused on a specific task and hadn't thought once during that time about my bleak situation. As I exulted in this minor triumph, a further thought occurred to me: *I think I could write something tonight—a sentence, maybe.*

A few days earlier when I'd gone to the cabin's storage closet for an extra blanket, I'd noticed on an upper shelf, partially concealed behind a stack of board games, my dad's old portable typewriter. He'd brought it up to the cabin one summer with the intention of writing his life history, but that plan had been interrupted when Mom had had a heart attack. With her failing health, and then his own, he'd never gotten around to the life history, and the typewriter had languished in the closet of the cabin.

That night, then, after coming inside from the porch, I pulled the typewriter from the closet and set it up on the kitchen table. What had seemed so feasible out on the porch, though, proved another matter in practice. I'm normally a fast writer, able to produce a competent draft of a twenty-page article in less than a week. That night, though, the process was agonizing. I just needed one sentence—one subject, one predicate— but the ghost of my excommunication flittered out from behind every word I tried to commit to paper. I imagined Craig D. Ahlgren's voice telling me that by writing this article I was distancing myself even further from God and the principles of righteousness. What if he was right? And even if he wasn't, the arguments I was making about women and the priesthood in the Nauvoo Church weren't going to bring me any closer to rebaptism if the article was published.

It took all of my effort to stay seated at the table. Finally, though, just before dawn, my mind wore itself out and muscle memory kicked in to compose a drab, boilerplate introductory sentence that would do the job just fine. I'd done it. And so I stumbled off to bed and slept.

The next night I repeated the process. After waking in a sweaty panic, I stepped outside to say a brief hello to the Big Dipper, and then took up my post at the table and wrote another sentence. This time, it took me two and a half hours instead of four, and I only cried once. I did the same the next night, and the next night, and the next, and by the sixth night I had written a long introductory paragraph for the article.

Each writing session grew less and less harrowing. Bolstered by this minor progress, I gained more and more confidence until, after a month, I was writing a full paragraph every night. Bit by bit, that confidence carried over into the daylight hours, and I was finally able to restore some semblance of order to my life. I bathed every morning. I fixed meals for myself. I found a set of snowshoes and went for long, restorative walks in the woods every afternoon. Before long, I was even sleeping through the night, and my work on the article became a regular daytime habit rather than a 3:00 a.m. coping mechanism.

And so I finished my article. I finished it, and I revised it, and I drove it into town and photocopied it at the grocery store. Then I sent a copy off to the editor of *Dialogue*, and a few months later it was published.

From there my life started to come back together. I'd been dabbling in translation work for years before my excommunication, and now I pursued it more aggressively. I let my contacts in publishing know that I was available to take on a heavier load of projects, and while it would be an exaggeration to say the work poured in from there, I translated quickly and competently enough that before my savings ran out completely, I was earning enough to keep afloat. It helped that I didn't—and still don't—pay rent. In fact, my career wouldn't be possible if I did. I'm sure my siblings aren't thrilled that I've squatted at the family cabin for all this time, but none of them has explicitly asked me to leave, so I continue to squat.

My approach to religion in the ensuing years has been similar. In a development as surprising to me as to anyone else, a few months after I moved to the cabin, I decided I wanted to go to church. I hadn't been since my excommunication, and although part of me felt like I might burst into flames if I stepped into a wardhouse, I sorely missed the weekly opportunity to worship with the saints. So, one Sunday morning I jumped in the deep end and showed up for sacrament meeting at the nearest ward in Danesville.

I was nervous for the whole drive over there, pulling my car over and nearly turning around four or five times. I worried how people might treat me when they found out who I was. More frightening still, I wondered if, on occupying holy ground, I would feel more acutely alienated from God than ever before.

As soon as I walked into the chapel, though, I knew I would be fine.

There were the rumpled young men setting up the bread and the water for the sacrament. There were the harried young parents, already seated on the long, padded benches, frantically shushing their noisy children. There was the organist, playing upbeat prelude music whose bouncy pep was at odds with the general grogginess of the early (for a weekend) hour. I felt completely at home. No one in that congregation knew who I was, and for seventy minutes I could be just another worshipper.

After the meeting was over, the ward's bishop, excited to see an unfamiliar face, tracked me down and introduced himself.

"Marty Cox," he said, pumping my hand, his round young face aglow with enthusiasm.

I told Bishop Cox who I was and said that I'd been recently excommunicated. Unbothered by this information, he told me he was glad to see me here and he hoped I'd make myself at home in the ward—they'd love to have me.

True to his word, he and the other members of the ward were nothing—or almost nothing—but kind and supportive. For instance, in Sunday school that first day, a woman about my age sat down next to me and asked how long I'd lived in the area, how long I planned to stay—the typical getting-to-know-you questions.

"You should know," I said to her before she could ask me anything else, "that I've recently been excommunicated."

While I recognized that this was an awkward conversational salvo, I felt a compulsive need at the time to inform people of my official standing with the Church so that nobody felt tricked into associating with a known apostate. My new acquaintance—her name was Laura—took the revelation in stride, though.

"I'm sorry to hear that," she said, and then invited me over for dinner.

During the fifteen years since then, it's been more of the same from the people in my ward. They've brought over soups and casseroles when I've been sick or overworked; invited me to birthday parties, barbecues, and bridal showers; attended presentations I've given through the local historical society; read books I've translated and articles I've written—really, they've been so generous, so lovely over the years. Only occasionally have a few opprobrious ward members gone out of their way to remind me of my fallen state, of my need to renounce my apostate ways. But ultimately, those types are in the minority.

It's funny—by this point, with nearly twenty years of turnover, a lot of the congregation doesn't even know I've been excommunicated, although I've certainly not forgotten, because the inescapable fact remains that I am technically not a member of the Mormon Church, no matter how many Sunday meetings I attend. Although that's also something that, to their credit, several of the successive bishops in my Danesville ward have tried to remedy. Each time we discuss rebaptism, though, the sticking point is that the reinstatement of my membership would require a clear renunciation on my part of the offense that got me excommunicated. Since I still don't believe I ever committed an offense worthy of excommunication in the first place, the situation remains at a stalemate.

In theory, at least, it is possible that the Church could acknowledge that I was wrongly disciplined, and then I'd be back in, free and clear, but my church isn't one that makes apologies, so I'm not holding my breath. In any event, by this point in my life I don't believe it's up to other people to determine my standing with God. That's not a power I grant to the Church anymore, so if they decide not to acknowledge their mistake . . .

The steam curling up from the surface of the water wrapped itself around Harriet before a cold breeze dispersed it into the night. She half shrugged, half shivered.

"All told," she said, "it's not the life I anticipated for myself, but I'm far from unhappy."

Gazing down at his bobbing gut, a reclining Sérgio considered Harriet's account in contemplative silence.

In my own corner of the hot tub, I stared down into the water, refusing to look Harriet in the eye. Her story had left me feeling edgy and defensive. The whole thing seemed wrong somehow—inaccurate, I mean. I didn't think she was lying outright or anything like that, but her experience of Mormonism was so radically different from my own that I felt an impulse to challenge her story, to stand up for my church and for Craig D. Ahlgren, my recently acquired ally.

"But that's enough of that," said Harriet before I could muster a response. "I wasn't fishing for sympathy with that story—merely commiserating—so before either of you feel obliged to offer condolences that I'm not looking for, I'll wish you good night. If you'll excuse me then."

"Of course," said Sérgio. "And thank you for commiserating."

Harriet extricated herself from the hot tub, steam rising from her ghostly-pale body. Wrapping herself in the vast motel towel she'd left on the little stairway leading up to the tub, she slipped her wet feet into her shoes and made her way toward her lodge through the steadily falling snow.

"Ugly business," said Sérgio once Harriet had gone.

The look of disgust on his face was too much for me.

"You know what, Sérgio?" I said, a little more abruptly than I'd intended. "The whole thing's a lot more complicated than Harriet made it out to be."

Sitting up a little straighter, brow furrowed, Sérgio said, "How so?"

An old pickup truck rattled down Main Street. I actually had no idea. All I knew was that I was ready for this stupid road trip to be over—Harriet's story had sparked a fire of resentment in me, a resentment whose target I couldn't quite discern.

After an uncomfortable moment of silence, I said, "It's just complicated."

Sérgio regarded me through the steam like he was meeting me for the first time. I lifted myself from the water.

I dried off with the scratchy motel towel, my resentment expanding beyond my own doughy body, beyond Sérgio, beyond Harriet, beyond this hot tub, and the sorry confines of Fremont Creek to encompass something much, much bigger. I felt it so intensely that I was almost surprised its heat hadn't melted all the fresh white snow around me.

Wrapping the flimsy bath towel around my shoulders like a cloak, I stormed off to my room, leaving Sérgio alone again in the hot tub to watch the relentlessly falling snow blanket the parking lot.

## XV

woke up to the sound of someone pounding on my door. I'd been dead asleep, dreaming of an idyllic camping trip I'd once taken with a few friends the summer before I'd graduated from high school, but then the dream had been interrupted by a series of urgent knocks.

I sat up in bed and remembered where I was: the Teton Motor Lodge in Fremont Creek, Idaho.

"Daniel," came Sérgio's voice through the door. "Are you in there?"

"Yeah," I said, lying back down.

"We leave in five minutes," called Sérgio. "There's been a development."

I pulled the blankets more tightly around myself.

"I'm going to sit this one out," I yelled toward the door.

"What?" yelled Sérgio.

Thanks in part to our conversation in the hot tub the night before, I'd reached that inevitable road trip saturation point where I couldn't stand the thought of spending another minute with my traveling companions. Sérgio and Harriet were both fine people probably, but I'd spent just about every waking moment with them for the past five days, and I was ready for a break.

"I'm not coming," I called out.

There was a pause, and I burrowed down further into the blankets, trying to recapture the soporific warmth they still contained.

"I'm not sure you understand," yelled Sérgio. "We've found someone who might know Salgado-MacKenzie."

"That's fine," I yelled. "Let me know how it goes."

I fluffed my pillow and turned over, closing my eyes before sleep could entirely escape me.

There was a long pause.

"If you change your mind," yelled Sérgio, "we leave in five minutes."

I did not change my mind, and instead of joining them on another wild goose chase, I slept until 10:30 a.m. When I got up, I took a long hot shower, the water pressure in the jaundiced tile bathroom surprisingly strong. I ate a kingly late breakfast at the Spud. The Sunrise Bonanza: scrambled eggs, cheddar cheese, bacon, sausage, country potatoes, ham, and onions all griddle-fried together and then topped with white sausage gravy—an unforgettable meal. Then I headed down the bright, snowy street, listening to the new Tinted Windows album as I walked, an undeniable bounce in my step. At Fremont Creek's tiny public library, I found an open computer and spent a couple of hours planning out my new, improved life. I looked for apartments in Salt Lake. I read up a little on the LSAT and studied law school rankings.

I'd been crushed for so long under so many failures that I'd forgotten how good it felt to have real ambitions. I liked feeling smart and competitive and promising, and I loved the straightforwardness of the new path I'd chosen: How do you get into a good law school? You get decent grades as an undergrad, and more important, you do well on the LSAT. That's pretty much it—easier said than done, maybe, but undeniably more straightforward than what I'd been doing for the past few years.

By midafternoon, I'd worked up an appetite with my research, so I walked back up the street to the Spud for lunch. Inside I found Harriet sitting at the counter reading the weekend edition of the *Fremont Creek Crier*. She had shed several layers of wooly outerwear and draped them over the low, padded back of her barstool, but still wore an itchy-looking sweater and a cable-knit beanie, which, together with her wire-rimmed reading glasses, lent her the air of a shabbily genteel deep-sea fisher.

I was not thrilled to see her. Before I could back out the door, though, she looked up from her paper and waved me over.

"Daniel," she said. "I couldn't find you back at the motel."

She pushed up the sleeves of her sweater.

"I was at the library," I said.

"Well, feel free to join me," she said, nodding at an empty, ketchup-smeared plate, and a half-full basket of fries. "I'm just finishing up my lunch."

I rummaged for an excuse not to stay, but Harriet knew as well as I did that I had nothing else going on.

Defeated, then, I sat down at the barstool next to hers, and the waitress behind the counter asked what she could get for me. I ordered a huckleberry milkshake and a BLT and hoped silently that Harriet would leave soon.

I was surprised to see her there without Sérgio, and in spite of my still-lingering resentment, I felt a pang of concern for the man, given his gloomy spirits the day before.

"Where's Sérgio?" I asked Harriet.

She closed her newspaper and folded it in half.

"Chasing a red herring, I'm afraid," she said, unhooking the stems of her glasses from behind her ears—they were those kind of glasses—and removing them from her face.

"But he's okay?" I said.

She set her glasses on top of the newspaper.

"I hope so," she said. "He's somewhere near Lodgepole."

Lodgepole was an old resort town about forty miles up the road.

"What's he doing in Lodgepole?" I said.

"*Near* Lodgepole," she said, tapping the newspaper with her glasses. "I'm not sure where exactly. I left him in Lodgepole, though—that's the last place I saw him."

"And this was the lead he was so excited about this morning?" I said.

"Yes," she said. "I came over here for breakfast a little past seven and found Sérgio already halfway through a stack of pancakes. He wasn't happy by any means, but he did seem a little more resigned to the fact that he wasn't going to find Salgado-MacKenzie—you know, starting to come to terms with it, at least. We talked about maybe throwing in the towel on our search and heading up to Yellowstone for some sightseeing before Sérgio had to fly home.

"We were just about to leave when a couple of old-timers we hadn't seen before came in the diner. They looked like locals, so in the name of due diligence, we asked if they knew any writers in the area, or if not, any Brazilians. Boyd and Vern were their names, and they'd been off fishing all week, which is why we hadn't met them yet.

"They thought over our question, and although they didn't know any writers, Vern said he remembered a couple by the name of Fordis who'd lived here in town about twenty, thirty years back. They'd only lived here a year or so, but he was a hunting and fishing guide, and she sometimes helped out with the books at the old barbershop. Vern said he was pretty sure she was Brazilian."

"The barbershop connection sounds promising," I said, feeling drawn back into the search in spite of myself.

"Yes," said Harriet. "But then Boyd said that Mrs. Fordis wasn't Brazilian, she was Spanish. Vern said no, he didn't think so—he was pretty sure Anne Fordis was Brazilian, or at least her people were. Boyd disagreed and they went back and forth for a minute, until I stepped in and asked if it would be possible to get in touch with Mrs. Fordis and let her settle the debate herself.

"Boyd said he didn't see why not—the Fordises still lived in the area, just up the road in Lodgepole, in fact, but he could save us the bother, because Mrs. Fordis was definitely not Brazilian, she grew up in Spain. Vern said no, the woman definitely spoke Portuguese, but Boyd said Vern was completely mistaken on this one—she was Spanish of Spain, and old Gus the banker always used to sing a song about it, which was why Boyd was so sure she wasn't.

"Sérgio and I had already gleaned the information we needed, so before we could be drawn any further into their debate, we thanked the men for their help and went and found a regional phone book. The Fordises were listed and Sérgio gave them a call. Anne Fordis answered and Sérgio introduced himself. When he explained what we were looking for, Mrs. Fordis got cagey. She said she had lived in Brazil for a while when she was a girl, but when Sérgio asked if she'd ever heard of Eduard Salgado-MacKenzie, she wouldn't answer him one way or the other. Finally, she said she didn't want to talk about it over the phone, but if we wanted to come by the house she might be able to tell us more."

"Wow," I said. "That's a big break."

"That's what Sérgio thought," said Harriet. "But I was much more wary—if this woman knew anything about Salgado-MacKenzie, why wouldn't she say so over the phone? All signs pointed to Mrs. Fordis being very eccentric at best, potentially dangerous at worst. But Sérgio had to find out what she claimed to know, and I couldn't say I blamed him. So we walked back to the motel to get the car and wake you up—we figured you'd want to come along."

"I was very tired," I said.

"So I heard," she said. "We got the car, though, and made it up to Lodgepole in about an hour. We found the Fordises' house just at the edge of town—a handsome A-frame with red trim and a nice, wide porch.

I could tell Sérgio was nervous (continued Harriet). He'd asked me about fourteen times on the ride up if I thought this was a legitimate lead, and I told him each time that I didn't think he should get his hopes up. He knew that, I'm sure, but he obviously couldn't help himself. Once we arrived, he was so keyed up that he just sat there looking at the house, drumming his fingers on the sides of his legs.

"Well," he said after a minute. "I think I'm ready."

We approached the front porch with some trepidation, walked up the three steps, and knocked. Anne Fordis herself answered the door, a hearty woman in her late sixties. She didn't look eccentric—she was dressed conservatively in heavy slacks and a simple blouse—but really, what does that prove? She thanked us for making the trip up and showed us into the house. In the kitchen she introduced us to her husband, Ed, a big salt-of-the-earth-looking guy in a plaid shirt and work pants who sat at the kitchen table shelling nuts from a glass bowl and watching football on an ancient portable TV.

When he saw us, he held out a wide strong hand.

"I'd get up but my knees are shot," he said.

We said that was fine and shook his hand.

Anne said, "We'll just be in the living room if you need anything, Ed."

So far, she hadn't said a word about Salgado-MacKenzie, which worried me. I tried bringing up the purpose of our visit—Sérgio was being very deferential—but instead, Mrs. Fordis dodged the question, explaining instead that Ed had a lot of trouble getting around these days, which drove him crazy. He'd always been so active. Until fairly recently, in fact, he'd made his living as a hunting guide. Sérgio listened politely, but I could see him fighting back his curiosity. I was curious too—I wanted to get right down to business and find out if Fordis had anything useful for us or if she was just a lonely woman desperate for company.

In the living room, Sérgio and I sat down on a wide, floral couch. Anne sat across from us in a matching floral armchair.

She said, "Tell me again—why are you looking for this Eduard Salgado-MacKenzie?"

At least she remembered his name. That was a good sign, I had to admit. Sérgio recapped his history with the writer, and I explained about the translation I'd done for the *Faint Constellations* anthology, and the letters that Salgado-MacKenzie and I had exchanged.

Mrs. Fordis listened carefully, hands crossed and resting in her wide lap. When we'd finished explaining ourselves, she gave an evaluative *huh* and then looked us over for what felt like minutes. Then she stood up from her armchair and left the room.

Another tick mark in the *eccentric* column.

Sérgio said, "Do you think she's all right?"

I said, "All right in what way?"

Before he could answer, though, Anne Fordis returned wearing snow boots and a long wool coat. She held a pair of gloves and a stocking hat in one hand and a set of keys in the other.

She said, "Where we're headed, you need four-wheel drive. Your little Toyota isn't going to make it in this snow, but I have room for one of you in my truck."

Sérgio said, "Excuse me?"

"Which one of you is coming with me?" said Fordis, a little louder. "I only have room for one, and we don't have all day."

"Going where?" I said.

"You?" she said, pointing at Sérgio. "Or you?" She pointed at me.

I said, "Can you give us a little more information, please?"

She said, "You're looking a gift horse in the mouth right now. The third option is that you can leave right now, both of you."

"Could you give us a moment?" I said.

"You know I have other things I could be doing right now," said Fordis.

I said, "Thirty seconds, please."

"Well, we can't just dawdle away the morning," she said.

"Thirty seconds," I said.

With an exasperated sigh, she left us alone in the living room.

I turned to Sérgio.

"I don't think you should go," I whispered, fairly certain that Anne Fordis would be listening in on us.

"You want to be the one to go?" said Sérgio, who, to his credit, sounded willing to entertain the possibility.

"No," I whispered. "I don't think either of us should go."

"Why not?" he whispered, not very softly.

I took a step closer, lowering my voice even further.

"Because Anne Fordis gives every indication of being a crank," I said. "The only question for me at this point is whether or not she's also dangerous."

"I don't know about that," said Sérgio, looking away.

"Sérgio," I said. "Use your head. She won't tell us what, if anything, she knows about Salgado-MacKenzie. She acts put out when we ask her questions, and now she wants to take you somewhere in her truck, but she can't say where you'd be going or who you'd be meeting with. How do you know she doesn't plan to drive you into the mountains and kill you? Make a coat out of your skin or something?"

"You honestly think she's going to skin me?" whispered Sérgio.

"Okay," I said, "she probably won't skin you—although we don't *know* that she won't—but I do think she's going to disappoint you."

Fordis came back into the room, slapping her gloves together.

She said, "Have you made your decision?"

"I'm coming with you," said Sérgio.

"It's decided then," said Anne Fordis.

I said, "It is, although couldn't you have told us over the phone that only one of us should come?"

She seemed offended by this question and said she'd needed to make sure we were the right kind of people. Then she nodded at Sérgio and said, "Are you ready?"

He said, "Absolutely," and jumped up from the couch.

On their way out the back door, Sérgio turned and said over his shoulder that he'd meet me back at the motel. And then the door closed and that was that.

I let myself out of the house—I waved to Mr. Fordis as I passed the kitchen, but he was engrossed enough in his football game that he didn't notice—and then I headed back here to Fremont Creek.


Harriet dipped a stale French fry into the little ketchup tub and tossed it into her mouth.

I'd missed the most exciting development in days. I almost regretted sleeping in.

"Wow," I said. "So where do you think she took him?"

"Who knows?" said Harriet.

The waitress, dishes in hand, approached and said, "Huckleberry milkshake and BLT?"

"That's me," I said.

She set down the plate and the glass, and I dug in, reflecting on what Harriet had just told me.

"How long has it been since you got back?" I asked Harriet between mouthfuls of sandwich.

"Five, six hours," said Harriet.

My annoyance with Sérgio started to give way to real concern. In that amount of time, anything could have happened.

"So," I said. "How much time, do you think, before we start to worry?"

"I started about an hour ago," she said, turning her glasses over in her hands.

I thought of Sérgio alone somewhere in the snowy mountains to the north.

"What do we do?" I said.

Harriet set down her glasses.

"Well, let's not get carried away just yet," she said. "He's probably fine."

Outside, the sun was sinking low in the sky and the temperature was likely plummeting.

"I hope so," I said.

"Can I try your shake?" said Harriet, keeping her voice calm with obvious effort.

"Yeah," I said.

She flicked a straw from the dispenser to her left and I scooted the cup in front of her. While she took a drink, I looked at the birdsong-every-hour clock hanging above the diner's cash register. It was already past four. Soon it would be dark.

"That's good," she said halfheartedly, eyeing the birdsong clock.

"Yeah," I said, trying to imagine what could be keeping Sérgio this long. "Do you think we should call the police?"

She looked at the clock again and then at her watch.

Behind us, the little bells attached to the top of the door jingled as someone came into the diner.

"There you are," said a familiar voice.

We both turned around. It was Sérgio, his face shining with a strange intensity.

"Are you okay?" I said.

"Where did she take you?" said Harriet.

Sérgio took a deep breath.

"I'm very hungry," he said. "Let's find a table and I'll tell you everything."

## XVI

'm still trying to make sense of what happened," Sérgio began once we'd settled in and the waitress had brought him a bacon cheeseburger and a basket of fries. "I've preoccupied myself for so many years with the work of Eduard Salgado-MacKenzie and then to find out . . ." He popped a fry into his mouth. "To discover . . ." He shook his head. "I just don't know how to put it into words." He took a bite of his cheeseburger, chewing reflectively. Whatever Sérgio had experienced had catalyzed in him a palpable transformation. His gloom had dissipated entirely, replaced not with his former chatty enthusiasm but with a wide-eyed awe, a baffled reverence. He swallowed and looked to us in consternation. "I encountered Salgado-MacKenzie," he said, "but to articulate that experience is to give it narrative form, which—I don't even know where to begin."

"Take your time," said Harriet. "But if you'd like a suggestion, you might start your story where I left you. I've filled Daniel in up to that point."

"Yes," said Sérgio. "Very good. Give me just a moment."

As he thought this through, he polished off the rest of his cheeseburger with great alacrity. Each bite he took seemed to incrementally restore his vigor, but even as the burger rejuvenated his body, that strange, awestruck intensity lingered in his face.

. . .

So (said Sérgio after finishing off half the basket of fries as a chaser to his burger). We parted ways, Harriet, at the Fordis residence, and as you—I assume—drove back to Fremont Creek, Anne Fordis drove me to the base of a mountain maybe ten miles from her house, where we diverted from the state road onto an unplowed mountain path. The snow on this path was not deep, but our ascent was dramatic and Mrs. Fordis, though she obviously knew the road well, drove the old pickup at barely a crawl. She watched the road ahead of us so intently, in fact, that I didn't dare break her concentration with questions. As you might imagine, I had many: How did she know Eduard Salgado-MacKenzie? Why had she decided to trust me? Where were we going? I remained silent, though, reminding myself that in all likelihood this would be another dead end— that, as Harriet had suggested, Mrs. Fordis was merely an attention-hungry eccentric. I hoped she was a benign one.

Higher and higher we drove, climbing the mountainside with a steady determination. As our strange, silent journey wore on, I began to fixate, in spite of myself, on the other possibility Harriet had raised, that Anne Fordis might be dangerous. At what point, I wondered, should I become concerned? The farther we drove from civilization, the more vulnerable I became to this stranger's enigmatic whims. I grew quite nervous, I have to say, and to distract myself from these troubling thoughts I focused on the view from the pickup truck. Whenever a gap appeared in the trees I could catch a glimpse down into Lodgepole's famous caldera below us. Truly stunning, the view from where we were: rugged hillsides, lofty evergreens, meandering streams. Everything was covered in a thin layer of snow.

After some time, the road leveled out and turned inward, toward the mountain, where we came to a broad, flat stretch of ground with an even higher mountain towering above it. To my great relief, a few houses lay ahead of us. We drove just beyond them then down a long private path at the end of which lay a cottage. Maybe that's not the right word. A rustic house, not small but not big either. Next to the house was a large garage with its door open and darkness within. Anne Fordis stopped the car. Barring the appearance of weaponry, I no longer feared for my safety. I was in running distance of human habitation, if things came to that.

Mrs. Fordis said, "Here we are," and got out of the truck.

This was it, whatever *it* was. I wondered if, in this snowy house in the mountains, I would finally discover what I'd spent decades searching for. As I stepped down from the cab of the truck, I asked Mrs. Fordis where we were, but she ignored my question, looking past me instead into the darkness of the open garage. I followed her gaze. At the edge of the darkness, just inside the garage door, a man in blue coveralls stood at a long workbench, completely engrossed in some small mechanical task. Just behind him, a squat space heater glowed orange.

I shut the door of the truck and the man finally turned to look at us. His hair was completely white, his skin wrinkled and loose, but there was no mistaking the sad-faced figure I'd met at the party some twenty-five years earlier. I took a step forward, and then back. I must have looked as discombobulated as I felt, because as the man watched me, his face assumed an expression of concern, and he looked to Anne Fordis as if for reassurance.

She came around from behind the truck and gave him a nod, which seemed to put the man at ease. He wiped his hands on an oily towel and took a few cautious steps out of the cavernous garage. If he recognized me, his face didn't show it.

I'd rehearsed this moment so often in my mind that the adrenaline now coursing through my veins granted my actions an added surety and my consciousness an almost hyperreal clarity. I introduced myself and held out my hand. Instead of taking it, though, he turned his own grease-covered hand palm upward and said, "I'll have to wash up first."

I lowered my hand. A minor deviation from the scene I'd imagined, but by no means an insurmountable obstacle.

The man tucked the oily rag into the back pocket of his coveralls and said, "What is this about?"

Back on script, I said, "You may not recognize me, but we've met before, Mr. Salgado-MacKenzie."

He cocked his egg-shaped head and said, "What did you call me?"

Another unexpected deviation.

"You're Eduard Salgado-MacKenzie," I said. "Are you not?"

This elicited a sound somewhere between a snort and a chuckle from the man.

"Name's Cooper," he said. "Rex Cooper."

"Mr. Cooper, then," I said. "We met at a party in São Paulo about twenty-five years ago, and you introduced yourself as Eduard Salgado-MacKenzie—your pseudonym, perhaps?"

"What did you say your name was?"

I said, "Sérgio Antunes, but please, call me Sérgio."

"All right, Sérgio," he said. "You're looking for Eduard Salgado-MacKenzie? I can tell you for a fact that Salgado-MacKenzie doesn't exist."

I had no idea where to start. I'd prepared a painstaking apology for this occasion, as well as a carefully curated list of questions, but I had not anticipated that Salgado-MacKenzie would deny his own existence.

"You've heard of Salgado-MacKenzie, though," I said.

He said, "Like I told you, the man doesn't exist."

Behind me, the pickup truck's engine ticked softly as it cooled down. Anne Fordis leaned against the cab, watching our exchange with folded arms. I decided to try a new approach.

I said, "But you've been to Brazil?"

"Sure," he said, wiping his nose with the back of his hand. "I lived there off and on for a lot of years."

Now we were getting somewhere.

"The party where we met," I said. "It was at the old Capital Hotel, during the Great Lusophone Exposition of Science Fiction—do you remember it?"

He wiped the back of his hand on the leg of his coveralls.

He said, "That's not a time in my life I like to think about."

Recognizing that this was not an explicit denial of having attended the convention, I decided to proceed.

I said, "I'd like to apologize for that night. I was very happy to meet you, but we had something of a misunderstanding."

He said, "Is that right?"

"Yes," I said and then described the encounter in some detail. He listened with an expression of increasing discomfort, as if an unseen presence were slowly driving a thin metal blade beneath one of his fingernails. When I finished my story, he shrugged, his pained expression softening into a look of minor annoyance.

He said, "What do you want from me?"

"Mr. Salgado-MacKenzie," I began.

"It's Cooper," he said.

I exhaled heavily, my breath forming a cloud in the chilly air.

"It's a strange thing," I said. "I've spent so much time thinking about the story you told at that party that I can't tell—within my own mind—what's invention and what's reality anymore. What I mean is, do I remember that night I shut the door in your face, or am I just remembering your account of it, made vivid by my thinking of it over and over and over again? I don't know anymore. What I do know is that I want to apologize. I'm sorry for my reaction when you confronted me at the party, and I'm sorry for any pain I caused you before that."

He took this in for a moment, thumbs hooked in the pockets of his coveralls. A bird landed on the branch of a tree behind him, knocking the narrow pile of snow that had accumulated there to the ground with a soft *puff*. Cooper turned to look, and the bird flew away. He looked back at me and said, "You seem pretty upset about all this, but I have to say, whatever did or didn't happen between us, it's over. Like I said before, that was a very unhappy time in my life that I've worked hard to forget, and it's over now. It's all in the past." He waved a dismissive hand. "Don't you see that? It just doesn't matter."

I said, "It matters to me."

"Well," he said, "there's nothing I can do about that."

Anne Fordis shifted her weight against the truck, which responded with a faint creak.

I said to Mr. Cooper, "I need you to know that I'm sorry."

"Okay," he said. "Message received. Anything else I can do for you?"

He angled his body back toward the garage, ready to walk away.

I was not going to allow this to be the end of our conversation, so I said, "Yes, there is. I've admired your writing my whole life, ever since—"

"Stop," he said, looking away from me. "I told you. I'm not Salgado-MacKenzie."

I said, "Then who—"

"He needs to meet Madge," said Anne, speaking up for the first time since we'd gotten out of the truck. She pushed off against the truck and stepped forward to stand between me and Rex Cooper.

I said, "Who's Madge?"

Rex shook his head.

Anne said, "She's our sister."

I said, "And where would I find her?"

"Right here," said Anne, pointing to the snow-covered house next to the garage. She looked at Rex. "Let's go inside."


As if overcome by these recollections, Sérgio put a thick hand to his chest.

"Heartburn?" I said.

"I'm fine," he said.

He took two deep breaths and a long swallow of off-brand diet cola from one of the diner's white Styrofoam cups.


Since we'd arrived, the sun had come out from behind the clouds (continued Sérgio), and as we approached the blue-gabled house I had to squint against the white light reflecting off the snow. It was still so bright, though, that my eyes stung. I approached the house then, eyes watering, wondering what revelations might await me inside. By that point in my visit, I truly had no idea what to expect, the day so far having been such a convulsive series of excitements and frustrations. I'd already abandoned my imagined script, the product of so many years of careful speculation, giving myself over to whatever this house held in store for me.

We ascended the wooden steps of the front porch and I followed Anne through the front door, Rex trailing behind me. Inside the house, that overpowering snow sheen diminished only slightly, thanks to a vast picture window through which light flooded the room. The illumination overwhelmed me, and I felt as disoriented as if the room had been pitch dark. As I adjusted to my surroundings, I heard music and, looking for its source, saw a rail-thin, white-haired woman sitting on a simple wooden stool strumming an old Spanish guitar.

Without missing a note, she looked up and in a husky voice said, "Who's this you've brought me?"

I introduced myself. She played through a few more arpeggios and then set her guitar on the floor, leaning it gingerly against the wall. With none of the stiffness I might expect, given her age, she stood from her seat. She was a tall woman, dressed smartly in trim black slacks, Chelsea boots, and an oversized tailored dress shirt. A cloth headband held her white hair back from her face, which regarded me with preemptive amusement.

"Madge Cooper," she said, shaking my hand. "You're Brazilian?"

I said, "Yes, ma'am. Paulistano."

"A great pleasure to meet you," she said, switching to Portuguese.

"Likewise," I said.

"Sit," she said. "Please."

So I sat down and Madge asked what brought me all the way to Idaho. I said, "I'm looking for a writer named Eduard Salgado-MacKenzie."

"Eduard Salgado-MacKenzie?" said Madge, and gave a short, barking laugh. "Now that's a name I haven't heard in quite some time."

She looked at Anne and Rex, who sat at a long wooden bench that ran beneath the picture window. With the light behind them, I had a hard time making out the expressions on their faces.

Madge said to her siblings, "What does he already know?"

Rex said, "I told him Salgado-MacKenzie doesn't exist."

Madge arched an eyebrow at her brother. "That's not quite true, though, is it, Rex?"

Without looking at me, Rex jerked a thumb in my direction and said, "It's true as far as he's concerned." He folded his arms. "Far as I'm concerned too."

Anne leaned conspiratorially toward Madge. As if I wasn't there, she said, "You know, he claims to have read all the stories."

"He does?" said Madge, recoiling in mild horror.

I had the uncanny feeling that if I didn't reassert my presence to these three ancient siblings, I might literally disappear.

I said, "I have read the stories, and they mean a lot to me."

Madge wheeled around to face me, a look of concerned wonder on her wrinkled face.

She said, "You've read them all?"

"All the ones I could find," I said.

"Who would have thought?" Madge said to her backlit siblings, and then to me: "You say they've meant a lot to you?"

"That's right," I said.

She cringed and looked again at her siblings. Anne shook her head with apparent pity, and Rex rested his face in one broad, upturned palm.

"I'm afraid you've made a terrible mistake," Madge said to me. "The stories, they're just larks. They're not meant to be taken seriously."

"In any event," I said, undeterred, "they've meant a lot to me."

She sat there for a moment, regarding me with her wide dark eyes.

"Clearly," she said. "After all, here you are."

"If this is an intrusion," I said.

"No," said Madge. "It's not. The truth is, Mr. Antunes, that Eduard Salgado-MacKenzie is a hoax. We invented him—Anne, Rex, and I did—back when we were children, as part of a little time-killing game during one of our parents' interminable parties in the countryside of São Paulo."

Rex and Anne both opened their mouths, presumably in protest, but Madge lifted a silencing finger before they could speak.

"This is a story I want to tell," she said to them.


The particular party that birthed Eduard Salgado-MacKenzie (Madge said to me) began as a Festa Junina, our parents' normally cosmopolitan guests arriving by the carload on Friday night dressed in their ridiculous straw hats and painted-on freckles. That first evening they stuffed themselves with pamonha, quaffed gingery quentão, and danced a lively quadrilha by the light of a bonfire. From there, though, the proceedings shucked off their holiday trappings and sprawled forth into a long, disorganized weekend of decadent revelries, a devolution not atypical for parties hosted by my parents.

We were living at the time on our grandparents' majestic fazenda, which they only occupied a few weeks out of the year and had graciously offered up to my parents while they found their feet in the country. For many visitors, the fazenda itself was attraction enough. The main building, a colonial mansion built in 1850, sat nestled between two hillsides, with three guesthouses and a house for the help not far off. The fazenda could, and often did, sleep twenty guests, and in warm weather, with hammocks strung along columned terraces, it could sleep even more. Visitors might go all day without seeing another soul if they opted to take advantage of the many natural features the ten-thousand-acre property had to offer—a picnic by a stream, a ride on horseback through a flowering meadow, a hike to a scenic mountaintop.

Usually, though, a thick knot of people remained at the central cluster of buildings. In spite of its spaciousness, the fazenda, during weekends when my parents were hosting an event, often felt overstuffed to my siblings and me. Everywhere we turned, we found friends of our parents debating politics, seducing each other, arguing over the merits of the latest art-world craze, sleeping in the yard furniture, eating our food, drinking, and fighting. Although the world of adults was of increasing interest to me, three days of this revelry was usually too much.

I would have been fifteen then, Rex thirteen, and Anne only seven. We'd been in Brazil for a year and were adjusting with only mixed success. Our situation was unique—I could spend all day recounting the history of our family, but in short, our mother, Gabriela de Queiroz, was the scion of a fabulously wealthy Brazilian coffee dynasty, and Dad— Jack Cooper—was the oldest son of a reasonably successful hotelier in Lodgepole, Idaho. They met when Mother and a few of her globetrotting artist friends—I should tell you, incidentally, that Mother was a very talented painter. As a young woman, she'd studied at the Real Academia de Bellas Artes in Madrid before dropping out and falling in with a group of minor surrealists who worshipped the work of René Magritte. On returning to Brazil, she'd proselytized the aesthetic within the burgeoning São Paulo art scene, but that's another story for another time.

What concerns us now is the trip she took with a few of her friends to the wild and wooly expanses of Yellowstone National Park. Back then Lodgepole, Idaho, was the last train stop before the park, and so Mother and her friends stayed the night there in—as it happened—our paternal grandfather's hotel. She met Jack that night at dinner. It was peak tourist season and the hotel was understaffed due to a summer stomach flu making its rounds through the town, so Jack was filling in as a waiter. Somehow he caught Mother's fancy. He was not an especially handsome man, but there was something so quintessentially American about his looks— that's how Mother always explained that initial appeal. She waited until his shift ended, asked him what a girl might do to have fun in a town like Lodgepole on a night like this, and he responded by rustling up a pair of flashlights and leading her on a hike to the top of Moosehead Peak, where they sat talking until the sun came up.

The next week, after visiting Yellowstone, Mother's friends headed west for California. Mother stayed behind, though, and following an intense three-month courtship, she and Dad were married, much to the consternation of Mother's parents.

The newlyweds stayed in Idaho at first, Mother having been besotted by the region—this was virgin territory as far as surrealism was concerned, and Mother was convinced that the rugged Idaho landscape would inspire paintings such as the world had never seen: Old Faithful spewing bales of human hair, a bloody-mawed bear in a three-piece suit, aspen groves with their white bark replaced by soft pink skin. During those pleasant early years, then, while Dad helped his father run the hotel, Mother roamed the countryside, producing dreamlike renditions of the monstrous Tetons, of the relentless Snake River, of the already fanciful hot pots and geysers of Yellowstone National Park. I was born during those salad days, and then Rex came a few years later. Of course, Mother's painting slowed down bit by bit as each of us children arrived, and then unfortunately the war came. Dad went off to fight, while Mother stayed in Idaho with us—no time to paint, only to worry.

My earliest memories are from that period. It was always winter, as I recall it, and baby Rex was always crying. I didn't meet Dad until I was seven—or rather, I have no memory of meeting Dad before that. It was a strange time, our family fragmented and discouraged, but thankfully the war did eventually come to an end, and Dad came back in one piece not long after V-J day.

Not too long after that, Anne was born. With the family now complete, long-delayed plans to move to Brazil were finally set in motion. Mother wanted to reconnect with her community of artist friends, and Dad wanted to try his hand as a freelance journalist abroad, so after tying up their loose ends in Idaho and making the necessary preparations—a process that actually took a few years—we all moved to São Paulo.

The three of us kids spoke the language well enough because our mother had spoken it to us the whole time we'd lived in Idaho, but still,

we sounded and acted like the foreigners we were. Children more socially adept than us might have parlayed that foreignness into an alluring
mystique, but the three of us, socially competent at best, came across as
clumsy and gauche to our schoolmates. As a result, we had no friends
from among our new peers, only each other.

In a way, this wasn't so different from our life in Idaho, where we'd
inherited a patina of foreignness from our Brazilian mother and had
never quite been regarded as fully authentic Idahoans. Still, at least we'd
been born there, which counted for something, whereas in São Paulo we
couldn't even claim nativity. We children were foreigners who spoke the
language reasonably well, who were only tenuously connected to the
land by our native-born mother.

This distance solidified a dynamic that had been developing for years
within our family, a sense that we were a sovereign, indissoluble nation
of five, having been united by our highly peculiar shared history, our
insular mishmash of cultures, idioms, and classes. We pledged allegiance
to each other, and as long as our family remained together, we children
felt like we had a place in the world.

I realize I'm making it sound as if we were outcasts in Brazil, which
wasn't really so. Mother and Dad fared much better in our new country
than the three of us did, quickly establishing themselves as the toast of
the São Paulo art scene. Mother had been much missed during her years
away, and everyone took an instant liking to Dad, which was the case
wherever he went. The man had a genius for likeability. Their parties
were numerous and legendary, and in addition to Mother's immediate
circle of friends, over the years they hosted such luminaries as Carlos
Lacerda, Alexander Calder, Clarice Lispector, Elizabeth Bishop, and
Lota de Macedo Soares, to name just a few.

Our parents' friends, it must be said, did treat us well, but in the way
an indulgent human dotes on an inoffensive dog. They brought us gifts,
laughed at the things we said—whether or not they were meant to be
funny—and told us repeatedly how delightful we were. We rarely felt
delightful, though. Resentful mainly, and as I said, bored.

. . .

$M$adge looked to her backlit siblings, who nodded in affirmation, while I shivered beneath my coat. Their ratification of her memories had all the weird potency of an incantation. It was as if by an act of shared will, they were reanimating the chilled corpse of the distant past.

$S$uch was the case, Mr. Antunes, two days into that fateful weekend-long Festa Junina (continued Madge). The trouble began when, in a fit of pique, Anne created a flipbook in the blank, creamy pages of a leather-bound notebook that Emílio Lazaretti, one of my parents' guests, had acquired in Florence. Lazaretti was Anne's bête noir thanks to an unfortunate incident several visits previous when he had accidentally, he claimed, thrown away an elaborate yarn doll that Anne had spent two days creating. On this visit, he had not only made an ill-advised joke about the yarn doll incident—the joke's supposed humor springing more from Anne's distraught reaction on that infamous occasion than from his own blunder—but he had also disparaged Lobinho, a rangy farm dog that Anne had recently taken under her wing, calling the dog one of the ugliest, stupidest mutts he'd ever seen.

About an hour after the slight had occurred, we found Anne on the porch of the second guesthouse, pen in hand, hunched over the notebook that, two evenings previous, Lazaretti had boasted he would fill with a series of poems destined to redefine the literary landscape of Brazil. To Anne's credit, the flipbook was very amusing, depicting a bear in a tutu executing a clumsy pirouette. Anne was the only one of us children to inherit Mother's genius for visual art. Given Lazaretti's famous temper, however, we thought it best to return the journal to his room and concoct an alibi for our guilty sister.

Later that day, then, when Lazaretti came storming across the grounds, defaced journal in hand, we were ready. He'd deemed us the most likely culprits, so we were the first ones he confronted. The three of us stood in a little cluster next to the swing set our grandfather had built for us near the main house. Waving the journal under our noses, he demanded to know the meaning of this obscenity. My siblings and I looked at each other uncomfortably, just as we'd planned. He asked which one of us had done it, flecks of spittle flying from his mouth.

At fifteen I had an honest, sensible face that adults trusted, so when I responded, voice breaking, that all three of us had promised the guilty party that we wouldn't reveal his identity, Lazaretti didn't doubt me for a second. Instead, he cajoled and threatened until, with a tremulous plea that he not be angry with us, I told him that Mr. Salgado-MacKenzie was the flipbook's creator.

"Who?" said Lazaretti.

I said, a little louder, "Mr. Eduard Salgado-MacKenzie."

Lazaretti said, "I heard you the first time. Who is this Salgado-MacKenzie?"

I said that he must remember the young man who had tripped and fallen into him during the quadrilha on Friday night.

"No," said Lazaretti.

I said, "But he fell right into you. And when he picked himself up, you shoved him back to the ground, you were so upset."

Lazaretti had consumed a prodigious quantity of quentão that Friday night, so I counted on his memory of the evening's events being more than a little hazy.

Rex chipped in, "He was one of the only people not to come to the party in costume, remember, and you called him an elitist swine?"

Lazaretti *had* called someone an elitist swine for failing to arrive in costume, but it was the painter José de Moraes, not the fictional Eduard Salgado-MacKenzie. We could see the wheels turning in Lazaretti's head.

"And when he defaced my notebook," he said, "what did he say to you?"

Anne said it was a very rude thing, what Mr. Salgado-MacKenzie had said, and we didn't want to repeat it.

"Now I must know," said Lazaretti.

I said, "If we tell you, you have to promise not to be angry with us."

He said he promised. I told him we'd found Mr. Salgado-MacKenzie on the porch of the second guesthouse writing in the journal.

I'd said, "Isn't that Mr. Lazaretti's notebook?"

Mr. Salgado-MacKenzie had smiled at us and said, "I'm filling these pages with something far more consequential than anything Emílio Lazaretti will ever be capable of producing," and then he'd held up the notebook, flipping through its pages to show us the little cartoon he'd drawn.

After a moment's silence, in a very quiet, very controlled voice, Lazaretti thanked us for our honesty and asked us where he might find Mr. Salgado-MacKenzie. We told him we were sorry, but he'd left soon after we'd spoken with him.

Tucking his notebook under his arm with great dignity, Mr. Lazaretti thanked us again and took his leave. For the rest of the afternoon we heard him raging around the fazenda complaining of the great slight against him by that putrid upstart, Eduard Salgado-MacKenzie. I think the other guests found the anger off-putting enough that—not wanting to prolong the abrasive interaction with Lazaretti any longer than they had to—they didn't inquire further about this mysterious Salgado-MacKenzie, even though they'd never heard of this young offender before in their lives. Everyone loved a good Emílio Lazaretti anecdote, though, so our story grew legs and began to travel among our parents' friends and acquaintances.

During lunch one day about a week after the party, our parents brought up the nascent feud between Lazaretti and Eduard Salgado-MacKenzie, saying that for the life of them they couldn't figure out who this Salgado-MacKenzie was. He was supposed to have been at their Festa Junina, but they'd never heard of him. Could it be that Emílio had begun to imagine things?

"No, Dad," said Rex, feigning confusion at their confusion. "Salgado-MacKenzie was the one who brought that bouquet of flowers that sat in the vase in the library all weekend."

Anne added that he'd also played fetch with Lobinho for some time, and had been very complimentary of the dog's intelligence.

"Then you met him?" said Dad.

"Yes," we all said.

"But who is he?" said Mother.

I told our parents that Ms. Elizabeth Bishop had told me that Salgado-MacKenzie was a very talented young novelist, only just arrived from Scotland. He'd been born and raised in Fortaleza, but when he was fourteen, his mother—Charlotte MacKenzie, the famous Scottish botanist—had moved back home to Edinburgh to accept an appointment at the university, and she'd brought young Eduard with her. His father had died, or otherwise abandoned the family, a few years earlier. Young Eduard had spent twelve years in Scotland, but now he was back in Brazil working on a novel that held great promise, according to everyone who'd read excerpts from it.

We were generally very honest children, so our parents had no reason to disbelieve our story.

Dad said, "How did we miss meeting him?"

Mother said, "You know how these parties can be," and the matter was settled.

The hoax may have ended there, more or less, if not for a rainy Saturday a couple of weeks later that kept us all indoors. Mother and Dad were visiting friends in Pernambuco for the weekend, and we had opted to stay behind. I was old enough to keep an eye on little Anne, and Maria de Jesus—our cook—and Neuze—our maid—were on hand to keep us well fed and out of any real trouble.

Madge smiled briefly at this memory before continuing.

As much as we'd looked forward to having the place to ourselves, though (she said), boredom soon got the better of us. An empty house was no less tiresome than a crowded one, and after a half day spent diverting ourselves—me with my guitar, Rex with an illicitly obtained book of off-color jokes, and Anne with a children's watercolor set—we were ready for some excitement.

The three of us were sitting in the library trying to teach the stubborn and lethargic Lobinho to roll over, when Rex said, "Do you know what would be funny?"

Anne shook her little head.

I said, "What?"

Rex said, "If Eduard Salgado-MacKenzie published a story."

Rex and I laughed and little Anne looked deeply puzzled. "But he's pretend," she said.

I said that yes, he was, and that this would be part of the game. *We* would write a story, but say that Eduard Salgado-MacKenzie had written it.

Once she caught on, Anne was delighted. We had to do it, she said. Rex and I agreed. We snuck into Dad's office—a big no-no—uncovered his typewriter, and got to work. All three of us were avid readers, and Rex and I were both burgeoning science-fiction fans, thanks to a crate of pulp magazines that an artist friend of Mother's had dropped by the house so Mother could check out the covers—this friend was in a proto-pop-art phase and evangelized the aesthetic to everyone who would listen. Mother hadn't been interested in the magazines, but Rex and I got a kick out of the stories we'd found inside: rocket ships, telepathic humans, penal asteroids, space pirates—a cavalcade of novelties. Given our enthusiasm for the genre, then, we decided that Salgado-MacKenzie's story would be set in outer space. Rex and I took turns typing, but all three of us shouted out ideas. We'd become so tightly knit since our move to Brazil that collaboration was second nature.

As I remember it, the story takes place in a large colony on the far side of the moon. The colony's governor, a petty megalomaniac named Ian MacTavish—we were leaning pretty hard on the Scottish angle—gets the idea one day to convince the other colonists that Earth's been destroyed by a nuclear war. Everybody is half expecting this to happen anyway, so there's very little resistance to the idea at first. The colony observes three days of mourning for their fellow humans, and then on the evening of the third day, Governor MacTavish convenes a colony-wide meeting in the giant stadium next to the government offices.

Once everyone arrives, MacTavish gets up on an elaborate platform in the middle of the field and, speaking into one of those booming stadium microphones, tells the colonists that before he was dispatched to the moon, he was given an elaborate set of protocols to follow if the Earth were ever destroyed. He tells the colonists that for the sake of humanity's future, it's essential that they follow these protocols to the letter.

He says that for starters, his gubernatorial stewardship now extends over all of humanity, given the recent and tragic demise of all more senior government leaders on Earth. He is, in essence, the supreme ruler of the universe, although of course they don't need to address him as such, except on very formal occasions. The rest of the time, "Governor MacTavish" will do just fine. As for the rest of the protocols, he'll reveal them as they become relevant, and everyone should just go about business as usual until the next such colony-wide meeting becomes necessary.

Many of the colonists are still so rattled by the news of Earth's destruction that they don't think to question MacTavish's decree, but there are a handful of colonists who are understandably skeptical. They send a delegation to Governor MacTavish, asking to see, in print, the protocols he alluded to. They just want to make sure, they explain, that everything is on the level. MacTavish hears them out, and when they finish he says he would love to help them but unfortunately the protocols dictate that only he can see them, and before the delegation can protest he has them escorted out of the government office building—newly renamed the Palace of MacTavish Triumphant—by an armed cadre from the just established Glorious Security Force.

In the ensuing months, the majority of colonists continue to stand behind MacTavish, and not without good reason. He treats his supporters well, listening carefully to their concerns and suggestions, and granting them a fairly active role in governing the colony. It's only his detractors who feel the squeeze of his iron fist, although not in the form of imprisonment or secret executions. MacTavish, it turns out, is something of a rhetorical genius, and he thoroughly convinces his supporters of the speciousness of the dissenters' claims. So effective are the governor's arguments that his supporters become more aggressively pro-MacTavish than MacTavish himself. Fearing for their safety, then, the dissenters cease speaking out against the MacTavish administration.

That changes, though, with the unexpected arrival of a spaceship from Earth. The rocket in question touches down in the dead of night, an emergency landing en route to Mars. The five astronauts emerge from the ship and are astonished to discover that the colonists believe Earth has been destroyed. The astronauts tell the colonists that no it hasn't, that they've been misled.

Initially it seems like the arrival of these five Earth astronauts is going to shatter MacTavish's carefully constructed illusion, and indeed the colony's dissidents seize upon the opportunity to expose MacTavish in his lies. They go door to door with the astronauts, explaining to their fellow colonists the falsehoods that MacTavish has been disseminating.

In spite of the astronauts' earnest testimony that Earth has not been destroyed, though, MacTavish's supporters become convinced that it's the astronauts who are lying, that they're actually moon colony dissidents in disguise, perpetrating a malignant hoax to unfairly besmirch their honorable governor. So they take the astronauts into police custody, put them on trial for high treason, find them guilty, and execute them. With this development, the dissidents give up hope. Some of them renounce their views and some just keep quiet, but the net effect is that MacTavish reigns supreme.

Meanwhile, on Earth, the Imperial Space Agency has no idea what's happened to their Mars-bound mission. For the sake of the missing astronauts, and for the edification of future crews, the ISA launches an investigative mission whose first stop will be the moon colony. This second ship lands in the middle of the colony's massive stadium just after lunchtime, which makes it difficult for anyone to question the rocket's provenance. Furthermore, the investigative team consists of over two dozen astronauts, all well armed and prepared for trouble. It's still an uphill battle, but they convince MacTavish's supporters that their governor has been lying to them and that Earth is fine, or as fine as it was when they all left it. At any rate, it hasn't been destroyed by nuclear war.

By this point, MacTavish has fled the colony, although there aren't many places to hide on the moon, so the investigative team finds him without much trouble. They place him under arrest and fly him back to Earth, where he's sentenced to life in prison. A new governor—honest and just—is sent to replace MacTavish, but, to a person, the colonists who survived the MacTavish years find the man's thoroughgoing decency intolerable, and some months after his swearing-in, an investigative team from Earth finds him bludgeoned nearly to death in a dark, dust-filled crater. The moon colony project is ultimately abandoned.

Our story was not a very original piece of work, more a collage of elements from some of our favorite stories we'd found in *Contos Astronômicos*, *Argonauto*, *FC*, and *Contos Fantásticos*. We were inordinately pleased with it, though, and it took great restraint not to show it to our parents as soon as they arrived home from Pernambuco. Instead, we sent it, under Salgado-MacKenzie's name, to the editor of *Contos Astronômicos*, our favorite magazine. We used our own address, the only time we would ever do so, and for weeks we were vigilant about checking the mail, careful to bring it in before our parents could see it. And about a month later, in what I recognize now as a stroke of very good fortune, we got a letter back from the editor saying *Contos Astronômicos* would be thrilled to publish the story.

When our copy of the magazine arrived—along with a check we had no way of cashing—we opened it to the first page of Salgado-MacKenzie's story and marveled at the sight of it. Seeing our creation's name in print made us feel like minor gods; we had summoned into existence a human being, or at least the illusion of one. Giddy with the thrill of it, we left the open magazine lying casually next to Dad's typewriter and waited for the magic to spread.

When Dad sat down to do some work later that day, he picked up the magazine to set it aside. When he saw the name of the author, however, he did a double-take, and unable to resist, he read through the whole story right there. When he finished, he went and found Mother, handed her *Contos Astronômicos*, and said, "You'll never guess who has a story in the kids' magazine." Mother was as intrigued as Dad, setting down her brushes to devour Salgado-MacKenzie's story on the spot. Of course, they shared it with their friends, and over the ensuing weeks, this concrete artifact of Salgado-MacKenzie's existence made the rounds among São Paulo's artistic elite.

The story in *Contos Astronômicos* not only confirmed he was a real person, but it also added an intriguing new wrinkle to his persona. If he was such a promising young talent, then what to make of this publication? It was science fiction, for one thing, but even judging by the standards of that decidedly unserious genre it was a lackluster specimen, not terrible enough to be fully derided and certainly not good enough to transcend its pulpy trappings. Some speculated that the young émigré must be desperate for money but too proud to ask his friends for help.

His detractors, Lazaretti most vocal among them, wondered if Salgado-MacKenzie's talent hadn't been massively overblown to begin with. Here was evidence of yet another big-mouthed young pretender whose self-promoting reach far exceeded his grasp. It was Lazaretti, in fact, who watched more diligently than anyone for every new story we produced in Salgado-MacKenzie's name so that he could flaunt its weaknesses before an informal jury of his peers until they came to the undeniable conclusion that he, Lazaretti, was the greater talent, and Salgado-MacKenzie merely a flash in the pan. And so, for some time, Lazaretti's legendary ego sustained not only himself but also the imaginary rival we had created for him.

In turn, Eduard Salgado-MacKenzie sustained our family, or rather, held it together over the following decade as diverging interests pulled us each in new and different directions that threatened to tear asunder our sovereign nation of five. Mother, for instance, though less and less active as an artist in her own right, came into her own during this time as an important social connector and an arbiter of taste in the upper echelons of the Brazilian art scene. Her opinion could make or break careers, so young artists sought her out, looking for guidance, approval, and the latest gossip. She could usually be found holding court with her young protégés, either at my grandparents' fazenda or at the luxurious downtown apartment that she and Dad had acquired a few years after our move.

Dad, for his part, carved out a role for himself as a kind of gentleman reporter, traveling sporadically throughout Latin America to cover events that caught his interest, wiring the pieces he produced to his newspaper contacts back in the States, who published them with avuncular indulgence, as they all thought the world of our gentle and lovable father.

As for me, in the late fifties I caught bossa nova fever and moved briefly to Rio, where I pestered the scene's young movers and shakers—Carlos Lyra, mainly, and Nara Leão—into helping me parlay my classical guitar skills into credible bossa nova chops. I spent some time—a few years, I guess—playing boozy nightclubs in Copacabana for restless crowds of hipsters and tourists until, feeling the absence of my treasured siblings, I moved back to São Paulo, where I continued pursuing my career as a third-tier bossa nova artist.

Rex, during this time, fell in with a group of ambitious young poets who sought to revolutionize the genre by abandoning language altogether. In the context of their late-night, pot-fueled summit meetings, I believe this decision made very good sense, and if memory serves, they even produced a manifesto for their movement in the form of a manhole cover they stole from a street in front of the newly opened São Paulo Zoo, a manifesto that hung on the apartment wall of one of the young poets until subsequent political developments led to the young man's imprisonment, as well as the confiscation of the manifesto, although the movement itself had all but died by that point, so the loss of the manhole cover was the least of their worries.

Anne, as I believe I've already mentioned, was the only one of us to have inherited any natural talent for visual art. Recognizing this for the rare gift it was, Mother constantly had her apprenticed out to this or that painter or sculptor in hopes that one day Anne might become a truly great artist, someone with global, historical significance. The potential was there, Mother always insisted; Anne just needed to catch the right spark. As is sometimes the case with savants, though, Anne had little interest in the gift that came so easily to her, so she seized upon every excuse not to paint or collage or sculpt or photograph—student government, volleyball, camping.

Madge looked affectionately at Rex and Anne, their younger selves now buried deep within their wrinkled faces. She turned back to me with a sad smile.

As I said before (continued Madge), we most likely would have drifted apart entirely during this time if it hadn't been for Eduard Salgado-MacKenzie. Amid all our other pursuits, Anne, Rex, and I always found time to keep our invented author alive. Whenever we were together— during holidays or family events—we'd find a quiet room where, over the course of a few days we'd hash out a new story to attribute to our secret creation. Sometimes we'd even collaborate by mail if one of us had an idea that couldn't wait. We'd set up a post office box and a bank account for our melancholy Scots-Brazilian author—we split all the money three ways—and it was with great glee that we received each sporadic acceptance letter. By the early sixties, his publication history had grown robust, at least for a writer who didn't exist. The stories we wrote had grown increasingly elaborate and had been greatly enriched by the introduction of the intrepid Captain Irena Sertôrian, a fictional alter ego for our fictional alter ego. We found this layering delightful, and in a way Irena Sertôrian felt more real to us than Salgado-MacKenzie ever had, or if not more real, more vivid somehow, as if some deep mathematical principle were at play by which a fraud multiplied by a fraud produces something unshakable and true.

In spite of this potency, and in spite of the project's longevity, we never stopped thinking of it as a joke, although on whom we really couldn't say. Our parents' crowd had long since forgotten about Salgado-MacKenzie, even Lazaretti, whose grudge, starved of fresh insults from its target, had slowly withered and died. What was the point of the whole charade then? All we knew was that we found continuing hilarity, even as Rex and I passed from our teens into our early twenties, in maintaining the illusion that Salgado-MacKenzie existed as a living, breathing person, a charming mutual friend who bound the three of us together.

However, that bond, arising as it did from a fictional entity, could not hold forever. Even the powers of Irena Sertôrian couldn't prevent the utter dissolution that visited our family in the late 1960s.

Ever since we'd moved to Brazil, there'd been a running joke among some of my parents' friends that, given his nationality and his penchant for solitary travel, Dad must be a CIA agent. Whenever he returned from one of his trips, these friends would laughingly ask him how many democratically elected heads of state he'd helped depose this time. Of course, none of these friends really believed that Dad was a shadowy agent of US imperialism—not at all. That was the joke: Dad was such a sweetheart, such a gentle soul, that he'd be the last person who might work for the CIA.

During the years of the military dictatorship, however, the jokes stopped. Given the USA's involvement in the coup of '64, the CIA had ceased to be funny, and anyway, many of the people who had made the joke in the first place were now fleeing the country to avoid imprisonment or worse, and no one who remained wanted to accuse my father, even in jest, of something so ugly. They liked Dad. A sweet, sweet man, they always said.

It was about six months after President Costa e Silva shut down the National Congress with the AI-5 when Mother discovered that Dad actually did work for the CIA. Even now, none of us is quite sure what the damning bit of evidence was, or if instead the discovery came about after years of accumulating suspicions. What we do know is that one night in July they had a spectacular fight behind closed doors after a family dinner at the fazenda celebrating Anne's first one-woman show: *Abstractions and Apologies*. Their private conversation escalated in volume very quickly, so that the three of us, still sitting in the dining room, could hear every word.

Dad denied everything at first, laughing off the accusation, but then Mother said if he had any respect for her and for all the years they'd been together, for all the trust they'd built during that time, he would tell her the truth. From the dining room table we strained to hear his response, which apparently was too quietly spoken for my mother as well.

"Say it so I can hear you," she said.

There was a long pause, and then he said, "I work for the CIA, but it's not what you think."

Another long pause. When conversation resumed, our parents—likely remembering our proximity in the dining room—spoke with discreetly lowered voices. According to the terse report Mother gave us two days later, she'd told Dad that their marriage was over, that he was no longer part of the family. Stung less, perhaps, by the political implications of what Dad had done—Mother was always considerably more conservative than she let on—and more by the personal betrayal, Mother demanded that Dad leave the house immediately, that he return to the States on the first flight he could catch. There had been pleading and cajoling, but Mother stood firm. Finally, Dad said he'd move out, if that was what she wanted, but he couldn't leave the country. It just wasn't in the cards. Mother said that if he didn't leave, she'd blow his cover, telling everyone she knew who he really was and what he'd secretly been up to for all these years. Whether he liked it or not, Dad was finished as a spy in her homeland.

So he left. Before we had time to process any of this, rumors of Dad's nefarious CIA involvement began circulating among Brazil's artistic elite. I don't think Mother ratted him out. I think instead that their friends merely put the same pieces together that she had. The talk was ugly, though, and we as his children weren't shielded from it in the least. At poetry readings and gallery openings, our own contemporaries and those of our parents spat vile tales of Dad's espionage directly in our faces.

Our father, they said, had slipped like a shadow into the private chambers of left-wing activists and government leaders and murdered them by means as sinister as they were undetectable—exotic poisons, impossibly thin knife blades, complex strangleholds. These methods, as well as the latest CIA torture strategies, he'd taught to local police forces throughout Latin America so that they could interrogate, and when necessary eliminate, factions the US government found undesirable. And with a voice like the buzzing of carrion flies, our father had spoken out via pirate radio stations to rural villages across the continent, urging them to embrace their basest impulses, fomenting chaos so the United States could step in and set things right. In essence he'd been an imperialist vampire drinking the blood of nubile young republics and turning them into unstoppable fascist monsters just like himself.

Years later, we would discover—or I should say, Anne would discover, as she was the one who dug through declassified records in drab government buildings—the truth about our father's career as a spy. During World War II he'd done intelligence work with the OSS. Not long before we moved to Brazil, he had been recruited by some wartime colleagues who'd found their way into the administration of the fledgling CIA. Dad's specialty was disinformation and psychological warfare. So, in regions the agency hoped to destabilize, Dad had actually, as some rumors went, launched pirate radio stations from forested hillsides, disseminating alarming false reports of local government plots to imprison large swaths of the populace or burn whole villages to the ground. On more than one occasion, according to the dry, bureaucratic language of the official reports, he had "successfully destabilized Soviet-friendly regions," providing his superiors with sufficient justification to "tactically intervene." Dad was very good at his job, from what Anne could surmise, and when the agency lost him it must have come as quite a blow. Because, thanks to Mother, they did lose him, at least as a Latin American operative.

With some distance, all three of us have been able to forgive Dad for what he did and even, to varying degrees, understand why he did it. At the time, though, we were as revolted by his alleged actions as anyone, if not more so. Should we have seen it coming, we wondered? *Did* we see it coming? Rex pointed out a handful of parallels between Dad's shadow career and the stories we'd published as Salgado-MacKenzie. The first one, for instance, about MacTavish and his great campaign of disinformation—had we intuited our father's secret vocation and, unable to confront it directly, channeled it into these ridiculous stories? Who could say. In any event, it wasn't long before none of us could stand to show our faces in public, and so, in shame and horror, we all retreated to our grandparents' fazenda.

At their sister's retelling of this memory, Anne lowered her head and Rex stared grimly at an empty corner of the light-filled room. I felt like an intruder, unsure whether to apologize or offer absolution. My eyes fixed on the elderly figure at the center of the room, and I chose to remain silent.

The three of us siblings were willing to lie low for a while and wait for things to blow over (said Madge), but Mother needed more dramatic relief. Nine days after decamping to the fazenda, Mother said she couldn't take it anymore. She told us she'd booked a flight to Paris, where she would spend some time recuperating from the trauma of her separation from Dad. It was all too much, she said to us. All too terrible. We didn't disagree.

And so, kissing each of us on the forehead, she wished us the best and said she didn't know when she might return, but we would be in her thoughts and in her heart throughout our separation.

"Goodbye," we said.

Mother's departure left the three of us alone in Brazil, sans parents, and although we were all technically adults by this time, Mother and Dad's departure left us feeling abandoned and afraid. Our entire lives, our family had served as the only context in which we could truly make sense of ourselves. Ultimately, we were not Americans, not Brazilians, not musicians, artists, or poets. First and foremost, we were the Coopers, whatever that signified, and we drew strength and purpose from that intimate fellowship. For decades, our family had withstood the devastating powers of entropy, huddling doggedly together as the forces of chaos and decay swirled around us. Now, those forces had found a way in, sundering us into disorderly, vulnerable little pieces. All that awaited us now was further chaos, further decay.

The day after Mother left for Paris, the three of us found ourselves idling listlessly in the library of the great fazenda, just as we had on so many bored Saturday mornings as children—Anne lazily scratching the belly of the latest farm dog she'd informally adopted, Rex sprawled out on the room's magnificent Persian rug, clutching my guitar with far less care than I would have preferred, mindlessly strumming the three chords he'd once taken the time to learn, and me, leafing through the oversized and beautifully illustrated pages of *The Guide to the Birds of Southeastern Brazil*, a book I'd loved as a girl. I don't remember which of us first suggested, half jokingly, that we should hold a wake for our family, but after batting the idea around with increasing seriousness, we decided we *should* hold a wake, that very night. We could gather right here in the library to contemplate the shattered body of our family, commemorating what it once was and would never be again.

We began preparations immediately. Anne picked a bouquet of flowers from the garden outside the kitchen. Rex cadged a bottle of bourbon from Dad's private store, which he'd no longer be needing, anyway.

And I selected a dozen or so records to lend the proceedings an appropriate aural atmosphere: Brahms's *Requiem*, of course, as well as Fauré's; some Britten in there too, I believe, though I can't remember what else. Then we all exhumed our most somber evening clothes from the backs of our wardrobes and, now more suitably attired, reconvened in the library just as the sun went down.

Drinks in hand, the stately strains of the *Selig sind die Toten* movement filling the air, we stood stiffly in our mourningwear around the antique Norwegian sea chest that we'd dragged over from the sunroom to serve as the casket for our family's imagined remains. After a few minutes spent inhabiting this solemn tableau, however, we recognized that we were going about the thing all wrong. We'd convened the wake semi-ironically, but after a few glasses of bourbon, we were willing to admit that we needed a more potent ceremony through which to channel our loss. So we decided to regroup.

I exchanged the Brahms for some Leonard Cohen. Rex doffed his jacket and tie. And Anne and I traded our gowns for a kimono and a festive party frock, respectively. Sitting cross-legged in a circle on the library rug, we took stock of our pharmacological assets. I had a shampoo bottle full of pep pills that I kept on hand for late-night club gigs, Anne had a half-empty dime bag and a few off-brand Quaaludes, and Rex had nine bars of blond Moroccan hash.

Our inventory impressed me, and I said as much to Rex and Anne, who nodded in agreement. The room had grown dark, but rather than switch on any of the room's many lamps, we lit six votive candles and placed them at the center of our circle. With nothing beneath them, they dripped translucent white wax directly onto the ornately patterned rug, but by that point, none of us cared.

I said, "The problem with a wake is, it's a gesture of defeat, an acknowledgment that death has won the day."

My siblings' faces, eerily illuminated by the flickering candles, looked somberly back at me. I think we'd forgotten that no one had actually died.

"But we don't *have* to concede to death tonight," I said. "There are other rituals we might explore."

A tremor of excitement ran through my body, and I pulled my kimono tighter, half worried that my body would fly into pieces from the moment's dark thrill. I told my siblings that I'd been reading a lot lately about the ancient Greek mystery cults. Not the Dionysians so much, with their ostentatious bacchanalia, but the Eleusinians, whose clandestine, drug-fueled rites celebrated—and some say harnessed—the power of Persephone's ascent from the underworld.

"What I'm saying," I said, "is that we don't have to just roll over and accept entropy as some kind of unstoppable universal force. If we perform the proper rituals, if we utter the ancient incantations and write the necessary symbols in the soft clay of our creation's forehead—"

I was wildly muddling my mystical traditions now, the Golem of Prague having lumbered its way into my vision of classical mystery rites. Rex and Anne nodded along, their eyes glowing in the dim room.

"If we harness these powers," I said, "we can reverse entropy. We can summon life from death." I looked from Rex to Anne, willing them through my gaze to feel the weight of this sentiment. "We can become immortal."

I should note that the bourbon was gone by that point, and we'd set to work on the first of Rex's nine bars of hash.

"But how will we do it?" said Anne, leaning forward.

Her question opened up a silence in the dimly lit room.

"Irena Sertôrian," said Rex after a few moments. "We'll bring her to life."

As soon as Rex spoke those words, I knew that he was right. Thrilled, I reached out and grabbed each sibling by the hand.

"Yes," I said. "Precisely. We'll create a body for our ethereal space captain, one she can inhabit for millennia to come. Rather than clay, though, or a patchwork cadaver, we'll use paper and ink for our raw material. What we'll do . . ." I paused to look meaningfully into each sibling's eyes. "What we'll do is, we'll write a new book of scripture," I said. "A sacred text to rival the Bible or the I Ching."

Rex jumped to his feet "Yes!" he said. "Exactly. Exactly!"

Pushing a swatch of hair back from his forehead, he said that the problem with the stories we'd written up to that point was their evanescent medium; magazines just didn't last. They were made to be thrown away, and with them, the words that constituted Irena Sertôrian's being. A whole book, on the other hand, especially if we constructed it in the proper manner, would stand through the ages, holding firm against the winds and rain of indifference and death. There was also the matter of Dad's betrayal—of both us and our adopted country—and though none of us was willing to say as much, I think we all hoped that such a book could somehow atone for everything our father had done.

We were all giggling by this point, a bit edgily, it must be admitted—equal parts delighted and frightened by our own audacity. We had to catch hold of this feeling, though, before it slipped through our fingers, so I kept talking, interrupting Rex to agree with him that during all these years we'd been over-focused on Salgado-MacKenzie when the true power lay much, much deeper than that, in the fictional creation of our fictional creation—the dream within the dream. Irena Sertôrian was the answer; Irena Sertôrian in all her mystical glory. We would call her forth, imbibe her everlasting power.

With a purpose in place, then, we relocated to Dad's old study, the site of Salgado-MacKenzie's first birth. We hadn't written a story there since the first one, and the keys of the typewriter felt, to my eager fingers, replete with untapped power.

We spent most of that first night composing a wild précis of what our monumental text would contain. At first all we did was free-associate, committing every concept that left our mouths to the creamy bond paper our father had stocked by the ream. A book of futuristic spells synthesized from centuries of global witchcraft traditions, for instance, or a handwritten epic inked with a pot of our commingled blood. I remember a madcap account of Sertôrian's childhood on Mars that eschewed any letters that appeared in her name—*U* was the only vowel we could use! No idea was too outrageous, but as the hastily typewritten pages accumulated, they failed to generate any accompanying transcendence.

Our enthusiasm momentarily flagged.

"What do we know about Sertôrian anyway?" asked Anne, perched feet up on the cracked leather club chair in the corner of Dad's office. She'd been manically pacing the room for the past hour, and her sky-blue frock was now soaked through at the armpits, her face damp with sweat.

Lying on the floor, a bronze letter opener balanced on his forehead, Rex rattled off a handful of biographical details from the dozens of stories we'd written.

"That's not what I mean," said Anne, drumming her fingers on her raised knees. "I guess what I'm really asking is *how* we know what we know about Sertôrian."

This stumped Rex, and me too, at first. Trying to think, I rested my head against the cool metal casing of the typewriter.

"*We* don't know anything about Irena Sertôrian," I said after a moment. "The only person who does is Eduard Salgado-MacKenzie. We don't have anything more than what he's written."

"Right," said Rex, catching on. "So if we want a new perspective on Sertôrian, we need to figure out what *other* people have written about her. Or will have written about her, I suppose. In the future."

He was close but not quite there. Closing my eyes, I could feel the answer barely tickling my fingertips, like a silk scarf snatched away by the wind on a stormy day. Then, with a fleet mental leap forward I said, "Almost. *We* don't need to figure out what these people will write. *Salgado-MacKenzie* needs to figure it out."

I explained that if we wanted to draw more fully on the latent potential of our beloved space captain, we needed to maintain, or even enhance, Sertôrian's embedded nature, as this was the essence of our relationship to her. The only way in, after all, was further out.

We were all on such a sympathetic high that this all made as much sense to Rex and Anne as it did to me. We'd discovered the key that fit the metaphysical lock of our current predicaments—the frustrated aimlessness of young adulthood, the crimes of our father, the dissolution of our family—and just like that, we all knew exactly what the project needed to look like.

Assuming the persona of Salgado-MacKenzie, we would peer into the future at the mesmerizing galactic religion that would spring up around Sertôrian in the centuries after her death. We would conjure the heartfelt testaments of her not-yet-existent devotees. Then, as far-seeing amanuenses, we would copy down their psalms and mystic visions, their exegeses and spiritual biographies, their rants and their ecstasies. Our book would not be a novel so much as a single-volume library, its page count running into the thousands.

The practical question arose at this point of how long it might take us to compose such a work. After running the numbers on an unused page of one of her sketch pads, Anne informed us that if we wrote five thousand words a day—and with our powers combined, we could certainly do so—we would have a million-word novel in under a year, thousands and thousands of pages that would serve as a sturdy receptacle for the powerful as-yet-unembodied spirit of Irena Sertôrian.

We began work immediately, then, on the first chapter—or rather, the first book—in our quasi-boundless single-volume library, the light of dawn already leaking into our father's office. *The Agony and the Ecstasy of Sister Úrsula*—that was our unofficial name for that first entry. It's an account written some twelve hundred years after the death of Captain Irena Sertôrian: As the galaxy descends into political chaos, the narrator—a historian-nun—examines a troubling episode from the life of Sertôrian as the nun's own life is imperiled by the approach of hostile armed forces. As good a place as any to begin, we supposed.

With the help of the pep pills and the Moroccan hash, composition of *The Agony and the Ecstasy of Sister Úrsula* moved quickly. We worked day and night, sleeping in shifts and eating much more sporadically than is generally advisable. Somehow we maintained the fervor of that first night throughout the whole process, and in six weeks, we had finished a two-hundred-page draft, fast work for us, but if it was any indication of what our pace might be on the dozens of narratives we had yet to write, our project would take at least twice as long as we'd originally estimated. Discouraging as that was, what ultimately killed our novel was the unfortunate decision we made one morning to read—while sober—what we'd spent the previous drug-fueled weeks writing.

Sitting in a row at the dining room table, we passed each page of the manuscript around, from me to Rex to Anne, until we'd read the whole thing. It took us four hours, with no snacks or bathroom breaks, and when Anne set the last page facedown on the half ream of paper to her right, we all looked at each other in grim dismay.

It wasn't that the story was *bad*, per se. It was fine—maybe even pretty good. The real problem was that it seemed so ordinary. We'd hoped that the outlandish circumstances of the story's conception and composition would have imbued it with some otherworldly splendor, some quality that would make up for everything Dad had done, that would guarantee the book's place in the canon of world religions until the end of time. But this stack of paper was, tragically, just another story, different perhaps from Salgado-MacKenzie's other work, but in no way transcendent.

Rex said, "That's it then."

And I said, "Looks like it."

We were done with Salgado-MacKenzie. He'd failed us or we'd failed him, but in either case, he would never finish his Sertôrial book of scripture, would never even write another story.

We watched a hummingbird flit past the flowering hibiscus outside the dining room. Anne said, "I meant to tell you this before now, but I'm going home tomorrow." Although Anne had lived in Idaho more briefly than any of us, it had always been her home—she'd felt its pull in ways that Rex and I never would. She explained that she'd been in touch with Dad, that he was back in Lodgepole, and that she'd decided that was where she wanted to be. It was her chance to make a clean break from the art world, a world that had never held much interest for her and that she'd occupied for as long as she had primarily to appease Mother.

Madge paused, looking at the now elderly Anne, who turned away with a grimace.

And so continued the sad dissolution of our remarkable family (said Madge). In light of this development, I decided it didn't make much sense for me to stick around either. I started gigging at nightclubs up and down the coast, never letting on to my fellow musicians as we shared flea-ridden motel rooms and late-night meals at dingy lanchonetes that this lifestyle was a choice for me, that I had recourse to an immense family fortune that would grant me access to all the luxury I desired as soon as I grew weary of life on the road.

Rex was the only one who stayed in São Paulo, the only one of us who tried to keep Salgado-MacKenzie from expiring completely. We had a whole back catalog of stories that nobody had picked up the first time we'd submitted them, and so, over the years, Rex kept submitting them, though only a few intrepid stories made it into print. I believe he did the same with *The Infinite Future*, sending queries to every press in the country that had ever published science fiction. On the rare occasions that an editor showed interest, Rex would send them *The Agony and the Ecstasy of Sister Úrsula*, supplemented for the sake of volume with a handful of whatever assortment of stories remained unpublished at the time.

Madge raised her bony shoulders in a melancholy shrug before continuing.

"And, as I'm sure you're aware, Sérgio, the novel was never published."

As Madge spoke my name, I realized I'd been listening to her account with an almost disembodied attentiveness, my awareness of myself and my own body having dissolved for a time into the sound of her rich and creaky voice. I took quick stock of myself in that still, light-flooded room, and a disorienting weariness engulfed me. Every part of me was tired, I realized: my mind, my body, my soul. I'd traveled so many miles in so few days—the flight from São Paulo, the drive from California to St. George to Salt Lake to Fremont Creek, and then, this morning, the ascent from Lodgepole to the top of this mountain. Humans, I believe, are not psychically equipped to cover so much distance in so little time, and I had to struggle to remember why I was there, what my objective had been in traveling so far.

Madge peered at me in concern, her folded hands resting lightly on a bony knee. To her right, her siblings stared in my direction, the light that streamed in through the window casting shadows on their now inscrutable faces. For a brief, panicked instant, I believed I might lose myself, that my mind might evaporate into the snow sheen that filled the simple room. Oblivion stretched out its gaping maw.

And then, as if some capricious god had snapped its well-manicured fingers, the strangeness passed. Once again, I was Sérgio Antunes, sublibrarian, guest in the home of the Cooper siblings, three senior citizens who had, many years before, pseudonymously written a handful of short stories that had given me inordinate pleasure over the course of my lifetime. They had also written a novel, never published, and I was here because I wanted to read it. The situation was as simple and mundane as that.

I said, "*The Infinite Future*—and excuse me if I'm overstepping here— would it be possible for me to read it?"

My request elicited a wheezing sigh from Madge.

"I wish you could," she said, "but I'm sorry to tell you that the manuscript is gone. Lost to the ages, I would imagine—none of us wanted to hold on to that reminder of our greatest collective failure."

I stifled a despairing sigh of my own. Even though I'd prepared myself for this possibility, I could feel the disappointment seeping into my tired muscles. Not only had Salgado-MacKenzie's masterwork never been completed, but its one existing fragment was lost. This was the end of the line. Any enlightenment I hoped to obtain from Irena Sertôrian would elude me forever.

All was not lost, though. I thought back to my first encounter with Rex Cooper at that smoky hotel room party—it must have been toward the end of his tenure in Brazil—and if nothing else, I suddenly had a clearer picture of the events he'd so angrily described at the party.

"That's why I didn't know who you were," I said to Rex, who looked back at me, puzzled. I realized what a non sequitur my comment appeared to be, and so I explained. "At the old apartment building," I said. "That's one detail from your story—the story you told at the hotel—that I've never been able to reconcile. Our names were on our mailboxes in that building, and if Eduard Salgado-MacKenzie had lived there, I've always reasoned, then surely I would have noticed his name. But I didn't notice, because it wasn't there. Because *your* mailbox would have said *Rex Cooper*, not *Eduard Salgado-MacKenzie*."

I laughed in triumph, but Rex Cooper only stared blankly at me in response. "But that means . . ." I began. "Or does it?"

Rex's face remained impassive.

"*Did* you stop by my apartment that night?" I said. "What I mean to ask is, did I truly slam my door in your face? Is that story *really* true?"

A pleading note had crept into my voice, and it was Madge and Anne who now sat at the edge of their seats, eager to hear what would come next.

Rex, though, only looked down at his thick-fingered hands and said, "Why would I make up something like that?" Which was both a deft evasion and an apt question, one I'd been wrestling with myself for decades.

I said, "It would mean so much to me—"

"It's like I told you before," Rex said. "Whatever did or didn't happen between us, it's over now. It's in the past."

"But—"

"No," said Rex, slipping his hands into the pockets of his coveralls. "This conversation is over."

Nobody, I think, knew quite what to do with their eyes. We all shifted our gazes awkwardly, searching for a comfortable nook where we might rest our uneasy attention.

Then Rex broke the silence. "As for *The Infinite Future*, though," he said, his voice gentler now, "I think I have a copy in a box under my bed."

I didn't dare speak but instead looked from Madge to Rex then back to Madge.

"Well," said Madge finally, with a light shrug. "Then I suppose Sérgio's in luck."

From her miffed expression, I got the sense she'd known about Rex's copy all along.

"If you don't want me to read it," I began.

"No," said Madge. "It's fine. No reason not to."

"I'll be right back then," said Rex, walking out of the room.

Anne checked her watch.

"We should head down the mountain soon," she said. "Snow's melting. The road will get soupy."

"Yes," I said. "I'm ready when you are."

Anne folded her arms with a satisfied nod.

"In a few minutes then," she said.

On her wooden stool, Madge, lips pursed, examined her knobby fingers.

"One more question," I said. "If I may."

"Go ahead," said Madge.

It was then (said Sérgio, addressing me and Harriet in the diner) that I asked about your letters, Harriet, if either Madge or Anne remembered corresponding with a young translator about thirty years earlier. It took her a moment, but when she remembered, Madge's face lit up.

"Yes," she said. "I do remember. A delightful young woman, by all indications. A friend of yours, you say?"

I explained how we knew each other, and told her you've been concerned for years that the anthology had offended Salgado-MacKenzie.

"I wasn't offended," said Madge, "because I never read the anthology. Should I be offended?" She waved a hand. "Never mind. No, I stopped writing because Dad died. You see, I was in Idaho because he was sick, and I hadn't seen him since he left Brazil. We'd never had a formal falling-out; we'd just lost touch. So I wanted to get reacquainted while I still had a chance. I stayed with Anne and Ed at first—they were living down in Fremont Creek then, I think—but then I came up here to stay, to help take care of Dad. This was his house, you know. We rented it out to vacationers for several years after he was gone, but then after Mother died, Rex and I decided to move back to our native land, spend our golden years with what remaining family we had. When was that, Anne, that we moved up here?"

"Ten years ago," said Anne. "No, fifteen."

"Right," said Madge. "In any event, I started corresponding with your friend while I was staying with Anne and Ed, and then I kept it up when I came up here to be with Dad. It can be so tedious, caring for the sick, even when it's breaking your heart. I needed something to keep my mind busy, and the letters proved a pleasant distraction. I believe they're the only venue in which I ever committed my famous Filamental Theory of the Universe to paper."

A groan from Anne.

"Would you like to hear my Filamental Theory?" said Madge, ignoring her sister.

"We have to go soon," said Anne.

"Well," said Madge, looking hurt. "Another time, perhaps. You should tell your friend, though, to come see me sometime. I'd hoped to meet her in person, back when we were corresponding, but then, as I said, Dad died here in Idaho and I flew back to Brazil as soon as the funeral was over. So." She lifted a hand palm up, as if she were handing me her excuse.

"I'll be sure to pass that along," I said.

A creak of the old wooden floor signaled Rex's approach, and a moment later he stepped through the door holding a stack of paper about an inch thick. He handed the manuscript to me and when the old worn paper touched my skin, a shiver ran through my body.

"May I read it?' I said.

"Take it," said Madge. "We have no more use for it here."

And so—

Sérgio reached for a paper grocery bag he'd brought into the Spud with him, but stopped mid-reach and picked up his napkin instead. In the lull between lunch and dinner, the Spud had emptied out and grown as quiet as an abandoned church. Even the waitress had nipped off for a break at some point, leaving the three of us to bask in reverential silence as Sérgio wiped his hands on his napkin, cleaning each individual finger with care. As Harriet and I watched on, mouths slightly agape, Sérgio set down his napkin, reached into the grocery bag, and withdrew a sheaf of worn, yellowing papers. Holding the manuscript with both hands, he lifted it up before us, and I knew I was not meant to touch it, not yet. The front page of the manuscript read *O Futuro Infinito, um romance por Eduard Salgado-MacKenzie.*

"*The Infinite Future,*" I said. "You found it."

"I found it," said Sérgio, his face still gleaming with mystical intensity, an unexpected note of sorrow in his voice.

# XVII

I didn't read *The Infinite Future* myself until several months later.

It was a smoggy February day in Salt Lake during one of those freezing late-winter stretches where all the snow on the ground is dirty and hard, when all the cars are coated with salt grime, when all the smog gets trapped inside the valley, turning the air toxic and gray. It was one of those days when the city looks like the dystopian pictures of the Soviet Union I remember seeing in *The Weekly Reader* back when I was in elementary school. An ugly day, in other words, although I didn't see much of it, because the sun hadn't come up yet when I got to work, and it had been down already for hours by the time I left.

When I got home to my apartment—an old but charming place at the edge of downtown Salt Lake—I saw I had an email from Sérgio. We hadn't been in contact at all since he'd found Salgado-MacKenzie, or the Cooper siblings, or whatever you want to call the author of all those stories. Sérgio had flown home out of Salt Lake the next day, and Harriet had dropped me off in Provo on her way back to Danesville. We'd all parted ways on friendly enough terms, but with no promises—at least on my part—to keep in touch, or get together again sometime.

Sérgio's email was brief and to the point. He told me he'd been having trouble finding a publisher for *The Infinite Future* in Brazil and wondered if I'd be interested in translating the manuscript into English and shopping it around stateside. The Cooper siblings had given their permission. He hoped his email found me well and that he'd hear back from me soon.

That afternoon in Fremont Creek, we'd photocopied the manuscript right away—a copy for me, a copy for Harriet, and a backup copy for Sérgio. I'd slipped my copy, still warm from the old Xerox machine's clanking innards, into an oversized manila envelope, which had remained unopened during my trip back to Provo and throughout my last few weeks in the storage room beneath the doughnut shop, my move to the apartment in Salt Lake, and my first months of employment as a filing clerk at Craig D. Ahlgren's law firm.

That same envelope, still unopened, currently sat on a dusty shelf above my washer and dryer, and every time I did a load of laundry, that manila revenant would dredge up feelings of guilt and embarrassment as I remembered the pathetic, flailing version of myself that had first met Sérgio, the version of myself I'd gratefully left behind when I'd been rescued by Craig D. Ahlgren. That was the version of myself that would have cared about the envelope's contents, but I wasn't that person anymore.

Still, though, Sérgio had been kind to me, had shared with me the thing he valued most in the world: the writings of Eduard Salgado-MacKenzie. At the very least, I told myself as I reread the email, I should skim through the manuscript before I told Sérgio I wasn't interested in translating it. I figured I owed him that much.

So I fixed myself a bowl of chicken noodle soup from a packet, pulled the envelope down from the laundry shelf, dusted it off, settled in at the crumb-covered drop-leaf table in my kitchen, and started to read.

Although I had to be at work early the next morning, I read late into the night, pulled through the text by the literary equivalent of highway hypnosis. I just couldn't stop turning the pages. When I finished reading, it was closer to morning than night, and I leaned back in the kitchen chair, rubbing my tired eyes. My first reaction to *The Infinite Future* was one of pity, both for Sérgio and the Cooper siblings. *The Infinite Future* was nothing more than a pulpy space thriller with stunted longings to be something more profound. The text held no arcane secrets, no occult spiritual power.

But then, as I was sliding the manuscript back into its manila envelope, a thought occurred to me: What if Madge Cooper had been lying when she'd told Sérgio that this text was a botched attempt at something greater? What I mean is, what if this text was *exactly* what the Cooper siblings had meant to produce—a magical gateway to some ethereal realm of higher understanding? Maybe Madge's claim that it was a failure was merely a distraction to throw the unworthy and the incredulous off the scent. Maybe she had created a ruse that a true devotee of Sertôrian would deftly sidestep and thus be led into the sanctum sanctorum of *The Infinite Future*.

With that possibility in mind, I reconsidered what I'd just read—a gripping and bizarre adventure of Irena Sertôrian embedded within a larger story of a nun in a futuristic convent under siege. As I contemplated that movement from the Sertôrian tale to the nun's frame story, and then followed that movement out to me sitting at my kitchen table reading, I had what I can only describe as a mystical experience.

What happened was this: As I sat at my table, manuscript in front of me, the room took on a shimmery, unstable sheen, like everything might just disappear around me. I felt such a profound sense of instability, in fact, that I had to grab the seat of my chair with both hands to anchor myself in place. That feeling of instability intensified into a primal terror, a certainty that my own existence was not as stable as I'd always believed it to be. A tingling sensation ran through my arms—was I having a heart attack?—and I fought back an urge to vomit. Flexing my fingers against the wood of the chair, I squeezed my eyes shut and hoped for the best.

Then, just as suddenly as the feeling had arrived, it passed.

The experience unsettled me for days, instilling in me an unshakable urge to return to the text. The following weekend, then, I sat down and read it again.

On the second time through, I found a more compelling explanation for why the novel might have affected me so powerfully a few nights earlier. How I'd missed it the first time, I'm not sure, but as I turned the pages of the manuscript, I saw—in this melancholy adventure of Irena Sertôrian—unmistakable shadows of my recent escapade with Sérgio and Harriet. Or I guess, since the manuscript was written decades before I was born, I saw in my own recent experiences shadows of *The Infinite Future*.

To be clear, I'm not talking exact parallels here—no "this person equals that person" kind of stuff. Instead, as you'll see soon enough, it's more the broad narrative strokes that overlap, as well as a smattering of more specific details that get chopped up and transmuted between one story and the other. Three travelers questing for an elusive prize, for instance, though the searchers themselves differ vastly from one story to the other. Or a shared interest in inconvenient religious histories, though again the details bear only a shadowy resemblance to one another.

You'd think I would have been more astonished by these fuzzy reflections than I was, but given the oracular weirdness of the rest of Salgado-MacKenzie's work, I would have been more surprised, honestly, if something like this *hadn't* happened. I'd been prepared for it, in fact, by one of his own stories, "A Metallic Flutter of Wings," in which the mad despot of a glassine cloud city proclaims that "there exists in the universe a finite, though vast, repertoire of narrative forms. Consequently, at this late stage in human history, the experience of every woman and man becomes a loose, unwitting translation of lives already lived and stories already told."

And so, this fragment of *The Infinite Future* functions (for this reader, at least) both as another charmingly strange tale by the elusive Eduard Salgado-MacKenzie and as a scrambled, anticipatory quasi-memoir of *my* life written by a trio of authors I have never—and will never—meet.

How could I resist?

Before I knew it, then, I had unearthed my multivolume Portuguese dictionary and was spending my evenings translating *The Infinite Future* into English.

Now, with the project complete, I'd like to be able to tell you that all the time I spent with this eerily reflective manuscript has helped me

understand my own life better, or even that my own experience illuminated, in some rare and valuable way, hidden nooks and crevices of *The
Infinite Future*. Instead, every time I tried reading the events described
in this translator's note as an uncanny iteration of Salgado-MacKenzie's
novel fragment (or vice versa), I felt like I was shooting at someone in a
Magic Mirror Maze, the multiplied images only confounding my aim
and leaving me dizzily vulnerable.

But that's enough from me. You'll be reading *The Infinite Future*
yourself in just a few pages, so I'll let you come to your own conclusions
about the book, and I'll use the rest of this translator's note—which has
already run much, much longer than I'd intended—to address a few con-
siderations that might interest you.

**First:** The Cooper siblings, though on board with the translation,
made it very clear that they didn't want to be bothered with questions about the manuscript's preparation. So I didn't bother them,
and all translation and editing decisions were made following my
own best judgment.

**Second:** I'm not a scientist, but it's clear to me that many details in
the story do not conform to accepted principles of astronomy,
physics, medicine, etc. Many of these departures don't seem especially deliberate, and I considered footnoting all the errors I could
catch, as I understand that many SF readers do care about the scientific principles at play in a story. Ultimately, though, it seemed un-
true to the spirit of the original work, which blazes proudly forward
through its delirious conjectures, treating all accepted wisdom as
mere inconvenience on the route to enlightenment. Annotating
such oversights felt like publicly correcting the false but harmless
utterances of a distinguished elderly relative.

**Third:** I've tried hard to recreate for you the experience of reading
the text in Portuguese, but it hasn't been easy. For reasons that

should make sense if you've read the preceding narrative, *The Infinite Future* doesn't always read like it was written by a native speaker. The syntax, usage, and presence of false cognates give the original Portuguese text the feel of a so-so translation from English, which made my job tricky, as I often felt like I was back-translating, even though strictly speaking I was not. How, then, to preserve that effect for you—the feel of a very Englishy Portuguese? I ultimately decided to embrace, and slightly enhance, the scholarly formality of the nun-narrator's prose style.

With all of that out of the way, then, you know as much as I do about the biography of Eduard Salgado-MacKenzie and the provenance of his strange, hubristic novel. Now I'll step aside and let the text speak for itself.

THE
INFINITE
FUTURE

· · ·

EDUARD
SALGADO-MACKENZIE

*Unfix'd yet fix'd,*
*Ever shall be, ever have been and are,*
*Sweeping the present to the infinite future,*
*Eidólons, eidólons, eidólons.*

— WALT WHITMAN, from "Eidólons"

# ONE

I was emptying rattraps in our convent's dusty undercroft when I heard the news of our impending destruction. Or rather, the rumors of our impending destruction, as the whispers of a Delegarchic death sentence had not yet been confirmed by Sister Kim, our chief communicant. One must always, I have learned, be skeptical of such unsubstantiated talk in a small, isolated community such as the one I occupy.

There was the time, for instance, when Sister Bilta mistakenly inferred from a bit of intercepted radio chatter that one of our sister convents on the other side of the galaxy had been beset by a scourge of Andromedan Bone Flu. Somehow, by the end of the day, half the convent was laboring under the mistaken impression that forces hostile to our order were systematically attacking our outposts throughout the galaxy with invidious biological weapons. The reality of the situation was that the almonatrix at our sister convent had contracted a mild case of food poisoning from an undercooked drumel egg, and Andromedan Bone Flu had never even entered the picture.

And so, when I heard that rogue Delegarchic forces intended to annihilate every last member of our order, I was understandably skeptical.

"But there was a teleprint," said Sister Aqueo, an excitable young novice who was on rattrap duty with me that morning. She'd just informed me of the terrible news, and I had responded with an incredulity that had dismayed her.

(By the way, we have no rats here in the convent, only moon-gophers that stowed away once in a poorly inspected shipment of barley we received from the farm planet of Bacchus II, and then multiplied like the tenacious vermin they are.)

"If there was a teleprint," said Sister Beatriz, also on rattrap duty, and my oldest friend here at the Astral Cenobium of Outer Hyperion, "then I'm sure Sister Kim will read it to us at vespers, whatever it might say."

We didn't have to wait until vespers, though, to receive confirmation of the rumor. When we ascended to the Greater Courtyard with our burlap sacks of rodent corpses, a flustered Sister Genoveva—normally so unflappable—breathlessly informed us that Sister Kim had convened an emergency meeting in the Chapter House, and our presence was required immediately.

We found the Council Room—the inner sanctum of the Chapter House—bustling with dozens of our sisters. Our arrival, in fact, brought the head count to forty-eight—in other words, every last person who lived in the convent. The room buzzed with anxious chatter, but when Sister Kim, standing on the Speaker's Platform at the room's exact center, saw we'd arrived, she lifted her hands above her head, and the entire Council of Forty-Eight fell instantly silent.

"Just a few hours ago," began Sister Kim gravely, "our convent teleprinter received a disturbing communication from the central governing offices of the Third Galactic Delegarchy. Under the pretense of protecting our safety, the communiqué requests that we vacate our convent, dissolve our order, and divest ourselves of all religious authority, effective immediately. The teleprint cites the threat of fundamentalist violence, such as the gruesome children's riot on Menelaus VII a few months ago and the recent and bloody uprising of a Pyuritic sect on Andromache II as a justification for the Delegarchs' so-called request. Using the politest of bureaucratic doublespeak, it further informs us that the Delegarchs have deployed military forces to 'aid us in complying with these requests.'"

Angry murmurs coursed across the room, but when Sister Kim again raised her hands, the murmurs ceased.

She continued: "Given the brazen and illegal government takeover last week by seven rogue Delegarchs, a takeover that left nineteen of their fellow lawmakers literally eviscerated on the floor of the OctoSenate and sent the remaining dozen into terrified hiding, as well as the unprecedented carnage that has lately beset our sister convents, we have no doubt that these troops are under orders to slay every last one of us."

More furious murmurs broke out, and this time Sister Kim did not try to quell them. With her news delivered, she ceded the Speaker's Platform, as per protocol, to whichever sister next chose to address the Council.

In some ways, Sister Kim's report should not have come as a shock. Our order represents a bothersome impediment to the rogue Delegarchs' final assumption of executive galactic powers, and for that reason we—both as a group and as individuals cannot be allowed to survive. This teleprint was merely a formality, a counterfeit proof of due diligence that these Delegarchs can later adduce to justify their atrocities to the acolytes of their new regime.

And so, with the truth of the morning's rumors thus established, we debated, following the anciently established parliamentary procedures of our order, how we might react to this veritable death sentence. I can reveal little of the discussion, given the vow of secrecy under which we operated in that room, but I can say that the Council unanimously decided that we should all continue in the work of our order—researching, experimenting, theorizing—until the approaching troops force us to stop.

What we do not know is when that might be. Our convent—a self-contained space station shaped like a spider gourd—is situated in an obscure corner of the galaxy, thirty days' journey from the nearest military outpost. If the rogue Delegarchs deployed the troops at the same time they sent the teleprint, then we have some time yet to live, maybe as much as a month. But if the Delegarchs deployed the troops preemptively, as may well be the case, armed forces could be knocking down our door at any moment.

The mood as we exited the Chapter House was an odd one, equal parts gloom and urgency. Sister Beatriz and I—Sister Aqueo was too distraught at the moment and had requested a few minutes alone in her quarters to collect herself—returned to the Great Courtyard to retrieve our hastily abandoned sacks of dead moon-gophers. As I hefted a pair of burlap bags over my shoulder, I considered the vast and frightening emotional terrain that had opened up within me. So overwhelming were my feelings that I couldn't even begin to express them to Sister Beatriz. And so the two of us walked in silence to the hall of waste disposal.

"Well Sister Úrsula," said Sister Beatriz after we'd emptied the bags into the astrochute. "I suppose we've no time to lose."

"No," I said. Wishing each other a good morning, we parted ways to work on our respective projects.

## TWO

As a student of history I understand the fleeting nature of any given way of life. What may seem to its occupants to be a state of unalterable stability will soon—in months, years, decades, or centuries—give way to chaos. Barbarian hordes will invade. Disease-ridden ships will arrive. Nuclear weapons will be deployed. When the way of life in question is my own, however, my perspective becomes markedly less academic.

It's been four days since the teleprint arrived, and you may well wonder what I've done with that precious time, representing, as it does, such a large portion of the truncated life I have left to live. I'm sorry to report that too many of those hours have been frittered away as I try to distract myself from such unpleasant questions as: *What if the troops arrive while I'm in the toilet?* Or: *Who will water my lykantos plant when I'm gone?* Or: *Does one feel the pain of a blast-gun shot before that shot causes one's death?*

(The answers, by the way: I die embarrassed. Nobody. And, according to Sister Yan, our resident trauma biologist, probably so.)

To keep these fears at bay, I've tried quantum meditation, jigsaw puzzles, pemlon stacking, gardening, nibo stretches, and painting. I've even tried doing research on my current project, but that only adds new worries to the already considerable existing ones. It appears that no matter what remedy I employ, my brain will continue to pester me with its grim and impertinent questions.

You may also be wondering, incidentally, why my comrades and I aren't preparing to defend our convent—or, better yet, to flee. Our rationale is complicated—partly ideological and partly pragmatic. The troops dispatched by the Delegarchs will not only vastly outnumber and outgun us but will also consist entirely of young people. Such has been the practice in warfare for millennia, the carcasses of a civilization's youth serving as gruesome prophylactics for the aged ruling classes in their perpetual battle against any and all threats to their own desperately held power. Our order believes that to fight against such youthful troops is to validate the logic of empire, and so—not in passivity but in protest— we lay down our weapons (so to speak; we don't actually have any weapons).

Though our decision not to physically resist the approaching troops is partly ideological, our decision not to flee is solely pragmatic. Our convent is located far from sympathetic ports—a deliberate choice made during peacetime and rendered inconvenient in dire moments such as this one. Long-distance transport vessels, while dramatically more available now than, say, in Irena Sertôrian's time, remain a rare commodity. Here at the convent we have a single long-range galaxy cruiser, capable of transporting no more than half a dozen people at once.

And while I can reveal very few specifics, I will say that the vessel is currently being put to very good use. Directly following the Council meeting four days ago, six of our number, whose particular disciplines equip them well for certain subversive activities, boarded the galaxy cruiser and, wishing us a teary farewell, embarked on a high-risk, top-secret assignment. As I write these words, our brave comrades should just be arriving at the first of three destinations where they will gather *matériel* for their upcoming operations.

Here at the convent, we've maintained no contact with the ship so that no record exists of their location, and I should tell you nothing more about this ongoing mission, except that when our order does take up arms, it will use them to strike directly at the heart of oppression.

My larger point is that the brave and needful actions of our six comrades stand in sharp contrast to my own frightened waffling. With the little time that remains, I could certainly produce *something* of value— something that might, in some small way, benefit humankind. As much as I'd like to move forward on such a project, though, I remain overwhelmed not only by the prospect of a violent and early death but also by the specter of certain personal matters that I've left unresolved for far too long.

# THREE

Over breakfast in the refectory this morning, I laid out my dilemma to Sister Beatriz: How should I spend the remaining weeks (or days, or minutes) of my mortality? She was doubly occupied already, with one hand scooping oatmeal into her mouth and the other scribbling calculations for her current project, a vortemathical experiment she's spent months designing. She paused, though, and looked up at me, regarding my nervous face with those sharp dark eyes of hers. Licking a trace of oatmeal from the corner of her lips, she leaned back in her chair, resting her face in the palm of her ink-smudged hand.

"You should do what you do best, Sister Úrsula," she said, pointing her spoon as if the answer had been sitting in front of me all along.

"And what would that be?" I said.

She'd taken another bite of oatmeal, and she shook her head at me while she swallowed.

"You're a brilliant historian," she said impatiently, "so what you need to do is write some history. Another one of your insightful monographs that so concisely illuminate the life and teachings of Irena Sertôrian. *That's* what you should do."

She punctuated this last sentence with an emphatic wave of her spoon, inadvertently flicking me with tiny gobs of oatmeal.

"Fine," I said, wiping the oatmeal bits from my blouse with the side of my thumb. "Let's pretend I even have something concise and insightful to say about Sertôrian at this point in my career. Even if I did—at a time like this, what would be the point? What good is yet another arcane bit of scholarship in the already bloated canon of Sertôrial studies?"

Reopening her notebook and picking up her pen, Sister Beatriz said that that was a question I would have to answer for myself. She started to write, lowering her head until a dark curtain of hair obscured her face, effectively bringing our conversation to a close.

The truth is, I've been in a rut, writing-wise, since long before the arrival of that fateful teleprint. I've been in a rut, in fact, ever since the explosive galactic success of my previous monograph, *Sertôrian the Woman*. With that text, I attempted to single-handedly counteract centuries of scholarship, which has treated Sertôrian not as a flesh-and-blood person but as a kind of metaphysical Holy Grail (to summon up a truly ancient myth), a vessel whose sole function is to convey grand spiritual truths to her yearning and thirsty disciples, a mere receptacle whose own pains, desires, struggles, and flaws merit not even the slightest consideration. Such approaches deny Sertôrian her basic humanity, and so to remedy this, my *Sertôrian the Woman* focused entirely on Sertôrian's historically verifiable biography, on the mundane details of her life. As you might imagine, my exclusion of any and all mystical elements from my treatment of Sertôrian caused no small controversy among scholars and worshippers alike, and in the ensuing fervor, I dug in my heels in defense of my approach, arguing so vehemently in favor of *Sertôrian the Woman* that I find myself unsure how to proceed with my next piece of scholarship.

You see, I've come to believe that I did, in fact, *slightly* overstate my case in *Sertôrian the Woman*. Ideally, I've concluded, any biography of Irena Sertôrian should no more exclude her mysticism than her often troubling humanity. However, so aggressive was the ire and vitriol of my detractors that to walk back the arguments I made in my previous book has felt too fraught, too much like surrender, to even consider. And so, for over a year now, I've been stuck.

As I consider this morning's conversation with Sister Beatriz, though, I realize that nothing more remains to me but scholarship. After all, the academic and religious backlash I might receive pales in comparison to the death sentence that looms over me and my comrades here at the convent. With the time I have left, then, I'll attempt to make the very argument that's so frightened me for the past year—an argument that examines Sertôrian's humanity not apart from but in conjunction with her sibylline identity. And to do so I turn to an unpopular little tale from the life of Sertôrian—the Rhadamanthus IX episode.

# FOUR

Truly valuable knowledge comes at a price. In most cases, discomfort may suffice. For instance, sacrificing hours of sleep to memorize the irregular verb forms of an ancient language. Or slogging through a noxious bog to observe the previously unstudied courtship rituals of a rare species of toad. In other instances, however, learning exacts an even higher toll in exchange for its precious fruits. Such is the case with our current study of the Rhadamanthus IX episode. For centuries, followers of Sertôrian chose to discount the tale as bogus rather than engage its spiny heart. I can't say I fault them.

Readers of this tale are confronted with a painfully human Sertôrian—less wise, less holy, less radically egalitarian than the sibylline figure now venerated by billions. In the Sertôrian of the Rhadamanthus IX episode, it can be achingly difficult to discern even the seeds of the post-Syndicate Sertôrian, who on four separate occasions was received into the unfathomable presence of the Infinite Eremites.

At the outset, then, let me make myself clear: I do not embark on this study for sensationalism's sake. By scrutinizing the Rhadamanthus IX episode, I have no desire to tarnish the legacy of Irena Sertôrian—only to burnish our understanding of her life and thinking. Though I've chosen to devote an entire monograph to the tale, I've done so less in admiration and more in the spirit of whatever impulse leads us to pick at scabs. Although that gives slightly the wrong impression of my motives. I certainly feel a curiosity, an inability to leave the Rhadamanthus IX episode alone, but unlike scab-picking, I hope my attentions will engender a better understanding of both Sertôrian the woman and Sertôrian the mystic.

(The more apt metaphor, I realize now, is that of the oyster who transforms irritating grit into a luminescent pearl.)

What I mean to say is, if you find the events examined in the following chapters disturbing, know that I do too and that this study examines them not in the spirit of sensationalism but of learning. With death fast approaching (faster for me, I imagine, than for you) one can't help but take stock of one's life and ask what that life has amounted to, what has given it significance. As a disciple of Sertôrian, I certainly seek meaning in her great spiritual triumphs—her many sermons and, of course, her Four Shrouded Visions—but at this time, I'm drawn even more to her disappointments and failures. Though I don't know what we might find by examining the catastrophe that is the Rhadamanthus IX episode, I suspect the difficulty of the path predicts the luminosity of the knowledge that awaits us.

A final note before we jump into the narrative itself: We'll be using Bombal's version of the Rhadamanthus IX episode, from her *Household Tales of Our Sertôrian*. I draw from this particular collection not only because it is the oldest one and thus the most historically proximate to the life of Sertôrian but also because it is lesser known to my contemporaries than Wilson's iconic and ubiquitous *Sertôrian's Travels*. I hope the use of a more obscure text will productively defamiliarize the story for those who grew up with the Wilson. For a further justification of this choice, I refer my audience to Gretchen Tidewater's excellent *This Vast Canopy: A Re-Evaluation of Bombal*.

And now, to the narrative:

• • •

Inside their rain-pelted tent, the only human refuge in all the vast and muddy Plains of Chubbúhc, Captain Irena Sertôrian lay on her cot contemplating the possibility that her two surviving crew members—Star-Guard Ava Valenti and Technician Seventh Grade Ernst de Bronk—might soon betray her.

She had never worried about mutiny from these two before. As much as they might abuse each other, squabbling like siblings, de Bronk and Valenti each remained intensely loyal to Sertôrian. But earlier this morning, on completing her turn at the watch, she'd reentered the tent to find Valenti and de Bronk in a flat-out brawl, pummeling each other with near-death blows on the canvas floor. In an act of open defiance, they'd ignored her orders to stop fighting immediately, opting instead to continue punching each other until Sertôrian had zapped them both with a specimen stunner from the field bio-kit. Aside from the inherent ugliness of their messy infighting, the insubordination of Valenti and de Bronk had hinted at dangerous emotions in Sertôrian's two shipmates that could trump their longstanding loyalty to her.

This deterioration was in keeping with the general trajectory of their sojourn here on Rhadamanthus IX, which had so far been a dispiriting parade of failure and humiliation. They'd been forced to land on this hostile planet when the *Circe's* temperamental thrust system had caught fire. They'd managed an emergency landing—just barely—but the moment they'd disembarked from the ship, an armed cadre of guards had taken them captive and thrown them into a clammy prison block, where they'd been tortured to no apparent purpose for three long days.

Finally, though, on the evening of the third day, Sertôrian had been brought before the planet's ruler, a sandy-haired despot who styled himself the Arch-Kaiser Glenn Harrison. He'd told Sertôrian that the situation was a simple one—he would hang on to their ship (effectively preventing them from leaving the planet) until Sertôrian and her shipmates could bring him the Bulgakov Apparatus, which he believed to be hidden somewhere in the unsettled wilds of his planet.

More than a little taken aback by this demand, Sertôrian had asked if he was referring to *the* Bulgakov Apparatus—that legendary, long-lost piece of technology that was rumored to grant its possessor unimaginable, godlike powers.

"That's the one," the Arch-Kaiser had said.

"The same Bulgakov Apparatus that's been lost for centuries?" Sertôrian had asked. "The same Bulgakov Apparatus that may never have existed in the first place?"

"It exists," the Arch-Kaiser had said. "And if you and your shipmates ever want to leave this planet alive, you will bring it to me."

If she hadn't been tied to a chair, Sertôrian would have walked away at that point. Given her limited range of options, though, she'd agreed to the Arch-Kaiser's terms. He'd outfitted them with the necessary equipment, and then bestowed upon them the blinking Green Beacon, an ancient artifact he'd claimed to have recovered on a recent archaeological dig.

"If I've correctly interpreted the glyphs on the outer casing," he'd told Sertôrian, "you just need to take the Green Beacon to the lowest point of the Plains of Chubbúhc and wait. And from there, the Beacon will lead the way to"—he'd lowered his voice with an unfailing instinct for melodrama—"*the Bulgakov Apparatus.*"

Unfortunately, a month into their sojourn on the wet and dreary Plains of Chubbúhc, the Green Beacon had refused to do anything more than blink.

It would be an understatement to say that morale within the little party was grim. Valenti and de Bronk were constantly at each other's throats, and Sertôrian—currently lying supine on her cot—felt stymied by their situation's smothering torpor. She had a creeping sense that if she couldn't turn things around soon, all three of them would die here.

What they needed, what Sertôrian's leadership thrived on, was a change in the status quo.

That change came as de Bronk, out on watch duty, reentered

the tent, his elderly, wrinkled face creased even more than usual in consternation.

Sertôrian sat up in her cot.

"It's raining maggots out there," said de Bronk, wiping the mud from his boots on their improvised doormat.

"What?" said Sertôrian.

"Maggots," said de Bronk, pointing back at the door. "They're falling from the sky."

"That's impossible," said Valenti, looking up from cleaning her binoculars at the folding camp table.

De Bronk picked up a tin mug from the table, leaned over, and held it outside the tent. A few moments later, he pulled in his arm. With a smirk, he handed the mug to Valenti. She set down her binoculars and peered inside. The freshly gathered rainwater teemed with flailing maggots.

"Well?" said de Bronk.

Rain drummed down on the canvas roof of the tent.

"Valenti?" said Sertôrian.

"They do look like maggots, Captain," she said with great reluctance.

"Get moving then," said Sertôrian, springing up from her cot.

The demeanors of Valenti and de Bronk transformed instantly. With an obvious crisis before them, their murderous petulance dissolved into a high-caliber professionalism. The three shipmates gathered in formation at the front of the tent and Sertôrian pulled open the door flap.

They stared in wonder at the scene before them. The surrounding field crawled with maggots, and as the rain fell, the tiny, writhing figures multiplied, creating a soggy carpet of speckled white over the formerly muddy ground.

Sertôrian's momentary relief at the change in the status quo gave way immediately to the pressing concerns of the moment. So maggots were, in fact, falling from the sky. Never mind the absurdity of it—what dangers might ensue? Although no immediate threat presented itself, Sertôrian began formulating a plan of action.

"We need to establish a perimeter around the tent," she said. "If the maggots start getting inside—"

"I don't think they want to come inside," said Valenti.

And Valenti was right; even though maggots now covered the ground like snowdrifts, not one of them had entered the tent. Looking out over the field, Sertôrian found herself transfixed by the concerted movement of the white masses of larvae. They were, if anything, crawling away from the open door flap. As each maggot hit the ground it moved in concert with its fellows toward a single point—the flashing Green Beacon that the Arch-Kaiser had sent with them.

Barely breathing, Sertôrian and her crew watched the maggots converge on the green flashing light and, clinging to one another, envelop the beacon until it disappeared within an undulating mound of glistening larvae. The mound grew and grew and grew until the surrounding field was devoid of the white drifts of maggots that had formerly covered it. The resulting mass—a living boulder—squirmed within itself, the collective sound of so many tiny movements generating a soft wet sucking noise.

Then, out of the indistinct lump, a shape began to form. The boulder elongated itself into a vertical pillar over two meters tall before sprouting four symmetrical branches.

"A body," said Valenti. "It's turning into a body."

Even as she said it, the figure became more distinct, the branches resolving themselves into arms and legs, the top of the pillar forming a head, the writhing, larval surface becoming a horrible simulacrum of muscles, tendons, and sinews. The mass of maggots now resembled an upright cadaver stripped of its skin, its muscles bleached an awful, gleaming white. A faint green glow, the only trace of the Beacon, blinked like a heartbeat from inside the figure's trunk.

With uncanny fluidity, the maggot creature turned its head to the left and then to the right. It flexed one arm then the other, bent its left leg then its right. Then, after beckoning to the crew with a squirming hand, the figure turned its body toward the distant Rathdrum Mountains and started to walk. Sertôrian, Valenti, and de Bronk stood motionless in the open doorway of the tent.

"What's the word, Captain?" said de Bronk.

"Break camp," said Sertôrian. "We follow the maggot man."

## FIVE

t's at night that I feel most acutely the stark isolation of our convent. I've just awoken (from a nightmare, as it happens) and though the night is far from over (several hours remain until the call for lauds will pull my sleeping comrades—fuzzy-eyed and yawning—out of their warm beds, out of their snug quarters and into the perpetually under-heated Chamber of Contemplation), I fear that further sleep will elude me, the sharp terror of my dream having flushed the slumber from my pulsing veins.

Though many specters flit at the edge of my consciousness, I'm especially haunted at this midnight hour by an inner vision of the sinister spacecraft that holds our callow executioners in its metal belly, bringing them closer and closer to our convent with each breath I take. Will they arrive on a night like this, I wonder, with my sisters and me at our most vulnerable, already reposing in that semi-death that is sleep? Even as I wonder, I can see it in my mind's eye: armored troops kicking in the sturdy doors of our private quarters, shooting us down as we groggily rise to the noise, our lives ending before we've determined if the sudden commotion is dream or reality.

Troubling as this vision is, though, it was not the subject of my nightmare, at least not directly.

In my dream, I was sitting at an old wooden desk in the convent library reading an oversized leather-bound manuscript whose pages were filled with exquisite symbols, the meanings of which I was entirely unable to decipher. They seemed important, though, so I was giving the book my full attention, searching for any linguistic toehold to give me purchase on the text's slippery face. To this end, I was flipping from page to page with an increasing sense of urgency when I felt a gentle but distinct tap on my shoulder.

"Just a moment, please," I said, engrossed as I was by the task at hand.

But my interrupter disregarded the request and tapped me again, more firmly this time. I was about to turn around with a mild rebuke, when a chill ran through my body. I knew suddenly, without quite knowing how, that the person behind me was no person at all, was instead some otherworldly being.

I ignored a third tap on my shoulder and realized with dismay that the library's only exit, which moments before had been directly in front of me, had vanished.

My fear only increased when a voice behind me, more terrible for its beauty, whispered, "You need to turn around. You need to look at what I hold."

I did not turn around, and so the figure behind me reached forward, the cool, papery skin of its cheek brushing against my face as it set a book down on the desk before me. Gone was the leather-bound manuscript, and in its place was a small, enchantingly assembled codex, its cover an intricately tooled leaf of platinum, its pages edged with shining black ink.

"Open the book," said the voice, less gently this time, but still I refused.

Curiously, I found I desperately wanted to open the book, but at the same time I feared its contents. Hands folded in my lap, then, I stared down at the codex, its cover gleaming.

"The book is yours," said the voice, and then a third time commanded: "Open it."

And still I refused. Behind me, the figure groaned mightily, and in an unsettling turn, I understood that my refusal, and not this visitor's command, was the truly monstrous act. Before I could amend my decision, though, a hand shot out from behind me, snatching away the beautiful book. I gave a cry of pain and awoke in my bed, my soul beset by an unsettling blend of horror and regret.

I recognize that in its retelling, this dream loses its ghastly edges. That is, in part, why I've just written it down. Though some dread lingers, my terror has largely dissipated, because, as Sertôrian teaches us in an often overlooked passage from the Bellerophon Sermon, "to recount a dream is to render it benign, for our dreams evade even the most basic narrative logic, and by so doing, shuck off the great ordering principles of the universe." In other words, a dream can't truly be recounted, only replaced with a tidier, less threatening narrative that only broadly approximates the dream, ultimately undercutting its bizarre formidability.

The boundlessness of dreams and visions is a theme that slithers between the lines of much of Sertôrian's sibyllic teachings, a preoccupation that raises a pressing question among believers and nonbelievers alike: how to account for Sertôrian's transformation from the pragmatic, no-nonsense captain of a warship to the mystical figure who, immediately following her trial before the Syndics of Mars, experienced the first of her breathtaking Four Shrouded Visions.

As it happens, three strange dreams lie at the heart of this chapter's selection from the Rhadamanthus IX narrative, dreams that a handful of pseudo-scholars have touted as marking the essential transitional moment between Sertôrian the ship captain and Sertôrian the sibyl. I must confess, however, that the three dreams you'll read about in this chapter fail to satisfy me as explanative precursors to the unwieldy and empyrean Four Shrouded Visions. Although some scholars treat the three dreams as if they should disturb or upset the reader, I find them overly neat. Where is their chaos? Where is their splendor? True, they contain spatial and temporal shifts typical of dream states, as well as certain striking images, but on the whole the reading experience is a decidedly straightforward one.

Contrast that with the experience of reading Sertôrian's reports of the Four Shrouded Visions. Though she insisted these accounts failed to capture even a fraction of the visions' resplendence, Sertôrian's radical yet lucid deployment of language manages to convey at least some of the destabilizing grandeur of her sibylline dream-voyage through the realm of the Infinite Eremites. Her accounts simultaneously invite us to learn from the Infinite Eremites and to understand that the Infinite Eremites will always evade our understanding, that they can only be seen, as it were, from the corner of the eye.

I must tell you, though—and this is something I'm loath to reveal to my sisters of the Order—reading Sertôrian's accounts of the Four Shrouded Visions never fails to unsettle me. And yes, I understand that that's their purpose, but if I'm being completely honest with myself (and with you), I must acknowledge that I'm of two minds regarding the tendency of visions and dreams to destabilize and upset.

For example, when I'm sitting at my favorite desk with the sun slanting in through the convent windows, and my life is following its relatively happy and stable course, I am fascinated, even delighted, by the disruptive power of dreams. If my surroundings are not so bright, though, if my head is not so clear, if I'm sitting up in bed in my dark room as I am right now with a tightness in my chest and the long fingers of a nightmare still troubling the pools of my mind, I say dreams are brutish, nasty things. Sleep offers us the illusion of escape from the cares of the waking world. How cruel, then, when those cares follow us into our repose, their teeth growing ever sharper as they do so.

But if narrative can defang a dream, the rigors of scholarship might put a bullet between its greedy, yellow eyes. And so while I wait for sleep—or armed Delegarchic forces—to arrive, we'll turn our attention back to the Rhadamanthus IX narrative, rejoining Sertôrian, Valenti, and de Bronk as they follow the maggot man into the shadowy groves of the Declo Forest.

·  ·  ·

Sertôrian woke just before dawn in the middle of the Declo Forest, her blanket-top wet with dew, her body sore from sleeping across a gnarled tree root. The night before, she'd been so tired that she hadn't bothered to find a comfortable patch of ground; she'd lain down right where she'd stood and fallen asleep immediately. Now, after what passed for a night's rest these days, she propped herself up on her elbows to take stock of the situation. Valenti and de Bronk lay on either side of her, still sleeping. A few yards in front of them, the maggot creature stood perfectly still, waiting for the sunrise.

This had been the routine for the past three days: While the planet's sun shone, the maggot man led them on a relentless march deeper and deeper into the wilderness of Rhadamanthus IX. As soon as the sun went down, though, the maggot man froze in place, granting Sertôrian, Valenti, and de Bronk a much-needed respite until the sun rose again the next morning.

All this walking, Sertôrian supposed, was not entirely a bad thing. If nothing else, it left Valenti and de Bronk with very little energy for bickering or mutiny. Although if that was the silver lining to this situation, then this cloud was a dark one indeed.

During the years they'd spent stuck here in the Minoan System searching for a way back home, Sertôrian and her crew had experienced scores of misadventures, ranging from the inconvenient (the time they'd accidentally ingested a lenticular sleeping draught and slumbered away a week of their lives on chilly Sarpedon IV) to the deadly (the time a Gracchan potentate had locked Sertôrian and each member of her crew inside a separate hanging razor casket and left them all to die). Somehow, though, none of those episodes had felt as dire as this one.

In the past she'd been driven not only by a need to survive but also by a sense of possibility, a sense that if they could just make it out of whatever scrape they currently found themselves in, then better, happier times lay waiting beyond the horizon. But the recent bruising months—in which three-fourths of her crew had died in mishap after grisly mishap—had put an end to that optimism. This mission to find the Bulgakov Apparatus felt like the end of the line, like Sertôrian's last chance, although to do what, she couldn't quite say. To make it back home with some semblance of a crew still remaining? To acquit herself of her recent leadership blunders? To simply not die? Who could say? All she knew was that she woke up each morning now with the acid tang of failure at the back of her throat.

This morning was no different. She took a swig from her canteen, trying—unsuccessfully—to wash down the taste, and wondered how much goodwill remained in Valenti and de Bronk. They'd followed her and the maggot man this far, if not with a heartening esprit de corps then at least without complaint. Sertôrian knew, though, that this compliance wouldn't last forever. Each day that the maggot man didn't lead them to some concrete token of the Bulgakov Apparatus's existence was a day that saw the further erosion of her shipmates' confidence in her leadership. And once that confidence eroded away completely, there was no telling what might happen.

As she contemplated this state of affairs, the sky grew lighter, and Sertôrian stood up, shaking out her blanket and then folding it into a compact parcel. Awakened by the sounds of her movements, Sertôrian's shipmates stirred to life, greeting one another with bleary salutations and hurriedly consuming their morning rations. They all packed up their sparse gear, loaded it onto their backs, and approached the maggot creature. Their mood in doing so was one of resignation, of mechanical willingness to walk behind this gruesome figure for hours on end, because what else could they do?

Drawing closer to their guide, however, they saw that something had changed. Usually, even in repose, the maggot creature's flesh squirmed constantly, animated by the writhing larval bodies that constituted its being. Sometime during the night, however, the creature's flesh had gone brittle and stiff, its terrible luster fading to a dull shade of yellow.

Sertôrian could feel the morning's bile reasserting itself in her throat as every instinct she possessed told her that this change in the maggot man would only complicate their situation further. Before she and her crew could fully react to this development, though, the sun inched its way up past the horizon, and the maggot creature, rather than striding immediately forward as it had every morning previous, began to violently tremble.

"Hit the ground," said Sertôrian, her battle instincts kicking in.

The three of them dropped with soldierly precision, and as they did so, a wave of tiny crackles tore through the maggot man. Then, with a deafening buzz, their erstwhile guide exploded into a swarm of newborn flies.

With a terrible drone—the sound of apocalypse if Sertôrian had ever heard it—the dense cloud of flies descended on the three shipmates, who tried in vain to simultaneously cover their noses and their ears against possible invasion. Tiny probing legs tickled every inch of Sertôrian's exposed skin, and it was only with great effort that she resisted the nearly overpowering urge to swat at them, to shoo them away. To do so, she recognized, would leave her face entirely undefended, and it didn't take much imagination to picture thousands of flies swarming into her nose, filling her lungs, suffocating her struggling body from the inside out and then laying their eggs in her vanquished carcass.

With that vision sharp in her mind, then, Sertôrian kept her mouth and nose tightly covered.

She held fast in that position, and just when the tickling of thousands of tiny feet against her exposed skin was becoming almost unbearable, the flies dispersed, lifting off from the shipmates' bodies and dissipating into the misty morning air of the Declo Forest.

Cautiously, Sertôrian, Valenti, and de Bronk rose from their defensive crouches. A few stray flies described erratic paths in the air before them, but otherwise the clearing was still. The Green Beacon, former heart of the maggot creature, lay blinking like a distant star on the leaf-strewn ground.

Sertôrian took a deep breath. During that unexpected entomological bombardment, the sense of failure and desperation she'd felt upon awakening that morning had been replaced by an even stronger sense of failure and desperation. Her two shipmates looked at her expectantly.

"What now?" said de Bronk.

For a moment, Sertôrian ignored the question. Resisting the daunting call of leadership, she focused instead on the smell of pine, on the far-off chatter of a squirrel, on the mist still clinging to the trunks of ghostly aspens.

"Captain?" said Valenti, adjusting her pack.

Sertôrian looked at her shipmates. Couldn't they just give their captain a much-needed rest? Perhaps if she remained completely still, Valenti and de Bronk would eventually wander off to sort out the situation for themselves. But even as she stood there, not responding, she could see the malaise of the Plains of Chubbúhc creeping back into their features.

No, they needed her firm direction. That much was clear.

Sertôrian said, "The maggot man or the Green Beacon or whatever's calling the shots here brought us to this clearing by design. So what we're going to do is establish a grid and search for our next clue until we find it. Right?"

"Right," said Valenti and de Bronk, and they all started combing the area for clues.

In all honesty, Sertôrian had trouble believing that the Bulgakov Apparatus even existed, let alone that it might be hidden somewhere here on Rhadamanthus IX. Given their dismal situation, however, she couldn't afford the luxury of skepticism. She needed the Bulgakov Apparatus to exist because delivering it to the Arch-Kaiser was the only way they would ever get off this wretched planet alive. And so they would root around in the dirt of this clearing all day and all night if necessary, until they found some sign—or something they could construe as a sign—pointing them toward the fabled Apparatus.

Much to Sertôrian's surprise, though, their search was rewarded almost instantly.

As Valenti bent down to retrieve the blinking Green Beacon, she found just beside it, buried in some leaves, a sturdy metal handle helpfully labeled "OPEN," with an arrow indicating which way to turn it.

"Captain," she said, pointing to the handle.

"Well," said Sertôrian. "Let's see what we have here."

She pulled her trenching tool from her pack, and Valenti and de Bronk followed suit. Working quickly, the shipmates cleared away the shrubbery that surrounded the metal handle, uncovering with a bit of digging a heavy steel door the size of a small coffin.

"The Bulgakov Apparatus," said de Bronk. "It's inside there, I can feel it."

Valenti—a staunch disbeliever in the existence of the Apparatus—shot him an acid glance and was about to say something when Sertôrian intervened.

"Stand back," said Sertôrian. "I'm going to open it."

De Bronk and Valenti, setting their quarrel on the back burner, took several precautionary paces away from the metal door.

"Ready?" said Sertôrian.

"Ready," said Valenti and de Bronk.

Sertôrian squatted down a couple of feet from the edge of the door, maintaining as much distance from it as possible. She had no idea what they might find beneath the door, but any risk, she had decided, was preferable to the deadly stasis that had beset them on the Plains of Chubbúhc. And so, leaning forward, she turned the handle. From there, the door opened under its own power with a hydraulic hiss, and out of the ground, amidst a cloud of fog, arose a pristine glass box.

Sertôrian stepped instinctively back. Standing shoulder to shoulder with her crew, she looked on in wonder as the contents of the box slowly revealed themselves.

"Wait," said de Bronk once the fog had fully cleared. "What?"

Inside the box, resting on fluted pedestals, were three frosted cakes: one pink, one beige, and one brown.

The three shipmates drew in close, leaning toward the box, resembling pilgrims before a holy relic, their lips parted in wonder and admiration. The cakes looked freshly baked, no more than a few hours old, the shiny frosting barely set. Atop each cake, in vivid white icing, someone had written, "DAY ONE," "DAY TWO," and "DAY THREE," respectively.

"The fabled Bulgakov Apparatus," said Valenti, but if de Bronk caught the sarcasm, he chose to ignore it.

"No," he said. "It's the next clue—the next step." His face was pressed against the glass. "We're supposed to eat the cakes."

"I'm not eating that," said Valenti, standing up straight and backing away from the box.

Normally, Sertôrian would have sided with the star-guard. Eating the cake presented too great a risk—they had no idea what effect it might have on them, and furthermore, this mission to find the Bulgakov Apparatus (or whatever they were being led to) remained subordinate to their greater goal of escaping the planet and trying to find a way home. It wouldn't do to have the cake compromise or even kill them.

That said, the Green Beacon hadn't led them astray so far. (Or maybe it had, but in any event, the time they'd spent on this dreary planet had sapped from Sertôrian the initiative required to come up with a better plan of her own.)

"Star-Guard Valenti," she said. "Run a sample of that first cake."

"Captain?" she said.

"You heard me," said Sertôrian.

With a you-know-best shrug, Valenti unsheathed her field knife and gingerly cut a narrow wedge from the pink DAY ONE cake. As she fished the bio-tester from her pack and dropped the bit of cake into the specimen drawer, Sertôrian and de Bronk sat down on the nearby trunk of a fallen tree. Valenti's bio-tester whirred to life, and a moment later a slip of paper emerged from its face. Valenti read the results aloud: "Grain flour, dairy product, egg, sodium bicarbonate, acid salt, sugar, strawberry."

"But that's just a normal cake," said de Bronk with dismay.

Valenti returned the bio-tester to her pack and handed the paper containing the results to her incredulous shipmate.

"There was nothing else?" said Sertôrian, taking the paper from de Bronk and confirming the results herself. "Did you test the frosting?"

Valenti sat down next to Sertôrian on the trunk of the fallen tree.

"I tested the cake *and* the frosting," she said.

Sertôrian handed the test results back to Valenti and gazed into the thick forest in front of them. Pine trees stood tall and dark, towering over quaking stands of aspens. A few birds flitted from tree to tree emitting irregular, nervous chirps. A rabbit emerged from the undergrowth, eyes wide, and darted to the safety of a clump of bushes.

After spending a few minutes pretending to think things over, Sertôrian said, "We'll eat the cake."

The truth was, the bio-test had been a mere formality; she'd made up her mind before Valenti had even run the sample. What other viable options did they have but to eat the cake?

Valenti said, "With all due respect, Captain, that's a very bad idea."

Even de Bronk looked markedly less gung-ho about the proposition than he had when the box had first surfaced, the implications of eating this centuries-old mystery cake having no doubt caught up with him.

Sertôrian stood from the fallen tree. Unsheathing her field knife, she opened the glass case and cut the pink DAY ONE cake into three equal pieces.

"Here," she said, handing a third each to Valenti and de Bronk, who received their shares with looks of mild alarm.

"Eat," she said, pointing at the cake slices with the tip of her knife.

Valenti and de Bronk looked down dubiously at the pink-frosted wedges in their hands.

With her own third of the cake, Sertôrian wandered to the edge of the clearing and, after an exploratory nibble, ate the entire piece. It tasted wonderful—springy and sweet, its smooth savor overpowering that acrid bitterness that had clung to the back of her throat all morning.

Sertôrian licked the frosting from her fingers and wondered what, if anything, would happen now. Paying close attention to her body, on high alert for even the slightest effect, she felt nothing. And then more nothing.

Sertôrian turned around to look at her shipmates and saw that their cake, too, was gone.

"Anything?" she said.

"No," said de Bronk.

"No," said Valenti. "I feel fine."

The cake had to serve *some* purpose, but after standing at the edge of the clearing for an uneventful half hour, Sertôrian grew doubtful. Unsure what else to do, she ordered her crew to set up camp. Working silently, the three of them spread and anchored their tarp next to the box of cakes, dug a shallow fire pit, hung their bag of remaining rations from a tree branch, and inventoried the meager gear in their packs. They filled their canteens at a nearby spring then set about the routine tasks that had been left undone during their days of marching—polishing their boots, mending rips in their clothing, cleaning their equipment.

Periodically Sertôrian asked, "Anything going on yet?" and every time, Valenti and de Bronk answered in the negative. By evening, an all too familiar fug of resentment and despair had beset the shipmates, and they ate their evening rations around the stinking chem-fire in qualmy silence.

It wasn't until after dinner, when the three of them went to bed, that something strange finally happened.

That night, Sertôrian dreamed for the first time since before the war. For years, her sleeping hours had passed with resolute blankness, but tonight a vivid scene filled the stage of her mind.

She stood in a dry, grassy field, the sun overhead bleaching the color from the sky and soaking her body with arid heat. Shielding her eyes against the light, Irena saw a figure approaching from a long way off. As the figure drew closer, Irena remembered that she'd had an appointment with this mystery person. How lucky it was, then, that she happened to be here. She would have been so embarrassed to have broken her commitment.

Relieved that she hadn't, Irena watched the figure come nearer and nearer until she could see that it was her older sister, Rosa, dressed in the same dusty jeans and ratty undershirt she'd always worn during their childhood forays into the red Martian desert where they grew up. Her face was older, though, older than Irena had ever seen it, beset by the incipient looseness of late middle age.

Rosa stopped a few feet in front of her. Irena wanted to hug her sister but felt a restraining impulse; a hug would not be appropriate to the business they were about to conduct.

"I've missed you," said Rosa.

"I've missed you too," said Irena.

But Rosa shook her head.

"We haven't spoken for years, though," she said accusingly.

"I know that," said Irena. "And I'm sorry. But it wasn't on purpose. We just led very different lives."

"We didn't talk for years," said Rosa, shaking her head more forcefully.

"But we can talk now," said Irena.

"No," said Rosa, still shaking her head.

"Yes," said Irena, feeling more and more panicked. This meeting wasn't going like she'd hoped it would. "We can talk right now."

"No," said Rosa. "No."

Her head shook violently back and forth.

Then she said, "There's something I need to do."

Rosa reached up with both hands and held the sides of her own head until it stopped shaking back and forth, until it was perfectly still.

"There's something I need to do," she said again and put her right hand inside her mouth.

"What are you doing?" said Irena.

Ignoring her, Rosa opened her mouth even wider and shoved her hand in farther—it was in there up to the wrist—and then her jaw slung down, almost like a snake's, and with a bone-crunching contortion she reached the whole arm down her own throat until it was buried up to the shoulder, her head turned sharply to the side, her arm at a sickening angle.

"No," said Irena. "You don't need to do this. What I need is the Bulgakov Apparatus. Can you help me find it?"

Rosa eyed her pleading sister with undisguised contempt, her arm twitching as it rummaged around inside her torso. Irena wanted to look away but somehow she couldn't. For one thing, she knew Rosa wouldn't let her. But Irena also knew that, for some reason, she needed to watch what was going to happen.

"Rosa," said Irena.

In response, Rosa, with a short, sharp tug of her right arm, extracted from within herself her stomach, turned sloppily inside out. She threw the dripping mass at Irena's feet, and by the same crunching, contortive process, removed the rest of her insides, from her liver and spleen to her heart and intestines.

Irena looked down at the pile of shining viscera, still warm from her sister's body.

"Is this the Bulgakov Apparatus?" she said.

Rosa took a step closer, and with a probing thumb, popped out her own left eye, and then her right. Then she yanked dripping orbs free of their optic nerves and threw them onto the pile.

Growing more and more desperate, Irena said, "I need to find the Bulgakov Apparatus, Rosa. Do you know where it is?"

Taking another step closer, Rosa pulled her tongue from her mouth and set it in the palm of her left hand.

"You want to know where the Bulgakov Apparatus is?" said the flopping tongue in Rosa's hand.

"Yes," said Irena.

Rosa clenched her hand into a fist, silencing the tongue.

"No," said Irena. "Please."

Rosa threw the lifeless tongue onto the viscid pile of organs and walked away into the bright white heat. As she did so, the fabric of the dream rotted away, leaving Sertôrian fully awake again, firmly back in reality. The sun, she could tell, was just about to creep over the horizon.

During those first moments of consciousness, the dream she'd just had felt supremely important—she needed to discuss it with de Bronk and Valenti immediately—but as the sun rose, filling the clearing with soft light, that sense of importance gave way to an intense and perplexed embarrassment. She had felt certain as she'd woken up that the dream had been a product of the cake she'd eaten the day before, but if that were the case, what was she supposed to make of it? The dream had been so strange yet so useless, bringing her no closer to the Bulgakov Apparatus, leaving her with no clue as to how they might proceed.

As the rising sun woke Valenti and de Bronk, Sertôrian shook off the last scraps of nocturnal uneasiness and assumed an assured attitude of command.

Still, though, so many questions remained, and thus, while they ate their meager breakfast by the warmth of a chem-fire, Sertôrian asked Valenti and de Bronk if they had experienced any noticeable effects from eating the cake.

"No," said Valenti.

"No," said de Bronk.

Probing more directly, she asked how they had slept the night before.

"Fine," said Valenti.

"No complaints," said de Bronk.

Still lacking a better plan, they spent the day searching the area around their camp for any additional clues that might point them in whatever direction the makers of the Green Beacon intended them to go. They found a hollow tree, but there was nothing hidden inside of it. They found a cluster of granite boulders—could they form an arrow, a glyph, a compass rose?—but on careful inspection, the arrangement appeared completely natural. They also, not far from the boulders, nearly walked right through a patch of stinging hemlock, but Valenti spotted the distinctive flower clusters just in time. Other than that, it was standard forest as far as the eye could see.

When late afternoon rolled around, they returned to camp, the stagnation already turning Valenti and de Bronk vicious again. They'd sniped at each other all morning, and now, sitting at opposite ends of the fallen tree trunk behind the cake box, they glowered at each other with undisguised malice.

Trying to keep the focus on the task at hand, Sertôrian opened the chilled glass box and, as she had with the strawberry cake the day before, divided the vanilla DAY TWO cake into three equal pieces. She felt again the impulse to eat alone, so she walked to the edge of their campsite, her share of the cake cradled in her hands. Once again, it was delicious and once again Sertôrian ate her entire piece. She dusted the crumbs from her fingers and savored the taste in her mouth for another moment or two before she and her crew continued their surveying while they still had some daylight.

Eventually dusk fell and Sertôrian's mind returned to the previous night's dream, the haunting unease creeping through her body. Again, she felt an impulse to bring it up with Valenti and de Bronk, to see what they might make of the strange, imagined encounter she'd had with her sister, but again, discretion prevailed and she said nothing. When the time came to turn in for the night, Sertôrian lay between her shipmates, wrapped tightly in her blanket, resisting sleep.

She didn't last long.

In her second night's dream she relived with horrifying fidelity her vision of the previous night, beginning with Rosa's bitter accusations and ending with her gleaming innards sitting in a pile at Irena's feet.

She woke lying perfectly still on her back, every muscle in her body tightly clenched, the sky above her gray with predawn light.

The second day passed much as the first one had, with a lackadaisical reconnaissance of the area, and a lack of any apparent effects from eating the cake. Sertôrian worried as they tromped through the Declo Forest that their time here would become nothing more than a less-rainy sequel to their sojourn on the Plains of Chubbúhc. How long would they have to wait here, she wondered, before the next move became apparent, assuming a next move even existed? And how much longer would it be before Valenti and de Bronk would be—quite literally—at each other's throats again?

That afternoon, Sertôrian cut up the third and final cake, observing the same solitary ritual of the previous two days and eating her portion at the edge of the campsite, looking off into the forest. Today's was the best of the bunch, a rich chocolate cake with a bittersweet frosting that Sertôrian relished.

Earlier that day, she'd wondered aloud if they needed to eat all three cakes before the intended effect would kick in. Valenti and de Bronk had both allowed that this could be the case, although they hadn't sounded too convinced. Sertôrian wasn't too convinced herself, and she understood as she ate the last of her chocolate cake that if something didn't happen soon to point them in the right direction the onus was on her to fix things somehow.

By dinnertime, though, nothing had happened. Sitting around a chem-fire, the three shipmates chewed thoughtfully on their night's rations, Sertôrian growing more and more uneasy. Night had fallen and darkness hugged the small circle of light cast by the fire. A small moth circled nearer and nearer to the flickering flames, until an incautious dive brought it too close to the heat and the fire consumed its papery body.

"This reminds me of the night Berezhnoy died," said Valenti.

*Why bring that up now*, Sertôrian wondered.

Lieutenant Anton Berezhnoy had been her third-in-command, an amiable giant of a man with an encyclopedic knowledge of galactic imperial military history.

"How so?" said de Bronk, sounding inexplicably annoyed.

"The waiting," said Valenti. "The waiting for him to come back, and then him not coming back. We were sitting around a fire, remember?"

"No," said de Bronk, his voice rising. "There was no fire."

"There was," said Valenti, with condescending patience.

"No," said de Bronk. "There wasn't. And he didn't die at night."

"There was definitely a fire," said Valenti.

She and de Bronk were standing now, fists clenched, teeth bared.

Wearily intervening, Sertôrian said, "There was no fire, Valenti."

"I remember a fire," said Valenti with a growl.

Sertôrian said, "Berezhnoy was stabbed on Catreus V, and it was too hot on Catreus V to ever build a fire."

Though she didn't look convinced by this reasoning, Valenti sat back down, unclenching her fists, and de Bronk followed suit. Still, a palpable tension remained.

"Maybe," said Sertôrian to the now sulking Valenti, "you're thinking of the night Dr. Ivanova died."

Ilsa Ivanova, their ship's surgeon, had been buried by an icy avalanche on the treacherous slopes of the Promethean Mountains on Chryses II, a virtually uninhabited planet that Sertôrian had believed would give them no trouble at all.

"I'm definitely thinking of Berezhnoy," said Valenti.

"Fine," said Sertôrian. "Can we just let it go?"

The chem-fire crackled and popped.

"Wasn't Ilsa the first?" said de Bronk, ignoring Sertôrian's suggestion. "To die, I mean."

The fire settled in on itself with an eerie flutter.

"Yes," said Valenti. "And then it was Katkov and Robinson."

Midshipman Oleg Katkov had gone space mad while their ship, the *Circe*, had been hiding from a fleet of reputed cannibals in an asteroid belt. In the grips of the disease, Katkov had become convinced that First Gunner Grace Robinson was an imposter plotting to destroy them all. He'd strangled Robinson in her bed and then slit his own wrists in the pantry, all while the rest of the crew had slept.

"Do we have to talk about this right now?" said Sertôrian, almost inaudibly. She could feel strength ebbing from her body with each death they mentioned.

Again ignoring Sertôrian, Valenti said, "And then it was the three: Ogawa, Araújo, and Teixeira."

Commander Masaki Ogawa, Midshipman Bruna Araújo, and Second Gunner Leonardo Teixeira had disappeared into a cavern on Euxanthius XII in pursuit of a hermitic scientist they'd been tracking for days on the strength of some rumors they'd heard on the previous planet that this scientist had developed a super-efficient rocket fuel that could get Sertôrian and her crew out of the Minoan System once and for all. Ogawa, Araújo, and Teixeira had never emerged from the cavern, and the search party Sertôrian had sent after them had found no clues explaining their disappearance.

A bat fluttered through the illuminated clearing and then back into the darkness of the forest.

Sertôrian couldn't see the point of this catalog of fatalities. It was just too much right now—couldn't they see that?

"Then Carr," said de Bronk.

In an absurd and tragic bit of bad luck, Sublieutenant Greg Carr had slipped in the shower one morning and hit his head on the hard, metal floor, losing consciousness immediately. He'd died two days later of complications from the injury.

"Then it was Berezhnoy," said Valenti.

"Yes," said de Bronk. "And then a lull."

"And then Ribeiro," said Valenti.

The most recent casualty, Quartermaster Igor Ribeiro, had died in a tragic fluke just two months earlier, fatally bitten by a mortitius spider on Deucalion VI.

Sertôrian poked at the dwindling chem-fire with a long stick, stirring the flames back to life.

The unspoken question—*who would be next?*—hung awkwardly in the air. De Bronk and Valenti both stared mournfully into the fire. Sertôrian, no longer able to bear it, decided to introduce a new topic of conversation.

"I've been having strange dreams," she said, "ever since we started eating the cake."

Valenti and de Bronk looked up at her.

"And I don't want to talk about the dreams themselves. I didn't even want to tell you I've been having them," said Sertôrian. "But it's the only thing that's been different in the past three days. What I want to know, then, is if you've been having dreams as well. On their own, the dreams I've been having make no sense, but if you've been having dreams as well, perhaps if we put them all together . . ."

She left her question at that. Valenti and de Bronk looked ill at ease, had looked deeply uncomfortable since she'd started talking, de Bronk especially. The chem-fire shot a spark at her foot and she watched it extinguish on the damp ground.

The silence stretched awkwardly forward.

"No dreams then?" said Sertôrian.

De Bronk looked away, his brow furrowed, and when he turned back to Sertôrian, he said, "We didn't eat any of the cake."

As soon as the words left de Bronk's mouth, Valenti shot him a look of aghast displeasure. Sertôrian was sure she looked no less shocked, no less displeased herself. She felt like she'd just been hit upside the head. Dropping the stick she'd been using to tend the chem-fire and sitting up straighter, Sertôrian said, "Explain yourselves."

Valenti, who'd already composed herself, held out a placating hand.

"De Bronk and I decided not to eat the cake," she said. Full stop, as if that were an adequate justification.

Sertôrian said, "Star-Guard, that's a restatement, not an explanation."

"I believe our decision was well within the bounds of acceptable protocol," said Valenti.

"Acceptable protocol?" said Sertôrian, feeling the ire rising in her chest. "Acceptable protocol? You disobeyed a direct order. I should court-martial you right here in the field, do you understand that?"

"I don't remember any direct orders," said Valenti, poking at the chem-fire with the toe of her boot. "Do you, de Bronk?"

De Bronk, avoiding Sertôrian's gaze, shook his head ruefully.

For a moment, Sertôrian doubted herself—*had* she issued a direct order?—before realizing that the question was a moot point. Her crew had willfully lied to her for three full days, conspiring together to perpetuate the deception. Sertôrian understood perfectly well why they hadn't wanted to eat the cake. It was a heavy risk. But that didn't excuse the lying. A dangerous rage bubbled up inside her.

Had this kind of incident occurred years earlier, Sertôrian would have castigated the offenders without a moment's hesitation. Trust was essential to a well-functioning unit, and lying was antithetical to trust. Now, though, lost in the Declo Forest on an obscure planet in a remote system of the galaxy, she couldn't see the point anymore. How, after all, could she punish them without hurting herself? And so the rage subsided, quenched by a bracing splash of despair.

Sertôrian stared into the dwindling chem-fire, darkness encroaching nearer and nearer.

In the end, there was nothing to do but spread their blankets and go to sleep.

In her third night's dream, Sertôrian stood in an empty gallery, where the only work of art on display was a framed painting nearly as large as the wall on which it hung. The scene swarmed with tiny people—ancient peasants—the women clothed in simple dresses of red and blue and green, the men wearing rough brown trousers and heavy shirts of the same vivid colors as the women's dresses. At first glance, the painting appeared to depict a pleasantly bucolic scene, a merry picnic by the side of a deep blue lake, with the peasants dancing, eating, and otherwise enjoying themselves.

But as Sertôrian took in the entirety of the canvas, she saw, emerging from the lake in the bottom right-hand corner of the painting, an enormous crablike creature equipped not only with two claws but with eight flailing tentacles as well. Although *flailing* was the wrong word, as it implied a lack of control. The artist had painted the tentacles moving deliberately across the canvas in twining arabesques that artfully and organically framed the chaos spreading toward the still-festive upper-left-hand corner of the scene. Beginning at the green, shell-encrusted body of the crab monster, its mighty claws brandished at the viewer, Sertôrian allowed one tentacle and then another to guide her eye across the canvas. Each appendage wended its way around clusters of peasants in varying degrees of distress. One tentacle slithered right by a family huddled together for dear life. Another tentacle wrapped around a man holding a now useless axe, his eyes bulging as the creature squeezed the life out of him. Another tentacle pursued a group of men fleeing toward the left side of the canvas, trampling one another in the process. Another tentacle crept up on a man and a woman locked in a passionate embrace, oblivious to the approaching danger.

Sertôrian felt curiously distant from the whole scene—or perhaps not so curiously distant, given that it was a painting. She stepped forward for a closer look.

"Amazing," said a voice from behind her. She turned to find Valenti and de Bronk sitting on a velvet upholstered bench. They wore crisp new uniforms and both looked ten years younger.

"Yes," said Sertôrian, turning back around, and she took the painting down from the wall, or someone took it down, or it fell and it was gone, and the only thing on the wall, the only thing that had ever been on the wall, was a military-grade map, unframed and thumbtacked in place. A red dotted line twisted across the topographic terrain and terminated in a heavy, black **X**.

Sertôrian tore the map down to get a better look.

She recognized part of the area depicted. The dotted line began where they currently camped, deep in the Declo Forest. The line then made its way northeast, winding through the Bogs of

Challis, past the Ucon Cliffs, and over the Meridian Hills before culminating at the black **X** at the Twin Falls.

This time when she woke from her dream, there was no fuzzy transition to consciousness, just a sharp, lucid jolt. She scrambled for her bag, found a pencil, and tore a blank page from her logbook. On the paper's clean white surface she recreated the map from her dream before it could vanish from her mind. She looked down at her handiwork as the morning birds began to sing.

"I know where to find the Bulgakov Apparatus," she said, waking up her shipmates. "I know where it's hidden."

# SIX

n a fitting coincidence, today we observed Adastra Peraspera here at the convent, the twice-yearly ritual that commemorates Sertôrian's suffering during the bleak Minoan years. Given our current circumstances (as far as we know, murderous Delegarchic troops draw closer by the minute), today's Adastra was an especially somber affair, although not without its moments of beauty:

There was the fog-enshrouded ice sphere passed from sister to sister, the sting of its frozen surface against the pads of our fingers reminding us of the cold loneliness of Sertôrian's tribulations. There was the precise geometry of the ceremonial hexagons into which we arranged ourselves, following carefully the patterns on the floor, which had been etched with such loving exactitude by the convent's sacral architect, now deceased. There was Sister Beatriz, this cycle's designated cantrix, declaiming in her lovely, ringing voice the forty-third stanza of the *Astral Passion*, that centuries-old blank verse epic that describes Sertôrian's deepest suffering in lines of stately, relentless iambic pentameter.

As I listened to Sister Beatriz's striking recitation, however, I found my thoughts turning not to Sertôrian but to Star-Guard Ava Valenti and Technician Ernst de Bronk. Though the Rhadamanthus IX narrative features two or three honest-to-goodness villains, none of them are so reviled in the popular imagination as Sertôrian's last two surviving shipmates.

Over time, I've come to feel that such sentiments do a great disservice not only to the memory of Ernst de Bronk and Ava Valenti but also to the scholarship of those critics who condemn them. Today we all too readily disregard this pair's admirable qualities (of which they had many) to focus solely on their actions following the discovery of the Apparatus. We should remember as the events of the Rhadamanthus IX episode unfold, though, that it required no small loyalty for Valenti and de Bronk to stick with Sertôrian during their quest for the Bulgakov Apparatus. *Traitor* is not a word to be used lightly, but too many scholars apply it too eagerly to Valenti and de Bronk. Their entire lives get read through the filter of a couple of admittedly unfortunate decisions made during the latest in a harrowing series of misadventures. I certainly don't defend their decisions, but I'm uncomfortable with the impulse to search out nascent traces of their supposed treachery from the earliest points in their biographies.

Read in such a way, the lives of Valenti and de Bronk become . . . Is there a word for the opposite of a hagiography? If I had more time I would scour the lexicon to see if such a term exists, but I'm afraid such pleasures are behind me now. We'll call such a disparaging approach a villiography, then, and condemn the practice out of hand, because if we approach their lives with more nuance, we can better understand not only de Bronk and Valenti but Sertôrian as well.

For such a purpose, we turn to Yu-Jin Kim's *An Archival Excavation of the Minoan Years*, brilliant in every way, but especially in its biographical sketches of Sertôrian's shipmates. In this monograph, her magnum opus, Kim pulls illuminating tidbits from the historical record like so many rabbits from the hat of a profligate magician. Because interest in Valenti and de Bronk generally takes such a vilifying tack, Kim's *Archival Excavation*—more sympathetic to the two than most studies—is criminally under-read. Her biographical sketches of Valenti and de Bronk remain unrivaled, however, so I will summarize them for the purpose of our current study.

Popular portrayals of Ernst de Bronk, Bombal's narrative included, show us a weak-willed old man, highly superstitious and simperingly nostalgic for a version of Earth that never really existed. He was born either just before or just after the Treaty of Moros. A citizen of the

Lachesian Empire, de Bronk would have experienced none of the cultural amenities about which he waxes rhapsodic throughout the Minoan narratives: ubiquitous automobiles, affordable real estate, jetpacks. This could be inaccuracy on the part of the tales or simply aggressive nostalgia on the part of de Bronk. In any case, it doesn't help his credibility with contemporary readers.

Nor does his lowly status as technician seventh grade. Many presume gross ineptitude as the reason behind such an old man holding such a low rank. And this is where the research presented in *An Archival Excavation of the Minoan Years* comes to de Bronk's rescue.

Within an archive of military files long believed to be lost, Kim discovered de Bronk's service records: Graduating first in his class from Starhaven, Earth's finest space academy, de Bronk was given command at age eighteen of a Tiger-Class raiding ship that, on its first mission, successfully liberated eighteen kilotons of crentonium from an Atropian space freighter. Proving this was not just beginner's luck, young Captain de Bronk further distinguished himself through a series of increasingly daring raids on Atropian mining stations. As a result of these successful missions, he made admiral by age thirty, a truly stunning accomplishment.

Shortly thereafter, however, his military career jumped the rails. Increasingly disturbed by the Lachesian Empire's ruthless exploitation of its own colonies on the moons of Saturn, de Bronk commenced an escalating campaign of resistance against his native empire's presence on the Saturnine Colonies. He began civilly enough with strongly worded letters to his superiors, but when that failed to achieve results, his activism escalated, culminating a few years later in a guerilla attack on the Empire's colonial government headquarters on Titan.

De Bronk was captured, court-martialed, and convicted of treason, and he would have been executed if the Forty-Day War hadn't drawn his superiors' attention elsewhere. De Bronk escaped and—here's the remarkable thing—reenlisted six months later under an assumed identity (Dirk Starr, Venusian gas farmer). After three years of cautious obedience, he won the rank of master sergeant, a position whose privileges he exploited to gather resources and sympathetic soldiers. Then he staged yet another guerilla attack on Titan. And just as he'd been before, De Bronk was apprehended, unmasked, and condemned to death. But once again he escaped at the eleventh hour, this time when Klothian Empire raiders blitzed the penal asteroid where de Bronk was imprisoned. His military records are silent regarding the next two decades of his life, but it would seem that at the beginning of the Great Aurigan War, de Bronk—presumably finding his own empire the lesser of three evils—reenlisted yet again, this time under his own name, and the Lachesian Empire so desperately needed soldiers that he was brought on under the stipulation that he never advance above the rank of technician seventh grade.

In the popular imagination (and in much reputable scholarship), de Bronk holds the dubious distinction of being labeled both a traitor and a lucky fool, because what else but luck could explain his surviving for so long in the Minoan System when other members of Sertôrian's crew so renowned for their competence died long before he did? Kim's findings provide a compelling explanation for de Bronk's ability to stay alive. Even the skeletal biography found in his military record suggests a man with a genius for survival—not a chronic bumbler but a tenacious idealist. What reads as temperamental weakness in the Sertôrial biographic canon could simply be exhaustion after a lifetime dedicated to losing causes. And as we will see in a few chapters, it may well have been idealism, rather than spineless malleability, that led him to join forces with Valenti to such unfortunate ends.

Ava Valenti, for her part, is generally portrayed as an equal and opposite foil to Ernst de Bronk (or vice versa, I suppose), a skeptical woman of science—young, hypercompetent, and an inveterate questioner of Sertôrian's orders. Many construe this final tendency as symptomatic of an acrid, combative relationship between Valenti and Sertôrian. This, according to Kim, couldn't be further from the truth.

To support her claim, Kim turns once again to obscure military archives, this time the student records from the Excelsior Space Academy Annex of Iopetus. This top-secret military facility trained the Lachesian

Empire's most elite young warriors in the years leading up to the Great Aurigan War. It not only served as Ava Valenti's alma mater, but it almost certainly employed Captain Sertôrian as an instructor during the time that Valenti would have been a student.

Prioritizing security as they did during the buildup to the war, the Excelsior Space Academy Annex referred to their instructors in all official documents solely by color-based code names, an attempt to hinder enemy intelligence efforts to track the Lachesian Empire's best officers. However, allusions in Sertôrian's later teachings to a prewar stint working with young cadets lead scholars to a near-consensus opinion that Sertôrian did in fact teach at the ESAA.

Many reputable thinkers, Kim included, also find it likely that Sertôrian taught and took a shine to a young Ava Valenti during their overlapping time at the ESAA, which is how Valenti later came to be part of such an elite team at such a young age. Out of Kim's indefatigable research came a document that serves as, if not a smoking gun, then the next best thing in establishing a prewar acquaintanceship between Valenti and Sertôrian. Toward the end of Valenti's student file is a summative evaluation of her performance written by one of her instructors, code-named Amaranth. Kim constructs a meticulous argument that identifies Amaranth as Sertôrian. Rather than summarize that argument here, I'll refer the reader back to *An Archival Excavation of the Minoan Years* for more details, and utilize this space to reproduce the letter itself. Watch for brief glimmers of distinctly Sertôrial sensibilities:

●　　●　　●

*Dear Admiral Peridot,*

*Ava Valenti is the smartest person in her class and she knows it. And when I say smart, I mean it in the most holistic way possible. She absorbs and retains every bit of knowledge that comes her way. She manifests impeccable battle instincts. And she interacts easily with her classmates. The last one impresses me most of all.*

*I said she knows how smart she is, and she does. Most students mismanage that kind of awareness, either blatantly patronizing their peers and ultimately alienating them or dumbing themselves down and limiting their own education in a misguided attempt to be well-liked.*

*Cadet Valenti does neither, embracing her own intelligence while simultaneously cultivating a genuine respect for her peers. She admires and learns from those around her and is, in turn, well regarded by her fellow cadets.*

*I am aware that some of my colleagues have expressed reservations regarding Cadet Valenti's behavior toward her superiors. I certainly agree that Valenti does not respect authority for authority's sake. But even in the military this is no fatal flaw. We're not looking for mindless sycophants after all.*

*Of course, my colleagues might argue that in the heat of battle, the last thing a commanding officer needs is a soldier who questions orders. That may be true in some situations, but in my own experience, dissenting viewpoints can also save lives.*

*My colleagues have recommended putting Valenti behind a desk for the rest of her career. I disagree and recommend field duty, and I would be pleased to have Valenti as a member of my own team.*

*If you wish to discuss the matter further, you know where to reach me.*

> *Sincerely,*
> *Captain Amaranth*

Although we won't examine the supposed treachery of Valenti and de Bronk for a few chapters yet, I bring these details up at this point in the study to help us better understand the dynamics among the three wandering shipmates. Reading Valenti and de Bronk not as villains but as multifaceted human beings helps us perform a parallel task with their captain. The ensuing chapters will show us a Sertôrian whose behavior contradicts many of the values she later espoused. Tempting though it may be to push all the fault for these inconsistencies onto Valenti and de Bronk, a rigorous reading of the Rhadamanthus IX narrative will not allow it. With that in mind, we'll rejoin Bombal's narrative as the three travelers continue their journey:

•   •   •

Sertôrian's dream map led the intrepid party on a several-day trek through some of the planet's most dangerous regions. Functioning, by necessity, as cohesively as they ever had, the three shipmates made their way through the Bogs of Challis, whose noxious centine gas nearly cost the travelers their lives; past the Ucon Cliffs, where deadly rock monkeys lurked in the shadows, gently gnashing their sharp little teeth; and over the Meridian Hills, home to the carnivorous lucifex moth, which the shipmates narrowly avoided before they crossed the Inhk-Omn River and reached the base of the Twin Falls, where, on the map, **X** marked the spot.

"We made it," said Sertôrian as they finally emerged from the thick vegetation at the edge of the Meridian Hills, the majestic Twin Falls towering above them. For a brief moment Sertôrian felt a wave of relief. Her dream map had been unfailingly accurate, from start to finish, which was no small wonder given Sertôrian's near-complete unfamiliarity with the planet's terrain. Their arrival at the Twin Falls, then, meant that the map had to have come from a source other than her own mind, from an external intelligence that was purposefully guiding them toward a specific and deliberate objective.

This fleeting reverie was sharply interrupted, however, by that oft-repeated question that Sertôrian had come to loathe in recent months:

"What now?" said Valenti, looking up at the misting falls.

"Yeah," said de Bronk. "I don't see anything here that looks like the Bulgakov Apparatus."

Taking a deep, steadying breath, Sertôrian unslung her pack from her shoulders and set it down at her feet.

"Let's look around more carefully then," she said, "and see what we can find."

Hoping it might trigger some secret door, some hidden sign-post, Sertôrian removed the Green Beacon from her pack and stepped farther into the clearing at the base of the falls, walking methodically back and forth across the sunlit ground while Valenti and de Bronk watched her expectantly. Her shipmates' minor revolt in the Declo Forest had been forgotten in the ensuing days, or rather, all three of them had refused to mention it. Sertôrian had no idea if Valenti and de Bronk felt shame or remorse for what they'd done, or if they were merely biding their time until the opportunity for a greater insurrection emerged.

Whatever their intentions, her crew had opened a rift with Sertôrian that, in spite of the group's current outward unity, bode ill for their future together. They needed to find the Bulgakov Apparatus, or something they could pass off as the Apparatus, deliver it to the Arch-Kaiser, and get off this planet. If they couldn't do that— and soon—then Sertôrian had grave doubts about their ability to survive not only this misadventure but also any further misadventures on the few Minoan planets that had not yet waylaid them.

Still pacing methodically at the base of the falls, Sertôrian held the blinking Beacon up higher and watched her surroundings carefully. Thick green moss—encouraged no doubt by the constant mist from the falls—covered every stationary surface in sight: boulders, logs, the sappy trunks of the lofty pines.

"Captain," shouted de Bronk over the roar of the falls. "Here!"

He pointed at the ground, his wrinkled face animated with glee. There, at the edge of the trees, a sunken arrangement of stones formed a thick black **X**. Sertôrian felt another too-brief wave of encouragement, the Beacon and its creators having apparently come through for them again. De Bronk stood aside and Sertôrian strode to the marker, Beacon in hand. With her back to the tall, mossy trees, she stood at the center of the **X** and waited.

For a moment nothing happened. Sertôrian tried holding the Beacon higher, then lower, then closer to her body, and then farther from it. Nothing seemed to make a difference. With a churn of dread, she wondered if this would turn into a repeat of the Plains of Chubbúhc, if they would be forced to wait for weeks and weeks before the Beacon triggered the next phase of their journey.

But then Valenti called out urgently, "Captain, behind you!"

She pointed to a nearby tree and Sertôrian spun around. The tree's thick green blanket of moss slowly unpeeled itself from the trunk and stretched toward Sertôrian, writhing through the air like a charmed snake. Gasping in spite of herself, Sertôrian tried to anticipate what this sinewy, stretching blanket of moss might be up to. She had no idea, but she decided to stand her ground. Slowly, the strip of moss reached closer and closer until, in a cobra-like strike, it shot forward and curled itself tightly around Sertôrian's head.

With a cry of alarm, Sertôrian dropped the Beacon and clawed at her face, trying to force her fingers under the edges of the moss. The grasp of her velvety captor only grew tighter, however, fitting itself intimately to Sertôrian's head, tethering her to the tree. She fell to her knees, her heart battering her ribs. She clawed at the moss, panic rising, until with a reflexive click, her battle instincts took over and she got control of herself.

Breathing deeply, Sertôrian took quick stock and realized to her minor relief that her nose and her eyes remained unobstructed by the still-writhing moss. She could see and she could breathe, which meant she still had more than a fighting chance; she'd been in worse situations than this before and had lived to tell about it.

Her relief lessened, though, as a warm sap oozed out from the underside of the moss, adhering it even more snugly to her head. Maintaining her breathing, she tried to keep a level head. Her discomfort only grew, though, as the syrupy streams oozed into her ears, filling the canals with sap. She fought against her rising panic, taking regular breaths and performing the mental stabilization techniques she had learned so long ago in her academy training.

With the panic once again contained—she could still breathe and she could still see, after all—she stood up, brushed the dirt from the knees of her pants, and saw Valenti and de Bronk watching on, horrified. Sertôrian signaled to them that she was okay. She wasn't sure if this was true or not, but for better or for worse, the process seemed to be complete. The helmet of moss and the warm, sticky sap beneath remained motionless. She held very still, feeling the sap harden and cool. Valenti and de Bronk stood poised and ready to intervene. She gave them another placating hand signal, and waited.

It began as a tickle in her ears, a tickle that evolved quickly to a buzz, and then to a rattling, whispery voice. Earphones. The hardened sap probes in her ear functioned as vibrating earphones, an ingenious mechanism that she would have admired if it hadn't been foisted on her so alarmingly. The voice from the hardened sap, in its glottal buzz, told her not to be afraid, at least not yet.

"To attain your final objective," it said, "you must beat me at liar's gammon—best two out of three. The rules of the game are not overly complex, but winning requires cunning, foresight, and nerve. You must complete this challenge because the object you seek requires wisdom in its use, and not without wisdom can you defeat me at this game. I will now explain the rules of—"

"Hang on a second," said Sertôrian, realizing as she did that the hardened sap had formed a cavity around her mouth, allowing her lips to move freely. "Who am I talking to right now?"

"I imagine you have many questions," said the voice. "And I'll apologize right now because I can understand none of them. I respond to voice commands that directly relate to the game of liar's gammon. Anything else falls outside of my cognitive purview. I should add that the use of *I* and *my* is primarily a matter of efficiency. I am not a person nor a sentient being, but an electronically preserved catalogue of winning strategies utilized by history's most accomplished players of the game. With these strategies at my disposal, I've been programmed to follow complex algorithms that help me respond to moves you make on the board. Such are the parameters of my cognition, so again, I apologize that I lack the ability to comprehend your questions."

There was a brief pause before the buzzing voice resumed.

"I will now explain the rules of liar's gammon," it said. "Please turn around."

Sertôrian turned around. The thick pine tree before her split open lengthwise with a mechanized whir. From within its hollow trunk a small table emerged.

"Please sit down," said the buzzy voice in her ear.

Sertôrian sat down at the low stool attached to the table.

"In front of you is a regulation gammon field with the game pieces positioned to commence play," said the voice, and Sertôrian looked over the hexagonal board as the voice explained the rules. By this point in their quest, Sertôrian didn't even question the premise of this absurd challenge. She was too exhausted, and more than willing to turn their fates over to someone (or something) with a plan—whatever that plan might be. If she needed to learn and master the rules of an archaic board game to save the lives of her crew and herself, then she would learn and master the rules of an archaic board game, no questions asked.

Listening carefully to the voice's explanation of the game, Sertôrian was heartened by the resemblance that liar's gammon bore to mag-zhadrez, with a few notable exceptions. Instead of squares, this game utilized a track of interlocking triangles, and instead of standing figurines, it used red or blue tiles, each one's function and rank inscribed in white on the surface. Bluffing also featured heavily, apparently, as did a wagering component. But Sertôrian could already see that the same strategies that made her so formidable at mag-zhadrez would serve her well here. She had at least a fighting chance of winning. The voice finished its instructions and told Sertôrian that as a visitor she was granted the first move.

She heard a muffled voice from outside her mossy helmet and looked up to see de Bronk waving his arms while Valenti stood by, field knife in hand. Sertôrian had forgotten that they were there, that they had no idea what the buzzy voice in her ear was telling her. Touched by their concern, Sertôrian pointed to the game board, gave her shipmates the hand signal for all systems go, and nodded reassuringly. They nodded hesitantly in return and took a step back.

Turning back to the hexagonal board before her, Sertôrian contemplated her first move. She felt the old, familiar, sickening thrill of a high-stakes battle, fully aware as she thought through the implications of various openings that her decision would make or break their mission. Placing her finger on a red marauder tile, Sertôrian slid it onto triangle G13, an opening move reminiscent of the cantor's gambit in mag-zhadrez. Almost immediately, her opponent's blue first-rank constable tile slid—apparently under its own power—onto triangle T13 on the opposite corner of the board. A bold and clever counter.

· · ·

I'll interrupt the narrative at this point because even the most dedicated readers find the ensuing passage impenetrably dull. What follows is an intricate, bone-dry account of the three games Sertôrian played against her invisible opponent. We're given a move-by-move summary of play with no description of Sertôrian's emotional state, the reactions of her shipmates, or any details outside the game board. Making matters worse, after the first paragraph, complete sentences are abandoned in favor of a shorthand game notation. For example: RBn to J/Q 36; BBn to J/Q 34; RBn to J/Q 38. And on it goes for pages.

In terms of style, this section of text is unlike anything else in the Sertôrial biographic canon. For this reason, many scholars believe that the Gammon Log, as it's called, was appropriated from an earlier source, most likely written by one of Sertôrian's earliest followers or, as some argue, by Sertôrian herself.

That last idea has proven irresistible to generations of scholars, and unfortunately pseudo-scholars, some of whom use the possibility of Sertôrial authorship as a springboard to a more radical thesis, perhaps most coherently (or least incoherently) articulated in Belle Carey's *The Gammon Cipher: An Explosive Secret Revealed*. Carey holds that not only did Sertôrian write the Gammon Log, but the meticulous notations also function as a coded message concealing a secret too dangerous to reveal openly. Utilizing the crackpot methodology typical of her ilk, Carey decodes the message using a key derived from the diameters of the planets in the Minoan System, the year in which Sertôrian experienced her First Shrouded Vision, and the text of Sertôrian's opening statement before the Syndics of Mars. And what dangerous secret does this key reveal? We're given the following decoded message: ABLE SAW I THE HAPTIC BRIGHT ENSCRIBED ORDER WITHAL. You may ask what this vague, semi-coherent nonsense is supposed to mean. Carey is quick with an interpretation that should, she says, be obvious to us all.

Through tortured logic too exhausting to reproduce here, Carey claims that this message reveals that Sertôrian's entire biography leading up to her appearance before the Syndics of Mars is pure fabrication—a work of fiction composed by Sertôrian herself. This of course raises the question of what Sertôrian *did* do with her life up to that point if not grow up on Mars, captain a battleship, and wander the Minoan System until returning to the planet of her birth. Never one for modest claims,

Carey claims that Sertôrian did nothing before the trial, did not even *exist* in the sense that we understand it. Invoking sketchy metaphysics, alternate dimensions, and the spontaneous generation of matter, Carey argues that Sertôrian was essentially and literally a self-created entity, a nonhuman organism with incomprehensible powers, and that the fictional biography she composed is simply an extended religious allegory meant to convey occult truths to her more discerning followers.

I certainly agree that there's much to be learned from the careful study of Sertôrian's biography, but beyond that I find Carey's theory to be undiluted nonsense. Despite its vapidity, though, Carey's argument has gained traction in certain circles, not because of its scholarly rigor or even its plausibility, but because like all conspiracy theories, it is as intriguing as it is improbable. I reproduce it here partly for the sake of curiosity, but largely as a useful contrast against which we can better appreciate the more rigorous and responsible ideas of my fellow scholars.

Because the fact of the matter is, some credible thinkers do argue that Sertôrian is the author of the Gammon Log, though not in the same way that Carey proposes. Their much more reasonable theory holds that the dialogue is not a secret code but a record of events as they transpired. This gammon log might have come directly from Captain Sertôrian's journal, they argue, her own firsthand account of the events that she witnessed during the wandering years.

As a follower of Sertôrian's teachings, I sometimes feel the woman herself growing ever more distant the more time I spend with her writings. Her words become so well worn in my mind that they feel infinite—hewn from eternal stone rather than generated from the mind of a living, breathing woman similar in many respects to myself.

Any new bit of language, then, however dry it may be, presents the possibility of a fresh encounter with Sertôrian. Though I have less confidence than some that the Gammon Log was written by Sertôrian, I'm deeply sympathetic to the impulse to search for her there. My greatest motive in conducting this study of the Rhadamanthus IX episode is to generate—for myself and for you—that vital spark necessary to reanimate Sertôrian the person in our minds and in our hearts. Actually doing so, however, proves a challenge indeed.

But we mustn't lose the thread of this chapter. Perhaps I feel a special affinity with Ava Valenti and Ernst de Bronk at this time, given the nature of my order's current covert actions. Treachery is such a slippery concept after all, so dependent on the vantage point from which events are viewed, and of course, on who survives to write the definitive history of what transpires. With that in mind, then, we'll return to Bombal's narrative. Strange though it may be to describe these passages as the calm before the storm, they do depict some of the trio's last fully unified moments.

Here, then, is a quick summary of the section I've passed over:

Having defeated her electronic opponent, Sertôrian receives her promised reward. The mossy helmet congratulates her and detaches itself from her head. As it slips to the ground, a brilliant beam of light shoots out from the game board, illuminating a secret chamber between the two churning waterfalls before them. Holding the Green Beacon in front of her, Sertôrian approaches the stone door, which swings smoothly open. Sertôrian sets down the Beacon and enters the chamber.

Now back to Bombal:

•  •  •

"What do you see?" said de Bronk from outside the doorway.

Sertôrian lit a holo-torch, revealing a little cube of a room with just enough clearance for her to stand upright. The perfectly flat stone walls met at precise ninety-degree angles and the space was unadorned except for a bronze plaque on the wall opposite the door and on the ground beneath it, a suitcase-sized object covered in an oily canvas sheet.

"Captain?" said Valenti. "Everything okay in there?"

Sertôrian couldn't look away from the canvas-covered object on the ground.

"It's fine," she said. "You two can come on in."

Valenti and de Bronk passed through the doorway, commenting on how dry the air was inside the chamber. When they saw the plaque and the object on the floor, though, they fell silent.

"Is this it?" said de Bronk in a whisper.

The room did have an ineffably sacred feel to it—still and cool and ancient.

"What does the plaque say?" said Valenti.

"I haven't read it yet," said Sertôrian, unease tingling through her extremities. Like de Bronk, she spoke in a whisper, though she couldn't say why.

"I think we should read it," said de Bronk.

"Yes," said Sertôrian, and the three shipmates stepped forward with reverential caution until they could make out the letters on the plaque, which read as follows:

### TO THE FINDER OF THIS VAULT,

*Congratulations. Through your bravery, wisdom, and perseverance, you've successfully navigated the path we laid before you. This in itself is a laudable achievement, but your reward, if we can rightly call it that, is far more than just satisfaction for a job well done.*

*The machine beneath this plaque will change the course of human history. Possessing a power that far surpasses any of our previous creations, it represents both our highest achievement and our deepest weakness. Nobler people than we would have destroyed it immediately. Sad experience has taught us that the craven powers of the world possess a preternatural ability for turning our inventions—each one created with the aim of bettering the situation of humankind—to their own bloodthirsty purposes. Through our own lack of foresight we have become unwitting accomplices to some of the Three Empires' most ruthless deeds.*

*In developing the device that sits concealed before you, we had hoped to subvert or even overthrow the tenacious power of the Empires, but we've realized too late this machine's awful potential for misuse. Common sense dictates we destroy the machine, but vanity—or perhaps a grain of optimism—has led us to preserve our creation. And so, fully acknowledging that there's no restitution for what we've already done, we've hidden our greatest achievement here in this chamber, hoping that it might be discovered in a nobler time, by a nobler people who will have the courage to put it to a noble purpose.*

*May wisdom guide you as you move forward.*

*Sincerely,*

*The Bulgakov Collective*

Sertôrian took a step back.

It was too much to take in all at once. De Bronk had tears streaming down his wrinkled face, and he wiped unashamedly at his running nose with a crumpled handkerchief. Valenti regarded the plaque with an appraising eye, searching for the telltale sign that would reveal it as a hoax. Sertôrian herself still hadn't discounted the possibility that this whole enterprise was actually an elaborate and malicious prank. Nonetheless, ever since she'd had those vivid dreams in the Declo Forest, she'd been more willing to entertain the notion that they were being guided by the artful machinations of the legendary Bulgakov Collective, the organization that had, among other things, pioneered the web of technologies that had made it possible to transform non-Earth planets into habitable spaces for humans.

She read over the plaque again, and though she found its message a bit too melodramatic, her gut told her it was genuine. And if the plaque was genuine, then the canvas-covered object below it would have to be the Bulgakov Apparatus.

Sertôrian's stomach flipped.

The Bulgakov Apparatus.

Her first impulse was to walk away—to seal up this chamber with the Green Beacon inside and find an exit strategy that didn't involve handing over the massively powerful Bulgakov Apparatus to an erratic thug like the Arch-Kaiser Glenn Harrison. She hadn't until now really thought through the implications of their assignment, as she hadn't believed in the Apparatus's existence. She'd not worried, then, about what Harrison might do if he got his hands on the device, because she hadn't thought they would find it. But now here they were, gathered around a canvas-draped box that could very well be the most powerful technology the galaxy had ever seen.

Did they *have* to hand it over to the Arch-Kaiser, though? After all, if it *was* the Bulgakov Apparatus they'd just discovered, couldn't they harness its legendary power—whatever that might be—to get themselves off this planet? If even a fraction of the rumors surrounding the Apparatus turned out to be true, not even the Arch-Kaiser and his secret police could stand in the way of whoever wielded this technology.

And if the object before them was *not* the Bulgakov Apparatus, if it was instead one of the many pseudo-Apparati that still littered the galaxy, then they could deliver the useless machine in good conscience to the Arch-Kaiser, declare their mission accomplished, and bid Rhadamanthus IX a not so fond farewell.

The only thing to do was test the device.

She laid out her rationale to Valenti and de Bronk.

De Bronk said, "Captain, I don't know how else to say this, but I don't think any of us are worthy to activate the Apparatus." He ran a hand through his sparse white hair. "It's all right there on the plaque—they wanted people with nobility to use it, and I'm not sure that's us. It's not me anyway." He looked at the canvas-draped bundle on the floor. "I say we leave it alone and find another way off this planet."

This was not what Sertôrian had been hoping to hear.

"Valenti?" she said.

The star-guard looked from the canvas-covered object to her expectant captain.

"De Bronk is right," said Valenti. "I mean, he's wrong—we don't know for sure that this is the Bulgakov Apparatus—but he's right that we should leave it alone. We have no idea what this thing is, which means we have no idea what it might do if we switch it on. Regardless of whether or not it's the Apparatus, it still might be incredibly dangerous. It could be nothing more sophisticated than a bomb, but it would still kill us all. And even if it does nothing, if it is a pseudo-Apparatus, how do you think that will go over with the Arch-Kaiser? Do you think he'll still give us our ship back like we've just done him a big favor? I don't think so. We need to pretend like we never saw this thing and start working on a plan B."

Valenti and de Bronk both moved toward the door. Sertôrian looked at the canvas-shrouded object on the floor and felt a twinge of resentment toward her shipmates. She couldn't fault their reasoning. Leaving the device behind was certainly the prudent course of action, no doubt about it. But couldn't Valenti and de Bronk feel the seductive pull of the unknown? If they walked away now, wouldn't they be tormented forever by the fact that all that had stood between them and the solution to a centuries-old mystery had been an overdeveloped sense of caution and a dirty canvas sheet?

"This is a big decision," she said. "We need to sleep on it."

Valenti and de Bronk exchanged one of the worried glances that had been passing between them so often lately.

"Captain," said Valenti, "I think the sooner we get out of here, the better."

"I agree," said de Bronk.

"I wasn't asking for a vote," said Sertôrian. "We'll set up camp nearby."

So without further ceremony, they extinguished the holo-torch and exited the stone chamber. Sertôrian removed the blinking Green Beacon from its slot in the rock face and the door slammed shut behind them.

That night at their camp, Sertôrian didn't sleep. Wrapped in her blanket, lying on her back, she listened to the slow, steady breathing of Valenti and de Bronk—the young officer's breathy wheeze and the old man's slight snore. Somewhere in the distance, a nocturnal bird whistled a melancholy tune. The night grew colder and darker, and Sertôrian worked to justify the decision she'd already made.

For one thing, the plaque's admonition to leave the Apparatus hidden for a nobler people in a nobler time rested on flawed reasoning. The truth was, a people in a nobler time wouldn't need something like the Bulgakov Apparatus, whatever it did. The people who needed it most were alive right now, caught in the midst of galactic turmoil, victims of the Three Empires' violent death throes. It would be irresponsible, Sertôrian reasoned, not to investigate if the Apparatus could be the means of changing billions of human lives for the better.

Lurking in the shadowy recesses of Sertôrian's mind, though, was a different impulse. She felt a metaphysical duty to examine the Apparatus, although she couldn't quite say to whom or to what she felt obliged. All she knew was that the imperative had an indescribable rightness to it, a burning necessity.

A light breeze swayed the towering pines surrounding their campsite.

Sertôrian knew what she had to do. De Bronk and Valenti were deeply asleep by this point, oblivious, she hoped, to the waking world. Still, she moved as quietly as possible. She carefully slipped on her boots and crept off into the night, taking the Beacon with her.

Back inside the stone chamber, she lit the holo-torch. The Apparatus, shrouded in canvas, remained just where they had left it. Illuminated from the ground by the even light of the torch, it cast a tall crisp shadow on the stone wall. Arms folded, Sertôrian reread the text of the plaque. Then she crouched down, grabbed a corner of the oily shroud, and pulled.

Beneath the sheet sat a compact tangle of wires, motors, hinges, circuit boards, spigots, and thin metal bars. A plastic band around the suitcase-sized bundle read, "Remove this band carefully and stand back: device will self-assemble." Attached to the band with a bit of string was a handwritten note that said, "Do not remove the band while inside this chamber. Not enough room."

Sertôrian realized she was holding her breath and exhaled. While the plaque had imbued the shrouded Apparatus with a mysterious grandeur, these bland instructions lent the squat cube all the mystique of a household appliance. Rather than disappoint, though, the machine's mundane tangibility filled Sertôrian with a wonderful sense of accomplishment. Uncovering the Apparatus drove home the sensation that this was very real, that she may well have discovered the Bulgakov Apparatus, one of the most sought-after artifacts in human history.

Feeling an irresistible urge to bask in the long-unfamiliar glow of success, Sertôrian lay down on the cool ground and curled her body around the compacted machine. Draping her arm over the top of it, she held the device close, drawing comfort from this tangible manifestation of resolve, genius, and idealism. She closed her eyes, breathing in the smell of metal and clean plastic.

She didn't know how long she'd been asleep when she heard

footsteps entering the chamber. Still wrapped around the device, she opened her eyes to see Valenti and de Bronk standing in the open doorway, their faces troubled at the scene before them. Sertôrian scrambled to her feet, assuming what she hoped was a posture of easy authority but knowing that nothing could erase for Valenti and de Bronk the sight of their captain embracing a piece of machinery.

She had never presented her shipmates with such an unguarded view of herself, and the terrible novelty of doing so, along with the shame of being caught so blatantly disregarding their collective decision to leave the Apparatus alone for the night, set off in Sertôrian a bitter chain of defensive thinking. Wasn't this their fault too? Shouldn't they have agreed with her the evening before and examined the Apparatus together? She was the captain, after all, and if they didn't respect her, then how could they ever hope to function as an effective unit? They were the ones who had made a mistake, weren't they? Her exhaustion, which not so long ago had manifested as relief, now enveloped her in frightening uncertainty. Everything was suddenly all wrong, and her shame combusted into a jagged rage that she fought to contain.

"Hello, Captain," Valenti said gently. "De Bronk woke up and saw you were gone. We wanted to make sure you were okay."

"You mean you wanted to check up on me," said Sertôrian, her rage further inflamed by Valenti's careful tone. "And you knew right where to come."

"No," said Valenti. "That's not it at all."

"We were worried," said de Bronk, looking from Sertôrian to the now unveiled machine at her feet.

"Suspicious, you mean," said Sertôrian, the shame-fueled rage egging her on.

"No," said de Bronk, looking back up at her, sounding hurt.

"Well, you've caught me red-handed." She gestured at the uncovered device. "Is that what you want me to say?"

"No," said de Bronk. "That's not . . ." He broke off with a sigh, the holo-torch in his hand casting the wrinkles of his face in sharp relief.

"Tell me the two of you weren't waiting for me to slip up," said Sertôrian, suddenly unable to stop her most paranoid fears from slithering out of her mouth. "Just lying in wait for days. You wanted this to happen."

"No," said de Bronk, shoulders slumping, voice breaking.

"Captain, listen," said Valenti, holding out a conciliatory hand and taking a step forward.

"No," said Sertôrian. "Tell me, is this the first place you came when you saw that I'd gone?"

They didn't answer.

"Is it?" said Sertôrian, looking directly at de Bronk.

"That's not a fair question," he said.

"Answer it anyway," she said.

"Fine," said de Bronk. "Yes. We talked it over and decided to look here first."

Sertôrian took two long steps across the chamber and stood nose to nose with de Bronk, who hadn't moved from his position in the open doorway.

"You and Valenti talked it over, huh?" said Sertôrian, poking him in the chest.

De Bronk grimaced.

Sertôrian said, "This seems to be a new habit with you two, plotting things behind my back."

De Bronk shrugged.

"Maybe we talked some things over," he said. "But it wasn't like you're saying."

"Then what was it like?" said Sertôrian, practically shouting now. "Because it seems to me that there's a whole ghostly decision-making process going on without me."

"Captain," said Valenti.

"I'm not talking to you," said Sertôrian, holding de Bronk's watery eyes in her gaze.

De Bronk looked away.

"What concerns me most," said Sertôrian, "is that my crew is either too afraid or too conniving to apprise me of their sentiments."

"Listen," said Valenti, the light from her holo-torch flickering across her face. "It's nothing systemic—just some informal conversations that happen here and there, catch as catch can. I have the same kinds of discussions with you."

"Is that right?" said Sertôrian, stepping closer to the starguard.

"Yes, it is," said Valenti, standing firm. "Yesterday while de Bronk was resting, you and I talked about how we might secure long-range transport once we make it off-planet. And the day before that, while you and I inventoried supplies, we talked about stretching our rations with some edible plants I'd spotted. And a couple of days before that—"

Sertôrian waved a hand, cutting Valenti off.

"All right, Ava," she said, her intensity waning. "You've made your point."

Sertôrian turned her back to her shipmates and looked down at the squat device she'd risked so much to uncover. As she stood there, taking in the silence of the stony chamber, her rage imploded, leaving behind it a cold, sucking hole of shame. She hadn't felt this embarrassed, this vulnerable and frustrated, since adolescence. How had she botched this encounter so horribly? How could she still salvage some functioning scraps of her crew's respect?

She turned back around to see Valenti and de Bronk still standing at the entrance of the chamber, watching her with wide, nervous eyes.

"Listen," said Sertôrian, with just a hint of apology in her voice. "You surprised me and I overreacted. Can we start over?"

De Bronk nodded and Valenti regarded her warily.

"Okay," said Sertôrian. "All right. So. The reason I'm here is, I've been thinking things over and I've decided we need to take a thorough look at the Apparatus. We need to figure out what it's supposed to do and how it does it."

She stepped back and pointed down at the compact bundle of wire, plastic, and metal.

"Just consider the possibilities," she said, "if this *is* the Bulgakov Apparatus. Just think about—"

"We've already talked through this, though," said Valenti. "And I agree it's an exciting idea, but—"

"Ava, let me finish," said Sertôrian, the hot anger prickling back to life. "We're going to examine the Apparatus because we can't allow ourselves to be ruled by fear. That's not how progress happens. That should be clear to you two, but if there's—"

"If I can speak freely, Captain," said Valenti, "nothing you're saying is very clear to me. I agree that fear is a bad thing, but what you're proposing sounds less like courage and more like recklessness. So before we do anything, I'd like some more details about how you intend to avoid a disaster here."

Sertôrian didn't respond immediately, instead maintaining steely eye contact with the junior officer. The encounter was unmistakably a lost cause and in her once again rage-blasted brain, Sertôrian could think of no recourse but scorched earth.

"Star-Guard Valenti," she began softly, "we are going to unwrap this machine and see what it can do. And then we're going to figure out how to get it off this planet without the Arch-Kaiser finding out. Do I make myself clear?"

Valenti shook her head. "Honestly, that doesn't allay any of my concerns," she said.

Sertôrian nodded, her fury building, and turned to de Bronk.

"Technician de Bronk," said Sertôrian. "What are your thoughts on the situation?"

De Bronk squirmed, his pale eyes begging for an escape.

"Captain," he began, and hesitated. "Captain, I have to say I agree with Star-Guard Valenti."

Sertôrian breathed out a hot snort of air.

"I'd just like some rational justification for all this," said Valenti, again reaching out with a conciliatory hand.

"All right," said Sertôrian, turning back to Valenti, swatting away her hand.

Valenti stepped back as if she'd been shot.

"All right," continued Sertôrian. "You want justification, Star-Guard? How's this for justification? You're going to examine this device because, in case you've forgotten, I'm the captain. My job is to tell you what to do, and your job is to do it—not to ask questions, not to come up with secret plans of your own, but to do what I say. Understood?"

Eyes wide, Valenti regarded her captain without a sound. De Bronk sighed, a defeated, wheezing rattle.

"I said do I make myself clear?" said Sertôrian.

"Yes, Captain," said Valenti and de Bronk in unison.

"Good," said Sertôrian. "Now we carry the Apparatus back to camp."

# SEVEN

The passage you've just read may be the most controversial moment in the entire Sertôrial biographic canon. For centuries, certain followers of Sertôrian have performed rhetorical acrobatics to discount this portrayal of Sertôrian's behavior, insisting that not only this scene but the entire Rhadamanthus IX episode must be a scurrilous fabrication—character assassination of the lowest order. Nowhere else, they argue, is Sertôrian cast in such a thoroughly unflattering light; in her flustered confrontation with Valenti and de Bronk, she comes across not only as tyrannical but inept.

And while such leaderly ineptitude might be plausible—the argument goes—in an unseasoned commander, Sertôrian had led her crew through countless battles in the Great Aurigan War and numerous misadventures on the renegade planets of the Minoan System. Certainly she had dealt with internal dissent before this episode, and given the fierce loyalty of her crew up to this point, she had to have done so with great efficacy. It strains plausibility for many readers, then, that Sertôrian would blunder so spectacularly through this encounter with her shipmates, and worse, that she would attempt to compensate for that inefficacy with such a coercive abuse of power, pulling rank to silence the not-unreasonable qualms of Valenti and de Bronk. And in fact, the entire Rhadamanthus IX episode teems with similar, albeit lesser, missteps on Sertôrian's part. Many claim, then, that this account is a dangerous piece of anti-Sertôrial invective, fabricated or embellished by those who would discredit her supernal teachings.

I disagree, largely because I'm wary of the urge to bleach any possible blemish from Sertôrian's past. Of what use to us is a sibyl who made no mistakes? What could such a person possibly teach us? Tempting though it may be to construe Sertôrian as an ethereal innocent, all the better to explain her mystic profundity, such an approach creates a flimsy foundation on which to build one's faith. To a large extent, my devotion to Sertôrian grows out of her very real fallibility. I don't dispute, then, that her behavior in the stone chamber is out of character. Clearly it is. But does that necessarily mean it didn't happen? Of course not. Though I generally hesitate to make universal claims about human behavior, I can comfortably say that it is not characterized by absolute consistency.

So. So what now? As I read over the preceding lines, I can't help but suspect that I'm only restating arguments I've already made at greater length in *Sertôrian the Woman*. And beyond that, of what use—I can't help but ask myself—is any of this scholarship in the face of impending death? In my previous book, I criticized those who co-opt and misconstrue Sertôrian to fill whatever spiritual or metaphysical gaps they find in their own ramshackle lives. Having examined my own life in light of recent developments, I can't help but notice significant gaps of my own, gaps that the Sertôrian from *Sertôrian the Woman* does little to remediate. And if my exegesis of the Rhadamanthus IX narrative can't even help me, then what good can it possibly do for anyone else? Since writing the previous paragraph, I've spent two full days composing and discarding half a dozen different conclusions for this chapter, each of which fails to solve the argument's (and my own) problems. I am, I must confess, at a loss as to how we might proceed.

Yesterday in the library I was discussing these very problems with my friend Sister Beatriz as we each hunted down books for our respective projects. She and I took our vows within weeks of each other, and for decades now she has been my closest confidante and best critic. We've not spoken as much lately, though, as everyone in the convent has been so absorbed in completing as much work as possible before the Delegarchic troops arrive to carry out our death sentence. Sister Beatriz, however, has decided to take a break, as she explained to me yesterday. She studies vortemathics—is one of the foremost scholars in her field, in fact—and is currently working on a three-volume critique of quantified metaphysics.

"And it's good, noble work," she said about the project. "I truly believe that, but I also don't want to spend my final hours calibrating lexiquations."

"What would you do instead?" I asked, climbing one of the library's many rolling ladders to reach an ancient atlas of the Minoan System.

"I'm planning a picnic," she said, "for starters."

This took me aback, as a picnic reeks of whimsicality and Sister Beatriz is anything but whimsical. I found the atlas I was looking for and pulled it from the shelf.

"A picnic?" I said, descending the ladder with the atlas under one arm. "Where would you have a picnic?"

"There's that bay window up in the observatory that looks out on Persephone III," said Sister Beatriz, paging halfheartedly through a philosophical survey of the Imperial Space Age. "I've always had a soft spot for that view. There's no place nearby to sit, so I plan to spread a blanket and eat on the floor while I look out the window at the beautiful view."

She hefted the book of philosophy up onto the shelf—the volume was almost as big as she was—and rolled her shoulders in relief, looking for a moment like a weary, middle-aged prizefighter.

"Hmm," I said, laying down my atlas on one of the library's study tables and consulting my list of books to retrieve. "That does sound pleasant."

And it did sound pleasant, but I had so much work I still needed to do.

"Yes," said Sister Beatriz, lifting another enormous book and examining its frontispiece. "You should come along."

"I can't," I said. As I scanned the shelves of the history section, I explained the problems I'd been having with this chapter. I hoped that Sister Beatriz might help me, as she had on so many previous occasions, to find a way past this apparent dead end.

Rather than provide any useful advice, though, she set down her book and said, "All the more reason to join me tomorrow."

"But there's no time," I said. "I really must finish this monograph."

I rolled a ladder into position and started up it in pursuit of a green-spined monograph on the ethics of leadership.

"You know, Úrsula," said Sister Beatriz, pausing until I looked her in the eye. "If you've run out of things to say, perhaps you've already finished."

This was not a sentiment I wanted to hear, and it irked me that Sister Beatriz could be so blasé about a problem that was causing me so much turmoil. In a bluster, I pulled the ethics book from the shelf and descended the ladder. The look of amusement on Beatriz's face only made me angrier, so I gathered my other books from the study table and excused myself on the pretense that I needed to get back to work. I told Beatriz, with what I hoped was sufficient sarcasm, to enjoy her picnic.

"I will," she said, unfazed. "Although I'd enjoy it more if you joined me."

"I don't think that will be possible," I said, heading out the door.

"Well," she said, "I'll stop by your desk tomorrow on my way out to see if you've changed your mind. I think you might."

"I wouldn't plan on it," I said, and took my leave.

Unfortunately, as is generally the case, Sister Beatriz was right and I have changed my mind. This monograph appears to have reached its logical end. Although much of the Rhadamanthus IX episode remains to be examined, I can muster no consequential scholarly or spiritual response. This morning, the narrative only summons a stream of memories from my own life, moments of shame and anger like the one Irena Sertôrian experienced in the stone chamber behind the waterfall. I think of opportunities squandered, damages inflicted, deep sentiments left unexpressed. And since such glum, self-focused thoughts have no place in the realm of scholarship, I can only thank you for your patience up to this point, apologize for any disappointment, and bring this monograph to an early close.

All that's left for me is to join Sister Beatriz on her foolish picnic.

## EIGHT

I still remember the first time I met Sister Beatriz. I was so young—we both were—and had just entered the postulancy here at the Astral Cenobium of Outer Hyperion. At the welcome mixer in the great-cloister, I had already met and exchanged pleasantries with a handful of fellow postulants, as well as some of the sworn votaries, when a short, angular girl with a little plate of chocolate cake in each hand introduced herself. Her name was Beatriz. I said it was nice to meet her.

"You have to try this," she said, giving me one of the little plates of cake. "It's phenomenal. Here." She extracted a fork from the pocket of her skirt and handed it to me. "It's clean, I promise."

"Thanks," I said, pleasantly taken aback by the warm but unoppressive familiarity of this person I'd barely met. I took a bite of cake. It *was* very good.

"Phenomenal, right?" said Beatriz, taking a bite from her own plate.

"Yes," I said. "It's delicious."

For a moment we just stood there, enjoying the cakes together. With the other postulants, I'd felt that first-encounter imperative to keep the energetic small talk at a constant flow. This Beatriz had approached me, though, as if we were already old friends, and so the temporary silence hung comfortably between us as we ate our cake.

"So what's your field?" said Beatriz, scraping up the last bits of crumb and frosting with the edge of her fork.

"History," I said, hoping her follow-up questions wouldn't be too specific.

"Oh!" she said. "Have you read *The Phoenix of Empire*? I love that one. Or what about *The Private Lives of Ancient Martians*? Figueira is just so meticulous about recreating what life was like in those early settlements. It's so vivid but it's rigorous too. Like that description of their hydroponic suspension gardens? Or the scripts of those early radio programs they produced—the one about the woman on Mars who falls in love with a future version of her next-door neighbor? Unbelievable. It blew me away the first time I read it. Do you like that one?"

I lied and said I loved both books. At seventeen I brimmed with grand, scholarly ambition, but the reality was that I had read almost nothing. My high school on Argus II had been adequate and I had applied myself to my studies, but farm duties had demanded so much of my attention. I helped my parents with everything: mixing feed, wrangling the calves, cleaning the milking parlor—all of it. To finish my schoolwork each day I stole five minutes here and ten minutes there, completing my chores with as much speed as the task allowed and working out a geometry problem or writing a paragraph for an ethics paper before my parents required my help with the next task. And so, while I completed all of my assigned homework with as much thoroughness as I could manage, I had no time for extracurricular reading or study. Still, I thrived at school and graduated at the top of my class.

It was on the day of my high school graduation that I learned of the Astral Cenobites' existence. We are by no means a secret order, only a quiet one, and as a result we tend not to attract much outside interest. Of course that's changed recently, but at the time I had never heard of the order until at the graduation ball, Ms. Sturgess, my history teacher, pulled me aside to tell me she'd submitted my name for consideration to the order's postulancy program.

"You should find out in about a month if you've been accepted or not," she said. "And you don't have to go if you don't want to. But I think you should."

Ms. Sturgess was one of the few people to whom I'd confided my scholarly ambitions—not even my parents knew—and this vote of confidence in my potential thrilled me. I waited on tenterhooks for the next month, my body performing its duties in the requisite farm chores but my mind completely preoccupied with dreams of becoming a historian. When, a month to the day after graduation, I received a letter admitting me as a postulant, I was dumbstruck with joy. My parents, when I'd explained the situation, were both shocked and proud. No one in our family, they told me, had ever had such an opportunity. I wrote back accepting the position and began my preparations.

Then reality set in. What did I know, after all, about history? Yes, I had read my high school textbooks with care, had given passionate dinnertime speeches on the importance of understanding our past, and had stayed after class not infrequently to learn more from Ms. Sturgess on whatever topic we had covered that day. But that made me nothing more than a relatively precocious student from a backwater agricultural planet whose standards of education were none too high.

I became convinced that I would flounder at the Cenobium, and I came close to turning down the offer I'd already accepted with an explanation that I just wasn't qualified. Ms. Sturgess talked me down from this ledge with a kind letter outlining what she saw as my scholarly virtues. I would, she allowed, find the order challenging, but she was certain that, given my work ethic and my tenacity, I would thrive under pressure. As my departure date approached, I squared my shoulders and resolved to become the student my history teacher thought I could be.

I know now that Beatriz, and not I, was the anomaly among the postulants. The Astral Cenobites accept applicants based primarily on their eagerness to learn and their willingness to consecrate their studies to the objectives of the Order. Preexisting expertise is not necessary, and therefore most postulants have yet to receive any significant training in their presumptive fields. But I didn't know that then. I felt quite the imposter and reasoned that it wouldn't do to let on to the others. Especially not to this Beatriz, who epitomized the sophisticated young scholar I wanted to be.

Eager to change the subject away from history, then, I asked about Beatriz's field.

"I study vortemathics," she said.

"Vortemathics," I said neutrally.

"Yes," she said. "Have you heard of it?"

I hadn't, and knew I couldn't bluff past my ignorance.

"No," I said, ashamed.

"It's okay," she said, taking my empty plate from me and dropping it with her own into a garbage bag proffered by one of our fellow postulants. "Nobody's heard of it. Hardly anyone at least. It's a new discipline that some of the sisters at the Appoline Institute have pioneered. Basically what it is is an attempt to map out the general contours of reality using a combination of preexisting disciplines, like philosophy and mathematics, as well as some new methodologies that involve very precise, very high-caliber instruments that can measure certain emotions and feelings, or at least that's what their inventors claim. It's essentially about exploring what happens at the intersection of the subjective and the objective. Does that make sense?"

"Kind of," I said.

By this point, the other postulants were trickling out of the great-cloister to find the breakout groups that constituted the next part of our orientation day. Beatriz showed no sign of wrapping things up, which made me feel oddly flattered.

"You're right," said Beatriz. "That's not very helpful." She pinched her lower lip. "Maybe think of it this way," she said after a moment's consideration. "Do you know how to poach an egg?"

"I can fry an egg," I said. "Or boil one."

"But you've at least eaten a poached egg before, right?"

"Yes," I lied.

I wondered if Beatriz was trying to intimidate me, to establish from day one her unassailable superiority. If so, she was doing a marvelous job.

In due time I would understand that intimidation wasn't her goal, that Beatriz had, and has, no interest in such games, and that her social style grows out of a persistent and usually flawed assumption that her comrades are as quick thinking, as perceptive, and as well read as she is.

"Well, this is how you poach an egg," she said, pivoting around so that we both faced an imaginary stovetop. "You fill a saucepan with about two centimeters of water, add a pinch of salt and a dash of vinegar, and you put that on a burner set to medium. While that's heating up, you crack your egg into a teacup. Once your water comes to a boil, you stir it around with a whisk until a whirlpool forms. Got that so far?"

"Yes," I said, listening as carefully as I knew how.

"Okay," she said. "So, you keep the whirlpool going with the whisk in your one hand, and then with your free hand you pick up the teacup and drop the egg into the center of the whirlpool. And be sure to drop it gently. Then what you do, you keep the whirlpool going until the egg just starts to set, because the vortex at the center is what's keeping the egg from feathering out into the water. Then, once the egg starts to set, you cover the pan, turn off the heat, and wait for exactly three minutes. Finally you uncover the pan and pull the egg out immediately with a slotted spoon." She smiled. "Did you get all that?"

"Yes," I said, already entranced by her apparent cosmopolitanism.

"Good," she said. "Now this oversimplifies everything, but it should start to give you an idea of how vortemathics works. The egg is truth. I mean, it's actually much more complex than that—what is truth, even?—but we're keeping things simple. So the point of the whole process is to make the egg, or truth, consumable or comprehensible for people. Again, I'm really simplifying here, so I apologize."

"It's not a problem," I said a little too quickly.

"All right," said Beatriz. "So if the egg is truth, in this instance the heat under the pan represents traditional philosophy. You know—Plato, Hegel, Wittgenstein, Samovanti, Taghut. And the pan, the thing that's holding this all together, is mathematics. Which leaves the water. The water is what vortemathics brings to the process. Oh, and it's only when it's spinning. The water, I mean. That little contained whirlpool is vor-temathics. Does that make sense?"

"Well," I said, feeling a bit spun around myself.

She said, "It's okay if it doesn't. Like I said, vortemathics is really hard to explain and I'm still pretty new at it. I could loan you *A Short Introduction to Vortemathics*, though. It explains everything much better than I can."

I was already learning to treat, as Beatriz did, the considerable voids in my education not as flaws in my character but rather as exciting journeys yet to be taken. I've learned much over the years from Beatriz's complete transparency regarding the holes and limitations in her own knowledge, as well as her habit of eagerly seeking illumination from the expertise and experience of others.

"Thanks," I said. "I'd like that."

All of the other postulants had moved on now to their breakout groups, leaving the two of us alone in the great-cloister. Beatriz seemed not to notice.

"But what about history?" she said. "What period are you interested in?"

I mustered a half-coherent answer about the inception of the Imperial Space Age, a genuine interest of mine, albeit one I knew little about beyond its treatment in my high school history book. Beatriz, in a manner both endearing and intimidating, hung on my every word, asking thoughtful questions about the influence of cryptodiplomacy and the role played by the threat of nuclear war.

We were interrupted finally by one of the older cenobites telling us we needed to move along, and quickly. As we made our way to our separate breakout groups, Beatriz said we'd have to pick this conversation up later. She'd see me at lunch? I said she would and she waved a cheery goodbye. So began our friendship.

On our picnic a few days ago, I recounted this memory to Sister Beatriz as we idled next to the broad picture window overlooking Persephone III.

"Do you remember that?" I asked.

"Of course," she said, wiping the corners of her mouth with a napkin.

We had finished our egg sandwiches, our pickled beets, our rind of cheese, and our fruit salad, and were sipping some earthy cashew wine that Sister Constance had bottled the previous fall. Bracing myself for the inevitable sadness that overtakes me after a hearty lunch, I looked out at the pink-and-green surface of Persephone III. Sister Beatriz, meanwhile, produced a casqada from the laundry bag that served as our picnic basket and began plucking out a halting tune on the instrument's seven strings.

The cashew wine, rather than render me more maudlin, dulled my afternoon sorrow, inviting a tentative contentment to sidle up next to the ache in my heart. Sister Beatriz's pluckings, meanwhile, grew more fluent as her fingers loosened, and soon a near-festive atmosphere permeated the observatory. I tapped my fingers in time with the music, a catchy dance tune I recognized from my girlhood. Swallowing the last of the wine from my mug, I lay on my back and closed my eyes. I could almost forget that death lurked just at the edge of this happy tableau.

We spent the better part of that afternoon with the sweeping vista of Persephone III beside us, reminiscing about our brash misadventures as youthful postulants. In recalling our exploits, we wondered at that maddening combination, endemic to the young, of guilelessness and bravado.

Perhaps in an attempt to recapture that spirit, we spent the next two days shirking our duties and, while strolling the lesser-trafficked stairways and cloisters of the Cenobium, making grand plans for the future. We would tour the far-flung outposts of our Order, sampling their libraries and striking up new friendships with our fellow cenobites. We would cultivate a warmer sense of community here at the convent. We would take our scholarly fields by storm.

We mentioned nothing of the Syndicate forces' imminent arrival.

I've since returned to my writing, as you can see. After three days spent in pure diversion, Sister Beatriz and I both found ourselves yearning for the tethering influence of our unfinished projects. So we will balance our flights of fancy with a few hours a day spent in our respective studies, laboring at our respective projects. The urge, I have found, to spend my final days examining the Rhadamanthus IX episode ultimately proves too strong.

## NINE

Just three years after her appearance before the Syndics of Mars, Irena Sertôrian delivered a short sermon to a group of early followers at the Palladium of Novo Pernambuco. Many of her teachings from this period have been collected into what we now know as *The Shadow Doctrines*, and though they lack the full majesty of her late-period thinking, these sermons hint at the theological heights she would later ascend to. The Palladium Sermon, as it's called, is no different. Sertôrian begins this discourse with the claim that "just as nature abhors a vacuum, our minds abhor a mystery." After exploring that claim at length, Sertôrian arrives at her conclusion. If I might take a chronological liberty here, I'd like to cite those final thoughts to set the stage for the events awaiting Sertôrian on Rhadamanthus IX decades before the speech was given: "A prohibition and a mystery are one and the same—a locked room whose inscrutable door beckons us closer. Human curiosity impels us to open it, and the enlightenment we find inside—if it's truly worth our while—will invariably devastate us."

The Rhadamanthus IX narrative shares with the Palladium Sermon a preoccupation with enlightenment and transgression, authority and dissent, and like the Palladium Sermon, it yields no easy answers to the reader seeking a blandly inspiring portrait of Sertôrian and her thinking. When examined with a discerning eye and a strong stomach, however, this narrative can productively illuminate uncomfortable yet vital dimensions of Sertôrian's life and teachings. Disconcerting as these

revelations may be for a devout follower of Sertôrian, a better understanding of our beloved and holy sibyl will only aid us in following her
precepts.

As we rejoin Bombal's narrative, then, consider carefully, with open
mind and open heart, the destruction that unfolds:

•   •   •

Fully assembled, the Bulgakov Apparatus resembled nothing so
much as a domed birdcage, but with dimensions best suited not to
a parakeet or a canary but a human being. Heavy straps hung from
the top of the cage to form what looked like a harness, and the
cage's flat plastic base was filled with tiny holes like a shower-
head's. Between the metal bars, a gauzy, jellyfish-like material
glistened in the morning sun. A close inspection of the device revealed no on-off switch, no levers, no instrument panel of any sort.

"It doesn't make sense," said de Bronk, circling the device, his
wrinkled face twisted in perplexity. "Was there a remote control
box that we overlooked?"

"I don't think so," said Valenti.

A breeze rustled the jellyfish membrane, flapping it against the
cage's metal bars. There had to be a way to activate the Apparatus,
but none of the three shipmates could find one. They tried waving
the Green Beacon at it, tried issuing voice commands. They even
tried kicking the base to knock some loose component into action.

Then Sertôrian noticed the door, hardly distinguishable from
the rest of the cage structure yet large enough to allow a full-
grown adult to enter the Apparatus. A closer look revealed a delicate hasp flush against a metal bar. Sertôrian unfastened it and
opened the door. As she did so, the hanging harness descended to
ground level. Sertôrian took a step toward the open doorway.

"Captain, before you go in there," said Valenti.

"Yes?" said Sertôrian, turning away from the Apparatus. She wasn't having second thoughts exactly, but the magnitude of the situation was becoming increasingly apparent. She was willing at this point to wait just a moment before committing herself to the Apparatus in all its formidable potentiality. It couldn't hurt, after all, to listen to what her junior officer had to say.

"Let's say this is the Bulgakov Apparatus," said Valenti, who remained skeptical. "What if it's a trap?"

"They wouldn't—" began de Bronk.

"Let her finish," said Sertôrian.

"Just think about it for a second," said Valenti. "The Bulgakov Collective hated the way the Three Empires kept repurposing their inventions—that's why they split up, right? Well, what if they *wanted* this invention to be repurposed? Not repurposed exactly, but what if it was designed all along to be used by the Empires? What if it's designed to destroy whoever uses it?" Valenti shook her head. "We just need to walk away."

That would certainly be the prudent course of action, but Sertôrian was sick to death of such caution. How had prudence, after all, benefitted her crew? Nearly all of them were dead now and if she were a betting woman she would not lay great odds on the survival of those who remained. If—and this was a big if— they made it off Rhadamanthus IX, it was only a matter of time before another backwater Minoan planet pulled them into its squabbling, deadly grasp. Their odds of returning home felt so remote that Sertôrian had a hard time seeing the downside of taking a chance on the Bulgakov Apparatus.

"I appreciate your concern," said Sertôrian to Valenti, "but we'll proceed as planned."

Sertôrian stepped into the cage and pulled the door shut behind her. Valenti and de Bronk took several paces backward. Sertôrian slipped her arm through the straps of the harness and buckled the thick belt around her waist. When she had cinched the leg straps tight, the harness lifted Sertôrian until her feet dangled several feet above the ground. From the top of the dome, a small metal bowl, previously unnoticeable, descended and fitted itself to Sertôrian's head. She looked down at her shipmates, who stared back up at her, their necks craned. The Apparatus began to hum, a steady liquid sound that under other circumstances might have been quite soothing.

The humming rose in pitch and the jellyfish membrane between the bars of the cage glowed pink and green. Sertôrian shifted in her harness, and all but three of the dome's bars unfastened themselves from the base and lifted upward like the spokes of an umbrella. The jellyfish material remained in place, forming a ghostly dome. The humming grew louder, accompanied now by an industrial sucking from the holes in the base of the Apparatus.

Sertôrian felt an alarming hollowness spreading through her body and found that she couldn't move her limbs. Up above her head, the raised bars began to spin, cutting through the air with a dangerous whistle. The feeling of hollowness grew more intense, permeating her bones. Sertôrian would have doubled over midair from the unpleasantness of it, but the movements of her body remained beyond her control. As the bars spun faster, the jellyfish membrane, now glowing a deep red, suddenly went limp and hung like a cloak around Sertôrian's body. The hollowness inside her dissipated, replaced with a melting warmth, and Sertôrian could move again.

She looked up through the translucent material, which cycled frantically now from one color to the next, and saw the metal bars spinning faster and faster and faster, heard the sucking from below growing louder and louder and louder. The warm, melting feeling inside her grew less and less pleasant.

And then, with disturbing abruptness, everything stopped. The metal bars descended and refitted themselves to the now silent base. The jellyfish material expanded outward, reattaching itself to the bars of the cage. And the cables by which Sertôrian hung lowered her until her feet touched the floor. She tested her weight on her legs and discovered she could stand comfortably. Any strange feelings had dissipated the moment the device shut off. Unsure of how else to proceed, Sertôrian freed herself from the harness and stepped out of the cage. She closed the door behind her.

"Well," said Sertôrian.

"Do you feel different at all?" said Valenti cautiously.

Briefly taking mental stock, Sertôrian shook her head. Valenti eyed her suspiciously.

"Nothing?" said de Bronk.

"Not that I can tell," said Sertôrian.

But the Apparatus hadn't finished. From the tiny holes in the base of the cage, a fleshy vapor arose, pouring out in greater and greater profusion until it filled the space inside the domed machine. The three shipmates watched in wonder as the meaty cloud touched the walls of the cage. The jellyfish substance glowed a rich purple, and the long metal bars once again unfixed themselves from the base and rose upward. The glowing purple membrane contracted around the cloud of vapor, and the metal bars spun with a wobbly kineticism.

"Is it broken?" said Valenti.

Before anyone could respond, arcs of electricity danced across the spinning bars with ear-numbing crackles. The jellyfish membrane contracted tighter and tighter, and the erratic spinning of the bars set the Apparatus wobbling on its base.

De Bronk fell to the ground, facedown, hands covering his neck. Valenti followed suit. Sertôrian remained standing, unable to look away from the spectacle before her. The noise grew even more terrible, the sparks even more frightful, and Sertôrian considered dropping to the ground next to her shipmates. Just as she began to crouch down, though, the Apparatus fell silent with a heavy mechanical sigh. The metal bars descended to re-form a dome and the glowing membrane ballooned back out to meet them. The mist inside the machine was gone. Everything had returned to normal, except that now a woman hung from the harness inside the cage.

Sertôrian stood and nudged her prone shipmates with her toe. She told them it was safe to get up, and they rose to their feet. When they saw the woman hanging from the harness inside the cage, they approached the Apparatus with awed trepidation. Sertôrian followed close behind. Though the woman's eyes were closed, her chest rose and fell with vital regularity. She seemed to be alive.

The presence of a previously nonexistent woman was, in itself, remarkable enough. But that alone was not the most striking aspect of this apparition.

"It's you," said de Bronk, turning to face Sertôrian. "It's a copy of you."

Indeed, the woman bore a strong resemblance to Captain Irena Sertôrian—the same lean, athletic build; the same dark hair and coppery skin; the same strong jawline; and on her face, the same expression, manifest even in repose, of flinty competence.

"It's you," repeated de Bronk, this time urgently.

Mouth agape, eyes on the woman in the harness, Valenti nodded in confirmation.

"It's not," said Sertôrian, already moving to the door of the cage. "Look again."

A closer look revealed a smattering of subtle physical differences between the woman and Sertôrian—a wider set to the woman's mouth; thicker, more dramatic eyebrows; streaks of gray in her hair; and altogether a slightly older appearance.

De Bronk said, "Then what—"

"It's Rosa," said Sertôrian, fumbling with the hasp of the door. "It's my sister."

## TEN

A person might keep a secret for any number of reasons—shame, self-preservation, caution, generosity—but no matter how base or elevated the motives, secrets corrode their keepers. They're potent things, secrets are, and by sad experience I've come to know how the decades-long concealment of a certain truth can nibble and gnaw at the iron girders of the soul until rust threatens to consume the entire structure. I often wonder if the maintenance of such secrecy represents a strength or a weakness of character, but that might be the wrong question entirely.

With cryptic rigor, Irena Sertôrian kept secret her views on the afterlife. Nowhere in her writings, her sermons, or her Four Shrouded Visions does she endorse or oppose the possibility of a life after this one. Articulating a view held by many scholars and lay believers alike, Vladimir Petrokoff, in his *Visions of the Eternal: Irena Sertôrian's Silent Eschatology*, argues that such silence represents a tacit approval of status quo religious beliefs held by citizens of the Lachesian Empire in Sertôrian's day, a more or less bifurcating afterlife in which worthy souls enjoy an eternity dwelling in paradise while the wicked are consigned to a realm of endless torment. If there were no afterlife, argues Petrokoff, then it would have been incumbent on Sertôrian to say so. Silence, then, can be taken as confirmation of Lachesian beliefs regarding the hereafter, and no significant mystery exists.

I say nonsense. I know a secret when I see one, and Sertôrian's absolute silence on the possibility of an afterlife fits the bill. Such a spotless omission suggests not a lazy endorsement of prevailing beliefs but a vigorous preemptive scrubbing of any trace of the idea from her public discourse.

But why the compulsive vigilance? For a compelling theory, we need look no further than the Rhadamanthus IX narrative.

It's a testament to the story's unpopularity that as I reviewed the key scholarly literature on Sertôrian and the hereafter over the past few days, I found nothing—nothing!—that considers the uncanny fruit of the Bulgakov Apparatus as a possible contributing factor to Sertôrian's reticence on the subject. As we'll see to an even greater degree as the Rhadamanthus IX narrative progresses toward its finale, no rational person could argue that Sertôrian's silence on all things eschatological could arise from apathy.

Earlier this evening, I was holding forth on this very topic to Sister Beatriz. We sat at a metal folding table in the calefactory playing two-handed oubliette, the most popular game on Hermes VII, Sister Beatriz's home planet. She taught me how to play it on our first rest day as postulants, and we've had a standing appointment every Steladay evening since. We both know the game so well by this point—the rules, the odds, the favored strategies of the other player—that any given round holds little suspense for either of us. Our back-and-forth gambits with the well-worn cards have become an amicable ritual, the gestures, the objects, and the sequence of play sacralizing and cementing our friendship. With our hands and certain portions of our brain pleasantly occupied with the tasks of the game, we devote our remaining attentions to airing and discussing the week's grievances and triumphs.

Such was the case this evening. I was working myself into a fine, righteous lather on the topic of Sertôrian's eschatology when Sister Beatriz, normally such a patient listener, cut me off mid-sentence.

"Excuse me?" I said. So unexpected was her interruption that her words flew straight past my ears.

"I said I have a question for you."

The holo-fire crackled in the hearth. At the other end of the calefactory, Sister Greta, a youngish cenobite who specializes in astronomy, manipulated a three-dimensional scale model of the Orpheus System with her magno-wand, completely absorbed in her task. Otherwise, we had the room to ourselves.

"You think my reasoning is unsound?" I said.

"No," she said. "It's nothing to do with that." She executed a neat waterfall with the impossible-to-shuffle round oubliette cards and dealt a new hand. Eyes still on the cards, she said, "Do *you* think there's an afterlife?"

From time to time, when my musings ratchet up into heated diatribes, Sister Beatriz will respond with a well-crafted question that nudges me toward an alternate perspective or an oversight in my thinking. She's a firm believer in this type of dialogue, though I often wish she would just come out with what she has to say rather than shepherding me toward it like a beleaguered work dog.

But this query about the afterlife was not like that. No, there was a plaintive quality to it, a distinct vulnerability opening up in its wake.

I wasn't sure how to respond, so I reminded Sister Beatriz that among Sertôrian's followers, various conceptions of the afterlife exist. While nearly all versions agree that the soul, once it's in the afterlife, will live on forever, dissent exists regarding whether the respective punishments and rewards will also be eternal. Many believe that once the soul has suffered sufficiently, it will be released from its hell and allowed into paradise. Others argue that this would be a travesty of justice.

But that, I said to Sister Beatriz, was only one of numerous debates surrounding the afterlife. Other topics of speculation include what form the eternal soul will take—corporeal? spiritual? recognizably human? And then there's the question of the Infinite Eremites. Will we encounter them in the afterlife? Or do they occupy a separate plane of existence altogether? As this question requires a grafting of Sertôrial cosmology onto ancient eschatology, searching for an answer with any degree of scholarly rigor proves nearly impossible.

Of course, I said, hundreds, even thousands, of smaller debates, questions, and theories exist, but those ideas I've mentioned constitute the key features of the afterlife as envisioned by followers of Sertôrian.

I also reminded Sister Beatriz that not all of Sertôrian's disciples believe in a hereafter. Some argue that Sertôrian's silence on the topic reflects the post-mortal oblivion that awaits us all, but that this should not be cause for despair. They argue that a finite human existence renders the teachings of Sertôrian, as well as her visions, all the more significant—a major implication of death's finality being that life is a precious, rare commodity that should always be treated as such. Though they have the textual support—or rather, the strength of textual absence—on their side, their position remains perennially unpopular.

"That's an impressive abstract of the field," said Sister Beatriz, laying a card down on the table. "But what do *you* believe?"

I played the three of knives to her three of spoons and thought for a moment.

"I'm not sure," I said. "I suppose I'm something of an agnostic on the question."

"Do you like the idea, though?" she said. "Of an afterlife, I mean."

Sister Beatriz played the three of forks and I laid down the seven. At the other end of the room, Sister Greta muttered an angry string of words in her native tongue and erased a long thread of calculations with her magno-wand.

"The notion of hell frightens me," I said. "I certainly wouldn't want to end up there, if it exists. I've striven to live an ethical life, but who knows?"

"But if you avoided hell?"

These questions were beginning to irritate me, and I wasn't sure why.

"Oh, I don't know," I said, pretending to examine my cards.

Sister Beatriz tossed the ten of forks onto the table.

"Do you find any comfort in the possibility of a post-mortal paradise?" she said.

"Don't you?" I said, laying down the hound of forks.

Sister Beatriz leaned over and turned down the volume on the crackling holo fire. Then she played the thief of forks and took the trick. I dealt a new hand.

"The more seriously I contemplate death," Sister Beatriz said, "the more terrifying I find the prospect of a life after this one."

"Terrifying?" I said.

"Yes," she said. "I've come to realize that for me to be happy in the afterlife"—she ran her finger along the round edges of her card—"for me to be truly happy . . . Well . . . Certain elements would have to be in place."

"Like what?" I asked. She had my full attention now, and I waited for her to answer with a nervous jangling in my chest.

"Well." She opened the trick with a jailer's double: the ace of spoons and the map of knives. She looked up at me in triumph. "Care to redact your bid?"

"That won't be necessary," I said, though it was clear to both of us that she would now, in all likelihood, take the trick. It didn't matter; our conversation had decisively trumped my interest in the game. I knew what I wanted Sister Beatriz to say about the afterlife—something I'd thought myself on many occasions—but I didn't dare believe she might say it. As casually as possible, as if I wasn't aching to hear what she said next, I played a prisoner's delight—the ace of knives and the hound of forks. Sister Beatriz responded with the deuce and the ten of spoons.

"So?" I said, finding it increasingly difficult to feign disinterest.

"I just played a digger's double," she said. "It's your turn."

"I know that," I said. "But you haven't answered my question."

Her bottom lip shrugged upward.

At the other end of the room, Sister Greta, still engrossed in her three-dimensional map, uttered a relieved "of course," and scribbled furiously in the air above the ghostly planets before her.

"I don't know," said Sister Beatriz. "It's not . . ."

She turned and stared into the holo-fire.

Turning back to look at me, she said, "You do understand what I mean, though, don't you? Aren't there certain things that would have to be true about paradise for you to be happy there?"

I laid down a pair of moons, not meeting Sister Beatriz's eyes.

"I suppose so," I said. "If paradise *does* exist, though, I imagine I'd be happy there."

"But would you be happy there no matter what?" she said. "The trick's yours, by the way—well done." She pushed the cards toward me, and I gathered them into my pile.

"If it's paradise," I said, "by definition I think I'd have to be happy."

"Really?" she said. "No matter what it's like?"

Did I detect a pleading strain in her voice, or was that just wishful thinking?

"Well, if it's paradise," I said.

Sister Beatriz turned in her chair, her gaze resting on the wide map of the Hyperion System that hangs on the wall of the calefactory. She was rarely like this, rarely so at a loss for words. Without looking at me, she said, "But what if you couldn't be . . ."

The light of the holo-fire flickered across her face.

"Couldn't be what?" I said, my heart pounding.

A shake of the head and she turned back to look at me.

"I don't know. Forget it," she said. "I can't think of a good example of what I mean."

I leaned back in my chair, not wanting to betray my acute desire to know what she'd wanted to say. Sister Beatriz dealt a new hand.

"Are you sure?" I said, unwilling to let it go so easily. "Because it seemed like you might have had something specific in mind."

"Well, I didn't," she said. "It's your turn."

I laid down an ace of forks next to the dwindling round deck. We played the entire round in silence. Sister Beatriz took the trick.

"I suppose that all I was trying to say," Sister Beatriz said as we tallied our points from the first triad, "was that once we arrive in the afterlife, if it exists, we will never cease to be. Our post-mortal existence will stretch on forever. I don't know. The thought of such an infinite future leaves me feeling claustrophobic. A little short of breath. With no exit and no end, eternal life could be a very small cage indeed."

"But what if it's mostly pleasant?" I said.

She said it was that *mostly* that scared her, that even small deprivations played out endlessly become a hell of their own. Tapping the edges of her cards against the table, she cast her eyes downward.

I could sense that the moment of potential revelation had long passed. If Sister Beatriz had a secret to confess, she wouldn't be doing so this evening.

"Did you meet your bid?" she said, looking up from her score pad.

"Yes," I said. "You?"

She shook her head and I gathered all the cards. Still clumsy after all these years, I awkwardly shuffled the deck.

"I'd also be lying if I said I take comfort in the notion of death as oblivion," said Sister Beatriz. "But it also doesn't scare me more than an inescapable eternity. I don't know." She rubbed at a smudge on the table with her long middle finger. "Who knows what happens when we die?"

I dealt the opening hand.

"Either way," I said, thinking of the approaching Delegarchic troops, "we'll find out soon enough."

She frowned at her cards and said, "That's not a foregone conclusion, you know."

I looked over the ten cards in my hand and calculated the points I would bid for.

"Do you really believe that?" I said, penciling the figure onto my score pad.

"Yes," she said. "I do. There's every chance that we'll be playing two-handed oubliette again at this time next week, and the week after that, and the week after that, and on until we die of more natural causes."

As it happens, she's not entirely wrong. A chance for escape does exist. I mentioned earlier in this monograph that, on receiving the teleprint from the office of the Delegarchs, we deployed a galaxy cruiser with six specially trained cenobites inside. I can divulge no significant details about their mission, except to say that if all goes according to plan—and there's certainly no guarantee that it will—then a relief party with a ship capable of transporting us all to safety should—*should*—arrive here at the Cenobium before Delegarchic forces do. As I said, such a possibility is a remote one, and I refuse to allow hope, that winged menace, to find purchase in my heart.

"Still, though," I said, arranging the cards in my hand, "this could be our last game."

She shrugged and opened with the deuce of spoons.

Arranging and rearranging the cards in my hand, I tried hard not to picture the impending spacecraft, packed to capacity with armed Delegarchic troops.

"Do you feel ready to die?" I said, not sure what I wanted her answer to be.

She considered this as I lay down the three of spoons.

"Given the choice, I would prefer to live longer," she said. "And truly, I believe that we will. But if we die, I have no real regrets about how I've spent the time I've been given. Do you?"

Though they shouldn't have, both her answer and her follow-up question rattled me. I thought of secrets and corrosion and remorse. Sister Beatriz played the four of forks. I composed my thoughts.

"There are certain things I'd like to clarify before I die," I said. "To get out into the open."

"Is this to do with your monograph?" she said.

This was not to do with my monograph. This was to do with something far more personal, but I simply said, "Yes. The monograph."

If the words rang false, Sister Beatriz either didn't notice or chose to let them pass. Instead, she played the thief of forks and took the trick.

What I didn't tell Sister Beatriz is that when one contemplates one's own death, one reconsiders long-held decisions to keep certain sentiments to oneself, sentiments that, if disclosed, could render a once easy friendship an uneasy one, or worse yet, a non-friendship. There's nothing I value more than my relationship with Sister Beatriz, and isn't having part of what one yearns for better than having none of it? Close though we are, I remain uncertain as to how Sister Beatriz might receive such a revelation, and while I have no desire to imperil our friendship, I'm also loath to leave this life behind without first revealing that secret chamber of my heart to the person who resides within it.

## ELEVEN

. . .

Despite what she'd said to de Bronk, Sertôrian knew that the unconscious woman hanging from the top of the Bulgakov Apparatus could not be Rosa. No matter how closely this strange being resembled her sister, the fact remained that Rosa had been killed years earlier when a necrotic missile launched by a rogue Klothian battleship obliterated a holo-theater in the busiest neighborhood of Rosa's hometown on Mars, a civilian target whose destruction violated dozens of tri-imperial codes of war and signaled the dawn of a frightening period of political chaos.

That person in the harness, then, if it was a person, could only be a superficial replica. Its resemblance to Rosa—a cruel joke perpetrated in the poorest taste—slighted the dead woman's memory. Why, Sertôrian wondered, would the Bulgakov Collective have devoted their considerable genius to the creation of a device that produced such a disgusting product? Just then, as if she had read Sertôrian's thoughts, the woman opened her eyes.

Lifting her head to take in her surroundings, the woman appeared confused and slightly worried. When she saw the three shipmates standing around the perimeter of the cage, however, her eyes grew bright and confident, and her chapped lips stretched into an angular smile.

"It worked," she said, and as soon as she had spoken the words, the cables fixing the woman to the top of the cage lowered her at a regal pace to the floor of the Apparatus. When her feet touched the plastic base, her legs flexed, testing her weight. Wobbling only slightly, the woman held herself upright. After a few seconds, the wobbling ceased and she stood before Sertôrian, Valenti, and de Bronk in fixed, marmoreal grandeur.

Still smiling, she gazed at Sertôrian, maintaining uncomfortable eye contact as she unfastened the straps and ties of the harness. The woman held herself like a feared and respected monarch, her posture suggesting that anyone who failed to genuflect in her presence would do so at their own peril. Sertôrian felt equal parts horror, wonder, and disgust as she looked into the eyes of this pseudo-Rosa.

Once freed from her restraints, the woman strode forward until she stood mere inches from Sertôrian, separated only by the thin bars of the cage. With the added height of the plastic base below her, the woman towered over the three shipmates. Sertôrian fought back an urge to bow.

The woman licked her lips with a bright, pointed tongue—a tongue far longer and sharper, Sertôrian was nearly certain, than her sister Rosa's had ever been. Otherwise, the resemblance was nearly perfect, better than perfect, in fact; she looked fifteen years older than the last time Sertôrian had seen her, with the ever so slight sags and wrinkles of the woman's face and body accounting for the decade and a half that had passed between the sisters' last encounter.

"Hello, Irena," said the woman.

It was Rosa's deep, throaty voice, more distinctively hers than this body, even, and Sertôrian couldn't help but respond with: "Rosa. Hello."

As if unfrozen by the exchange, Ava Valenti pushed past Sertôrian to stand closer to the woman inside the Bulgakov

Apparatus. Valenti feigned nonchalance, or perhaps she was truly unflapped.

"I have to say," said Valenti, peering clinically at the woman, "I'm beyond impressed. The product appears very nearly human."

Valenti's cold condescension raised Sertôrian's hackles, even though she found the woman in the cage at least as uncanny as Valenti did. The emotional effect of the resemblance to Rosa—her face, and more than anything, her voice—was hard to shake.

Ignoring Valenti, the woman walked magisterially to the door of the cage and began to undo the mechanism that held it closed. Sertôrian wanted to stop her, to hold the door shut with the weight of her body, but she couldn't bring herself to move. As the woman unfastened the hasp, however, the metal recoiled at her touch, re-twisting itself shut and locking her inside the Apparatus. She tried again and again to open it, and each time, the metal squirmed beneath her fingers, resisting her increasingly frantic efforts with a lightning responsiveness of its own. Her queenly carriage dissolved into animal-like panic.

"Irena," said the woman, failing to keep the fear altogether out of her voice. "Open the door for me, would you?"

"No," said de Bronk, his elderly voice cracking. He had been silent to this point, mouth agape and eyes wide. Now his wrinkled face creased itself even further into an expression of anger and dismay.

Sertôrian was about to tell him that she had no intention of opening the door, but before she could, the old soldier emitted a long, rattling yell—half moan, half growl.

"This is all wrong," he choked out.

"De Bronk," said Valenti.

"This is all wrong," he said again, his voice strained and guttural. "All my life I dreamed of the Bulgakov Apparatus. But it was not this." He pointed an accusing arm at the cage, refusing to turn his head to look at it. "That thing inside there is not what I expected. It's not what I expected, Captain. This is not what—"

"All right, de Bronk," said Sertôrian. "Pull yourself together."

Instead, de Bronk let out another long low growl.

"De Bronk," said Sertôrian.

He took a deep, shuddering breath and fell silent. Sertôrian and Valenti exchanged a quick, worried glance.

"This is all wrong," de Bronk repeated one more time.

Sertôrian, Valenti, and the woman in the cage watched de Bronk shuffle off toward the tarp and their gear. Though usually as robust as a person half his age, he looked every bit the frail octogenarian as he curled up in a spare blanket, shaking his head and moaning.

Almost as rattled by her shipmate's collapse as by the appearance of this Rosa doppelgänger, Sertôrian turned her back on the Bulgakov Apparatus, staring off into the shadowy depths of the forest while she took a moment to collect herself.

"Captain," said Valenti, sounding cool and clinical again. "I'd like to ask that thing in the cage a few questions. With your permission, of course."

Sertôrian turned around, but before she could answer, the woman inside the Bulgakov Apparatus said, "You can ask me whatever you like, but I'd feel a lot better about all of this if I had some clothes to wear."

Within the greater strangeness of the situation, Sertôrian had failed to register the woman's nakedness, and up to this point it hadn't seemed to bother the woman either. But a new vulnerability had entered the woman's voice, and even though Sertôrian knew she should mistrust this new rhetorical tack, the woman's plaintiveness impelled her to action. Beyond that, Sertôrian was glad for a clear-cut task to focus on in this otherwise bewildering situation. She and Valenti scrounged through their gear for spare scraps of clothes, ignoring the now sleeping body of de Bronk. They handed what they found through the bars of the cage, allowing the woman to functionally, if not fashionably, attire herself in torn camo pants and a threadbare sweater.

"Thank you," said the woman, sounding even more like Rosa. "Now, are you going to introduce me to your friend?"

After a moment of confusion, Sertôrian realized the woman meant Valenti.

"This is Star-Guard Ava Valenti," said Sertôrian, "my next-in-command. Valenti, this is . . ."

She caught herself before introducing the woman as her sister, but the figure in the cage stepped in without missing a beat.

"Rosa Sertôrian," said the woman.

"Fascinating," said Valenti. She pulled a portable reel-to-reel tape recorder from her knapsack and aimed its microphone at the woman, who, for her part, sat down cross-legged at the edge of the cage.

"Why do you think this door won't open for you?" said Valenti, nodding at the Bulgakov Apparatus and beginning her line of questioning with no further preamble.

The woman licked her dry lips with her pointed tongue.

"Security measure, perhaps," she said.

"Do you pose a threat to us then?" said Valenti.

The woman smiled her sharp, angular smile. "No."

"Then why are you smiling like that?"

Though Sertôrian objected to Valenti's condescending tone, the questions had merit. The woman's smile had taken on a sly, predatory gleam, producing a double discomfort for Sertôrian; not only was it unsettling in itself, but it was also unpleasantly familiar. How many times had she seen that very expression on Rosa's face as an outward sign of her sister's tightly contained and potent rage? Was that what this woman felt right now? If so, she had good reason. How could she not be infuriated by Valenti's condescension and Sertôrian's apparent detachment?

"Well?" said Valenti.

"I'm smiling because I can help you," said the woman.

"Is that right?" said Valenti.

"It is," said the woman, her smile gone, impatience manifesting in the tightness of her voice.

"And what could we possibly need your help with?" said Valenti.

The woman stood up and, disregarding Valenti's question, turned to Sertôrian.

"Irena," said the woman. "You need to let me out of this cage."

Sertôrian didn't move. Not sure whether she felt more anger, fear, disgust, or most horrifying of all, affinity with this woman, Sertôrian didn't trust herself to respond out loud, fearing her voice would betray her trembling uncertainty.

"What do we need your help with?" repeated Valenti, like a parent humoring a stubbornly mendacious child.

"Irena," said the woman, her nostrils flaring.

"Answer Valenti's question, please," said Sertôrian, the *please* slipping out as the pseudo-Rosa's face took on a dangerous, stormy expression. The woman's gleaming eyes swept over Sertôrian's face.

"Fine," said the woman, her face relaxing. She leaned forward against the bars of the cage and beckoned Sertôrian closer.

"You can tell me from there," said Sertôrian.

The woman smiled. Was there a smugness there now, a satisfaction that her victims had finally opened their mouths to receive the deadly bait?

"I can get you off this planet," said the woman.

Valenti snorted at this claim, and Sertôrian felt an involuntary surge of hope. If this were true, the woman inside the Bulgakov

Apparatus had the power to resolve most, if not all, of the three shipmates' most pressing problems. But it had to be a lie.

"How?" said Sertôrian.

"There are things I understand now," said the woman, "that I didn't before I died."

"Like what?" said Valenti, lifting her tape recorder.

"Nothing I can put into words," said the woman. "Although if I had to describe it, I'd say I now have an intuitive understanding of the hidden workings of the universe."

Sertôrian felt her disgust waning by just a sliver, replaced by a proportional admiration for the woman's audacity.

"I see," said Valenti. "And how, specifically, will that help you get us off this planet."

The woman shook her head, lips pursed.

"I can't really explain it," she said. "I'd have to show you."

"Which means we'd have to let you out of the Bulgakov Apparatus," said Valenti.

"That's right," said the woman.

"Then I'd say we've reached an impasse," said Valenti.

"I can promise you," said the woman, "that you have more to lose by keeping me locked up than I do."

"Is that right?" said Valenti, starting to lose her cool.

"Irena," said the woman, looking over Valenti's shoulder, more relaxed now that she was gaining the upper hand. "Who's the one making decisions here? Are you going to let me out of this cage, or do I have to respond to more of your friend's inane questions?"

"I have a question for you, actually," said Sertôrian, increasingly intrigued by the woman's daring gambit. "You said you were dead before this?"

"That's right," said the woman patiently.

"What was it like?" said Sertôrian.

The woman appeared to think carefully about this, her brow furrowed, her lips pressed together.

"Let me guess," said Valenti. "It's not something you can put into words."

"I can certainly explain it," said the woman. "But I don't think you'll believe me."

"Go ahead," said Sertôrian. "I'm listening."

The woman took a moment to compose herself.

"I remember I was buying a bucket of popcorn at the concession stand of the holo-theater," she began, "when the room was filled with a horrible white light." The woman closed her eyes, either straining to remember or flinching at the picture in her mind. "I looked up and the ceiling had torn open. I was looking at night sky, and then there was this scraping, screeching explosion. Or maybe the explosion came first. Everything happened so quickly that it's hard for me to remember. Next thing I knew, though, I was on the ground, feeling kind of dizzy, and my clothes were very wet and very warm. At first I thought it was urine, but then I looked down and realized it was blood, lots of blood coming from my leg and my gut, and from there I guess I died pretty quickly. Which was like falling asleep—the dying, I mean. No great surprise there, but the feeling of sleep lasted only for a moment.

"I woke up in a new location that resembled a barren tundra—a flat, rocky landscape as far as the eye could see, no trees to speak of, and a sad, yellow groundcover in scattered patches. Above it all loomed a frosty gray sky. Somehow, though, I wasn't cold. A little chilly maybe, but not freezing. The other thing was, there were little clusters of animals everywhere, and my first thought was, *This is what happens when you die?* That disbelief lasted only a moment, however. As I looked at the animals nearest to me—a heron, a crocodile, and a wildebeest—I felt an overwhelming compulsion to lead them someplace else. I had no idea how I might go about it, or even where I wanted to lead them, but the longer I stood there, the stronger the compulsion grew. So I stood up (I'd been lying down) and I set about herding them the best I could,

320 | TIM WIRKUS

walking behind the animals, waving my arms, and yelling when it felt appropriate, as they waddled and flapped and trudged their way forward.

"It was all a bit haphazard, but still we made steady progress, maintaining our loose cohesion as a group and traveling in a more or less consistent direction as we went. After many, many days of this (and I use the term *days* loosely; it never grew dark, or light for that matter, the terrain bathed instead in constant twilight) I reached a gnarled old tree and knew that I had arrived. I allowed my three animals—the heron, the crocodile, and the wildebeest— to disperse, and then I curled up on the ground and slept.

"When I awoke, I began the whole process anew, gathering a different group of animals—this time a skunk, a tapir, a chimpanzee, and a tortoise—and setting off resolutely in a new direction, though I had no idea where this course would take us. I did know, though, in some instinctual part of my body, that we were going in the right direction.

"And so it went, the process repeating itself each time I delivered my latest group of animals. There was *some* variability to the process. Each group of animals took anywhere from a few hours to a few weeks to move, and of course the quantity and species of creatures in my group varied wildly from journey to journey. The one thing that didn't change, though, was that after I'd left the animals behind, I'd go off by myself and fall asleep. Then when I'd wake up, I'd start over again with another group of animals.

"From time to time, I ran into other people, and I might give them a nod or even a wave, but that's where the interaction always ended because we both had animals that we needed to move.

"And that's another thing. I've been saying, 'my group of animals,' like they belonged to me or I was in charge of them, but that wasn't it at all. I wasn't some rancher or farmer trying to get his fox and hare and carrots to the market. No. What it was . . . Well, I can't describe it. I'm not even sure there's a corollary in this life to that relationship, or if it was even a relationship at all. There was a strong logic underlying the process, though, albeit a very different logic than the one we use here—like a different language. Moving animals was just the exigent thing to do.

"So that's what I did for what felt like many years, with no break or significant variation in the general routine.

"Then one morning I woke up having deposited my latest group of animals at a nearby lake the evening before. I sat up, and a few yards away from me an enormous black bear lay dead on the ground. As soon as I saw it I knew what I needed to do. It wasn't like a revelation or anything; it was just what the logic of the situation dictated. It was clear to me that I needed to skin this bear and then wrap myself in its hide.

"I won't go into too much detail, but obviously I didn't have a knife so I had to do the whole job with some chipped obsidian I found not too far from the body. It was bloody, sweaty, stinking work, but after some amount of time, I had a peeled bear carcass on one side of me and a more or less intact bearskin on the other. The skin had taken on a faint glow, and I knew I had no time to waste. I shrugged the hide up onto my body. It weighed a ton. I put my arms inside the empty arms, my legs inside the empty legs. I flipped the skin of the head up over my own head. It felt terrible in there and smelled even worse.

"I'm not sure what prompted this, but once the bearskin was wrapped around me, I felt an intense desire for this to work. Before I could wonder what *this* even was, my vision went blurry and I passed out. When I woke up, I was hanging from the harness inside this cage."

She gestured at the Bulgakov Apparatus, whose barred dome glinted in the high afternoon sun.

"That's completely absurd," said Valenti.

"I recognize that," said the woman. "But it's also completely true."

Sertôrian, for her part, found in the woman's account of the afterlife a vast, feral quality that rendered the woman if not more trustworthy then at least more compelling. Her vexing cosmology, her very being, reminded Sertôrian of the vast Martian wilderness of her childhood, a landscape as austerely enticing as it was unpredictable. As a girl, Sertôrian had been unable to resist such a combination, and in her current circumstances she felt herself drawn deeper and deeper into this woman's story. Though she doubted all of the woman's claims, Sertôrian felt an intense desire to explore, even for a few minutes, the situation's treacherous landscape.

"I'm going to let you out of the Apparatus," said Sertôrian, "and you're going to get us off this planet."

The woman licked her lips with her pointed tongue, and her pupils gleamed semi-violet—a trick of the light? She practically sprang to the door of the Apparatus, clinging eagerly to its bars.

Valenti's body slumped in defeat. She switched off her tape recorder and returned it to her pocket.

"I realize," said Valenti to her captain, "that you're going to do what you want to do no matter what I say, but I can't, in good conscience, stay silent. That thing in the cage is not your sister—you know that, right?" Sertôrian said nothing. The woman inside the cage grinned, baring her teeth. Valenti continued. "What you're doing is unleashing havoc on us—I can guarantee that."

"Are you finished?" said Sertôrian.

"I am," said Valenti. "Do what you're going to do." Valenti gave Sertôrian a tired salute and wandered off to join de Bronk at the muddy tarp.

Inside the Bulgakov Apparatus, the woman took a step back from the door and held her hands clasped respectfully behind her back. Sertôrian undid the hasp that had so thoroughly foxed the Apparatus's occupant and opened the door.

Several minutes later, walking along the sandy banks of the wide Inhk-Ohm River, putting more distance between themselves and Sertôrian's shipmates with each step, the two women fell into a comfortable rhythm, the decisive forward momentum of their pace lending a false sense of purpose to an otherwise aimless, amorphous situation. They had left the camp on the pretext of gathering materials the woman needed to transport the three shipmates away from this troublesome planet. But the moment they had moved out of earshot of Valenti, the woman had turned to Sertôrian and confessed that she did not know how exactly to do what she had promised.

"So you lied," said Sertôrian, still walking briskly forward even though such a confession merited an immediate about-face and a return to the safety of camp.

"No," said the woman. "Not exactly. I'll be honest with you, Irena. I know I can get you off this planet; I'm just not sure how yet. It's like the answer's on the tip of my tongue; I know that I know it, I just can't quite access it. Does that make sense? It's an intuitive knowledge more than anything, so there might be some amount of trial and error."

"What are we doing heading into the forest then?" said Sertôrian.

"I thought a walk might jog my mind," said the woman.

"Well?" said Sertôrian.

"Give me a little more time," she said.

Although the Rosa doppelgänger was in no position to make demands, Sertôrian acquiesced and they continued on their stroll along the water's edge. A blue-green river crab scuttled along a sandy patch of the bank. A shadowy trout swam in place in the cool water beneath an outcropping log. Sertôrian's boots crunched through the marble-sized rocks that proliferated along the edge of the river. The more time she spent with this woman, the more seriously Sertôrian entertained a disturbing possibility:

What if—and Sertôrian understood the manifold improbabilities contained in this proposition—*what if* this actually was her sister Rosa? Truly, a device capable of summoning the dead would be a triumph worthy of the Bulgakov Collective's dazzling reputation. After all, the Collective had promised a device with a power beyond their wildest imaginings. Had years of combat and grim survivalism inured Sertôrian and her shipmates to the possibility of wonders and miracles? Why couldn't this be her sister?

If the Bulgakov Apparatus was a trap, as Valenti argued, then what would be this Rosa creature's function? To kill them all? If so, then why hadn't she done it already? She was, Sertôrian realized, leading her farther and farther away from Valenti and de Bronk, but if her plan was to lure them off one by one and murder them, then the Bulgakov Apparatus was one of the least efficient weapons ever created. Given the legendary prowess of the Collective, this seemed unlikely.

"This isn't permanent, by the way," said the woman, interrupting Sertôrian's train of thought. "I don't know exactly how long I have, or what will happen when the time runs out, but I don't get to stay forever."

Sertôrian resented this added pressure.

The woman licked her lips.

"If you were in my position," said Sertôrian, "would you trust someone who claimed to be your dead sister?"

"No," said the woman. "That's the thing—the reasonable position is to distrust me, and I understand that. I promise you, though, it's really me."

Sertôrian took a deep breath, fully aware that there'd be no coming back from what she was about to say.

"This is what we're going to do," said Sertôrian, her tone as businesslike as she could manage. "For the next few minutes, I'm going to play along with you, and I'm going to pretend that you're Rosa."

"Excellent," said the woman. "I feel like we're—"

"But I want to be perfectly clear," said Sertôrian. "I do not believe that you're actually my sister. I don't know who or what you are, but I do know that I miss my sister. I miss her very much. So. Rosa." Sertôrian paused, not meeting the other woman's eyes. "Rosa, it's nice to see you."

And with that, an alchemical reaction took place in Sertôrian's mind, transforming the situation from yet another wretched postwar misadventure to a not-unpleasant echo of her childhood on Mars. All of the ingredients had been there: a trek through a forbidding wilderness, a tinge of danger in the air, and Rosa, or at least a near approximation of her. But not until Sertôrian addressed the woman as her sister did the transmutation take effect.

Her thoughts returned to a Mars decades in the past, the Mars of her youth.

So much had happened since then, so much had changed, that when Sertôrian thought about her life on the Red Planet, it was like she was remembering the life of a stranger. In the intervening years, she'd lost nearly all access to that younger version of herself so that her memories of that time had taken on a distant, third-person quality.

Throughout their early years in the small town of Novo Lobato, the two Sertôrian girls had constituted a strange, isolated nation of two whose customs were inscrutable, and whose boundaries were impassable to all non-natives. The girls' parents— tenacious descendants of the convicts and political prisoners who'd been forced to settle this arid planet in its earlier days as a penal colony—were well respected in the community. Their mother, a space traffic controller, spent most of her waking hours fifteen miles from town in a tiny booth atop a lofty tower, monitoring rocket flights into and out of their Martian province. Maria Sertôrian staffed the little booth almost single-handedly, reprieved only by a night controller whose shifts granted Maria just enough time to catch a few hours of sleep before returning to the tower semi-rested.

Oskar Sertôrian, the girls' father, worked as a field medic for Red Planet Mineral, a mining company whose surveyors and diggers suffered regular bodily harm while operating the heavy, skittish machinery that located and extracted an assortment of valuable minerals from the depths of nearby Mt. Krummholz. He set broken bones, stitched lacerated flesh, and, when necessary, signed death certificates for those workers who'd died on the job.

Both careers, vital and difficult as they were, lent the Sertôrian parents a moderate prestige within the town.

For their part, the two girls—Rosa and Irena—were not disliked, and indeed there was much to admire about them. They were polite, responsible, self-sufficient, and bright. By all these measures, they should have been warmly regarded by all who knew them. Behind the girls' good manners, however, lurked a subtle but perceptible indifference to the affairs of anyone outside their sisterhood.

To outsiders, this insularity manifested itself in quick, intense glances exchanged between the sisters—who bore a striking resemblance to each other—in accidental allusions to elaborate private mythologies, and most of all, in the sisters' overwhelming preference for one another's company above all else, which led them to regularly reject the warmly extended invitations of classmates to birthday parties and sleepovers. Though they could not reasonably fault the sisters for their closeness, it rubbed many townspeople the wrong way.

Part of this exclusivity was a function of geography. Due to their mother's vocation, the family lived just outside town, as near as possible to the colossal observation tower. As a result, the sisters spent all of their free time playing in the vast surrounding wilderness—a red, rocky desert known as Veloq's Sand-Barrens, after an early settler who had perished there. Together, they scrambled over rock piles, played hide-and-seek among towering hoodoos, and carried picnic dinners up sloping peaks, where the setting of the distant sun served as a backdrop for their shared evening meal. In the eyes of the townspeople, the eccentric austerity of the Sand-Barrens rubbed off on the sisters, clinging to them like the region's inescapable red dust.

When, several years later, Irena left home to attend spaceflight school, leaving behind her parents, and more significantly, Rosa, she had no idea that her departure would sever that girlhood bond forever. The sisters had been so inseparable, so intertwined for so long, that Irena couldn't imagine their relationship being any different. But in the end, all it took to break that connection was physical distance. There was no shouted confrontation, no bubbling resentment, no bitter falling-out. Instead, the two sisters merely lost touch with each other, bit by bit.

They wrote letters at first while Irena was at spaceflight school, but neither sister was much at letter writing, so gradually the letters stopped. They still saw each other on the occasional holiday when Sertôrian visited home, but their lives had already begun to follow such separate trajectories that as time went by they had less to talk about, and while a vestige of that childhood affection always remained, there came a point when the two sisters had no idea what to do with each other—Irena the hotshot interstellar space captain, Rosa the small-town schoolteacher. Each sister had become as mysterious to the other as their sororal unit had been to the townspeople of Novo Lobato during their growing-up years.

So, yes, this machine-produced entity, this fleshy memento of her dead sister currently walking next to Sertôrian along the banks of the Inhk-Ohm River, did feel like a stranger. But so had the indisputably authentic Rosa the last time Irena had seen her at their mother's funeral a few years before the war. And when news of Rosa's own death had reached Sertôrian not long before she and her crew had been flung into the Minoan System, she'd felt a strange emptiness, followed by the uncomfortable realization that Rosa had already been lost to her for decades.

This whole situation, then, presented an irresolvable tangle of logical and emotional complications. Sertôrian had no idea where to begin, so she continued her charade of taking this Rosa doppelgänger at her word.

"What you said back at the campsite," said Sertôrian as she and the woman clambered over a fallen tree that blocked their path. "About the afterlife—herding animals and all that. Was it true?"

"In a way," said the woman, brushing bits of muddy bark from her hand. "Not literally, though—not by any means. The reality of it is much stranger, but what I said about the animals—that sums up the way I *felt* about the situation there. It was the best I could do at the spur of the moment."

Her eyes gleamed violet in the midday sun.

"Now that you've had a little more time to think about it then," said Sertôrian, "how would you describe it?"

They reached a small waterfall and the terrain along the riverbank grew steeper and rockier. Picking her way downhill, Sertôrian couldn't help but steal glances at her companion's familiar and uncanny face, resolute and not unhappy, her pointed tongue emerging intermittently to wet her cracking lips.

"Do you remember the first time we hiked into Ghost Grotto Springs?" asked the woman once they'd reached more level ground.

"The first time?" said Sertôrian. "Absolutely."

Ghost Grotto Springs was a legendary feature of Veloq's Sand-Barrens, an enchanting, watery nook so difficult to find that many assumed it didn't actually exist. It had taken the sisters an entire summer of systematic exploration—gridded maps, a homemade sextant—to find the Springs, but they'd done it.

"Well," said the woman, "do you remember how, without really realizing it, we built the place up in our minds so much that by the end of the summer we expected—or I did, at least—some mythic, tropical oasis?"

"Yes," said Sertôrian.

"The way I imagined it," the woman continued, "it was a crystal-blue lagoon, deep enough to dive into, with rock shelves at various heights around the water, where we could picnic or nap and then roll right into the water when we got too warm. There would be scenic shafts of light illuminating the grotto from artfully placed holes in the rock ceiling, and fish we could catch to fry up for our dinner. I think I'd stopped short of imagining mermaids who would teach us to breathe underwater, but only barely."

Sertôrian kicked a rock out of her path and into the river, where it landed with a hollow splash.

"Yeah," said Sertôrian. "I'd fantasized about building a raft we could float on. And cave paintings—I'd hoped there would be cave paintings."

"Right," said the woman. "And then we found it."

The reality of Ghost Grotto Springs had failed to live up to even a fraction of their expectations. They'd crawled through the hole in the rock that served as the Grotto's entrance to find a hollow in the cliffside the size of a high-ceilinged bathroom, an ankle-deep puddle of freezing, bubbling water on the ground.

The initial disappointment had been as shocking to Irena as the cold water on her feet. There would be no swimming, no fishing, no handmade rafts. As she'd adjusted to the reality of their discovery, though, Irena had come to recognize the charms of the real-life Ghost Grotto Springs, and the sisters returned frequently after that day, finding a cool respite from the desert heat in the secret stone cavern, eating picnic lunches with their feet in the cold clear water and talking excitedly about what adventures would fill the rest of the day.

"And that's what death is like?" said Sertôrian.

"Yes," said the woman, licking her lips with her sharp tongue. "It was not what I expected."

Sertôrian thought back to their pleasant sojourns in the Grotto.

"But then after the disappointment," she asked, "you came to enjoy it?"

The woman grimaced and said, "I never stopped being disappointed by what we found in that dingy little cave."

She looked at Sertôrian with those oddly colored eyes and Sertôrian looked away. The stretch of river beside them glared in the midday sun. Sertôrian veered away from the riverbank, heading for the cover of trees and the leafy shade they'd provide.

"Hang on," said the woman, reaching out her arm to stop Sertôrian. "Do you hear that?"

Sertôrian turned her head and listened. From the direction of their campsite she heard a series of clangs, followed by the unmistakable sound of wrenching metal.

"The Apparatus," said Sertôrian.

In a sprint, she set off toward camp, with the woman keeping pace just a few steps behind her. More wrenching screeches filled the air, followed by a silence that was abruptly broken by two people shouting at each other. Sertôrian recognized the voices as belonging to Valenti and de Bronk, and although she couldn't make out any words, the animalistic intensity of the yells clearly signaled the urgency, the potential for violence in the exchange. Sertôrian knew she would be too late to salvage the Bulgakov Apparatus, but as the shouting grew even more heated she hoped she would make it in time to keep Valenti and de Bronk from killing each other.

Then, just as she neared the campsite, the shouting stopped. Sertôrian trotted, panting, to the edge of the clearing and found it empty. The Bulgakov Apparatus lay in shambles on the ground, but her shipmates were nowhere to be seen. Where had they gone so suddenly? Her skin prickled, her body presaging an unseen danger.

Half a second before Ava Valenti's improvised blackjack—a woolen sock filled with marble-sized river rocks—made contact with her skull, Sertôrian sniffed out the ruse. But it was too late to defend against the blow. Sertôrian registered a sharp pain at the side of her head, and then darkness.

# TWELVE

The ambiguities of the previous chapter threaten to overwhelm me. I had never understood the extent to which my own scholarly affinity for uncertainty relied on the relative stability of my life at any given time. I have no problem embracing ambiguity, I now realize, as long as I am doing so within a larger context of regular, nutritious meals and a warm place to sleep at night, the pleasant companionship of sympathetic colleagues, and the absence of a threat of violent death at the hands of armed government forces. As long as such conditions hold, I'll sing the praises of dwelling in uncertainty when it comes to the complexities of Sertôrian's life and teachings, and I'll decry as cardinal sins the impulse to flatten and oversimplify. I'll argue with great vigor that we elevate our thinking as we suppress the urge to seek concrete resolutions.

A recent development has tempered such attitudes.

A spaceship approaches our quiet convent. We know the ship is a large one, capable of transporting dozens of passengers, and their attendant weaponry, over long galactic distances. We also know that if the ship maintains its current rate of speed, it will arrive at our docking station in three days' time. What we don't know is who's inside.

On the one hand, the ship's sinister bulk may harbor a panoply of Delegarchic soldiers, armed and ready to enact our death sentence.

Conversely, it may contain a relief party led by our six brave sisters, the ones we dispatched for help on the day we received the Delegarchs' teleprint. The ship might be fully equipped to whisk us away from the convent and on to the next phase of our daring plan to thwart the insidious government factions who currently seek to destroy us.

We have no way of knowing beforehand which it might be, as, following our reception of the fateful teleprint from the office of the Delegarchs, we destroyed every bit of machinery in our communications booth, having learned by calamitous prior experience that such devices may be deftly and secretly employed by our enemies to eavesdrop on our every word.

We lack, therefore, the ability to hail or be hailed by this ship before it docks, and I cannot pretend that one outcome—death or salvation—is as likely as the other. Though a timely rescue by our fellow cenobites certainly lies within the realm of possibility, the odds favor Syndicate troops, who, based on the timing of the Syndics' threatening teleprint, are due to arrive at any moment.

With this uncertainty looming large, I found myself unable in the previous chapter to do anything more rigorous than copy the words it contains from my dog-eared copy of *Household Tales of Our Sertôrian* to the pages of this manuscript. To engage any of the vexing questions raised by the arrival of the eerie doppelgänger, or by Sertôrian's subsequent reaction, required more fortitude than I could muster.

A lifetime of engagement with the Sertôrial canon has taught me that each time I construct an explanatory framework with which to dispatch one question, seven new questions rear their beastly heads in its place. What, then, is the point of trying? Would it not be easier, as so many have done before, to ignore these questions, or better yet, to ignore the tales that generate them, opting instead for narratives that soothe and reassure? To this last question I must answer yes, it would obviously be easier to do so. But would I be any happier than I am right now? Perhaps, but I'm also reminded of an apocryphal account of the origins of Bombal's *Household Tales of Our Sertôrian*.

I should note that the genesis of *Household Tales* lies concealed in a mythic obscurity typical of ancient, sacred texts, and I certainly don't have the time now to even begin to wade through that swamp of supposition and legend to present you with a concise account of how the book came to be. Although I could, I suppose, present you with the basics.

We find the first surviving external reference to the book in a letter from Catherine of Saturn, that early martyr to the Sertôrial cause whose witty epistles continue to garner admiration even today, and whose proclivity for self-mutilation in the name of enlightenment has thankfully been all but forgotten. Writing to her half brother and fellow believer, Catherine derisively refers to a group of disciples on Phoebe I who "spend more time mining brutish thrills from *Household Tales of Our Sertôrian* than bending themselves in contemplation of the more delicate wonders to be found in the Four Shrouded Visions." Such opprobrium for Bombal's book would only grow among self-appointed policers of the faith in the ensuing centuries. Respect for, and interest in, Bombal's book continued to decline until the recent discovery of the Tau Pakhomius audio reels drastically rehabilitated the tales' credibility.

But what of the book's origins? Who was Bombal (first name Greta or Gretjen or, a more remote possibility, Rosalinda)? And how did she come across the tales she so famously compiled? The answers to these questions remain so irreparably mired in legend and hearsay that I can in good conscience only say that we do not know.

With that caveat in mind, we'll turn now to an account of the book's origins that, while almost certainly fictional, contains a potency that transcends questions of historic truth.

The story goes that Gretjen Bombal, a prosperous zinc merchant from Galatea IV (I must remind you again that none of these details can be confirmed as historically accurate) met one day while walking down a crowded street in her home city, a grizzled old soldier whose penury was evident in the threadbare uniform he wore, a makeshift patch reading "DISCHARGED" sewn over its front pocket, lest anybody mistake him for an active trooper. The old soldier approached Bombal, who had already reached into her satchel to find a few coins she might give to the poor fellow. As she extended a handful of gold kopeks to the soldier, Bombal was surprised to see the old man shake his head.

He told her, "Before you give me anything, you must understand that in doing so you incur a serious obligation to me."

"No, no," said Bombal. "I'm giving you this money freely, with no obligations or—"

"I'll repeat myself," said the old soldier, "and this time listen carefully. If I accept this money, *you* incur an obligation to *me*."

The old soldier raised his eyebrows significantly.

"What kind of obligation?" said Bombal, withdrawing her hand with the money.

"There is something I must tell you," said the soldier. "And you must listen and remember."

Bombal considered the proposition.

"I accept," she said, and handed the old soldier the golden kopeks. He dropped the money into the trouser pocket of his threadbare uniform and explained that as a much younger man he had fought in a campaign on Bellerophon III with a very old soldier named Astrud Kalfa. One evening after their fellow troopers had fallen asleep, Kalfa, who lay next to him, turned over and quietly announced that she carried a valuable package of secret knowledge inside her elderly brain, knowledge that she needed desperately to pass on.

She told him that many years earlier, when she was a young soldier herself, she had served as the communications technician on one of the few transgalactic transport vessels to have survived the chaotic decades following the Great Aurigan War. During one especially delicate mission, the first officer of the ship had accidentally stumbled across a long-lost Lachesian war hero who had been stuck for decades in the Minoan System and reduced to a shattered wreck of her former self. The first officer brought the woman on board and debriefed her, primarily to discover whether she possessed any knowledge about the planets in the Minoan System that might come in handy during their current mission.

Kalfa acted as the stenoduler during this debriefing, and in the decades since then she had been unable to forget a single one of the harrowing tales the woman had recounted. Kalfa had carried the stories with her for all these years, and now it was time to pass them on to another. And so she spent the entire night relaying to her young comrade the monumental saga of the war hero's lost years in the Minoan System.

"That war hero, of course," said the old soldier to Bombal, "was Captain Irena Sertôrian. And that debriefing is the only firsthand account she ever gave of her postwar years of wandering. Kalfa is long dead, the transcribed account long since destroyed, and I alone have carried the saga within myself for too long. Now I've grown old and must transmit my knowledge, one episode at a time. So." The old soldier stood up a little straighter, chest out, and took a deep breath. "Captain Sertôrian and her crew had barely escaped the deadly machinations of the kryonauts when . . ." The old soldier stopped. "You need to write this down," he said to Bombal.

Bombal rummaged through her satchel until she found her dict-a-pad.

"Good," said the old soldier, and proceeded to tell the story. Bombal's stylus fled across the screen, and when the soldier finished, he asked if she'd got everything.

"Yes," she said, checking her pad.

"Good," said the soldier again, and walked away.

Only mildly surprised at his departure, Bombal watched for a moment as the old man disappeared into a teeming crowd of pedestrians.

Over the next few days, Bombal thought frequently of the story the poor old man had told her, and each morning on her way to work she watched carefully for the man, half hoping to reencounter him and hear another of his tales. But week after week she saw no sign of the old soldier. No great surprise, given the size of the city she lived in, but still Bombal was disappointed.

Then one day, while waiting for a rocket bus, she heard a bespectacled mecha-fish vendor recounting an experience almost identical to her own.

The young man had run across the poor soldier and given him an old coat, and in exchange the soldier had obliged the young man to listen to and record a tale of Irena Sertôrian's Minoan exploits.

To make a long story short, Bombal discovered that the old soldier had disseminated dozens of tales among the people of the city, enjoining each one to remember what he had told them. Intrigued by the poor old man's project, Bombal began tracking down the other people the old soldier had encountered and collecting the tales he had given them. Soon the project consumed every free minute she had, and truth be told, her dedication to her zinc trading slipped little by little until the project overtook her life. Doggedly pursuing the tales, Bombal worked tirelessly for decades until she was satisfied she had found all of the poor old soldier's stories. With her great undertaking thus accomplished, Bombal compiled the accounts into a single volume that we now know as *Household Tales of Our Sertôrian*.

You might ask what potency I find in such a fanciful little tale, and I would agree that on the whole it resembles so many others of its ilk in its preponderance of banal and wishful thinking. But every time I reencounter the story, one distinct moment slides between my ribs like a warm knife. The initial exchange between Bombal and the old soldier is often written off as an erratum, an accidental piece of narrative illogic generated and perpetuated over the centuries by the vagaries of folkloric transmission. It makes no sense, goes the reasoning, that Bombal's act of charity would put her in the old man's debt.

In considering that charge, I return to the question I posed earlier in this chapter: Given the current turbulence of my situation, would I not be happier if I set aside Bombal's thorny tale and instead passed my remaining time contemplating simpler, less jagged stories? Like the old man in the apocryphal account of the origins of *Household Tales*, the Rhadamanthus IX account makes ever-increasing demands on its reader, requiring more and more and more of the audience's attention. Other tales seem far more generous to their readers. *Sertôrian's Travels*, for instance, or *The Life and Voyages of Irena Sertôrian* contain story after story whose narrative logic conforms exactly to the values Sertôrian's later teachings seem to espouse.

In one such tale, Sertôrian's selfless act of kindness to a scarred, pus-ridden hermit ensures the safety of her crew. When a marauding band of aristocratic assassins attacks Sertôrian and her shipmates, the hermit turns out to be in possession of a weaponized level-nine pulse shield that keeps the assassins at bay.

In another story, Sertôrian's refusal to betray her comrades melts the heart of the bionic despot who holds them captive, and they are released from his magma dungeon with the despot's well-wishes and a month's supply of food and fuel.

These flattened, reassuring tales ask so little of their audience and appear to give so much in return: comfort, peace, and inspiration. But such candyfloss fails to provide the soul with the sustenance it needs to withstand the tireless slugs and sucker punches of lived experience. Conversely, my decades-long career spent sparring with difficult religious texts has cultivated in me a tenacity that I never would have developed reading more comforting tales.

Furthermore, to attempt to resolve every vexing question posed by Bombal's account is to forget that resolution is a minor species of death. I should cherish my struggle with these theological knots, knots whose sublime multiplicity intimates planes of existence beyond my ability to comprehend.

I grapple with uncertainties, and so I live.

Of course, that is nonsense. A shot from a trooper's blast-gun will kill me as dead as anything, regardless of what complex questions enliven my mind. This monograph, into which I poured so much early hope, will not save my life. And yet I race to complete it, and in so doing I treasure the ambiguities with which I have an increasingly ambiguous relationship, ambiguity spawning ambiguity, contaminating everything it touches with dark, shimmering uncertainty until the whole universe teeters on the brink of being one thing, or possibly another.

There does exist an arena in which I can no longer allow ambiguity to reign supreme. I have held too fast for too long to certain secret feelings whose revelation would forever alter, for better or for worse, a dear and treasured friendship. By withholding such feelings I have dwelled for decades in possibility, free to imagine consequences either happy or much less so if these sentiments were ever revealed. In the past I've found freedom in that ambiguity, but now the cold finality of death approaches (or might approach). If I continue to keep these feelings to myself, the great multitude of potentialities will vanish with my dying breath. The time has come to evict my secret from its ramshackle house of too many windows and too many doors.

## THIRTEEN

• • •

As Sertôrian regained consciousness, her first thought was that she could still turn the situation around. Things had taken an unfortunate turn—that couldn't be denied—but she could still fix this. She opened her eyes and took quick stock of her situation. She lay facedown on the ground at the edge of their campsite, a gag in her mouth, her limbs trussed up behind her, a throbbing pain at the side of her head. The afternoon sun shone down into her face, and she squinted against the light. Yes, things were very bad, but didn't she have a genius for survival, for pulling her team together when the going got tough?

Then came the scrape of a shovel cutting through dirt. She craned her neck toward the sound and saw Ava Valenti standing waist deep in a hole in the ground, her face, torso, and arms covered with dirt and still-drying blood. Valenti dug with steady strokes, tossing spadefuls of earth to the side with a short-handled trenching shovel.

All around them, pieces of the Bulgakov Apparatus lay scattered on the ground, and Ernst de Bronk, clutching a skull-sized rock in his hands, moved methodically through the rubble, smashing to bits any component that could still be functional.

Not far from the deepening hole in the ground, the woman who looked exactly like Rosa lay splayed in the dirt, her throat gaping open, her threadbare sweater soaked in blood. A wave of bile rose in Sertôrian's throat, but she fought it back down. The magnitude of this betrayal was greater than she could have imagined. She turned her head away and closed her eyes.

In the distance she could hear the roar of the Twin Falls, a deceptively soothing undertone to the regular *strick* of Valenti's shovel blade cutting through hard earth. As Sertôrian lay there with her eyes held tightly shut, her mind ran not to thoughts of punishment but of repairing the situation, whatever that might mean. Sertôrian recognized she was not blameless in all this, and furthermore blame was beside the point. Survival remained the top priority—survival and returning home so they could resume lives of civilized normalcy. Her team couldn't just dissolve like this, not this late in the game. They needed to talk things through, and they needed to pull together.

As best she could with a gag in her mouth, Sertôrian shouted for her crew's attention. The cries emerged muffled and weak, but Valenti heard them and paused her digging mid-stroke. She looked at Sertôrian for a moment with flat, empty eyes, then looked away and emptied her shovel-load of dirt onto the growing pile next to the hole.

Sertôrian shouted again, but this time, if either of her shipmates heard her, they gave no sign of it. And so, rather than yelling more, rather than struggling against her ropes, Sertôrian chose to conserve energy for whatever might come next. She lay very still, her cheek pressed into a sharp twig, and tried to control her panicked breathing.

She watched Valenti dig, and after a while the hole grew deep enough that Valenti was in up to her shoulders. Valenti paused, wiped her forehead, and hoisted herself out of the hole. She glanced at de Bronk still wildly flinging the last bits of the Apparatus into the surrounding forest. Then, tossing aside the shovel, Valenti crouched down at the dead woman's head and, hooking her own arms under the dead woman's armpits, dragged her into the open pit.

Although it was deep, the grave was not very long, and Sertôrian could tell by the way the dead woman's body folded as it fell into the hole that it would come to rest in an ungainly sitting position, where it would remain awkwardly bunched until the natural processes of decay ran their full course.

Shovel once again in hand, Valenti recommenced her project, this time in reverse, dropping spadefuls of dirt into the open grave with the steadiness of a grimy metronome. When de Bronk had finished scattering the remnants of the Bulgakov Apparatus, he joined Valenti in her task, kneeling down and pushing in heaps of dirt with his extended arms.

By the time evening arrived, they had finished, a bulge of dark earth the only testament to their actions. They brushed themselves off, drank some water, and hoisted their already packed rucksacks onto their backs. Valenti removed a long knife from the pocket of her bag—Sertôrian's knife—and set it on the ground a few meters away from her trussed captain. As she did so, she nodded to Sertôrian and then without a word, Valenti and de Bronk set out at a trot into the darkening forest.

A bird, perhaps the same one Sertôrian had heard the night before, trilled a melancholy reveille. Taking a deep breath, Sertôrian began to squirm across the ground toward the knife that Valenti had left behind. It was slow going. Moving even a centimeter required an ungainly combination of shimmies and heaves that dangerously sapped her already waning strength. Pebbles and twigs scraped her cheeks and jabbed through her worn clothing. Her feet and hands tingled with pain from being raised up behind her for so long, and her stomach twisted with pain, as she hadn't eaten since the night before.

Sertôrian well knew, however, that focusing on her discomfort would get her nowhere. So she jerked her body forward across the ground, centimeter by grueling centimeter. When she reached the knife, darkness had arrived in full force. The blade glinted in the starlight. Sertôrian sidled up next to the knife and with the last of her strength began rocking her body from side to side. After a few rocks, she gained enough momentum to flop onto her side, her bound hands just centimeters from the knife. She scooted backward until her fingers touched the handle. She grasped the knife and, moving clumsily but with purpose, positioned the blade against the rope that bound her. From there it was a sweaty half hour of grunting, sawing at the ropes, fumbling the knife, picking it back up, sawing, dropping, picking back up, until her hands were free. She untied the rest of the rope and then lay there waiting as the blood came coursing painfully back into her limbs.

As soon as it had, she stood up, stiffly, and started walking in the direction that her two mutinous shipmates had gone. She stole a sidelong glance at the dark mound of dirt to her left, but that wasn't something she could think about now. Right now she needed to catch up with Valenti and de Bronk, and she needed to salvage this wretched situation they'd all created for themselves. She started to run, but her adrenaline couldn't compensate for the toll taken by the physical and emotional traumas of the past twenty-four hours. She hadn't eaten in a day, hadn't had any water in nearly as long, and had just spent hours tied up on the ground. Before she even reached the trees, her head grew fuzzy and she collapsed once again into darkness.

Hazy confusion consumed her for what could have been hours or even days. She was aware of movement, of new, unfamiliar voices, but where her troubled sleep ended and her semiconsciousness began, she couldn't tell.

After some time, though, the haze cleared, and she woke up in what looked like a clean, inexpensive hotel room. The décor was bland and accommodating—lots of warmish, neutral colors, an inoffensive print of a field of flowers hanging on the wall opposite her bed—and everything was very clean. *She* was very clean, for that matter. Somebody had bathed her and dressed her in a pair of soft cotton pajamas. She currently lay beneath a blue quilt in a wide, comfortable bed. She propped the pillows behind her and sat up.

She had a dim recollection of a delirious night's sleep back at the Twin Falls, followed at dawn by the sound of engines and shouting, and then a bumpy flight spent tightly restrained. How long ago had that been? She needed to find Valenti and de Bronk, and to do so she had to get out of here, wherever *here* was.

Pushing the quilt aside—when was the last time she'd slept in a bed?—she swung her feet onto the floor. As she stood up, she realized she must have eaten or been fed during those lost hours. She felt stable and revitalized, and as she walked to the room's single, curtained window, a dim memory of hot soup and warm bread flickered at the back of her mind. Pulling open the window's heavy curtains, she looked down at a neatly landscaped park below. Her room was several stories up, and based on the human figures she saw inside the high-fenced enclosures and glassed-in habitats below, she surmised that what lay before her was the Arch-Kaiser's infamous zoo—stocked not with animals but with people, primarily the Arch-Kaiser's political enemies but also with individuals who possessed some remarkable physical attribute: great beauty or ugliness, a striking physique, and so on. That meant she currently occupied the zoo administration building.

He'd caught her then—the Arch-Kaiser had tracked them down. She wondered how long it would be before she'd have to meet with Harrison to receive her death sentence.

She closed the curtains, and as she did so a woman's voice addressed her through a speaker in the wall, which Sertôrian had failed to notice. Above the speaker was the small, glinting lens of a security camera.

"Captain Sertôrian," said the voice. "So glad to see you up and about. You gave us quite a scare when we found you. We worried we were too late."

"Too late for what?" said Sertôrian.

"To rescue you, of course," said the voice.

Why would the Arch-Kaiser send people to rescue her? Sertôrian looked directly into the lens of the camera.

"Who am I talking to?" she said.

"Where are my manners?" said the voice. "Ruth Aylesbury, at your service."

A strategically unhelpful answer.

"What am I doing here?" said Sertôrian.

"Yes, of course. You must have so many questions," said Aylesbury. "There's a shower in your bathroom, if you'd like to use it, and a fresh set of clothes in your closet. Why don't you get dressed—at your leisure, of course—and when you're ready one of your guards will escort you up to the roof of the garden. You and I will have lunch together—I'll put in an order with the cafeteria— and I'll explain everything."

"One of my guards?" said Sertôrian.

"Yes," said Aylesbury. "You have two of them stationed at your door. It's for your own protection, I assure you."

"You can dismiss them," said Sertôrian. "I'd prefer it that way."

"I'll see you at lunch as soon as you're ready," said Aylesbury, ignoring the question outright.

So that was how it was going to be.

While she bathed and dressed, Sertôrian strategized. If these people, whoever they were—Harrison's secret police?—had found her, they had most likely found Valenti and de Bronk as well. Which meant her shipmates were probably right here in the same building with her. The first step would be to establish contact.

Then, once they opened a line of communication, they could start scheming. They'd escaped before from facilities more secure than this one, and they could do it again.

Sertôrian suspected that this Aylesbury's cheery affect concealed a much more calculating disposition than she let on, which would make intelligence gathering a tricky endeavor. Tricky but not impossible.

As soon as she was dressed, a pair of armed guards entered the room.

"Ready?" said the first one.

"Yes," she said.

They led her down a forking series of hallways, up several flights of stairs, and onto a balcony arboretum at the top of the building. A compact woman in a crisp khaki uniform waited at a metal picnic table. When she saw Sertôrian and the guards, she rose with a smile.

"Ruth Aylesbury," said the woman.

Her brownish hair, in a tidy pageboy, framed a face that, through a studied blandness, rendered any inner secrets completely inaccessible to the world at large. At the moment, her wide smile conveyed a low-wattage warmth that might lead lesser adversaries to lower their defenses.

"Irena Sertôrian," said Sertôrian, shaking the woman's hand. "But it seems like you already knew that."

"Oh yes," said Aylesbury. "And I'm so looking forward to chatting with you."

Sertôrian suspected that any questions she posed at this time— *What happened to my shipmates? Where am I? Does the Arch-Kaiser know about this?*—would be deflected with a screen of inane pleasantries, so she merely returned the compliment and took a seat across from her.

The guards left the two women alone.

"I normally don't talk business on an empty stomach," said Aylesbury, "but I'd hate to keep you in suspense much longer. I imagine there's a lot you'd like to know."

Sertôrian gave a slight nod.

"Yes, well," said Aylesbury. "Where to start?"

She furrowed her brow, appearing to give the matter genuine thought. Sertôrian took the opportunity to examine her surroundings. Potted trees filled the balcony: birches, oaks, yews, willows, rowans, and alders. The shade from their leafy branches created a chilly twilight in the space even in the heat of the day.

Beyond the balcony, through the leaves of the potted trees, Sertôrian could just make out the carefully ordered landscaping of the Arch-Kaiser's zoo down below. Groups of visitors, appearing tiny from this height, wandered from habitat to habitat, pausing from time to time to gaze at their jailed compatriots.

Aylesbury lifted her head and Sertôrian returned her attention to the smartly uniformed woman across the table.

"I suppose I'll just come out with it," said Aylesbury. "We'd like to offer you a job."

This was not what Sertôrian had been expecting, was so far beyond the realm of anticipated possibilities, in fact, that her guard went down completely and out came a genuinely confused, "Hold on. What?"

"A job," repeated Aylesbury. "We've recently had a position open up—head of Tactical Operations—and we think you'd be a perfect fit."

Sertôrian didn't even know where to start with this proposal.

"So you're asking me to work for the Arch-Kaiser?" she said after a moment, working on the assumption that Aylesbury was part of Harrison's secret police force.

"Oh no," said Aylesbury. "Not the Arch-Kaiser. No. I'm asking you to work for us."

This clarified nothing. A breeze rustled the leaves of a nearby alder.

Sertôrian said, "And who would the *us* be, in this case?"

"Yes, right," said Aylesbury. "I suppose that's not entirely clear to you at the moment. The Arch-Kaiser, as you're well aware, has a secret police force at his beck and call. You met them when you first arrived on Rhadamanthus IX."

"Yes I did," said Sertôrian, recalling the thorough torture they had administered to her and her shipmates.

"Thing of it is, there's nothing secret about them. Everyone on the planet knows they exist, knows what they look like, knows what they do. So they're not *really* a secret police force, are they?"

"I guess not," said Sertôrian.

"No," said Aylesbury. "That's where we come in. We're the *truly* secret police. Not even the Arch-Kaiser is aware of our existence." She folded her arms with satisfaction. "With me so far?"

"Not completely," said Sertôrian, still disoriented by the unexpected job offer. "What use are you to the Arch-Kaiser if he doesn't know you exist?"

"An excellent question," said Aylesbury. "And the answer is, no use at all. The Arch-Kaiser Glenn Harrison, however, is of great use to us. You see, our friend the Arch-Kaiser only thinks he runs this planet. In point of fact, our secret police force predates Mr. Harrison's rule by decades. As we've done with his predecessors, we allow Harrison certain powers so he can maintain the illusion of his sovereignty. But the reality is, we're the ones running the show."

"And the Arch-Kaiser is just a distraction," said Sertôrian.

"Precisely," said Aylesbury. "And Glenn Harrison has proven an especially effective one. Such megalomania is a rare thing, and more valuable to us than he could ever know. He's temperamentally incapable of imagining power greater than his own, and so we exert very little effort to hide ourselves from him. And his eccentricities—his zoo, his penchant for outrageous disguises, his obsession with the occult—command the attention of the planet's citizenry. They can't keep their eyes off him, and so, without even knowing it, he provides the majority of the camouflage we need to hide from the common people." Aylesbury chuckled and shook her head. "This latest venture is a perfect example. What was it he sent you to look for? The Tablets of Metempsychosis? The Book of Futures Past?"

"It was the Bulgakov Apparatus," said Sertôrian.

"That's right," said Aylesbury with another broad grin. "The Bulgakov Apparatus. Believe it or not, when he develops his little fixations on these fairy tales and legends, he becomes absolutely convinced they're real."

Sertôrian raised her eyebrows in faux disbelief.

"I'm sure he expected you to actually come back with the Bulgakov Apparatus," said Aylesbury, "as absurd as that may seem."

Sertôrian took this in like a punch to the gut. So Aylesbury had no idea the Apparatus was real. *Was* being the operative word.

The door to the arboretum swung open.

"Ah," said Aylesbury. "Lunch."

A guard had stepped through the glass door holding two plastic cafeteria trays laden with food. Sertôrian was thankful for the distraction. She doubted her face could conceal her outrage at Aylesbury's flippant dismissal of the Bulgakov Apparatus, the discovery of which had cost Sertôrian nearly everything. She tamped down her fury, tamped down thoughts of her mutinous shipmates, of the dead woman she had left behind. She tried not to imagine the crawling insects and the gritty dirt finding their way into that tender, gaping gash in the woman's throat. It hadn't been Rosa—Sertôrian had to remember that—only a cunning replica.

She couldn't look Aylesbury in the face right now without betraying her anger, so she watched the guard set one tray in front of each woman, salute Aylesbury, and exit the balcony.

"Bon appétit," said Aylesbury.

Sertôrian tamped down her outrage as best she could. She needed to focus on finding her shipmates, and anger would only distract her. She would keep humoring Aylesbury until she saw a chance to dig for information about Valenti and de Bronk. It was a skill she'd been forced to develop during her time in the Minoan System—feigning sincere interest while a despotic captor unfolded their deluded pet philosophy, their deranged master plan.

But to do this, Sertôrian required energy, so she turned her attention to her meal.

The food on her plate was difficult to identify—an industrial slurry of beige—but inoffensive to the taste. The tray also contained five stalks of an unfamiliar vegetable and a cup of lukewarm, under-brewed tea. All told, it was an improvement on what she'd been eating for the past several weeks, and in spite of herself Sertôrian wolfed the meal down.

"So who are you?" said Sertôrian when the time seemed right to recommence their conversation. "Your organization, I mean."

"Do you mean what defines us, aside from being secret?" said Aylesbury.

"That's right," said Sertôrian.

Aylesbury took a sip of tea and nodded thoughtfully.

"An excellent question," she said. "And not an easy one to answer. There's been fervent internal discussion lately on this very issue. We've even organized a committee to craft a mission statement, but the delegates can only agree that our organization is and must remain a secret one. It's grown into quite a heated debate. Violent, even. The position you'd be filling—if you accept our offer, of course—was vacated as a result of a particularly unpleasant dispute."

Aylesbury gave an ironic moue of regret.

"You had my predecessor killed," said Sertôrian.

The skin around Aylesbury's eyes creased in a brief expression of annoyance or possibly satisfaction; she was a tough woman to read.

"It wasn't quite that simple," said Aylesbury.

"I suppose it never is," said Sertôrian. "I'd just like to know what I'm getting into."

"And that circumspection is partly why we want you for the job," said Aylesbury. "You truly are a legend, you know, and if you'll allow me to be so bold, if you turn this job down and return home to Mars, the skills you've developed will be wasted by whomever you find to be in charge. The age of the Three Empires has passed, and whatever regime rises up to take their place will want to put as much distance between themselves and the Great Aurigan War as possible. You will be nothing more than an inconvenient reminder of that costly and embarrassing conflict. Here on Rhadamanthus IX, though, your skills will be put to excellent use. It's a smaller stage than the one you're used to, I'll grant you that, but the role we're offering you is a juicy one."

"I don't doubt it," said Sertôrian, "and I'm very flattered by all this. Truly. But I need to know more about your organization."

Sertôrian hoped that if she kept Aylesbury talking, a chink in the woman's armor might become apparent.

"Yes," said Aylesbury. "Very good." She pushed aside the plastic cafeteria tray and folded her hands together. "You know," she said, "I told you a minute ago that secrecy was the only defining characteristic our committee could agree on." She paused. "The more I think about it, that's really not such a bad answer. Because, you see, our secrecy matters not only in terms of our efficacy but also our ideology. And what is our ideology? I don't mean to sound too circular here, but our ideology is, I believe, secrecy. That's what tripped up—what keeps tripping up—the committee.

"They're overfocused on superficialities, so some of them

believe that we exist to maintain order, much like a traditional police force, while others think we're here to advance civilization, whatever that even means. Still others say we're a new form of government, and I suppose none of them are outright wrong, but they are all missing the point. You see, we can't truly succeed if anyone outside of the organization knows that we're the ones behind it all.

"Secrecy is preeminent, because what this secret police force creates for the rank-and-file citizens of Rhadamanthus IX is the illusion of a neatly ordered universe in which events have explicit precedents and consequences. The unjust find punishment and the just receive a fitting reward. It's a hugely ambitious undertaking, yes, but we've broken it up into discrete and manageable components. Allow me to explain:

"If, for example, a fellow swindles his neighbor out of a year's salary, our organization makes sure that a misfortune of comparable severity befalls this same fellow at some point in the not-too-distant future. A broken leg, perhaps, or a flooded home. Depends on how much money he stole, of course, and what it meant to the person he stole it from. We have excellent algorithms to determine the severity of the punishments.

"We also do the opposite from time to time: reward people for good deeds performed. But that's actually much trickier—you might not have guessed that—so we primarily focus on punishment.

"What our ideological articulation committee keeps forgetting, though, is how essential it is that the consequences we engineer appear to come about naturally. Our involvement can never be discovered, whether we're administering a punishment or a reward, or the whole system shatters. Invisibility is vital. If nobody knows that we're the ones pulling the strings, then they're left to assume that what they're observing is the essential nature of reality and that the universe is undergirded by direct and observable laws of moral justice. Keeps people on their toes, certainly, but deep down it also comforts them, provides them with the stability and consistency they crave. It's a real gift, I believe."

"It's a fiction," said Sertôrian.

"Yes," said Aylesbury. "And it's a benevolent one."

Sertôrian shrugged.

"You don't agree?" said Aylesbury.

"It's a lot to take in," said Sertôrian.

Among all the dangerous cranks Sertôrian had met in her lifetime, Aylesbury and her secret organization certainly ranked among the most ambitious.

"You're a careful thinker," said Aylesbury. "I ask you not to rush to judge us until you've seen the full impact of what our organization can do."

Sertôrian could see the planet's sun hot and heavy in the sky, but the arboretum's trees kept the balcony pleasantly shaded. She took a moment to collect herself.

"Tell me more about the position I'd be filling," she said.

"Ah yes," said Aylesbury. "Head of Tactical Operations. A vital position. Vital. You would control the hands and the feet of this organization, as it were. You see, I run the Intelligence Branch of the secret police. The eyes and the ears, if you will. We gather information from around the planet, observing crimes, good deeds, and other notable occurrences, and then we share that information with the Assessments Department, who then analyze the intel and present their findings to Central Command, who grant approval to act. Once that approval is granted, the ball goes to you in Tactical Operations. Working closely with Intelligence, you will plan secret operations that will aid us in administering the types of consequences I was explaining to you a moment ago. You'll plan these operations, then, and once Central Command green-lights your proposed operations, you will oversee their execution."

"Interesting," said Sertôrian.

The longer Aylesbury talked, the more her respect for Sertôrian seemed, to a certain extent, genuine. This could be just the leverage Sertôrian needed.

"It's a splendid post," said Aylesbury. "You'll have over a dozen elite tactical units at your disposal. You'll sit in on weekly closed-door meetings with Central Command. You'll have the pleasure of observing a well-run planet whose inhabitants are blissfully unaware of all the work we do for them."

"Hmm," said Sertôrian. She tried to maintain a polite expression as the full magnitude of the organization's power and its lunacy became increasingly apparent.

"I'm going to lay all my cards out on the table here," said Aylesbury. "And I'm speaking not just for myself right now but for my superiors as well. We are very excited at the prospect of your joining our organization. When you arrived on our planet, it seemed far too good to be true. We believe that you have so much to offer us, and also that the organization has so much to offer you. What do I need to do in order for you to accept this position?"

"Like I said before," said Sertôrian, "I'm flattered."

"But?" said Aylesbury.

Sertôrian decided to trouble the waters a bit to see what happened.

"Here's a question that's been bothering me," she said, opening the valve on the torrent of emotions she'd been damming up during this whole conversation.

"Yes," said Aylesbury.

"If you were so excited to see me here on your planet, why did you allow the Arch-Kaiser to torture me and my shipmates? And why didn't you intervene when he sent us on what you yourself acknowledge was a wild goose chase?" said Sertôrian, allowing her voice to fill with indignation.

"Yes, that was regrettable," said Aylesbury, growing somber.

"And I do apologize. Had circumstances been different we certainly would have intervened and extricated you sooner from your difficulties. But I'm afraid we were involved in a very delicate operation of our own at that time, and your arrival served as a useful distraction for the Arch-Kaiser. I am sorry, but you know how it is."

A hint of steel undergirded the apology.

"I'm not sure I do," said Sertôrian.

"In time you will," said Aylesbury.

"My other question," said Sertôrian, ignoring the condescension, "is what happens if I say no?"

"What do you mean?" said Aylesbury.

"You know exactly what I mean," said Sertôrian. "You've just told me how important—how essential—secrecy is to your organization. And now I know your secrets, or at least the biggest one: I know you exist. If I say no, then I find it hard to believe you'll let me leave this building alive. It'd be too big a risk."

Aylesbury's eyes shone with a dangerous, uninterpretable light.

"In most circumstances," she said, "you'd be right. But you, my friend, are an exception. Truly you can't understand the degree to which we respect you here. You're a woman of honor, Captain Sertôrian, and if you turn this position down—and I still hope you won't—you're free to go, provided you promise to keep our secret. You won't be allowed to stay on Rhadamanthus IX, of course, but I don't think you would choose to anyway."

Sertôrian saw her window of opportunity open—just a sliver—to find out about her crew.

"I'm not sure I believe you," she said.

"I give you my word," said Aylesbury.

"I appreciate that," said Sertôrian, not trusting Aylesbury for a second.

"A professional courtesy," said Aylesbury. "It's the least I could do."

Now. The time was right.

"Another question, then, if you don't mind," said Sertôrian.

"Please," said Aylesbury.

As she opened her mouth to finally ask the question she'd been building up to throughout this entire interview, Sertôrian realized that she wasn't sure she wanted to know the answer.

"My crew," she said. "Star-Guard Ava Valenti and Technician Ernst de Bronk. Where are they?"

Aylesbury's face grew solemn.

"I'm sorry," she said. "I'm sorry to be the bearer of bad news, but I'm afraid your shipmates didn't make it."

Aylesbury lowered her eyes in mock respect for the dead.

Of course. Of course they hadn't made it.

Sertôrian clenched her fingers against the rim of the table. Why had she not anticipated this possibility? How had the thought not even crossed her mind?

"You killed them," said Sertôrian, keeping her tone neutral.

"Absolutely not," said Aylesbury, the glint in her eyes and the tilt of her head suggesting that she knew that Sertôrian knew that this was a lie. "We'd hoped to bring them in, just like we did with you. We even created positions for them within the organization—not as prestigious as yours, but important ones we wanted them to fill. No, we didn't kill them. They would have been so useful to us."

Up until this moment, Sertôrian had thought of the situation with her shipmates solely in terms of how it could be fixed. They'd done a very bad thing (Sertôrian pushed away images of the raw, gaping wound in Rosa's throat), but they could still rally together and cohere again as a crew. They would leave Rhadamanthus IX together, and they would return home together, all a little worse for the wear but still indisputably a crew.

Now there was just Sertôrian, and there was nothing else to be done.

"How did they die?" said Sertôrian, not expecting an honest answer.

"Their necks were broken," said Aylesbury.

"And how do you think that happened?"

"The day before we found you," said Aylesbury, "one of our aerowagons came across their sodden corpses at the base of the Shelley Ravine. The footpath along the edge of the ravine is treacherous even under the best of conditions, and it had been raining there for days. Even a skilled mountaineer could have slipped on that narrow path." Aylesbury pursed her lips in a savage imitation of sympathy. "I'm so sorry."

The whole charade was beginning to make Sertôrian sick.

"Can I see the bodies?" she said.

"We thought it would be best to incinerate them," said Aylesbury.

"I see," said Sertôrian.

This, she surmised, was no lie, and what surprised and horrified Sertôrian most of all was that as the news of her shipmates' deaths sunk in, it filled her not with rage, not with sorrow, but with a delirious sense of relief. The burden of leadership she had carried for years was, in an instant, lifted from her shoulders. She fought back a frightening urge to laugh, and before the full weight of their deaths could catch up to her, she braced herself against the table and said, "I'll take the job."

## FOURTEEN

must move quickly. Our time together nears its end. As I write these words, the clangs and creaks of a docking spacecraft fill the air. Within the hour, the convent's main gate will open and the entry hall will echo with either the happy laughter of our rescuing comrades or the sharp crack of gunfire.

At my feet sits the very suitcase I brought with me from my home planet of Argus II when I first arrived at the convent so many decades ago. Back then it contained a week's worth of clothing and a new set of zero-grav fountain pens that my mother had given me as a going-away present. Now its contents are far less innocuous. I can't reveal the specifics, but on the off chance that the approaching spacecraft contains not armed troops but our rescuing colleagues, we must be ready to board the ship immediately and depart for ports I cannot name, where we'll unite with our surviving sisters from around the galaxy to combat the tyrannical and ever-growing forces of the seven rogue Delegarchs.

Over the past three days, then, I have, to the best of my ability, put my affairs in order—a repulsively tidy phrase to describe the absurd process of preparing oneself for the terminus of one's own life. As mentioned previously, I packed my suitcase in the unlikely event of a rescue. I cleaned my quarters, cut my hair, and watered my plants. I made every effort to complete the composition of this study. And I played, presumably, my last game of two-handed oubliette with Sister Beatriz.

And I have, of course, packed my suitcase with care, including only what's necessary for the task that may lie ahead of us. Unfortunately, I could conjure no sound justification for including this bulky manuscript, so when I've finished copying out the end of the Rhadamanthus IX account, I'll leave the ink-stained codex here at the convent in hopes that someday it might find its ideal reader, whoever that might be.

Not all of my unfinished business, however, was as tangible as suitcases and houseplants. Previously in this manuscript, I wrote of a pressing need to unburden myself of certain long-hidden feelings. One might think that a deadline as nonnegotiable as death would quell any tendency to procrastination, but I'm chagrined to inform you that my impending mortality has left my capacity to delay some needful tasks completely intact. Rather than resolve the situation immediately after composing those lines, I waited until yesterday afternoon, when I'd finished transcribing the conclusion of the Rhadamanthus IX episode, to make an oblique and mealy-mouthed confession.

I was repacking my suitcase—having reconsidered, not for the first time, what I might want to bring with me on the off chance that we're rescued—and I couldn't find my pocketknife, as useful an item as any, I would suppose, for a possible galactic insurgency. I had a vague recollection of loaning the knife to Sister Beatriz, so I decided to pay her a visit.

I found her in her sleeping chamber, a menagerie of personal belongings strewn about the room.

"I don't mean to interrupt," I said.

"Please do," she said. "Sit down, if you can find a place to sit. I apologize for the mess."

"No need," I said, and then sat down on the edge of the wooden chest where Sister Beatriz keeps all of her ontoscope slides.

Her suitcase, a battered leather portmanteau, sat open and empty in the middle of the bed. I watched Sister Beatriz as she packed and then unpacked a series of items whose necessity she apparently could not decide on. Finally, after packing, unpacking, packing again, and then unpacking a gyroscopic sextant, Sister Beatriz turned to face me, one hand on her hip, the other holding her angular face.

"This is dreadful, isn't it?" she said.

"It's really not so messy," I said, looking theatrically around her rom.

"I don't mean my room," said Sister Beatriz in a small voice, almost a whisper.

"I know that," I said. "A small joke."

Sister Beatriz managed a weak smile, the corners of her eyes wrinkling almost imperceptibly.

"Yes," she said. "Of course."

Hands on her hips, she looked at the empty suitcase sitting on her bed, at the piles of clothing, books, tools, and knickknacks that lay in hopeless drifts about the room, and her narrow shoulders sagged.

"Well, as I said, I don't mean to interrupt," I said. "I'm only stopping by to see if you might still have the pocketknife I loaned you a while ago."

Unexpectedly, the question seemed to revivify her flagging spirits.

"Yes," she said, springing into action. "It's funny you should mention it. I saw it just a moment ago while I was emptying my closet. I was going to bring it by your bedroom as soon as I'd finished packing." She moved around the room like a scavenging bird, pecking and prodding at one heap of belongings and then another. "Now where has it gone?"

As she rummaged through a pile of sundries in the corner of the room, I stole a glance at her bustling form. I've often thought of the middle-aged body as a thing to be pitied, no longer possessing the sprightliness of youth and not yet earning the gravitas of old age. But as I watched Sister Beatriz in that moment, I experienced an unexpected and overwhelming illusion of atemporality brought about by that very liminality. In Sister Beatriz's middle-aged visage I could see the fresh-faced youth with whom I had become so ardently infatuated, as well as the familiar friend I currently loved so deeply, as well as the elderly woman she might never have a chance to become.

"Here it is," she said, and the illusion passed. She handed me the knife.

"Thank you," I said. I knew that this would be my last chance to unburden myself of my long-concealed secret.

"Is everything all right?" said Sister Beatriz. "You look like you've seen a ghost."

My hands trembled and my heart beat furiously.

"Would you sit down for a moment?" I said. "I have something to say."

Sister Beatriz took a step back and nodded warily. She sat down on the edge of the bed, bracing herself with her arms and narrowing her eyes, as if anticipating a physical blow.

I had no idea where to begin, so I simply started talking.

"Do you remember," I said, "the story of the three bandits who encountered Death?"

Sister Beatriz's face regarded me cautiously. "I'm not sure," she said.

"It's a very, very old story," I said. "A pre-Sertôrial folktale that dates back to the early days of the Imperial Space Age. Balinetti uses it to illustrate a minor point in his theory of dynamic historical displacement in *Understanding Time, Standing under Time.* And a somewhat modified version of the story is told by the Woman of the Hillside in Mori's account of Sertôrian's blindfolded pilgrimage. Does that ring any bells?"

"No," said Sister Beatriz. "It doesn't."

"All right," I said. "Then I'll tell it to you."

"All right," said Sister Beatriz, her arms still braced against the bed, her eyes still alert.

To keep my hands from trembling, I held them tight against the sides of my legs.


There were once three bandits (I began) who pillaged and plundered their way across the galaxy. Their ruthlessness was exceeded only by their loyalty to one another, and space travelers far and wide quivered with fear at the very thought of them.

One day, after narrowly escaping an imperial constable, the bandits' longship touched down on a strange new planet. The three bandits disembarked and, not far from their ship, found Death sitting outside a weathered wooden shack at the edge of a clear and sulfurous pool of water.

Death rose to greet the bandits, welcoming them with a courtly gentility and asking if they would care to join him for a restorative soak in the warm mineral waters of his pool. Not wishing to offend their host, the bandits accepted Death's invitation.

"Very good," said Death, shucking off his heavy robe and lowering his ashen body into the pellucid waters of the pool. The bandits followed his lead, unencumbering themselves of their gear and their spacesuits, and stepping cautiously into the steaming water.

Though Death's manners were impeccable, his conversational preferences were undeniably grim. As the bandits' skin grew wrinkled and hot in the waters of the pool, he spoke of war, pestilence, famine, and disease.

Eventually, growing weary of Death's bleak company, the three bandits thanked their host for his hospitality and began to take their leave of him.

"My hospitality I give without price," said Death. "But you have looked directly upon my face, a bold and foolish act for which there must be consequences." He lifted a pale, dripping hand from the water, index finger raised. "First, the punishment: Exactly one year from today, I will snatch the breath from your mouths and leave your cold, lifeless bodies to molder and to rot." Death's great gray eyes flashed with something resembling pleasure, and the three bandits felt a chill in the deepest part of their being.

"Second," continued Death, "the reward. Before you depart, each one of you will meet with me in private and reveal the dearest wish of your heart. I will fulfill this wish and you will enjoy its fruits for the remainder of your life."

He rose from the pool, skin drying instantly, and beckoned to the first bandit.

"Come," he said.

She followed him into the wooden shack, her wet skin prickling as it touched the cool air.

Over the course of so many years of shared adventures, the first bandit had fallen deeply in love with the second bandit, and in her heart she knew exactly what her request would be.

While the other two bandits waited in the sulfurous pool, the first bandit sat across from Death inside the wooden shack.

"What is your wish?" said Death.

The first bandit told Death of her love for the second bandit. She explained that if this meeting had taken place years earlier she might have wished for the second bandit to love her in return. But now her love for him had grown so pure that she only desired his happiness. Her wish, then, was for the second bandit's death sentence to be lifted.

"Granted," said Death. "Now go."

She stepped out the door and, shivering violently now, hurriedly dressed herself as the second bandit rose from the pool and, beginning to shiver himself, entered the shack.

Unfortunately, the second bandit cared nothing for the first bandit, having fallen in love with the *third* bandit. Like the first bandit, though, his love had grown so pure that he only desired his beloved's happiness. And so, sitting across from Death, the second bandit explained his love for the third bandit and asked for her death sentence to be lifted.

"Granted," said Death.

Then came the third bandit's turn. The third bandit, for her part, adored nobody, the love of wealth having entirely consumed her avaricious heart.

"What is your wish?" said Death.

"Money," said the third bandit. "Lots and lots of money."

"Granted," said Death.

As the third bandit got dressed, Death wrapped himself in his dark and heavy robe and turned his back to the bandits.

"Until we meet again," he said.

The bandits left as quickly as they could.

Though they all put on a brave face, each bandit inwardly trembled at the possibility of such an early death. Over the ensuing months, the lives of the three comrades gradually drifted apart as they sought to resolve as much business and fulfill as many aspirations as they could before the coming of the baleful deadline.

Unavoidably, the anniversary of their meeting with Death arrived.

That morning, the first bandit stood in a sunlit greenhouse admiring a spotted orchid that she had tenderly cultivated for months. It had bloomed only the day before and was as lovely as the first bandit had hoped it would be.

Death walked in through the door of the greenhouse.

"Hello," he said.

"Hello," said the first bandit. She had forgotten how fathomless Death's eyes were.

"Open your mouth, please," said Death, ever the gentleman.

Warmed by the thought that her earlier wish would spare her beloved bandit comrade a similar fate, the first bandit opened her mouth. Death reached inside and snatched her breath. The woman's lifeless body fell to the ground among the plant trimmings and the spilled soil.

The second bandit passed the day in great trepidation. Though, like the first bandit, his heart was warmed by the thought that his wish would spare the life of his beloved, he felt great sorrow at the thought of leaving this life behind so soon.

But the anniversary came and went, and not even the shadow of Death crossed the second bandit's threshold. Days went by, and with no sign of Death, the second bandit grew confident that a long and happy life lay before him.

For her part, the third bandit had dreaded the arrival of this ominous anniversary. Over the previous months, she had acquired quantities of money so vast that they had sated even her prodigious cupidity. Recognizing that half of Death's promise had indisputably been fulfilled, she felt certain that her demise lay close at hand. But when the designated day came and went without incident, she breathed a sigh of relief and laughed at her own credulity. The curse had been nonsense after all.

Years later, the second and third bandits encountered each other by chance in a dark and smoky tavern. Both had learned of their colleague's death on that long-ago anniversary, and both had long been troubled by the uncanny coincidence of it. The surviving bandits each spoke a brief, spontaneous eulogy for their deceased friend, and then, after an uncomfortable moment of silence, the two old friends fell to talking of happier things, which they did with relish until the small hours of the morning. At dawn, they parted ways with a backslapping embrace and a lingering recollection of their long-ago encounter with Death.

For several moments, neither Sister Beatriz nor I spoke. I had become so caught up in recounting the story that I'd nearly forgotten my purpose in doing so. My hands, which had been steady throughout the tale, began again to tremble.

"I have heard that story once before," said Sister Beatriz, glancing at my shaking hands. "A long time ago."

I folded my hands in my lap, fingers tightly clasped to steady the tremor. I could still back out of this; I had not yet said anything that I could not explain away.

"I recognize that this tale is a fanciful one," I said, screwing my courage to the sticking place, "but one element has always rung false to me."

"And what would that be?" said Sister Beatriz.

Though the usual brusque vigor had returned to her voice, a palpable wariness remained about her eyes.

"The bandits," I said. "That the bandits would work together so closely and be so unaware of the romantic feelings developing in one another."

"Really?" said Sister Beatriz.

"Yes," I said.

"I have no trouble believing that," she said, punctuating the sentence with a sad, sardonic laugh that evaporated as quickly as it had appeared. Lips tightening as if to stifle any further outburst, Sister Beatriz fixed her gaze downward on a sweater lying next to her on the bed.

"Very interesting," I said, eyeing her stolid face. "Very interesting. So

in your opinion, two intelligent people—or three people, in this case—
might harbor these kinds of feelings without their colleagues being any
the wiser?"

"Yes," said Sister Beatriz, her fingers worrying at a loose thread in
the sweater's sleeve.

"You see, I find that very improbable," I said. "What I mean to say is,
an intelligent person must perceive feelings of that nature in a close
colleague—how could they miss them?—and to not acknowledge those
feelings could only be interpreted as a diplomatic yet firm rejection of
the sentiments in question."

"I disagree," said Sister Beatriz.

I waited for her to provide the kind of cogent support for her position
that she always summons so effortlessly, but she did not elaborate or
even seem willing to. So I went on.

"But to work together so closely, and to know each other so well in so
many respects," I said. "How could they keep something like that
hidden?"

Refusing to meet my eye, Sister Beatriz said, "I suppose, Úrsula, that
you're asking whether my feelings for you might be in the least bit
romantic."

And here was the Rubicon, daring me to cross it. Whether I waited
seconds or minutes to make my final decision, I do not know. Whatever
the quantity of time, however, so saturated was it with dread and anticipation that the moment threatened to engulf me like a flood.

"Yes," I finally managed to say.

Sister Beatriz turned her body away from me in what I presumed to
be revulsion, and at that moment I felt that death could not come quickly
enough. Worse still, as I stood to leave, I saw that Sister Beatriz was crying, a thing that I had never before seen her do. The sight momentarily
arrested me. Was the disgust she felt at my confession really so great?
Ashamed and devastated, I hurried toward the door.

"Where are you going?" said Sister Beatriz through her tears.

The question caught me completely off guard, as did what happened next. In three long strides, Sister Beatriz crossed the room to where I stood. Taking my face in her slender hands, she leaned in and kissed me, her lips soft and salty with tears.

Relief blossomed in my shattered heart and grew into something even greater, something even more sublime. With still-trembling fingers, I unbuttoned Beatriz's blouse and slid it down her arms. Stepping briefly away from each other, we both undressed—not gracefully—shedding first our simple cenobitic uniforms and then, with awkward twists and hops, our remaining underthings.

Beatriz's skin against mine was cooler than I'd expected, bristling with tiny goose bumps. Kissing again, we sidestepped to the bed, easing ourselves down onto Beatriz's cluttered mattress, sweeping aside piles of clothes and heaps of knickknacks in the process.

Historiography has trained me well to depict sweeping battles, multigenerational dynastic conflicts, and the spread of revolutionary ideas, but it is at this point in my account, as I attempt to describe the thrill and relief I felt at Sister Beatriz's touch, that I realize my powers of more intimate representation are sorely lacking. On the one hand, a precise anatomical description of what transpired between us fails to capture the moment's thrilling mysticism. On the other hand, I might, as others have done before me, employ metaphor to capture that ecstatic thrill—exotic flowers? white lightning?—but I know that to metaphorize such bodily experience is to annihilate it, and so I reach a narrative impasse.

"It breaks my heart," said Sister Beatriz later that evening, the two of us lying side by side in her narrow bed. "It breaks my heart that we didn't have that conversation years ago."

But so it goes.

The truth is, Sister Beatriz and I should count ourselves lucky. To paraphrase ancient scripture, we have found, however briefly, our own insular Tahiti, a land of peace and joy amidst the appalling ocean of this half-known life. Many people live and die and never find such a pleasant refuge, although I would be lying if I didn't admit that I, like Sister Beatriz, feel no small loss when I consider what might have been.

## FIFTEEN

And now, reader, I bid you a hasty farewell. The ship has docked, the gate has opened, and our fate has been decided.

At the pivotal moment, Beatriz and I sat at the edge of her bed, our legs touching, her elbow gently prodding my side as she scribbled feverishly in her notebook to record the last of her experimental findings. When we heard the massive docking gate open, though, she stopped writing and looked over at me, her sharp eyes both seeking and offering consolation.

For a moment, neither of us breathed. In fact, I was so frightened in that vast and gaping silence that all conscious thought briefly ceased, overwhelmed by pure animal death fear. All I could do was grip Beatriz's proffered hand with all my faltering strength.

The spell was broken, though, when our ears were met with the unmistakable sound of happy laughter echoing through the halls of the convent.

We were—we are—rescued.

I must confess that my melancholy soul doesn't quite know what to make of so many happy developments occurring in such a short period of time. Soon enough, I'm certain I will find new and compelling reasons to revive the feelings of gloom and foreboding to which I've grown so accustomed, but for now, I suppose, I will make do with this foreign sentiment in my heart, this unexpected joy.

In a few minutes, Beatriz and I—along with the rest of our sisters—

will board the rescuing spacecraft and depart for safer shores. With the brief time that remains, then, let us turn our attention to the final paragraphs of the Rhadamanthus IX episode:

• • •

Ultimately, Captain Sertôrian did not so much outwit Ruth Aylesbury and the secret police force of Rhadamanthus IX, as outwait them. For seven long years she worked tirelessly within the organization, a model employee, applying the full extent of her talents to the execution of her duties, bringing to each tactical operation she oversaw a flair and precision that produced success after success after success. Her superiors interpreted such hypercompetence as zeal for the cause, and she quickly won their trust. The relentlessly shrewd Ruth Aylesbury remained the one holdout, always keeping a wary eye on Sertôrian, suspecting—and rightly so—that her star recruit might not be as devoted as she seemed.

But Aylesbury's scrutiny left Sertôrian unruffled, and doggedly she pursued her strategy of outward assimilation. She lived in the same gray, anonymous housing complex that all her colleagues preferred, drank in the same bars, vacationed at the same dumpy lake resort. Over time, she even grew accustomed to the appearance of the Arch-Kaiser Glenn Harrison's sneering image on the ubiquitous urban vid-screens, and at some point his face ceased to generate such sharp revulsion in Sertôrian. And when, inevitably, Harrison was violently deposed to make way for a fresher, younger demagogue, she hid from her coworkers any sign of personal satisfaction at having outlasted the tyrant, commenting only on the organizational adjustments that would need to be made in response to the planet's ostensible new leader.

Sertôrian's outward behavior, both on the job and off, was so immaculate, so above reproach as to stymie even Aylesbury's tenacious doubts.

Inwardly, however, Sertôrian's rage knew no bounds. Early in her tenure with the force, she had procured, through subterfuge and misdirection, the minutes of a meeting conducted just after her capture. The document revealed that the officers present, Ruth Aylesbury among them, had unanimously resolved that if Sertôrian turned down their offer of employment she would be executed on the spot by an assassin concealed within the balcony's dense foliage, and her body would be incinerated along with the corpses of her two shipmates, Ava Valenti and Ernst de Bronk, who, as the minutes of the meeting further revealed, had both been caught, interrogated, and beheaded the day before Sertôrian's capture. (For good measure, Sertôrian's ship, the *Circe*, had previously been demolished.)

Those present at that meeting were all her coworkers now, and to be forced to cheerfully interact each day with such a cabal of remorseless fiends stoked in Sertôrian a white-hot flame of hatred. In unguarded moments, she daydreamed labyrinthine and bloody revenge plots that baroquely punished those who had killed her crew and who currently held her captive. Because she *was* a captive, that much was clear. She may have been allowed to leave the building at night, to occupy rooms by herself, to move about the city as her coworkers did, but as she did so, she was under constant surveillance, and whoever was watching her—Aylesbury, most likely—didn't bother being overly subtle about it. Everywhere she went Sertôrian spotted tiny lenses, pinhead microphones, and clumsy tails, all meant to remind her of the situation's true nature.

In spite of the rage that simmered within her, Sertôrian understood that revenge had a tendency, even when successful, to destroy the avenger along with her targets, and since Sertôrian still hoped to leave this planet alive, she decided to bide her time until the right opportunity for escape presented itself. This strategy required no small amount of self-control, but if nothing else, her years of wandering the Minoan System had inculcated in her a nearly pathological capacity for patience.

With time, this focus paid off, enabling her to feign a loyalty so convincing that when Aylesbury was tapped to take over as commissioner of Central Command, she appointed Sertôrian her chief lieutenant. And while such a posting did not entirely liberate Sertôrian from the heavy surveillance she had been under since her arrival, it did grant her sufficient operational autonomy to move with some freedom throughout the towering administration building.

In the end, her escape was almost as simple as walking out the front door.

One day, not long after Sertôrian had assumed her new duties as lieutenant commissioner, one of the tactical units confiscated a spaceship from a band of smugglers foolish enough to make a pit stop on Rhadamanthus IX. It was just a little planet hopper, nothing that could get her out of the Minoan System altogether, but it would do the job for now.

The scarcity of vehicles capable of leaving the planet had long been the greatest impediment to Sertôrian's escape. Only once before had a vessel with such capabilities been so near. Years earlier, the force had confiscated a spaceship even more powerful than this current one, but Sertôrian had been so new to the organization, so hobbled by surveillance, that she hadn't been able to get anywhere near the craft without arousing the suspicions of her superiors. The ship had been sold through a fence to an influential spice merchant who'd stopped off for supplies on Rhadamanthus IX, and that had been that.

This time was different. Sertôrian could move more or less unrestricted, and so the moment she heard of the spaceship's presence in the building's aircraft hangar, she knew this was her chance.

She thought back, as she sometimes did, to those delirious moments when she'd first learned of the deaths of Valenti and de Bronk. She'd initially felt a dizzy unburdening—for the first time in decades she was responsible for no one but herself. She was finally unconstrained, finally unfettered. It hadn't taken long, however, for that relief to be replaced by a sense of failure more stinging than any she had ever experienced, a sense of failure commingled with grief, resentment, and fury. In the long run, only the fury had survived, filling Sertôrian until all that remained of her—she often felt—was raw, corrosive rage.

As she plotted the details of her imminent escape, then, her body shook, not with worry but with anger.

She waited until lunchtime to make her move. As she walked with a group of colleagues down the stairs to the cafeteria, Sertôrian said she'd forgotten something in her office and would catch up with them in a minute. Once separated from the group she moved quickly, veering down one empty hallway and then another. Heart pounding, Sertôrian found the hangar guarded by Cobb and Harris, two officers who had worked under Sertôrian on numerous tactical operations.

"Afternoon," said Sertôrian.

"Lieutenant Commissioner," said Cobb and Harris in unison.

Looking discreetly past them and behind several rows of aerowagons, she saw the spaceship—her means of delivery.

She said, "I'm taking an aerowagon out to meet an informant," which was just barely close enough to plausible to get her through the door.

"Very good, Lieutenant Commissioner," said Cobb and flipped the switch to open the runway exit portal.

"As you were," said Sertôrian.

Cobb and Harris saluted Sertôrian, and as she walked away they resumed their conversation. Sertôrian walked straight to the spaceship and climbed the ladder into its open cockpit.

It wasn't until the ship was lifting off the ground that Cobb and Harris, alerted by the sound of an engine more powerful than that of an aerowagon, noticed something amiss. They turned to watch the spaceship flying out the exit portal, and the last Sertôrian saw of them was their baffled faces trying to make sense of her unexpected departure.

As the ship passed through the planet's atmosphere and into the darkness of outer space, Sertôrian could feel seven years' worth of tightly compressed anger begin a strange metamorphosis, one that would stretch over many decades before producing in Sertôrian's heart an emotional state as potent as it was numinous. At the moment, though, what Sertôrian mainly felt was relief.

Consulting the onboard navigation system, she set a course for Daedalus IX, one of the few planets in the Minoan System that she had not yet visited. Autopilot engaged, she leaned back in her seat, rubbing her eyes. The instrument panel chirped pleasantly, confirming the vessel's course, and Sertôrian spared one backward look through the rear porthole at the shrinking sphere that had been her prison for more than seven years.

On her first day of work with the secret police, Sertôrian had found a small cedar box sitting on top of her desk. Next to it had been a slip of paper reading, simply, "Your shipmates." Sertôrian had looked inside the box at the cinders and ash and recognized the gesture for the threat that it was. The box had earned a permanent spot on her bedside table, where it would be the last thing she saw every night before falling into a tense and dreamless sleep.

Now, in the cockpit of the stolen planet hopper, she pulled the same cedar box from her canvas rucksack. With the ship still on autopilot, Sertôrian shook the contents of the box into the waste disposal chute and, commending the ashes to the cosmic emptiness around her, pushed the red eject button. Through the side porthole, Sertôrian watched the remnants of her once formidable crew drift into the vacuum of space, a fleeting constellation of dust. Her thoughts turned, as they often had in recent times, to the woman she had left buried near the Twin Falls seven years earlier. By now the woman's face would surely have been rendered unrecognizable through the ineluctable process of decomposition, a small mercy that instilled a dubious comfort in Sertôrian's heart.

She returned to the pilot's seat.

Unbeknownst to Sertôrian, a gory and long-running feud between the planet's two most ruthless families awaited her on Daedalus IV. She would, yet again, be kidnapped and tortured. She would be humiliated and threatened. She would be pressed into service as a spy for one infernally clever family and then the other. She would kill and nearly be killed.

But for now, there was only the quiet calm of a single person in a tiny vessel drifting through the dark and starry immensity of space. Hands tightly gripping the ship's yoke, Captain Irena Sertôrian savored the unfathomable stillness, drawing the moment into herself like a drowning sailor taking her last breath.

# AFTERWORD

This started out as an acknowledgments page, but as I was running through the list of people to thank, I realized there are a couple more things I need to tell you.

In late October 2016 I got a phone call from Tim Wirkus, an old college acquaintance of mine. I'd met up with him about a year and a half earlier after he read from his first novel at a local bookstore. It would be an overstatement to say we'd had a full-blown artistic rivalry at BYU—I was never that interested in the stuff Tim wrote—but there had been a palpably competitive undercurrent to every interaction we'd ever had. The first time we met, for instance, and discovered we'd both served missions in São Paulo, Tim spent the entire conversation trying to one-up me, to prove that he'd served in more interesting, more dangerous, more picturesque parts of the city than I had.

"Did you ever meet a witch?" he said.

"No," I said.

"I did," he said, and I could see him notching up a point on the mental scorecard he'd been keeping since he'd introduced himself. I should have called him out on his exoticization of the city and its people, but at the time I lacked the language to do so, and anyway he didn't seem worth the trouble.

Ensuing interactions followed a similar template, with one or the other of us casually bringing up a recently won university writing contest or an obscure online publication, and the other one scrambling to top it. We mostly avoided each other, though, with Tim keeping to his weird clique of *Secret History* wannabe writing center nerds, and me sheltering myself in the branches of my lofty principles.

I'd been interested to discover, though, that he'd recently published a novel, and I wanted to see what he had to say about it. As we talked after the reading, I told him about *The Infinite Future* and sent him a copy. Given our history, I suppose it's odd that I trusted Tim to help me get the book published. But it turns out that rivalry engenders an intimacy all its own.

Initially, that trust seemed to pay off. He finished the manuscript by the next afternoon and emailed to say he loved it, and would do everything he could to find a publisher. This was followed by a long stretch of radio silence during which I assumed Tim had deliberately forgotten about the book, just the kind of passive-aggressive move I should have expected from the guy.

A year and a half later, though, I was raking leaves in the backyard of my new house when I got a call from my mediocre old bête noir.

"Hey there, Danny boy," said Tim, his voice dripping with forced congeniality. "Guess who's about to make your day?"

"Is it you?" I said, unable to fully purge the annoyance from my voice.

"You got it," said Tim, and then told me he'd found a small but reputable science-fiction press that wanted to bring out *The Infinite Future*.

"Wow," I said, leaning on my rake and smiling into my phone in spite of the announcement's source.

"Yeah," said Tim. "You're welcome."

I ignored this and allowed the good news to sink in. It was like a ray of light through the clouds of that dreary autumn day.

"This is so exciting," I said.

"Yeah," said Tim. "Should be a fun little book!"

A sudden wind scattered the small pile of leaves I'd been gathering before Tim called, and the accompanying sharp chill through my wool jacket snuffed out the flame of my growing enthusiasm. Actually, no, it wasn't the wind. It was Tim's description of *The Infinite Future* that stopped me short, the diminutive he'd attached to the book rankling me like a deliberate flick to the ear.

"Well, I mean, it's not a *little* book," I said, not even trying to hide my irritation.

"No, it's definitely got some meat on its bones," said Tim, still not getting it. "I didn't mean to ruffle your feathers."

"They're not ruffled," I said, although they were. "I'm just surprised you described the book as *little*."

"Yeah, as a term of endearment," said Tim. "And it *is* a fun little book, so relax."

I tightened my grip on the handle of my rake.

"But you wouldn't call *War and Peace* a fun little book," I said. "Right? I mean, you wouldn't say that about, I don't know, *Ulysses*."

"Probably not," said Tim, his voice betraying an incipient boredom with the direction our conversation was taking.

"And I'm not saying that, quality-wise, *The Infinite Future* is necessarily on a par with *War and Peace* or *Ulysses*," I continued, "but in terms of its scope, it just feels evocative of so much more. It's like the tip of an enormous iceberg, you know?"

While I waited for Tim's response, I watched the dead leaves scuttling across my yard on the growing wind. What had seemed so self-evident to me about Salgado-MacKenzie's fragmentary work had apparently not manifested itself to Tim.

"How so?" he said finally. Was he even listening anymore?

"You read my introduction, right?" I said.

"Yeah," he said.

"So you know that *The Infinite Future* was originally intended to be a mega-novel with a page count in the thousands," I said.

"Yeah," said Tim.

"So?" I said. "Doesn't reading the existing manuscript feel so tantalizing to you? Like the little we have of what was intended just serves to emphasize how big the unrealized possibilities are?"

There was another pause on the line.

"Like I said," said Tim. "I really like the book, and I'm very excited that more people are going to be able to read it."

I ignored his condescending dodge and told him that every time I'd read *The Infinite Future* it had summoned the ghost version of its as-yet-unrealized self, inspiring a complicated awe that for me was the essential heart of the book.

"Yeah, that's pretty interesting, Danny," said Tim, and I could almost hear his thumb reaching over to end the call. He again offered his congratulations and said he had to go. He had a doctor's appointment in just a few minutes. Recognizing a brushoff when I heard one, I thanked him and hung up the phone. Looking around my yard, I saw that the wind had already undone a whole morning's worth of work. Letting my rake fall to the ground, I went inside and switched on *Side 3* by the Raspberries, then lay down on my new living room couch feeling indignant and a little embarrassed.

On an intellectual level I could recognize that Tim had just given me some very good news, but emotionally all that had registered was that maddening diminutive he'd attached to *The Infinite Future*—a "fun little book." Really? Was that all it was? Hoping to transform my zigzagging anxiety into something more celebratory, I decided to share the news with the only people who might be able to share my reaction.

Because it wasn't feasible for the three of us to meet in person, I was thrilled when Sérgio and Harriet both agreed to participate in a video chat the next afternoon. It had been seven years since I'd seen either of them, and while I'd exchanged a handful of emails with Sérgio during my time in law school, I hadn't heard a single thing from Harriet.

Well, I guess that's not completely true. The intervening years had been especially newsworthy for Mormonism, from Church leadership intensely opposing the legalization of gay marriage to *The Book of*

*Mormon* musical to Mitt Romney's presidential bid to the excommunication of a prominent women's rights activist. Reportage had abounded in national papers, and it was rare to read an article or a think piece without seeing a quote from Harriet Kimball. Her take on *The Book of Mormon* musical, for instance: "Funny enough, but not nearly as well researched as it pretends to be." Or here's this doozy from that *New Yorker* piece on mid-twentieth-century Mormon historians: "Look at all the backlash against Juanita Brooks for *The Mountain Meadows Massacre*. Church leadership didn't dispute its factuality, but there were still members of the Quorum of the Twelve who wanted Brooks excommunicated, because the massacre just wasn't something that was openly discussed. Compare that to Bruce R. McConkie's *Mormon Doctrine*, which, behind closed doors, even the Church president agreed was filled with dubious suppositions, doctrinal errors, and minor heresies. McConkie was a rising star, though, so nobody said one word about their problems with the book. McConkie's reputation was protected, and Brooks's was not, which just goes to show you that some Mormons are more equal than others."

The combination of her thorough expertise in Mormon history and culture, and her idiosyncratic relationship with the Church—you were never sure whether her perspective would be staunchly apologist or just as ardently critical—made her a great source. That much I had to admit, though like any member of a touchy subculture, I resented the way in which these articles portrayed their interviewees' opinions, however subtly, as being either universally typical of Mormon thinking or completely unique. I knew that this phenomenon wasn't Harriet's fault, though, at least not entirely, and that the articles were probably richer for her having commented. Not everyone I knew was willing to cut her that kind of slack, though.

Craig D. Ahlgren, for one, resented every public utterance Harriet made. After I'd finished near the top of my class at Vanderbilt, Craig's law firm had taken me on as an associate. To say that my first few years as an attorney were hectic would be an understatement. Not only did I make sure that I was always among the last to leave the offices each night, I also showed up to every work-related social engagement I was aware of: lunches, retirement parties, client functions, pickup basketball games, fishing trips. It was exhausting but seemed to be paying off. Each passing year yielded an increase of winking hints that if I kept this up I'd make partner before I knew it.

Anyway, the point is Craig Ahlgren was my boss and whenever he saw Harriet Kimball quoted in an article, he'd wander into my office, hands in the pockets of his dark suit pants, and say simply, "The papers can't get enough of your old friend." Then he'd raise his eyebrows in a look of teasing disapproval and wander right back out the door.

At first I wasn't sure whether this half-joking response was the tamped-down product of true outrage or displeasure feigned for the sake of some intra-office ribbing. I found out the answer one Thursday evening when I went to the Salt Lake Temple to do an endowment session— a ceremony in which participants ritualistically contemplate their relationship with the divine. I was sitting in the back row of the first ordinance room, and things were taking a little longer than usual to get started. Attention wandering, I looked around at the mural that covered the walls and ceiling of the crowded room—a primordial scene of roiling waters, jutting rocks, and thick clouds of blue, white, and faintest pink. Lost in contemplation, I didn't notice the latecomer enter the room until he was sitting next to me, and even then not until he'd whispered, "Danny, nice to run into you here."

It was Craig Ahlgren, looking very much at home.

"Hi Craig," I whispered back.

I wasn't unhappy to see him necessarily, but I had been looking forward to having a couple of hours to myself when I wouldn't have to think about work. Craig settled into his chair. At the front of the room an officiator announced that there'd been a mix-up with the ordinance workers assigned to this session but the ceremony would be starting as soon as things got straightened out. He thanked us all for our patience, and with those words a quiet restlessness filled the room—whispered conversations and the gentle susurrus of fabric sliding against fabric as people shifted in their seats.

"You know," whispered Craig, leaning toward me. "I've been thinking a lot about Harriet Kimball lately."

"Oh yeah?" I whispered. "What about her?"

With his left index finger he adjusted the dimple beneath the knot of his white tie, a gesture I recognized from high-stakes professional conversations as a sign that Craig was formulating the most precise possible expression of a strong and complicated sentiment.

"When it comes to Mormonism," he began, "the newspapers are always more interested in listening to people like Harriet—you know, people who have dissented from the Church—than to people like you or me. People like us are orthodox, devout, and comfortable in our faith. The press sees us as being either brainwashed or insidious, or both. We don't register as sentient, self-aware beings to them."

He paused, glancing around at the room's flawlessly maintained nineteenth-century craftsmanship—the white moldings, the mural, the intricately pieced glasswork above the door.

"People like Harriet," he continued, "could be doing so much to rectify that situation. She has the ear of the media, but what does she use it for? To lift herself up. To talk like one of *them* just so everyone's clear that she's not one of the ignorant, unwashed mass of savage Mormons."

Craig smiled, more a baring of teeth than an expression of happiness.

"What makes me most upset," he continued, working to keep his voice at a whisper, "is that she hides behind this screen of supposed intellectual idealism, telling everyone, including herself, that she's only after the truth, whatever that might mean to her. There's no self-interest there, according to her. No desire to cause trouble. It's all so obvious, though. What she's really after, Danny, is the acceptance of the world. She wants to fit in. She wants to be respected by all those who point their fingers and laugh at the Church. And she's succeeded is the thing. The media treats her like the only enlightened Mormon in America, and that's fine I suppose. That's her business. That's the decision she made a long time ago. But do you know what, Danny?"

And here a look of bone-deep satisfaction overtook Craig's face.

"Harriet can say whatever she wants to the media," said Craig. "Harriet can disparage the Church until she's blue in the face. At the end of the day, though, what really matters is that Harriet's out there, and you and I, Danny—we're in here."

He gestured at the ordinance room and, presumably, at the larger edifice that contained us.

"We have the temple," he said. "And we have everything it represents."

He clapped me on the shoulder.

"You're in the right place tonight," he said. "And I'm proud of you for making that decision."

"Thanks," I said, unsure of what else to say.

The tardy ordinance workers had arrived at some point during Craig's speech, so I was rescued by the beginning of the endowment ceremony.

Given Craig's regular disparagement of Harriet, when her face appeared on my computer screen the day after my phone conversation with Tim, I was surprised to see a bright, pleasant woman looking out at me rather than the glowering wraith I'd been subconsciously expecting. She looked really good, in fact—well rested, more fleshed out, much happier than the last time I'd seen her. The perpetual defensiveness that had hung about her in a cloud was gone as well, replaced by an easy air of authority. Here was someone capable of properly appreciating the news of *The Infinite Future*'s publication.

"Can you see me all right?" she said.

"Yeah," I said. "You're coming through just fine."

"Good," she said, reaching out and tilting her camera back so it no longer cut off the top of her head. "Earlier this week I was presenting remotely at a conference in Melbourne and my video feed was a mess, apparently."

With a what-can-you-do shrug, she made another minor adjustment to her camera.

"Are you at your cabin?" I said.

She sat in front of an overcrowded bookshelf, with several more books piled at her elbows on the desktop before her.

"No," she said. "I received a two-year research fellowship from the Arrington Institute in San Diego, so I'm in California right now."

"Wow," I said. "Congratulations."

"Thank you," she said. "I'm working on a history of late-twentieth-century Mormon feminism. It's slow going, but of course it is. Anyway, how about you? Are you still in Provo?"

"No," I said, and then told her how I'd gone to law school at Vanderbilt and was now an associate at Craig Ahlgren's law firm in Salt Lake.

"Congratulations," she said, sounding like she really meant it. "Where in town are you living?"

"I just bought a little house in the Avenues," I said.

"Good for you," she said.

"Things are going well for me," I said, unsure why I felt the need to reemphasize the point. I couldn't stop myself, though. "I've also been seeing someone for a few months now, so—yeah."

Harriet's supportive smile briefly turned to one of amusement before she recomposed her face and said I must be very happy.

"Yes," I said.

I wasn't lying about seeing someone, per se, but it also wasn't the kind of relationship I'd otherwise brag about. A few months earlier I'd run into Christine Voorhes, former stooge for the Coalition of Aggrieved Christians, on the steps of the Salt Lake City County Building. She recognized me right away, and after chatting for a few minutes—she was now a partner in a practice in town that had a reputation for not messing around—we exchanged numbers. Not long after, we started meeting up intermittently for late-night restaurant meals and sweaty make-out sessions in the backseat of her pearlescent Lexus GS. She never invited me over to her house, and I never invited her to mine, and so it went.

One time I asked her, as we crossed a restaurant parking lot toward her car, if she ever would have been interested in the younger, less successful version of me she'd met so many years earlier.

"The great thing about you, Daniel," she said, hooking her arm around mine, "is that you're whatever I want you to be."

"What's that supposed to mean?" I said.

Instead of answering, she pulled her keys from her coat pocket and with a squeeze from her leather-gloved thumb, unlocked her Lexus.

It was strange, this specter from my floundering past reappearing in my more successful present, a reminder of how far I'd come and, conversely, of my inability to completely free myself from that grim period in my life.

"Sérgio is joining us, isn't he?" said Harriet, glancing at her watch.

"He's supposed to be," I said.

I was about to check my email to see if something was up when a third chat square blossomed on the screen and there was Sérgio, sitting in the computer lab of the Biblioteca Anita Garibaldi, arms folded over the guitar-playing image of Nara Leão on the front of his black T-shirt.

"I apologize for my lateness," said Sérgio. "The library's been having trouble with its Internet today."

Where the passing years had invigorated Harriet, they seemed to have drained Sérgio of his vitality. His hair was grayer and his face, if not quite gaunt, possessed a troubled angularity.

"No need to apologize," said Harriet. "Daniel and I were just catching up."

"Very good," said Sérgio, nodding wearily. "Now I understand, Daniel, that you have some exciting news for us?"

I'd been hoping to build up to it, but Sérgio's briskness forced my hand.

"Yeah," I said and then told them what Tim had told me the day before.

"Wonderful," said Harriet. "That's very exciting. Welcome to the glamorous fellowship of published translators, Daniel."

"Thanks," I said, although her response wasn't what I'd been looking for. This wasn't about me—I'd long ago given up on my own literary dreams—but about Salgado-MacKenzie, that pseudonymous entity who still inspired a complicated awe within me. Hadn't I done something important here? Hadn't I contributed to a phenomenon so much bigger than myself?

"This is also good for the cause, though, right?" I said, half jokingly.

"The cause?" said Sérgio, and I could see heavy bags under his eyes that hadn't existed seven years earlier.

"Yeah," I said. "Spreading the good word of Salgado-MacKenzie."

"Ah," said Sérgio, scratching his beard. Maybe it was the Internet connection, but his voice sounded like it was coming from the bottom of a well. "Of course."

What was going on here? Why wasn't Sérgio as excited as I needed him to be—was it jealousy? I hadn't really thought through the fact that I would be the one with my name on the cover, or at least on the title page, below Salgado-MacKenzie's own.

"And really, Sérgio," I said, trying to make up for any possible envy, "it's all thanks to you."

"Yes," said Harriet.

There was an awkward pause as Sérgio's image froze on my computer

"Hello?" I said. "Sérgio? Are you still there?"

"Yes," said Sérgio, his response preceding his reanimation on the screen by just a few beats.

"You were just frozen," I said.

"Ah," said Sérgio.

For a second I thought he'd frozen again, but he was actually just sitting very still. This seemed less like jealousy and more like Sérgio had been drained of all his vital humors.

"So, Sérgio," said Harriet as the pause grew more uncomfortable. "What have you been up to lately?"

He looked somewhere beyond his computer screen, as if searching for a cue card.

"Oh yes," he said after a moment, looking back into the camera. "This will be of interest to the two of you. I've been given a remarkable opportunity recently."

"What's that?" I said, a little overenthusiastically in an attempt to compensate for Sérgio's lack of enthusiasm.

"About a year ago, I convinced the Cooper siblings to donate their papers to the Biblioteca Anita Garibaldi," he said, his weary eyes staring straight into his camera. "So I've been busy for the past several months scanning and cataloging everything the library acquired."

"That's great!" I said.

"Yes," said Harriet. "Congratulations!" She paused. "But I thought they hadn't hung on to much of their Salgado-MacKenzie material."

"That's the impression Madge gave when I first met them in Idaho," said Sérgio without relish, "but I suspected otherwise. Or rather, I hoped otherwise. You see, when the manuscript of *The Infinite Future* turned out to be less of a revelation than I'd anticipated . . ."

Had I been the only one to have such an otherworldly experience with the novel? Why was this not going the way I'd hoped it would? I fought back an urge to just shut off my computer and walk away.

Sérgio continued: "I remembered something Rex had mentioned, that when he submitted the novel to various publishers, he'd included unpublished stories of Irena Sertôrian. So what had become of those stories, I wondered? Given their penchant for mystique, I knew I couldn't ask the Coopers directly, so I began a long and patient correspondence with them.

"The first coup was convincing them to allow the extant portion of *The Infinite Future* to be translated and published, if we could find anyone willing to do so. For the next phase, which lasted three years, I slowly drew them out, playing hard to get as they fed me a detail here and a detail there about their pseudonymous career, until finally they admitted to me that they still possessed every single page they'd ever written as Salgado-MacKenzie. From there it was only a matter of time before I convinced them that for the sake of posterity, etc., etc., they should donate their papers to the library that employed me. And so," concluded Sérgio, "here I find myself."

"Good for you," I said, again with too much enthusiasm.

"Were there many unpublished stories?" asked Harriet.

"A couple dozen," said Sérgio with a sad and enigmatic smile.

"Wow!" I said. "You must be over the moon."

"Over the moon?" he said, brows furrowed.

"Yeah," I said. "Like really, really happy."

"No," said Sérgio. "I know what 'over the moon' means."

"Oh," I said.

Much to my dismay, Sérgio seemed even more deflated now than he had when our conversation had begun, a caul of grief clinging to his heavy head.

"What are the stories about?" I asked softly, the gloom beginning to infect me through the screen of the computer.

"Most of them are fairly minor entries in the Sertôrian saga—weaker versions of stories that actually made it into print," he said. "A couple are different. A couple aren't too bad."

"What are they about?" I said. "The couple of good ones, I mean."

"Oh, I don't know," said Sérgio. "Let me check the catalog I've been working on."

His hand moved to the mouse on the desktop, and after a few clicks he said, "Here, I'll read you a summary: The year is 4658, and the most popular sport in the galaxy is a much-evolved version of jai alai. As the new season commences, billions of fans follow with wonder the meteoric rise of a new team whose controversial style of playing wins them as many enemies as it does matches. The Twins of Boundless Fury, as the duo is known, confound opponents and commentators alike with their preternatural ability to hurl the pelota from their cestas at unprecedented speeds."

This prompted a soundless chuckle from Harriet.

"When the sport's governing body initiates an official inquest into the team's background, though, the Twins of Boundless Fury simply disappear," continued Sérgio, "prompting loyal fans everywhere to pore over scorecards, game films, and magazine interviews for any clues pertaining to the team's origins or current whereabouts. Over the ensuing months, this search comes to eclipse the sport itself in popularity, until a young fan-turned-researcher discovers a secret about the vanished duo that will redefine the sport—and humankind—forever."

Sérgio looked back into the camera, then intoned: "Both twins were, in fact, Irena Sertôrian."

"That sounds pretty good," I said.

Sérgio's baleful face stared out at me from the screen. He shrugged, and his image was fleetingly pixelated. Before the melancholy could engulf us all, Harriet, who'd been silent through this exchange said, "Sérgio, is everything okay?"

He drew a deep breath. He nodded, and then, contradicting himself, shook his head.

"On paper," Sérgio began, eyes averted, "I've found exactly what I've spent my whole life looking for. I've met Salgado-MacKenzie and I've read all of his—or rather *their*—published work. I should be, as Daniel put it, over the moon. As you've gathered, though, I'm not." Sérgio drew a hand down his face. "There's a dream I've been having ever since our trip to Idaho. Not every night, and sometimes I'll go months without dreaming it, but then it returns, jarring my slumber and clinging to my mind for hours after I wake."

Sérgio paused, his haunted eyes turned momentarily downward, and suddenly I didn't want to hear any more, didn't want to be consumed by this despondency that had overtaken my once jocular friend. Before I could open my mouth to stop him, though, Harriet gave Sérgio an encouraging nod, and he continued.

"In this dream," he said, "this anxiety dream—it's a nightmare, I suppose—I'm in the hotel room where I first met Salgado-MacKenzie. And just as it was in real life, the room is packed—people sitting cross-legged on the bed, sprawling out on the red-and-blue carpet, everyone drinking and talking, everyone having a very pleasant time.

"Or almost everyone anyway. As I'm looking around the room, I see someone standing alone over in the corner, but instead of Salgado-MacKenzie—or Rex Cooper, I should say—it's Irena Sertôrian I see, looking just as I always imagined she would: heroic and sad and so invitingly powerful. I feel an upsurge of an emotion that's not joy so much as an *anticipation* of joy, and I know I have to speak with her.

"As I cross the room, though, I realize that what I mistook for people are actually dozens of blue crablike creatures crawling over every available surface, their scuttling legs tapping against the walls and snagging against the softer surfaces of the bedspreads and carpet. I walk carefully, but whenever I get near one, it hisses and snaps its claws at me. I move very slowly.

"Finally, I make it past the crabs, whose ranks are growing as more and more of them spill out from a crack in the ceiling back by the bathroom. But it doesn't matter because now I'm standing just a few feet away from Irena Sertôrian herself. Unfortunately, though, I can't see her face. It's turned away from me toward the empty hotel wall, and somehow I know that the joy I'm anticipating will continue to elude me until I can look her in the eye.

"I clear my throat, then, and hold out my hand. 'Excuse me,' I say. 'My name is Sérgio Antunes, and it's an honor to meet you.'

"For a second she doesn't move, but then her head slowly turns to look at me, and for a moment—less than a moment—there's an expression of guarded pleasure, almost a smile on her face, and I feel my anticipation teeter on the cusp of becoming something much more powerful. And then, as Sertôrian opens her mouth to say something, her eyes take in my face, and there's a spark of recognition.

"She recognizes me, Harriet, and the joyful anticipation flushes out of me. I feel seasick instead—so uneasy. Irena Sertôrian knows who I am, and in that exact moment a doorway appears between us, and a dark wooden door swings shut."

*Daniel Laszlo*
*February 2017*
*Salt Lake City, UT*

**END**

## ACKNOWLEDGMENTS

Thanks to Ray Bradbury for *The Martian Chronicles*. Thanks also to Emily Anderson for the illuminating conversations about how reading works. For their insightful and generous feedback on early drafts of the novel, thanks to Aimee Bender and Yishai Seidman. More thanks to Yishai Seidman for being a terrific and indefatigable agent. Thanks to Ed Park for being an editor who knows his power pop (and much, much more). The whole team at Penguin has been lovely to work with—a big thank you to all of them. I'd also like to acknowledge the generous support of the University of Southern California's Provost's PhD Fellowship during the writing of this novel. Thanks also to Jessie, a diamond of the first water (minus the creepy purity connotations).

# SOURCES

As I was doing research for this novel, the following books proved essential:

*David O. McKay and the Rise of Modern Mormonism*, by Gregory A. Prince and Wm. Robert Wright

*Juanita Brooks: The Life Story of a Courageous Historian of the Mountain Meadows Massacre*, by Levi S. Peterson

*The Lord's University: Freedom and Authority at BYU*, by Bryan Waterman and Brian Kagel

*Mormon Enigma: Emma Hale Smith*, by Linda King Newell and Valeen Tippetts Avery

*Mormon Feminism: Essential Writings*, edited by Joanna Brooks, Rachel Hunt Steenblik, and Hannah Wheelwright

*The Mormon People*, by Matthew Bowman

*The Mountain Meadows Massacre*, by Juanita Brooks


*Bossa Nova: The Story of the Brazilian Music That Seduced the World*, by Ruy Castro; translated by Lysa Salsbury

*Brazil: Five Centuries of Change*, by Thomas E. Skidmore

*Rare and Commonplace Flowers: The Story of Elizabeth Bishop and Lota de Macedo Soares*, by Carmen L. Oliveira; translated by Neil K. Besner

*Why This World: A Biography of Clarice Lispector*, by Benjamin Moser